For Georgia Morris Bond

Contents

FOREWORD

"The last of the last," I wrote to a friend, during the yearlong process of bringing five newly discovered stories by Raymond Carver to publication. As a poet, I also hear in that phrase an echo of "lasting." Yet this is all the new work there will ever be from that extraordinary voice—its witnessing so clarified by relentless honesty that his stories have entered into over twenty languages around the world.

When Haruki Murakami, a fine novelist and Ray's Japanese translator, visited me with his wife, Yoko, after Ray's death, he confided that he felt accompanied by Ray's presence and dreaded finishing his complete edition of Ray's work. I know now the mixture of pleasure and sadness he must have been feeling.

The certain joy of this present endeavor has been in hearing something new from a voice it seemed had left the earth, of being glad for its unexpected entrance after a curtain has rung down. If a trunk of Kafka's or Chekhov's manuscripts were discovered today, there would be a scramble to see what it held. We are like that—curious, nostalgic, eager for the familiar ghosts of those we admire in our literature and lives.

These discoveries of new work by Ray are a separate, yet connected event in relation to work he published while he lived. There is value for those who wish it, for when we love a writer, we want to read on and on, to encounter the full range of what he or she wrote—the transcendent, the unexpected, even the unfinished. We're able. This value comes not only from the whole, but also from small things: phrasing and syntax, the recognition or surprise of characters, the line-by-line play of the telling.

The discoveries of these stories took place at different times and in different locales. The first occurred in March 1999 at Ridge House, the Port Angeles, Washington, home where Ray and I lived at the time of his death. Jay Woodruff, a friend and senior editor at *Esquire*, assisted me in this process. The second came that midsummer, when William L. Stull and Maureen P. Carroll, husband and wife partners in Carver scholarship, visited the William Charvat Collection of American Fiction at the Ohio State University Library. There, while examining a box of manuscripts, they found two complete unpublished stories. They phoned me excitedly, on my birthday, with this news.

It was bounty added to bounty when these two stories joined the three Jay and I had located. Moreover, it is grounds for a republication of Ray's uncollected writings. Many of these works had appeared earlier in *No Heroics, Please* (published by The Harvill Press in Great Britain, and Vintage Books in America). In addition to these unpublished stories, we have further enriched the book with four essays previously included in *Fires*, a 1983 miscellany of poetry, prose, and fiction.

Shortly after Ray's death, while writing the introduction to *A New Path to the Waterfall*, I had come upon folders containing typescripts and hand drafts of unpublished stories. At the time I wasn't sure these were complete manuscripts or, if they were, whether they should come to light. I felt that before unpublished work should be considered, all the writing Ray had clearly intended to see in print should first be made available. It would take nine years to accomplish that with the appearance of Ray's collected poems in *All of Us* (Harvill, 1996; Knopf, 1998).

There was plenty to do after Ray's too-early death at fifty in 1988 from lung cancer. I saw three of his books into print in British and American editions; finished *Carver Country*, a book of photographs by Bob Adelman; and advised on the Robert Altman film *Short Cuts*, which drew on nine of Ray's published stories. I participated in the making of three documentary films about Ray. Much of the above I did while teaching far from home. Somehow I also managed to write three books of poems, a book of stories, and a collection of essays.

Early in 1998, as the tenth anniversary of Ray's death approached, Jay Woodruff phoned to say he wanted to do something to honor Ray in *Esquire*. "There are these folders in the desk," I said. "There may be nothing whole or worthwhile," I told him. "But I could look sometime." I suspect Jay heard hesitation. At any rate he said, "Tess, when you get ready to look at those things I'll be happy to come out and help you."

Jay seemed exactly the person I'd been hoping might appear. He respected my work, loved Ray's writing, and understood the process of revision and publication. Moreover, as both a fiction writer and a magazine editor, Jay knew good stories when he saw them. In March 1999 he flew to Seattle and came three hours, by car and ferry, to Port Angeles. The next day, from nine in the morning until eleven at night, we carefully examined the contents of each drawer in Ray's desk. We read the pages in the folders, labeled and photocopied them, and finally made our choices. It was a quiet, intimate process, full of purpose. As we read, it became clear there were three fine stories. The dread I'd felt of coming to the last of Ray's work was subsumed by the prospect of doing right by these unpublished stories. It seemed especially fitting that *Esquire*, where Ray's stories found their first broad readership in the early 1970s, should participate in this discovery.

Jay took on the job of deciphering Ray's cramped handwriting to make accurate transcriptions. One manuscript was entirely handwritten, while others were in typescript with hand corrections. Far from finding this work tedious, Jay drew energy from the task. Having spent eleven years deciphering Ray's handwriting, I checked Jay's transcriptions word for word against the originals to fill in a few spots he couldn't make out. We were mindful that Ray would sometimes take a story through thirty rewrites. These stories had been put aside well short of that. (In Ray's final months, he turned from fiction to poetry for what became his last book, *A New Path to the Waterfall*.) Still, very little editing was needed on these stories. Characters and place names were standardized, so Dotty didn't become Dolores a page later, or Eureka did not become Arcata. Endings, where Ray always worked hardest, were, in some instances, left as one leaves a meal when the phone rings. We simply let those last moments reverberate, allowing the story to come to rest.

Ray had written several accounts of men trying to start over again, most notably "Where I'm Calling From." In "Kindling," the first of the new stories to be published in *Esquire*, a man desperately splitting a cord of wood tries to clarify his will toward going forward after alcoholism and the breakup of a marriage. The narrator is also a writer, and his tentative attempts to write again hark back movingly to that time in 1979 when Ray and I began our lives together in El Paso and he made his own fresh start at writing after a ten-year bout with alcoholism.

Of the five new stories, "Dreams" became my favorite and Jay's. Here a woman loses her children to a fire after the collapse of her marriage. The story seemed to bridge our lives in both Syracuse (where Ray and I had, like the couple in the story, slept in the basement to avoid the August heat) and the Northwest (where a fire had broken out on our street, although no lives had been lost). I recognized the echo of Ray's story "A Small, Good Thing," in which a child also dies. In both cases I admired Ray's audacity in taking on subject matter that easily could have gone sentimental. In "Dreams," the details curl forth like smoke from a roof, the action unfolding in chiaroscuro: the scene looms, glowers, then flares. These characters' lives are so plundered by circumstance that they become our own.

The two stories Bill and Maureen discovered date from the early 1980s, and both deal with the collapse of a marriage. One of them, "Call if You Need Me," anticipates a central image in the story "Blackbird Pie" and the poem "Late Night with Fog and Horses." In all three tellings, horses mysteriously appear through fog at a fateful parting. The other story, "What Would

You Like to See?", seems a cousin to "Chef's House"; in each a husband and wife, while attempting to bring their lives together again, remain so injured at the core that they must go their separate ways. The closing image of spoilage recalls Ray's story "Preservation" in its suggestion that relationships, like food on the thaw, are perishable, and beyond a certain point, you can't get them back.

When all but one of the stories had seen serial publication, Gary Fisketjon, Ray's friend and editor, went over them again with me. At one point we discovered ourselves taking out the commas we'd put in. We laughed and quoted Ray to each other—that if you find yourself taking out what you just put in, it's a sure sign the story is finished.

I recently reread the four essays from *Fires* included here. I felt about "My Father's Life" as I did when Ray first showed it to me in an early draft. It has to be one of the most moving expressions on record of a son's love for his father. In an emotionally implosive scene, Ray goes to his father, who's in the mental ward of the hospital where Ray's child has just been born, and tells him, "You're a grandfather." His father responds, "I feel like a grandfather." That sentence falls as softly as distant thunder, yet it has the effect of a hammer blow.

In "On Writing" we get Ray's literary credo. Eschewing what he calls "cheap tricks," he delights in the labor of rewriting. He's brave enough *not* to know where he's going as he writes his initial draft. He sees to it that the story has tension, or what he calls a "relentless motion." He knows what to leave out or to let rest "just under the surface." Above all, there is his injunction to use "clear and specific language," for which he set the mark for writers of his generation.

Ray's homage to John Gardner, his mentor and teacher, made me recall our driving through a snowstorm to visit John at his home in upstate New York. We'd talked into early morning, savoring the company of this man who had cared about Ray and his writing at a time when Ray desperately needed it—even loaning him the keys to his office so he had a place to write. Later, when John died in a motorcycle accident, Ray and I remembered John hadn't wanted to go to bed that last night we'd spent together.

It's natural to want to know where a writer we admire began, and Ray's first published story, "Furious Seasons," marks that beginning, with Faulkner and Joyce as mentors. Also there is the rough gem of a story, "The Hair," which seems antecedent to the later "Careful." In "The Hair" we witness the first moments of that honed "dis-ease" for which Ray became famous. "The Aficionados," also written at this time, is one of only two parodies he published. Here, under the pseudonym John Vale, he took his jabs at one of his clearly recognizable influences. Nonetheless, Hemingway remained an important literary model who would later give way to Chekhov.

The reviews, introductions, and remaining essays collected here remind us of Ray's enthusiasms: his love of a pure "good read," vagaries of character, turns and twists of plot. Always there is the mandate of having something important at stake. As we read what Ray says about teaching writing or the reasons behind his choices for an anthology, we draw instruction from his respect for "vivid depiction of place" or "demonic intensity" and his awareness of "what counts": "Love, death, dreams, ambition, growing up, coming to terms with your own and other people's limitations." Ray understood writing as a process of revelation, and his essay "On Rewriting" emphasizes the importance of revision as a means to open up the story and discover, in the deepest sense, why it was being written in the first place.

I have great respect and affection for the writings collected in this book, not only for their biographical and literary value, but for their passion and clarity. As at the initial publication of *No Heroics, Please*, I feel greatly indebted to William L. Stull, who did the work of collecting Ray's fugitive pieces from newspapers and periodicals. I will always be grateful to Jay Woodruff for his personal kindness and cooperation during all phases of presenting the three stories we discovered; our work enhanced an already great friendship.

Here in the Northwest we often set out rain barrels in order to catch some of nature's bounty. The rain barrel insures an ample supply of soft water for washing our hair, for watering our plants. This book is like rain collected in a barrel, water gathered straight from the sky. We can dip into it at any point and find something to refresh and sustain us—to bring us close again to the life and works of Raymond Carver.

TESS GALLAGHER
Ridge House
Port Angeles, Washington
January 2000

EDITOR'S PREFACE

Like its predecessor *No Heroics, Please* (1991), *Call if You Need Me* includes all the nonfiction left uncollected at the time of Raymond Carver's death: his statements on his work ("Occasions"), his comments on others' writings ("Introductions"), his book reviews, his two last-written essays ("Friendship" and "Meditation on a Line from Saint Teresa"). In addition, the present book contains four prose pieces—"My Father's Life," "On Writing," "Fires," and "John Gardner: The Writer as Teacher"—previously collected in the miscellany *Fires: Essays, Poems, Stories* (1983, 1989). Sections devoted to fiction include five of Carver's early stories and the sole fragment of his uncompleted novel, *The Augustine Notebooks*.

The impetus for issuing an expanded volume of Raymond Carver's uncollected work (and the source of this book's title) was the discovery in 1999 of five previously unpublished short stories. Three of these—"Kindling," "Vandals," and "Dreams"—were found in files at Carver's home in Port Angeles, Washington. The remaining two—"What Would You Like to See?" and "Call if You Need Me"—were found among Carver's papers in the William Charvat Collection of American Fiction at the Ohio State University Library. All five stories are printed here for the first time in book form.

The texts in *Call if You Need Me* are presented uncut and largely unedited. Obvious misspellings, word omissions, and errors of fact have been silently corrected. Direct quotations, whether from Carver's work or writings by others, have been checked against their sources. In general, works in each section are arranged chronologically, in the order of their first publication.

Information about copy-texts, sources, and publication history is provided in the notes.

For expert advice and assistance in locating and editing the texts that comprise this book, I thank my wife, research partner, and codiscoverer of two of the new stories, Maureen P. Carroll.

WILLIAM L. STULL
University of Hartford
Connecticut
March 2000

CALL IF YOU NEED ME

Years ago I read something in a letter by Chekhov that impressed me. It was a piece of advice to one of his many correspondents, and it went something like this: Friend, you don't have to write about extraordinary people who accomplish extraordinary and memorable deeds. (Understand I was in college at the time and reading plays about princes and dukes and the overthrow of kingdoms. Quests and the like, large undertakings to establish heroes in their rightful places. Novels with larger-than-life heroes.) But reading what Chekhov had to say in that letter, and in other letters of his as well, and reading his stories, made me see things differently than I had before.

RAYMOND CARVER
"The Art of Fiction LXXVI"
Paris Review, summer 1983

UNCOLLECTED STORIES

Kindling

It was the middle of August and Myers was between lives. The only thing different about this time from the other times was that this time he was sober. He'd just spent twenty-eight days at a drying-out facility. But during this period his wife took it into her head to go down the road with another drunk, a friend of theirs. The man had recently come into some money and had been talking about buying into a bar and restaurant in the eastern part of the state.

Myers called his wife, but she hung up on him. She wouldn't even talk to him, let alone have him anywhere near the house. She had a lawyer and a restraining order. So he took a few things, boarded a bus, and went to live near the ocean in a room in a house owned by a man named Sol who had run an ad in the paper.

Sol was wearing jeans and a red T-shirt when he opened the door. It was about ten o'clock at night and Myers had just gotten out of a cab. Under the porch light Myers could see that Sol's right arm was shorter than his other arm, and the hand and fingers were withered. He didn't offer either his good left hand or his withered hand for Myers to shake, and this was fine with Myers. Myers felt plenty rattled as it was.

You just called, right? Sol said. You're here to see the room. Come on in.

Myers gripped his suitcase and stepped inside.

This is my wife. This is Bonnie, Sol said.

Bonnie was watching TV but moved her eyes to see who it was coming inside. She pushed the button on a device she held in her hand and the volume went off. She pushed it again and the picture disappeared. Then she got up off the sofa onto her feet. She was a fat girl. She was fat all over and she huffed when she breathed.

I'm sorry it's so late, Myers said. Nice to meet you.

It's all right, Bonnie said. Did my husband tell you on the phone what we're asking?

Myers nodded. He was still holding the suitcase.

Well, this is the living room, Sol said, as you can see for yourself. He shook his head and brought the fingers of his good hand up to his chin. I may as well tell you that we're new at this. We never rented a room to anybody before. But it's just back there not being used, and we thought what the hell. A person can always use a little extra.

I don't blame you a bit, Myers said.

Where are you from? Bonnie said. You're not from anywhere around town.

My wife wants to be a writer, Sol said. Who, what, where, why, and how much?

I just got here, Myers said. He moved the suitcase to his other hand. I got off the bus about an hour ago, read your ad in the paper, and called up.

What sort of work do you do? Bonnie wanted to know.

I've done everything, Myers said. He set the suitcase down and opened and closed his fingers. Then he picked up the suitcase again.

Bonnie didn't pursue it. Sol didn't either, though Myers could see he was curious.

Myers took in a photograph of Elvis Presley on top of the TV. Elvis's signature ran across the breast of his white sequined jacket. He moved a step closer.

The King, Bonnie said.

Myers nodded but didn't say anything. Alongside the picture of Elvis was a wedding picture of Sol and Bonnie. In the picture Sol was dressed up in a suit and tie. Sol's good strong left arm reached around Bonnie's waist as far as it would go. Sol's right

8

hand and Bonnie's right hand were joined over Sol's belt buckle. Bonnie wasn't going anywhere if Sol had anything to say about it. Bonnie didn't mind. In the picture Bonnie wore a hat and was all smiles.

I love her, Sol said, as if Myers had said something to the contrary.

How about that room you were going to show me? Myers said.

I knew there was something we were forgetting, Sol said.

They moved out of the living room into the kitchen, Sol first, then Myers, carrying his suitcase, and then Bonnie. They passed through the kitchen and turned left just before the back door. There were some open cupboards along the wall, and a washer and dryer. Sol opened a door at the end of the little corridor and turned on the light in the bathroom.

Bonnie moved up and huffed and said, This is your private bathroom. That door in the kitchen is your own entrance.

Sol opened the door to the other side of the bathroom and turned on another light. This is the room, he said.

I made up the bed with clean sheets, Bonnie said. But if you take the room you'll have to be responsible from here on out.

Like my wife says, this is not a hotel, Sol said. But you're welcome, if you want to stay.

There was a double bed against one wall, along with a night-stand and lamp, a chest of drawers, and a pinochle table with a metal chair. A big window gave out onto the backyard. Myers put his suitcase on the bed and moved to the window. He raised the shade and looked out. A moon rode high in the sky. In the distance he could see a forested valley and mountain peaks. Was it his imagination, or did he hear a stream or a river?

I hear water, Myers said.

That's the Little Quilcene River you hear, Sol said. That river has the fastest per-foot drop to it of any river in the country.

Well, what do you think? Bonnie said. She went over and turned down the covers on the bed, and this simple gesture almost caused Myers to weep.

I'll take it, Myers said.

I'm glad, Sol said. My wife's glad too, I can tell. I'll have them pull that ad out of the paper tomorrow. You want to move in right now, don't you?

That's what I hoped, Myers said.

We'll let you get settled, Bonnie said. I gave you two pillows, and there's an extra quilt in that closet.

Myers could only nod.

Well, good night, Sol said.

Good night, Bonnie said.

Good night, Myers said. And thank you.

Sol and Bonnie went through his bathroom and into the kitchen. They closed the door, but not before Myers heard Bonnie say, He seems okay.

Pretty quiet, Sol said.

I think I'll fix buttered popcorn.

I'll eat some with you, Sol said.

Pretty soon Myers heard the TV come on again in the living room, but it was a very faint sound and he didn't think it would bother him. He opened the window all the way and heard the sound of the river as it raced through the valley on its way to the ocean.

He took his things out of the suitcase and put them away in the drawers. Then he used the bathroom and brushed his teeth. He moved the table so that it sat directly in front of the window. Then he looked at where she'd turned the covers down. He drew out the metal chair and sat down and took a ballpoint out of his pocket. He thought for a minute, then opened the notebook, and at the top of a blank white page he wrote the words *Emptiness is the beginning of all things.* He stared at this, and then he laughed. Jesus, what rubbish! He shook his head. He closed the notebook, undressed, and turned off the light. He stood for a moment looking out the window and listening to the river. Then he moved to get into bed.

*

Bonnie fixed the popcorn, salted it and poured butter over it, and took it in a big bowl to where Sol was watching TV. She let him help himself to some first. He used his left hand to good effect and then he reached his little hand over for the paper towel she offered. She took a little popcorn for herself.

What do you make of him? she wanted to know. Our new roomer.

Sol shook his head and went on watching TV and eating popcorn. Then, as if he'd been thinking about her question, he said, I like him all right. He's okay. But I think he's on the run from something.

What?

I don't know that. I'm just guessing. He isn't dangerous and he isn't going to make any trouble.

His eyes, Bonnie said.

What about his eyes?

They're sad eyes. Saddest eyes I ever saw on a man.

Sol didn't say anything for a minute. He finished his popcorn. He wiped his fingers and dabbed his chin with the paper towel. He's okay. He's just had some trouble along the way, that's all. No disgrace attached to that. Give me a sip of that, will you? He reached over for the glass of orange drink she was holding and took some. You know, I forgot to collect the rent from him tonight. I'll have to get it in the morning, if he's up. And I should have asked him how long he intends to stay. Damn, what's wrong with me? I don't want to turn this place into a hotel.

You couldn't think of everything. Besides, we're new at this. We never rented a room out before.

Bonnie decided she was going to write about the man in the notebook she was filling up. She closed her eyes and thought about what she was going to write. *This tall, stooped—but handsome!—curly headed stranger with sad eyes walked into our house one fateful night in August.* She leaned into Sol's left arm and tried to write some more. Sol squeezed her shoulder, which brought her back to the present. She opened her eyes and closed them, but she couldn't think of anything else to write about him at the moment. Time will tell, she thought. She was glad he was here.

This show's for the birds, Sol said. Let's go to bed. We have to get up in the morning.

In bed, Sol loved her up and she took him and held him and loved him back, but all the time she was doing it she was thinking about the big, curly headed man in the back room. What if he suddenly opened the bedroom door and looked in on them?

Sol, she said, is this bedroom door locked?

What? Be still, Sol said. Then he finished and rolled off, but he kept his little arm on her breast. She lay on her back and thought for a minute, then she patted his fingers, let air out through her mouth, and went off to sleep thinking about blasting caps, which is what had gone off in Sol's hand when he was a teenager, severing nerves and causing his arm and fingers to wither.

Bonnie began to snore. Sol took her arm and shook it until she turned over on her side, away from him.

In a minute, he got up and put on his underwear. He went into the living room. He didn't turn on the light. He didn't need a light. The moon was out, and he didn't want a light. He went from the living room into the kitchen. He made sure the back door was locked, and then he stood for a while outside the bathroom door listening, but he couldn't hear anything out of the ordinary. The faucet dripped—it needed a washer, but then, it had always dripped. He went back through the house and closed and locked their bedroom door. He checked the clock and made sure the stem was pulled. He got into bed and moved right up against Bonnie. He put his leg over her leg, and in that way he finally went to sleep.

These three people slept and dreamed, while outside the house the moon grew large, and seemed to move across the sky until it was out over the ocean and growing smaller and paler. In his dream, someone is offering Myers a glass of Scotch, but just as he is about to take it, reluctantly, he wakes up in a sweat, his heart racing.

Sol dreams that he is changing a tire on a truck and that he has the use of both of his arms.

Bonnie dreams she is taking two—no, three—children to the park. She even has names for the children. She named them just before the trip to the park. Millicent, Dionne, and Randy. Randy keeps wanting to pull away from her and go his own way.

Soon, the sun breaks over the horizon and birds begin calling to each other. The Little Quilcene River rushes down through the valley, shoots under the highway bridge, rushes another hundred yards over sand and sharp rocks, and pours into the ocean. An eagle flies down from the valley and over the bridge and begins to pass up and down the beach. A dog barks.

At this minute, Sol's alarm goes off.

Myers stayed in his room that morning until he heard them leave. Then he went out and made instant coffee. He looked in the fridge and saw that one of the shelves had been cleared for him. A little sign was Scotch-taped to it: MR. MYERS SHELF.

Later, he walked a mile toward town to a little service station he remembered from the night before that also sold a few groceries. He bought milk, cheese, bread, and tomatoes. That afternoon, before it was time for them to come home, he left the rent money in cash on the table and went back into his own room. Late that night, before going to bed, he opened his notebook and on a clean page he wrote, *Nothing*.

He adjusted his schedule to theirs. Mornings he'd stay in the room until he heard Sol in the kitchen making coffee and getting his breakfast. Then he would hear Sol calling Bonnie to get up and then they'd have breakfast, but they wouldn't talk much. Then Sol would go out to the garage and start the pickup, back out, and drive away. In a little while, Bonnie's ride would pull up in front of the house, a horn would toot, and Bonnie would say, every time, I'm coming.

It was then that Myers would go out to the kitchen, put on water for coffee, and eat a bowl of cereal. But he didn't have much of an appetite. The cereal and coffee would keep him for most of the day, until the afternoon, when he'd eat something else, a sandwich, before they arrived home, and then he'd stay out of the kitchen for the rest of the time when they might be in there or in the living room watching TV. He didn't want any conversation.

She'd go into the kitchen for a snack the first thing after she got in from work. Then she'd turn on the TV and wait until Sol came in, and then she'd get up and fix something for the two of them to eat. They might talk on the telephone to friends, or else go sit outside in the backyard between the garage and Myers's bedroom window and talk about their day and drink iced tea until it was time to go inside and turn on the TV. Once he heard Bonnie say to someone on the telephone, How'd she expect me to pay any attention to Elvis Presley's weight when my own weight was out of control at the time?

They'd said he was welcome anytime to sit in the living room with them and watch TV. He'd thanked them but said, No, television hurt his eyes.

They were curious about him. Especially Bonnie, who'd asked him one day when she came home early and surprised him in the kitchen, if he'd been married and if he had any kids. Myers nodded. Bonnie looked at him and waited for him to go on, but he didn't.

Sol was curious too. What kind of work do you do? he wanted to know. I'm just curious. This is a small town and I know people. I grade lumber at the mill myself. Only need one good arm to do that. But sometimes there are openings. I could put in a word, maybe. What's your regular line of work?

Do you play any instruments? Bonnie asked. Sol has a guitar, she said.

I don't know how to play it, Sol said. I wish I did.

Myers kept to his room, where he was writing a letter to his wife. It was a long letter and, he felt, an important one. Perhaps the most important letter he'd ever written in his life. In the letter he was attempting to tell his wife that he was sorry for everything that had happened and that he hoped someday she would forgive him. *I would get down on my knees and ask forgiveness if that would help.*

After Sol and Bonnie both left, he sat in the living room with his feet on the coffee table and drank instant coffee while he read the newspaper from the evening before. Once in a while his hands trembled and the newspaper began rattling in the empty house. Now and then the telephone rang, but he never made a move to answer it. It wasn't for him, because nobody knew he was here.

Through his window at the rear of the house he could see up the valley to a series of steep mountain peaks whose tops were covered with snow, even though it was August. Lower down on the mountains, timber covered the slopes and the sides of the valley. The river coursed down the valley, frothing and boiling over rocks and under granite embankments until it burst out of its confines at the mouth of the valley, slowed a little, as if it had spent itself, then picked up strength again and plunged into the ocean. When Sol and Bonnie were gone, Myers often sat in the sun in a lawn chair out back and looked up the valley toward the peaks. Once he saw an eagle soaring down the valley, and on another occasion he saw a deer picking its way along the riverbank.

He was sitting out there like that one afternoon when a big flatbed truck pulled up in the drive with a load of wood.

You must be Sol's roomer, the man said, talking out the truck window.

Myers nodded.

Sol said to just dump this wood in the backyard and he'd take care of it from there.

I'll move out of your way, Myers said. He took the chair and moved to the back step, where he stood and watched the driver back the truck up onto the lawn, then push something inside the cab until the truck bed began to elevate. In a minute, the six-foot logs began to slide off the truck bed and pile up on the ground. The bed rose even higher, and all of the chunks rolled off with a loud bang onto the lawn.

The driver touched the lever again and the truck bed went back to its normal place. Then he revved his engine, honked, and drove away.

What are you going to do with that wood out there? Myers asked Sol that night. Sol was standing at the stove frying smelt when Myers surprised him by coming into the kitchen. Bonnie was in the shower. Myers could hear the water running.

Why, I'm going to saw it up and stack it, if I can find the time between now and September. I'd like to do it before the rain starts.

Maybe I could do it for you, Myers said.

You ever cut wood before? Sol said. He'd taken the frying pan off the stove and was wiping the fingers of his left hand with a paper towel. I couldn't pay you anything for doing it. It's something I was going to do anyway. Just as soon as I get a weekend to my name.

I'll do it, Myers said. I can use the exercise.

You know how to use a power saw? And an ax and a maul?

You can show me, Myers said. I learn fast. It was important to him that he cut the wood.

Sol put the pan of smelt back on the burner. Then he said, Okay, I'll show you after supper. You had anything to eat yet? Why don't you have a bite to eat with us?

I ate something already, Myers said.

Sol nodded. Let me get this grub on the table for Bonnie and me, then, and after we eat I'll show you.

I'll be out back, Myers said.

Sol didn't say anything more. He nodded to himself, as if he was thinking about something else.

Myers took one of the folding chairs and sat down on it and looked at the pile of wood and then up the valley at the mountains where the sun was shining off the snow. It was nearly evening. The peaks thrust up into some clouds, and mist seemed to be falling from them. He could hear the river crashing through the undergrowth down in the valley.

I heard talking, Myers heard Bonnie say to Sol in the kitchen.

It's the roomer, Sol said. He asked me if he could cut up that load of wood out back.

How much does he want to do it? Bonnie wanted to know. Did you tell him we can't pay much?

I told him we can't pay anything. He wants to do it for nothing. That's what he said, anyway.

Nothing? She didn't say anything for a time. Then Myers heard her say, I guess he doesn't have anything else to do.

Later, Sol came outside and said, I guess we can get started now, if you're still game.

Myers got up out of the lawn chair and followed Sol over to the garage. Sol brought out two sawhorses and set them up on the lawn. Then he brought out a power saw. The sun had dropped behind the town. In another thirty minutes it would be dark. Myers rolled down the sleeves of his shirt and buttoned the cuffs. Sol worked without saying anything. He grunted as he lifted one of the six-foot logs and positioned it on the sawhorses. Then he began to use the saw, working steadily for a while. Sawdust flew. Finally he stopped sawing and stepped back.

You get the idea, he said.

Myers took the saw, nosed the blade into the cut Sol had started, then began sawing. He found a rhythm and stayed with it. He kept pressing, leaning into the saw. In a few minutes, he sawed through and the two halves of the log dropped onto the ground.

That's the idea, Sol said. You'll do, he said. He picked up the two blocks of wood and carried them over and put them alongside the garage.

Every so often—not every piece of wood, but maybe every fifth or sixth piece—you'll want to split it with the ax down the middle. Don't worry about making kindling. I'll take care of that later. Just split about every fifth or sixth chunk you have. I'll show you. And he propped the chunk up and, with a blow of the ax, split the wood into two pieces. You try it now, he said.

Myers stood the block on its end, just as Sol had done, and he brought the ax down and split the wood.

That's good, Sol said. He put the chunks of wood by the garage. Stack them up about so high, and then come out this way with your stack. I'll lay some plastic sheeting over it once it's all finished. But you don't have to do this, you know.

It's all right, Myers said. I want to, or I wouldn't have asked.

Sol shrugged. Then he turned and went back to the house. Bonnie was standing in the doorway, watching, and Sol stopped and reached his arm around Bonnie, and they both looked at Myers.

Myers picked up the saw and looked at them. He felt good suddenly, and he grinned. Sol and Bonnie were taken by surprise at first. Sol grinned back, and then Bonnie. Then they went back inside.

Myers put another piece of wood on the sawhorses and worked awhile, sawing, until the sweat on his forehead began to feel chill and the sun had gone down. The porch light came on. Myers kept on working until he'd finished the piece he was on. He carried the two pieces over to the garage and then he went in, used his bathroom to wash up, then sat at the table in his room and wrote in his notebook. *I have sawdust in my shirtsleeves tonight,* he wrote. *It's a sweet smell.*

That night he lay awake for a long time. Once he got out of bed and looked out the window at the mound of wood which lay in the backyard, and then his eyes were drawn up the valley to the mountains. The moon was partially obscured by clouds, but he could see the peaks and the white snow, and when he raised his window the sweet, cool air poured in, and farther off he could hear the river coursing down the valley.

The next morning it was all he could do to wait until they'd left the house before he went out back to begin work. He found a pair of gloves on the back step that Sol must have left for him. He sawed and split wood until the sun stood directly over his head and then he went inside and ate a sandwich and drank some milk. Then he went back outside and began again. His shoulders hurt and his fingers were sore and, in spite of the gloves, he'd picked up a few splinters and could feel blisters rising, but he kept on. He decided that he would cut this wood and split it and stack it before sunset, and that it was a matter of life and death that he do so. I must finish this job, he thought, or else . . . He stopped to wipe his sleeve over his face.

By the time Sol and Bonnie came in from work that night—first Bonnie, as usual, and then Sol—Myers was nearly through. A thick pile of sawdust lay between the sawhorses, and, except for two or three blocks still in the yard, all of the wood lay stacked in tiers against the garage. Sol and Bonnie stood in the doorway without saying anything. Myers looked up from his work for a minute and nodded, and Sol nodded back. Bonnie just stood there looking, breathing through her mouth. Myers kept on.

Sol and Bonnie went back inside and began on their supper. Afterward, Sol turned on the porch light, as he'd done the evening before. Just as the sun went down and the moon appeared over the mountains, Myers split the last chunk and gathered up the two pieces and carried the wood over to the garage. He put away the sawhorses, the saw, the ax, a wedge, and the maul. Then he went inside.

Sol and Bonnie sat at the table, but they hadn't begun on their food.

You better sit down and eat with us, Sol said.

Sit down, Bonnie said.

Not hungry just yet, Myers said.

Sol didn't say anything. He nodded. Bonnie waited a minute and then reached for a platter.

You got it all, I'll bet, Sol said.

Myers said, I'll clean up that sawdust tomorrow.

Sol moved his knife back and forth over his plate as if to say, Forget it.

I'll be leaving in a day or two, Myers said.

Somehow I figured you would be, Sol said. I don't know why I felt that, but I didn't think somehow when you moved in you'd be here all that long.

No refunds on the rent, Bonnie said.

Hey, Bonnie, Sol said.

It's okay, Myers said.

No it isn't, Sol said.

It's all right, Myers said. He opened the door to the bathroom, stepped inside, and shut the door. As he ran water into the sink he could hear them talking out there, but he couldn't hear what they were saying.

He showered, washed his hair, and put on clean clothes. He looked at the things of his in the room that had come out of his suitcase just a few days ago, a week ago, and figured it would take him about ten minutes to pack up and be gone. He could hear the TV start up on the other side of the house. He went to the window and raised it and looked again at the mountains, with the moon lying over them—no clouds now, just the moon, and the snowcapped mountains. He looked at the pile of sawdust out in back and at the wood stacked against the shadowy recesses of the garage. He listened to the river for a while. Then he went over to the table and sat down and opened the notebook and began to write.

The country I'm in is very exotic. It reminds me of someplace I've read about but never traveled to before now. Outside my window I can hear a river and in the valley behind the house there is a forest and precipices and mountain peaks covered with snow. Today I saw a wild eagle, and a deer, and I cut and chopped two cords of wood.

Then he put the pen down and held his head in his hands for a moment. Pretty soon he got up and undressed and turned off the light. He left the window open when he got into bed. It was okay like that.

What Would You Like to See?

We were to have dinner with Pete Petersen and his wife, Betty, the night before our departure. Pete owned a restaurant that overlooked the highway and the Pacific Ocean. Early in the summer we had rented a furnished house from him that sat a hundred yards or so back behind the restaurant, just at the edge of the parking lot. Some nights when the wind was coming in off the ocean, we could open the front door and smell the steaks being charbroiled in the restaurant's kitchen and see the gray flume of smoke rising from the heavy brick chimney. And always, day and night, we lived with the hum of the big freezer fans in back of the restaurant, a sound we grew used to.

Pete's daughter, Leslie, a thin blond woman who'd never acted very friendly, lived in a smaller house nearby that also belonged to Pete. She managed his business affairs and had already been over to take a quick inventory of everything—we had rented the house furnished, right down to bed linen and an electric can opener—and had given us our deposit check back and wished us luck. She was friendly that morning she came through the house with her clipboard and inventory list, and we exchanged pleasantries. She didn't take much time with the inventory, and she already had our deposit check made out.

"Dad's going to miss you," she said. "It's funny. He's tough as shoe leather, you know, but he's going to miss you. He's said so. He hates to see you go. Betty too." Betty was her stepmother and looked after Leslie's children when Leslie dated or went off to San Francisco for a few days with her boyfriend. Pete and Betty, Leslie and her kids, Sarah and I, we all lived behind the restaurant within sight of one another, and I'd see Leslie's kids going back and forth from their little place to Pete and Betty's. Sometimes the kids would come over to our house and ring the doorbell and stand on the step and wait. Sarah would invite them in for cookies or pound cake and let them sit at the kitchen table like grown-ups and ask about their day and take an interest in their answers.

Our own children had left home before we moved to this northern coastal region of California. Our daughter, Cindy, was living with several other young people in a house on several rocky acres of ground outside of Ukiah, in Mendocino County. They kept bees and raised goats and chickens and sold eggs and goat's milk and jars of honey. The women worked on patchwork quilts and blankets too, and sold those when they could. But I don't want to call it a commune. I'd have a harder time dealing with it, from what I've heard about communes, if I called it a commune, where every woman was every man's property, things like that. Say she lived with friends on a little farm where everyone shared the labor. But, so far as we knew anyway, they were not involved in organized religion or any sort of sect. We had not heard from her for nearly three months, except for a jar of honey arriving in the mail one day, and a patch of heavy red cloth, part of a quilt she was working on. There was a note wrapped around the jar of honey, which said:

Dear Mom and Dad
    I sewed this myself and I put this Honey up myself. I am learning to do things here.
                                    Love,
                                    Cindy

But two of Sarah's letters went unanswered and then that fall the Jonestown thing happened and we were wild for a day or two that she could be there, for all we knew, in British Guiana. We only had a post-office box number in Ukiah for her. I called the sheriff's office down there and explained the situation, and he drove out to the place to take a head count and carry a message from us. She called that night and first Sarah talked to her and wept, and then I talked to her and wept with relief. Cindy wept too. Some of her friends were down there in Jonestown. She said it was raining, and she was depressed, but the depression would pass, she said; she was where she wanted to be, and doing what she wanted to do. She'd write us a long letter and send us a picture soon.

So when Leslie's children came to visit, Sarah always took a large and real interest in them and sat them down at the table and made them cocoa and served them cookies or pound cake and took a genuine interest in their stories.

But we were moving, we had decided to separate. I was going to Vermont to teach for a semester in a small college and Sarah was going to take an apartment in Eureka, a nearby town. At the end of four and a half months, at the end of the college semester, then we'd take a look at things and see. There was no one else involved for either of us, thank God, and we had neither of us had anything to drink now for nearly a year, almost the amount of time we had been living in Pete's house together, and somehow there was just enough money to get me back east and to get Sarah set up in her apartment. She was already doing research and secretarial work for the history department at the college in Eureka, and if she kept the same job even, and the car, and had only herself to support, she could get by all right. We'd live apart for the semester, me on the East Coast, she on the West, and then we'd take stock, see what was what.

While we were cleaning the house, me washing the windows and Sarah down on her hands and knees cleaning woodwork, the baseboards and corners with a pan of soapy water and an old T-shirt, Betty knocked on the door. It was a point of honor for us to clean this house and clean it well before we left. We had even taken a wire brush and scoured the bricks around the fireplace. We'd left too many houses in a hurry in the past and left them damaged or in a shambles somehow, or else left owing rent and maybe having to move our things in the middle of the night.

This time it was a point of honor to leave this house clean, to leave it immaculate, to leave it in better condition even than we had found it, and after we'd set the date we were going to leave, we had set to work with a passion to erase any signs of ourselves in that house. So when Betty came to the door and knocked, we were hard at work in different rooms of the house and didn't hear her at first. Then she knocked again, a little louder, and I put down my cleaning materials and came out of the bedroom.

"I hope I'm not disturbing you," she said, the color high in her cheeks. She was a little, compact woman with blue slacks and a pink blouse that hung out over her slacks. Her hair was short and brown and she was somewhere in her late forties, younger than Pete. She had been waitressing at Pete's restaurant and was friends with Pete and his first wife, Evelyn, Leslie's mother. Then, we had been told, Evelyn, who was only fifty-four, was returning home from a shopping trip into Eureka. Just as she pulled off the highway into the parking lot behind the restaurant and headed across the lot for her own driveway, her heart stopped. The car kept going, slowly enough, but with enough momentum to knock down the little wood rail fence, cross her flower bed of azaleas, and come to a stop against the porch with Evelyn slumped behind the wheel, dead. A few months later, Pete and Betty had married, and Betty had quit waitressing and become stepmother to Leslie and grandmother to Leslie's children. Betty had been married before and had grown children living in Oregon who drove down now and then to visit. Betty and Pete had been married for five years, and from what we could observe they were happy and well suited to each other.

"Come in, please, Betty," I said. "We're just cleaning up some around here." I moved aside and held the door.

"I can't," she said. "I have the children I'm looking after today. I have to get right back. But Pete and I were wondering if you could come to dinner before you leave." She spoke in a quiet, shy manner and held a cigarette in her fingers. "Friday night?" she said. "If you can."

Sarah brushed her hair and came to the door. "Betty, come in out of the cold," she said. The sky was gray and the wind was pushing clouds in off the sea.

"No, no, thank you, I can't. I left the children coloring, I have to get back. Pete and I, we just wondered if you two could come to dinner. Maybe Friday night, the night before you leave?" She waited and looked shy. Her hair lifted in the wind and she drew on her cigarette.

"I'd like that very much," Sarah said. "Is that all right with you, Phil? We don't have any plans, I don't think. Is it all right?"

"That's very nice of you, Betty," I said. "We'd be happy to come to dinner."

"About 7:30?" Betty said.

"Seven thirty," Sarah said. "This pleases us very much, Betty. More than I can say. It's very kind and thoughtful of you and Pete."

Betty shook her head and was embarrassed. "Pete said he's sorry you're leaving. He said it's been like having more family here. He said it's been an honor having you here as renters." She started backing down the steps. The color was still high in her cheeks. "Friday night, then," she said.

"Thank you, Betty, I mean that," Sarah said. "Thank you again. It means a lot to us."

Betty waved her hand and shook her head. Then she said, "Until Friday, then," and the way in which she said it somehow made my throat tighten. I shut the door after she'd turned away, and Sarah and I looked at each other.

"Well," Sarah said, "this is a switch, isn't it? Getting invited to dinner by our landlord instead of having to skip town and hide out somewhere."

"I like Pete," I said. "He's a good man."

"Betty too," Sarah said. "She's a good kind woman and I'm glad she and Pete have each other."

"Things come around sometimes," I said. "Things work out."

Sarah didn't say anything. She bit her lower lip for a minute. Then she went on into the back room to finish scrubbing. I sat down on the sofa and smoked a cigarette. When I'd finished, I got up and went back to the other room and my mop bucket.

The next day, Friday, we finished cleaning the house and did most of our packing. Sarah wiped down the stove once more, put aluminum foil under the burners, and gave the counter a last going over. Our suitcases and few boxes of books stood in one corner of the living room, ready for our departure. We'd have dinner tonight with the Petersens and we'd get up the next morning and go out for coffee and breakfast. Then we'd come back and load the car; there wasn't all that much left after twenty years of moves and disorder. We'd drive to Eureka and unload the car and put things away in Sarah's efficiency apartment, which she'd rented a few days before, and then sometime before eight o'clock that night she'd drive me to the little airport where I would begin my trip east, planning to make connections with a midnight flight leaving San Francisco for Boston, and she would begin her new life in Eureka. She'd already, a month before, when we began discussing these matters, taken off her wedding ring—not so much in anger as just in sadness one night when we had been making these plans. She had worn no ring at all for a few days, and then she had bought an inexpensive little ring mounted with a turquoise butterfly because, as she said, that finger "felt naked." Once, some years before that, in a rage, she had twisted the wedding band off her finger and thrown it across the living room. I had been drunk and left the house and when we talked about that night a few days later and I asked about her wedding ring, she said, "I still have it. I just put it in a drawer. You don't really think I'd throw my wedding ring away, do you?" A little later she put it back on and she'd kept wearing it, even through the bad times, up until a month ago. She'd also stopped taking birth-control pills and had herself fitted with a diaphragm.

So we worked that day around the house and finished the packing and the cleaning and then, a little after six o'clock, we took our showers and wiped down the shower stall again and dressed and sat in the living room, she on the sofa in a knit dress and blue scarf, her legs drawn up under her, and me in the big chair by the window. I could see the back of Pete's restaurant from where I sat, and the ocean a few miles beyond the restaurant and the meadows and the copses of trees that lay between the front window and the houses. We sat without talking. We had talked and talked and talked. Now we sat without talking and watched it turn dark outside and the smoke feather up from the restaurant chimney.

"Well," Sarah said and straightened out her legs on the sofa. She pulled her skirt down a little. She lit a cigarette. "What time is it? Maybe we should go. They said 7:30, didn't they? What time is it?"

"It's ten after seven," I said.

"Ten after seven," she said. "This is the last time we'll be able to sit in the living room like this and watch it get dark. I don't want to forget this. I'm glad we have a few minutes."

In a little while I got up for my coat. On my way to the bedroom I stopped at the end of the sofa where she sat and bent and kissed her on the forehead. She raised her eyes to mine after the kiss and looked at me.

"Bring my coat too," she said.

I helped her into her coat and then we left the house and went across the lawn and the back edge of the parking lot to Pete's house. Sarah kept her hands in her pockets and I smoked a cigarette as we walked. Just before we got to the gate at the little fence surrounding Pete's house, I threw down my cigarette and took Sarah's arm.

The house was new and had been planted with a tough climbing vine that had spread over the fence. A little wooden lumberjack was nailed to the banister that ran around the porch. When the wind blew, the little man began sawing his log. He was not sawing at this moment, but I could feel the dampness in the air and I knew the wind would come soon. Potted plants were on the porch and flower beds on either side of the sidewalk, but whether they had been planted by Betty or the first wife, there was no way of telling. Some children's toys and a tricycle were on the porch. The porch light was burning, and just as we started up the steps Pete opened the door and greeted us.

"Come in, come in," he said, holding the screen door with one hand. He took Sarah's hands in his hands and then he shook hands with me. He was a tall thin man, sixty years old or so, with a full head of neatly combed gray hair. His shoulders gave the impression of bulk, but he was not heavy. He was wearing a gray Pendleton shirt, dark slacks, and white shoes. Betty came to the door as well, nodding and smiling. She took our coats while Pete asked us what we'd like to drink.

"What can I get you?" he said. "Name it. If I don't have it we'll send over to the restaurant for it." Pete was a recovering alcoholic but kept wine and liquor around the house for guests. He'd once told me that when he'd bought his first restaurant and was cooking sixteen hours a day he drank two fifths of whiskey during those sixteen hours and was hard on his help. Now he'd quit drinking, had been hospitalized for it, we'd heard, and hadn't had a drink in six years, but like many alcoholics, he still kept it around the house.

Sarah said she'd have a glass of white wine. I looked at her. I asked for a Coke. Pete winked at me and said, "You want a little something in the Coke? Something to help take the dampness out of your bones?"

"No thanks, Pete, but maybe you could toss a piece of lime in it, thanks," I said.

"Good fellow," he said. "For me it's the only way to fly anymore."

I saw Betty turn a dial on the microwave oven and push a button. Pete said, "Betty, will you have some wine with Sarah, or what would you like, honey?"

"I'll have a little wine, Pete," Betty said.

"Phil, here's your Coke," Pete said. "Sarah," he said, and gave her a glass of wine. "Betty. Now, there's lots more of everything. Let's go in where it's comfortable."

We passed through the dining room. The table was already set with four place settings, fine china, and crystal wineglasses. We went through to the living room and Sarah and I sat together on one of the sofas. Pete and Betty sat across the room on another sofa. There were bowls of cocktail nuts within reach on a coffee table, cauliflower heads, celery sticks, and a bowl of vegetable dip beside the peanuts.

"We're so glad you could come," Betty said. "We've been looking forward to this all week."

"We're going to miss you," Pete said, "and that's a fact. I hate to see you go, but I know that's life, people have to do what they have to do. I don't know how to say this, but it's been an honor having you over there in the house, you both being teachers and all. I have a great respect for education, though I don't have much myself. It's like a big family here, you know that, and we've come to look on you as part of that family. Here, here's to your health. To you," he said, "and to the future."

We raised our glasses and then we drank.

"We're so glad you feel that way," Sarah said. "This is very important to us, this dinner; we've been looking forward to it more than I can tell you. It means a great deal to us."

Pete said, "We're going to miss you, that's all." He shook his head.

"It's been very, very good for us living here," Sarah said. "We can't tell you."

"There was something about this fellow I liked when I first saw him," Pete said to Sarah. "I'm glad I rented the house to him. You can tell a lot from a man when you first meet him. I liked this fellow of yours. You take care of him, now."

Sarah reached for a celery stick. A little bell went off in the kitchen and Betty said, "Excuse me," and left the room.

"Let me freshen those up for you," Pete said. He left the room with our glasses and returned in a minute with more wine for Sarah and a full glass of Coke for me.

Betty began carrying in things from the kitchen to put on the dining room table. "I hope you like surf and turf," Pete said. "Sirloin steak and lobster tail."

"It sounds fine, it's a dream dinner," Sarah said.

"I guess we can eat now," Betty said. "If you'd like to come to the table. Pete sits here always," Betty said. "This is Pete's place. Phil, you sit there. Sarah, you sit there across from me."

"Man who sits at the head of the table picks up the check," Pete said and laughed.

It was a fine dinner: green salad dotted with tiny fresh shrimp, clam chowder, lobster tail, and steak. Sarah and Betty drank wine, Pete drank mineral water, I stayed with the Coke. We talked a little about Jonestown after Pete brought it up, but I could see that conversation made Sarah nervous. Her lips paled, and I managed to steer us around to salmon fishing.

"I'm sorry we didn't have a chance to go out," Pete said. "But the sports fishermen aren't doing anything yet. It's only the fellows with the commercial licenses that are getting them, and they're going way out. In another week or two maybe the salmon will have moved in. Anytime now, really," Pete said. "But you'll be on the other side of the country then."

I nodded. Sarah picked up her wineglass.

"I bought a hundred and fifty pounds of fresh salmon from a guy yesterday, and that's what I'm featuring on the menu over there now. Fresh salmon," Pete said. "I put it right in the freezer and fresh-froze it. Fellow drove up with it in his pickup truck, an Indian, and I asked him what he was asking for it and he said $3.50 a pound. I said $3.25, and he said we had a deal. So I fresh-froze it and I have it over there on the menu right now."

"Well, this was fine," I said. "I like salmon, but it couldn't have been any better than what we had here tonight. This was delicious."

"We're so glad you could come," Betty said.

"This is wonderful," Sarah said, "but I don't think I've ever seen so much lobster tail and steak. I don't think I can eat all of mine."

"Whatever's left we'll put in a doggy bag for you," Betty said and blushed. "Just like at the restaurant. But save room for dessert."

"Let's have coffee in the living room," Pete said.

"Pete has some slides we took when we were on our trip," Betty said. "If you'd care to see them, we thought we might put up the screen after dinner."

"There's brandy for those who want it," Pete said. "Betty'll have some, I know. Sarah? You'll have some. That's a good girl. It doesn't bother me a bit to have it around and have my guests drink it. Drinking's a funny thing," Pete said.

We had moved back into the living room. Pete was putting up a screen and talking. "I always keep a supply of everything on hand, as you noticed out there, but I haven't touched a drink of anything alcoholic myself for six years. Now this was after drinking more than a quart a day for ten years after I retired from the service. But I quit, God knows how, but I quit, I just quit. I turned myself over to my doctor and just said, Help me, doc. I want to get off this stuff, doc. Can you help me? Well, he made a couple of calls. Said he knew some fellows used to have trouble with it, said there'd been a time when he'd had trouble with it too. The next thing I knew I was on my way to an establishment down there near Santa Rosa. It was in Calistoga, California. I spent three weeks there. When I came home I was sober and the desire to drink had left me. Evelyn, that's my first wife, she met me at the door when I came home and kissed me on the lips for the first time in years. She hated alcohol. Her father and a brother both died from it. It can kill you too, don't forget it. Well, she kissed me on the lips for the first time that night, and I haven't had a drink since I went into that place at Calistoga."

Betty and Sarah were clearing the table. I sat on the sofa and smoked while Pete talked. After he'd put up the screen he took a slide projector out of a box and set it on an end table. He plugged in the cord and flicked a switch on the projector. Light beamed onto the screen and a little fan in the projector began to run.

"We have enough slides that we could look at pictures all night and then some," Pete said. "We have slides here from Mexico, Hawaii, Alaska, the Middle East, Africa too. What would you like to see?"

Sarah came in and sat down on the other end of the sofa from me.

"What would you like to see, Sarah?" Pete said. "You name it."

"Alaska," Sarah said. "And the Middle East. We were there for a while, years ago, in Israel. I've always wanted to go to Alaska."

"We didn't get to Israel," Betty said, coming in with the coffee. "We were on a tour that went only to Syria, Egypt, and Lebanon."

"It's a tragedy, what's happened in Lebanon," Pete said. "It used to be the most beautiful country in the Middle East. I was there as a kid in the merchant marines in World War II. I thought then, I promised myself then, I'd go back there someday. And then we had the opportunity, Betty and me. Didn't we, Betty?"

Betty smiled and nodded.

"Let's see those pictures of Syria and Lebanon," Sarah said. "Those are the ones I'd like to see. I'd like to see them all, of course, but if we have to choose."

So Pete began to show slides, both he and Betty commenting as the memory of the places came back to them.

"There's Betty trying to get on a camel," Pete said. "She needed a little help from that fellow there in the burnoose."

Betty laughed and her cheeks turned red. Another slide flashed on the screen and Betty said, "There's Pete talking with an Egyptian officer."

"Where he's pointing, that mountain behind us there. Here, let me see if I can bring that in closer," Pete said. "The Jews are dug in there. We could see them through the binoculars they let us use. Jews all over that hill. Like ants," Pete said.

"Pete believes that if they had kept their planes out of Lebanon, there wouldn't be all that trouble there," Betty said. "The poor Lebanese."

"There," Pete said. "There's the group at Petra, the lost city. It used to be a caravan city, but then it was just lost, lost and covered over by sand for hundreds of years, and then it was discovered again and we drove there from Damascus in Land Rovers. Look how pink the stone is. Those carvings in the stone are more than two thousand years old, they say. There used to be twenty thousand souls who lived there. And then the desert just covered it up and it was forgotten about. It's what's going to happen to this country if we aren't careful."

We had more coffee and watched some more slides of Pete and Betty at the souks in Damascus. Then Pete turned off the projector and Betty went out to the kitchen and returned with carameled pears for dessert and more coffee. We ate and drank and Pete said again how they would miss us.

"You're good people," Pete said. "I hate to see you leave, but I know it's in your best interests or you wouldn't be going. Now, you'd like to see some slides from Alaska. Is that what you said, Sarah?"

"Alaska, yes," Sarah said. "We'd talked once about going to Alaska, years ago. Didn't we, Phil? Once we were all set to go to Alaska. But we didn't go at the last minute. Do you remember that, Phil?"

I nodded.

"Now you'll go to Alaska," Pete said.

The first slide showed a tall, trim red-haired woman standing on the deck of a ship with a snow-covered range of mountains in the distance behind her. She was wearing a white fur coat and facing the camera with a smile on her face.

"That's Evelyn, Pete's first wife," Betty said. "She's dead now."

Pete threw another slide onto the screen. The same red-haired woman was wearing the same coat and shaking hands with a smiling Eskimo in a parka. Large dried fish were hanging on poles behind the two figures. There was an expanse of water and more mountains.

"That's Evelyn again," Pete said. "These were taken in Point Barrow, Alaska, the northernmost settlement in the U.S."

Then there was a shot of the main street—little low buildings with slanted metal roofs, signs saying King Salmon Café, Cards, Liquor, Rooms. One slide showed a Colonel Sanders fried-chicken parlor with a billboard outside showing Colonel Sanders in a parka and fur boots. We all laughed.

"That's Evelyn again," Betty said, as another slide flashed on the screen.

"These were made before Evelyn died," Pete said. "We'd always talked about going to Alaska, too," Pete said. "I'm glad we made that trip before she died."

"Good timing," Sarah said.

"Evelyn was a good friend to me," Betty said. "It was a lot like losing my sister."

We saw Evelyn boarding a plane back for Seattle, and we saw Pete, smiling and waving, emerging from that same plane after it had landed in Seattle.

"It's heating up," Pete said. "I'll have to turn off the projector for a little while to let it cool off. What would you like to see then? Hawaii? Sarah, it's your night; you say."

Sarah looked at me.

"I guess we should think about going home, Pete," I said. "It's going to be a long day tomorrow."

"Yes, we should go," Sarah said. "We really should, I guess." But she continued to sit there with her glass in her hand. She looked at Betty and then she looked at Pete. "It's been a very wonderful evening for us," she said. "I really have a hard time thanking you enough. This has meant a good deal to us."

"No, it's us who should be thanking you," Pete said, "and that's the truth. It's been a pleasure knowing you. I hope that the next time you're in this part of the country you'll stop by here and say hello."

"You won't forget us?" Betty said. "You won't, will you?" Sarah shook her head. Then we were on our feet and Pete was getting our coats. Betty said, "Oh, don't forget your doggy bag. This will make you a nice snack tomorrow."

Pete helped Sarah with her coat and then held my coat for me to slip my arm into.

We all shook hands on the front porch. "The wind's coming up," Pete said. "Don't forget us, now," Pete said. "And good luck."

"We won't," I said. "Thank you again, thanks for everything." We shook hands once more. Pete took Sarah by the shoulders and kissed her on the cheek. "You take good care of yourselves, now. This fellow too. Take good care of him," he said. "You're both good people. We like you."

"Thank you, Pete," Sarah said. "Thank you for saying that."

"I'm saying it because it's true, or else I wouldn't be saying it," Pete said.

Betty and Sarah embraced.

"Well, good night to you," Betty said. "And God bless you both."

We walked down the sidewalk past the flowers. I held the gate for Sarah and we walked across the gravel parking lot to our house. The restaurant was dark. It was after midnight. Wind blew through the trees. The parking lot lights burned, and the generator in back of the restaurant hummed and turned the freezer fan inside the locker.

I unlocked the door to the house. Sarah snapped on the light and went into the bathroom. I turned on the lamp beside the chair in front of the window and sat down with a cigarette. After a little while Sarah came out, still in her coat, and sat on the sofa and touched her forehead.

"It was a nice evening," she said. "I won't forget it. So different from so many of our other departures," she said. "Imagine, to actually have dinner with your landlord before you move." She shook her head. "We've come a long way, I guess, if you look at it that way. But there's a long way to go yet. Well, this is the last night we'll spend in this house, and I'm so tired from that big dinner I can hardly keep my eyes open. I think I'll go in and go to bed."

"I'm going too," I said. "Just as soon as I finish this."

We lay in bed without touching. Then Sarah turned on her side and said, "I'd like you to hold me until I get off to sleep. That's all, just hold me. I miss Cindy tonight. I hope she's all right. I pray she's all right. God help her to find her way. And God help us," she said.

After a while her breathing became slow and regular and I turned away from her again. I lay on my back and stared at the dark ceiling. I lay there and listened to the wind. Then, just as I started to close my eyes again, I heard something. Or, rather, something that I had been hearing I didn't hear anymore. The wind still blew, and I could hear it under the eaves of the house and singing in the wires outside the house, but something was not there any longer, and I didn't know what it was. I lay there a while longer and listened, and then I got up and went out to the living room and looked out the front window at the restaurant, the edge of moon showing through the fast-moving clouds.

I stood at the window and tried to figure out what was wrong. I kept looking at the glint of ocean and then back to the darkened restaurant. Then it came to me, what the odd silence was. The generator had gone off over at the restaurant. I stood there a while longer wondering what I should do, if I should call Pete. Maybe it would take care of itself in a little while and switch back on, but for some reason I knew this wouldn't happen.

He must have noticed it too, for suddenly I saw a light go on over at Pete's, and then a figure appeared on the steps with a flashlight. The figure carrying the flashlight went to the back of the restaurant and unlocked the door, and then lights began to go on in the restaurant. After a little while, after I had smoked a cigarette, I went back to bed. I went to sleep immediately.

The next morning we had instant coffee, and washed the cups and packed them when we were finished. We didn't talk much. There was an appliance truck behind the restaurant, and I could see Betty and Leslie coming and going from the back door of the restaurant, carrying things in their arms. I didn't see Pete.

We loaded the car. We would be able to carry everything into Eureka in one load, after all. I walked over to the restaurant to drop off the keys, but just as I got to the office door, it opened and Pete came out carrying a box.

"It's going to rot," he said. "The salmon thawed out. It was just starting to freeze, then it began to thaw. I'm going to lose all this salmon. I'm going to have to give it away, get rid of it this morning. The fillets and prawns and scallops, too. Everything. The generator burned out, goddamn it."

"I'm sorry, Pete," I said. "We have to go now. I wanted to give you back the keys."

"What is it?" he said and looked at me.

"The house keys," I said. "We're leaving now. We're on our way."

"Give them to Leslie in there," he said. "Leslie takes care of the rentals. Give her your keys."

"I will, then. Good-bye, Pete. I'm sorry about this. But thanks again for everything."

"Sure," he said. "Sure, don't mention it. Good luck to you. Take it easy." He nodded and went on over to his house with his box of fillets. I gave the keys to Leslie, said good-bye to her, and walked back to the car where Sarah was waiting.

"What's wrong?" Sarah said. "What's happened? It looked like Pete didn't have the time of day for you."

"The generator burned out last night at the restaurant and the freezer shut down and some of their meat spoiled."

"Is that it?" she said. "That's too bad. I'm sorry to hear it. You gave them the keys, didn't you? We've said good-bye. I guess we can go now."

"Yes," I said. "I guess we can."

Dreams

My wife is in the habit of telling me her dreams when she wakes up. I take her some coffee and juice and sit in a chair beside the bed while she wakes up and moves her hair away from her face. She has the look that people waking up have, but she also has this look in her eyes of returning from somewhere.

"Well?" I say.

"It's crazy," she says. "This was a dream and a half. I dreamed I was a boy going fishing with my sister and her girlfriend, but I was drunk. Imagine that. Doesn't that beat everything? I was supposed to drive them fishing, but I couldn't find the car keys. Then, when I found the keys, the car wouldn't start. Suddenly, we were at the fishing place and on the lake in a boat. A storm was coming up, but I couldn't get the motor started. My sister and her friend just laughed and laughed. But I was afraid. Then I woke up. Isn't that strange? What do you make of it?"

"Write it down," I said and shrugged. I didn't have anything to say. I didn't dream. I hadn't dreamed in years. Or maybe I did but couldn't remember anything when I woke up. One thing I'm not is an expert on dreams—my own or anybody else's. Once Dotty told me she'd had a dream right before we got married when she thought she was barking! She woke herself up and saw her little dog, Bingo, sitting beside the bed looking at her in what she thought was a strange way. She realized she'd been barking in her sleep. What did it mean? she wondered. "That was a bad dream," she said. She'd added the dream to her dream book, but that was that. She didn't get back to it. She didn't interpret her dreams. She just wrote them down and then, when she had the next one, she wrote that one down too.

I said, "I'd better go upstairs. I need to use the bathroom."

"I'll be along pretty soon. I have to wake up first. I want to think about this dream some more."

I left her sitting up in bed, holding her cup, but not drinking from it. She was sitting there thinking about her dream.

I didn't have to go to the bathroom after all, so I took some coffee and sat at the kitchen table. It was August, a heat wave, and the windows were open. Hot, yes, it was hot. The heat was killing. My wife and I slept in the basement for most of the month. But it was okay. We carried the mattress down there, pillows, sheets, everything. We had an end table, a lamp, an ashtray. We laughed. It was like starting over. But all the windows upstairs were open, and the windows next door, they were open too. I sat at the table listening to Mary Rice next door. It was early, but she was up and in her kitchen in her nightgown. She was humming, and she kept it up while I listened and drank coffee. Then her children came into their kitchen. This is what she said to them:

"Good morning, children. Good morning, my loved ones."

It's true. That's what their mother said to them. Then they were at the table, laughing about something, and one of the kids was banging his chair up and down, laughing.

"Michael, that's enough," Mary Rice said. "Finish your cereal, honey."

In a minute, Mary Rice sent her kids out of the room to get themselves dressed for school. She began to hum as she cleaned a dish. I listened and, listening, I thought, I am a rich man. I have a wife who dreams something every night, who lies there beside me until she falls asleep and then she goes far away into some rich dream every night. Sometimes she dreams of horses and weather and people, and sometimes she even changes her sex in her dreams. I didn't miss dreaming. I had her dreams to think about if I wanted to have a dream life. And I have a woman next door who sings or else hums all day long. All in all, I felt quite lucky.

I moved to the front window to watch the kids next door when they went out of their house to go to school. I saw Mary Rice kiss each of the children on the face, and I heard her say, "Good-bye, children." Then she latched the screen, stood for a minute watching her children walk down the street, then turned and went back inside.

I knew her habits. She'd sleep in a few hours now—she didn't sleep when she came in from her job at night, a little after five in the morning. The girl who baby-sat for her—Rosemary Bandel, a neighbor girl—would be waiting for her and would leave and go across the street to her own house. And then the lights would glow over at Mary Rice's for the rest of the night. Sometimes, if her windows were open, like now, I'd hear classical piano music, and once I even heard Alexander Scourby reading *Great Expectations*.

Sometimes, if I couldn't sleep—my wife sleeping and dreaming away beside me—I'd get up out of bed and go upstairs and sit at the table and listen to her music, or her talking records, and wait for her to pass behind a curtain or until I saw her standing behind the window shade. Once in a while the phone rang over there at some early and unlikely hour, but she always picked it up on the third ring.

The names of her children, I found out, were Michael and Susan. To my eye they were no different from any of the other neighborhood kids, except when I'd see them I'd think, you kids are lucky to have a mother who sings to you. You don't need your father. Once they came to our door selling bath soap, and another time they came around selling seeds. We didn't have a garden, of course not—how could anything grow where we lived—but I bought some seeds anyway, what the hell. And on Halloween they came to the door, always with their baby-sitter—their mother was working, of course—and I gave them candy bars and nodded to Rosemary Bandel.

My wife and I have lived in this neighborhood longer than anyone. We've seen almost everyone come and go. Mary Rice and her husband and children moved in three years ago. Her husband worked for the telephone company as a lineman, and for a time he left every morning at seven o'clock and returned home in the evening at five. Then he stopped coming home at five. He came home later, or not at all.

My wife noticed it too. "I haven't seen him home over there in three days," she said.

"I haven't either," I said. I'd heard loud voices over there the other morning, and one or both of the children were crying.

Then at the market, my wife was told by the woman who lived on the other side of Mary Rice that Mary and her husband had separated. "He's moved out on her and the children," was what this woman said. "The son of a bitch."

And then, not very long after, needing to support herself because her husband had quit his job and left town, Mary Rice had gone to work in this restaurant serving cocktails and, pretty soon, began staying up all night listening to music and talking records. And singing sometimes and humming other times. This same woman who lived next door to Mary Rice said she had enrolled in two correspondence courses from the university. She was making a new life for herself, this woman said, and the new life included her children too.

Winter was not so far away when I decided to put up the storm windows. When I was outside, using my ladder, those kids from next door, Michael and Susan, came charging out of the house with their dog and let the screen door bang shut behind them. They ran down the sidewalk in their coats, kicking piles of leaves.

Mary Rice came to the door and looked after them. Then she looked over at me.

"Hello there," she said. "You're getting ready for winter, I see."

"Yes, I am," I said. "It won't be long."

"No, it won't," she said. Then she waited a minute, as if she was going to say something else. Then she said, "It was nice talking to you."

"My pleasure," I answered.

That was just before Thanksgiving. About a week later, when I went into the bedroom with my wife's coffee and juice, she was already awake and sitting up and ready to tell me her dream. She patted the bed beside her, and I sat down.

"This is one for the book," she said. "Listen to this if you want to hear something."

"Go on," I said. I took a sip from her cup and handed it to her. She closed both hands around it as if her hands were cold.

"We were on a ship," she said.

"We've never been on a ship," I said.

"I know that, but we were on a ship, a big ship, a cruise ship, I guess. We were in bed, a bunk or something, when somebody knocked at the door with a tray of cupcakes. They came in, left the cupcakes and went out. I got out of bed and went to get one of the cupcakes. I was hungry, you see, but when I touched the cupcake it burned the tips of my fingers. Then my toes began to curl up—like they do when you're scared? And then I got back in bed but I heard loud music—it was Scriabin—and then somebody began to rattle glasses, hundreds of glasses, maybe thousands of glasses, all of them rattling at once. I woke you up and told you about it, and you said you'd go to see what it was. While you were gone I remember seeing the moon go by outside, go by the porthole, and then the ship must have turned or something. Then the moon came by again and lit up the whole room. Then you came back, still in your pajamas, and got back in bed and went back to sleep without saying a word. The moon was shining right outside the window and everything in the room seemed to gleam, but still you didn't say anything. I remember feeling a little afraid of you for not saying anything, and my toes started curling again. Then I went back to sleep—and here I am. What do you think of that? Isn't that some dream? God. What do you make of it? You didn't dream anything, did you?" She sipped from her coffee and watched me.

I shook my head. I didn't know what to say, so all I said was that she had better put it in her notebook.

"God, I don't know. They're getting pretty weird. What do you think?"

"Put it in your book."

Pretty soon it was Christmas. We bought a tree and put it up and on Christmas morning we exchanged gifts. Dotty bought me a new pair of mittens, a globe, and a subscription to *Smithsonian* magazine. I gave her a perfume—she blushed when she opened the little package—and a new nightgown. She hugged me. Then we drove across town to have dinner with some friends.

The weather became colder between Christmas and the first of the year. It snowed, and then it snowed again. Michael and Susan went outside long enough one day to build a snowman. They put a carrot in its mouth. At night I could see the glare of the TV in their bedroom window. Mary Rice kept going back and forth to work every evening, Rosemary came in to baby-sit, and every night and all night the lights burned over there.

On New Year's Eve we drove across town to our friends' for dinner again, played bridge, watched some TV and, promptly at midnight, opened a bottle of champagne. I shook hands with Harold and we smoked a cigar together. Then Dotty and I drove home.

But—and this is the beginning of the hard part—when we reached our neighborhood, the street was blocked off by two police cars. The lights on top of the cars revolved back and forth. Other cars, curious motorists, had stopped, and people had come out of their houses. Most of the people were dressed up and wearing topcoats, but there were a few people in nightclothes wearing heavy coats that they'd obviously put on in a hurry. Two fire engines were parked down the street. One of them sat in our front yard, and the other was in Mary Rice's driveway.

I gave the officer my name and said that we lived there, where the big truck was parked—"They're in front of our house!" Dotty screamed—and the officer said we should park our car.

"What happened?" I said.

"I guess one of those space heaters caught on fire. That's what somebody said, anyway. A couple of kids were in there. Three kids, counting the baby-sitter. She got out. The kids didn't make it, I don't guess. Smoke inhalation."

We started walking down the street toward our house. Dotty walked close to me and held my arm. "Oh my God," she said.

Up close to Mary Rice's house, under the lights thrown up by the fire trucks, I could see a man standing on the roof holding a fire hose. But only a trickle of water came out of it now. The bedroom window was broken out, and in the bedroom I could see a man moving around in the room carrying something that could have been an ax. Then a man walked out the front door with something in his arms, and I saw it was those kids' dog. And I felt terrible then.

A mobile TV unit from one of the local stations was there, and a man was operating a camera that he held over his shoulder. Neighbors huddled around. The engines in the trucks were running, and now and then voices came over speakers from inside the trucks. But none of the people watching were saying anything. I looked at them, and then I recognized Rosemary, who was standing with her mother and father with her mouth open. Then they brought the children down on stretchers, the firemen, big fellows wearing boots and coats and hats, men who looked indestructible and as if they could live another hundred years. They came outside, one on either end of the stretchers, carrying the children.

"Oh no," said the people who stood watching. And then again, "Oh no. No," someone cried.

They laid the stretchers on the ground. A man in a suit and wool cap stepped up and listened with a stethoscope for a heartbeat on each of the children, and then nodded to the ambulance attendants, who stepped forward to pick up the stretchers.

At that moment a little car drove up and Mary Rice jumped out of the passenger side. She ran toward the men who were about to put the stretchers into the ambulance. "Put them down!" she yelled. "Put them down!"

And the attendants stopped what they were doing and put the stretchers down and then stood back. Mary Rice stood over her children and howled—yes, there's no other word. People stepped back and then they moved forward again as she dropped to her knees in the snow beside the stretchers and put her hands on the face of one child and then the other.

The man in the suit with the stethoscope stepped forward and kneeled beside Mary Rice. Another man—it might have been the fire chief or else the assistant fire chief—signaled the attendants and then stepped up to Mary Rice and helped her up and put his arm around her shoulders. The man in the suit stood on the other side of her, but he didn't touch her. The person who'd driven her home now walked up close to see what was going on, but he was only a scared-looking kid, a busboy or a dishwasher. He had no right to be there to witness Mary Rice's grief and he knew it. He stood back away from people, keeping his eyes on the stretchers as the men put them into the back of the ambulance.

"No!" Mary Rice said and jumped toward the back of the ambulance as the stretchers were being put in.

I went up to her then—no one else was doing anything—and took her arm and said, "Mary, Mary Rice."

She whirled on me and said, "I don't know you, what do you *want*?" She brought her hand back and slapped me in the face. Then she got into the ambulance along with the attendants, and the ambulance moved down the street, sliding, its siren going off, as the people got out of the way.

*

45

I slept badly that night. And Dotty groaned in her sleep and turned again and again. I knew she was dreaming that she was somewhere far away from me all night. The next morning, I didn't ask her what she'd dreamed, and she didn't volunteer anything. But when I went in with her juice and coffee, she had her notebook on her lap along with a pen. She closed the pen up in the notebook and looked at me.

"What's happening next door?" she asked me.

"Nothing," I said. "The house is dark. There are tire marks all over the snow. The children's bedroom window is broken out. That's all. Nothing else. Except for that, the bedroom window, you wouldn't know there'd been a fire. You wouldn't know two children had died."

"That poor woman," Dotty said. "God, that poor, unfortunate woman. God help her. And us, too."

From time to time that morning people in cars drove by slowly and looked at her house. Or else people came up to the front of the house, looked at the window, looked at how the snow had been churned up in front of the house, and then went on again. Toward noon I was looking out the window when a station wagon drove up and parked. Mary Rice and her former husband, the children's father, got out and went toward the house. They moved slowly, and the man took her arm as they went up the steps. The porch door stood open from the night before. She went inside first. Then he went in.

That night on the local news we saw the whole thing going on again. "I can't watch this," Dotty said, but she watched anyway, just like I did. The film showed Mary Rice's house and a man on the roof with a hose spraying water down through the broken window. Then the children were shown being carried out, and again we watched Mary Rice dropping to her knees. Then, as the stretchers are being put into the ambulance, Mary Rice whirls on somebody and screams, "What do you *want*?"

At noon the next day the station wagon drove up in front of

the house. As soon as it was parked, before the man could even turn off the engine, Mary Rice came down the steps. The man got out of the car, said "Hello, Mary," and opened the passenger's door for her. Then they went off to the funeral.

He stayed four nights after the funeral, and then the next morning when I got up, early as always, the station wagon was gone and I knew he'd left sometime in the night.

That morning Dotty told me about a dream she'd had. She was in a house in the country and a white horse came up and looked in through the window at her. Then she woke up.

"I want to do something to express our sorrow," Dotty said. "I want to have her over for dinner, maybe."

But the days passed and we didn't do anything, Dotty or I, about having her over. Mary Rice went back to work, only now she worked days, in an office, and I saw her leave the house in the morning and return home a little after five. The lights would go out over there around ten at night. The shade in the children's room was always pulled, and I imagined, though I didn't know, that the door was closed.

Toward the end of March, I went outside one Saturday to take down the storm windows. I heard a noise and looked and I saw Mary Rice trying to spade some dirt, to turn over some ground behind her house. She was wearing slacks, a sweater, and a summer hat. "Hello there," I said.

"Hello," she said. "I guess I'm rushing things. But I have all this time on my hands, you see, and—well, this is the time of year it says on the package." She took a packet of seeds out of her pocket. "My kids went around the neighborhood last year selling seeds. I was cleaning out drawers and found some of these packages."

I didn't mention the seed packets I had in my own kitchen drawer. "My wife and I have been wanting to ask you over for dinner for a long time," I said. "Will you come some night? Could you come tonight, if you're free?"

"I guess I could do that. Yes. But I don't even know your name. Or your wife's."

I told her and then I said, "Is six o'clock a good time?"

"When? Oh, yes. Six o'clock is fine." She put her hand on the spade and pushed down. "I'll just go ahead and plant these seeds. I'll come over at six. Thank you."

I went back into the house to tell Dotty about dinner. I took down the plates and got out the silverware. The next time I looked out, Mary Rice had gone in from her garden.

Vandals

Carol and Robert Norris were old friends of Nick's wife, Joanne. They'd known her for years, long before Nick met her. They'd known her since back when she'd been married to Bill Daly. In those days, the four of them—Carol and Robert, Joanne and Bill—were newlyweds and graduate students in the university art department. They lived in the same house, a big house on Seattle's Capitol Hill, where they shared the rent, and a bathroom. They took many of their meals together and sat up late talking and drinking wine. They handed the work they'd done around to each other for criticism and inspection. They even, in the last year they shared the house together—before Nick appeared on the scene—bought an inexpensive little sailboat together that they used during the summer months on Lake Washington. "Good times and bad, high times and low," Robert said, for the second time that morning, laughing and looking around the table at the faces of the others.

It was Sunday morning, and they were sitting around the table in Nick and Joanne's kitchen in Aberdeen, eating smoked salmon, scrambled eggs, and cream cheese on bagels. It was salmon that Nick had caught the summer before and then had arranged to have vacuum packed. He'd put the salmon in the freezer. He liked it that Joanne told Carol and Robert that he'd caught the fish himself. She even knew—or claimed to know—how much the fish had weighed. "This one weighed sixteen pounds," she said, and Nick laughed, pleased. Nick had taken the fish out of the freezer the night before, after Carol had called and talked to Joanne and said she and Robert and their daughter, Jenny, would like to stop on their way through town.

"Can we be excused now?" Jenny said. "We want to go skateboarding."

"The skateboards are in the car," Jenny's friend, Megan, said.

"Take your plates over to the sink," Robert said. "And then you can go skateboarding, I guess. But don't go far. Stay in the neighborhood," he said. "And be careful."

"Is it all right?" Carol said.

"Sure it is," Joanne said. "It's fine. I wish *I* had a skateboard. If I did, I'd join them."

"But mostly good times," Robert said, going on with what he'd been saying about their student days. "Right?" he said, catching Joanne's eye and grinning.

Joanne nodded.

"Those were the days, all right," Carol said.

Nick had the feeling that Joanne wanted to ask them something about Bill Daly. But she didn't. She smiled, held the smile a moment too long, and then asked if anybody would like more coffee.

"I'll have some more, thanks," Robert said. Carol said "Nope" and put the palm of her hand over her cup. Nick shook his head.

"So tell me about salmon fishing," Robert said to Nick.

"Nothing much to tell," Nick said. "You get up early and you go out on the water, and if the wind isn't blowing and it doesn't rain on you, and the fish are in and you're rigged up properly, you might get a strike. The odds are that, if you're lucky, you'll land one out of every four fish that hit. Some men devote their lives to it, I guess. I fish some in the summer months, and that's it."

"Do you fish out of a boat or what?" Robert said. He said this as if it was an afterthought. He wasn't really interested, Nick felt, but thought he had to say more since he'd brought it up.

"I have a boat," Nick said. "It's berthed down at the marina."

Robert nodded slowly. Joanne poured his coffee and Robert looked at her and grinned. "Thanks, babe," he said.

Nick and Joanne saw Carol and Robert every six months or so—more often than Nick would have liked, to tell the truth. It wasn't that he disliked them; he did like them. He liked them better, in fact, than any other of Joanne's friends he'd met. He liked Robert's bitter sense of humor, and the way he had of telling a story, making it seem funnier, probably, than it really was. He liked Carol, too. She was a pretty, cheerful woman who still did an occasional acrylic painting—Nick and Joanne had hung one of her paintings, a gift, on their bedroom wall. Carol had never been anything but pleasant to Nick during the times they'd been in each other's company. But sometimes, when Robert and Joanne were reminiscing over the past, Nick would find himself looking across the room at Carol, who would hold his look, smile, and then give a little shake of her head, as if none of this talk of the past were of any consequence.

Still, from time to time when they were all together, Nick couldn't help feeling that an unspoken judgment was being made, and that Robert, if not Carol, still blamed him for breaking up Joanne's marriage with Bill and ending their happy foursome.

They saw each other in Aberdeen at least twice a year, once at the beginning of summer, and once again near the end. Robert and Carol and Jenny, their ten-year-old, made a loop through town on their way to the rain forest country of the Olympic Peninsula, heading for a lodge they knew about at a place called Agate Beach, where Jenny would hunt for agates and fill up a leather pouch with stones that she took back to Seattle for polishing.

The three never stayed overnight with Nick and Joanne—it occurred to Nick they'd never been asked to stay, for one thing, though he was sure that Joanne would have been pleased enough to have them, if Nick suggested it. But he hadn't. On each of their visits, they arrived in time for breakfast, or else they showed up just before lunch. Carol always called ahead to make the arrangements. They were punctual, which Nick appreciated.

Nick liked them, but somehow he was always made uneasy in

their company, too. They'd never, not once, talked about Bill Daly in Nick's presence, or even so much as mentioned the man's name. Nevertheless, when the four of them were together Nick was somehow made to feel that Daly was never very far from anyone's thoughts. Nick had taken Daly's wife away from him, and now these old friends of Daly's were in the house of the man who'd committed that callous indiscretion, the man who'd turned all their lives upside down for a while. Wasn't it a kind of betrayal for Robert and Carol to be friends with the man who'd done this? To actually break bread in the man's house and see him put his arm lovingly around the shoulders of the woman who used to be the wife of the man they loved?

"Don't go far, honey," Carol said to Jenny as the girls passed through the kitchen again. "We have to be leaving soon."

"We won't," Jenny said. "We'll just skate out in front."

"See that you do," Robert said. "We'll go pretty soon, you kids." He looked at his watch.

The door closed behind the children, and the grownups went back to a subject they'd touched on earlier that morning—terrorism. Robert was an art teacher in one of the Seattle high schools, and Carol worked in a boutique near the Pike Place Market. Between the two of them they didn't know anyone who was going to Europe or the Middle East that summer. In fact, several people, friends of theirs, had canceled their vacation plans to Italy and Greece.

"See America first, is my motto," Robert said. He went on to tell something about his mother and stepfather, who'd just come back from two weeks in Rome. Their luggage had been lost for three days—that was the first thing that'd happened. Then, the second night in Rome, walking down the Via Veneto to a restaurant not far from their hotel—the street patrolled by men in uniform, carrying machine guns—his mother had her purse snatched by a thief on a bicycle. Two days later, when they drove a rental car about thirty miles from Rome, somebody slashed a tire and stole the hood off the car while they were in a museum. "They didn't take the battery or anything, you understand," Robert said. "They wanted the hood. Can you beat it?"

"What'd they want with the hood?" Joanne asked.

"Who knows?" Robert said. "But in any case, it's getting worse for people over there—for tourists—since we bombed. What do you guys think about the bombing? I think it's just going to make things worse for Americans. Everybody's a target now."

Nick stirred his coffee and sipped it before saying, "I don't know any longer. I really don't. In my mind I keep seeing all those bodies lying in pools of blood in the airports. I just don't know." He stirred his coffee some more. "The guys I've talked to over here think that we should have dropped a few more bombs, maybe, while we were at it. I heard somebody say they should have turned the place into a parking lot, while they were at it. I don't know *what* we should or shouldn't do over there. But we had to do something, I think."

"Well, that's a little severe, isn't it?" Robert said. "A parking lot? Like, *nuke* the place—you know?"

"I said I don't know what they should have done. But some kind of response was necessary."

"Diplomacy," Robert said. "Economic sanctions. Let them feel it in their pocketbooks. Then they'll straighten up and fly right."

"Should I make more coffee?" Joanne said. "It won't take a minute. Who wants some cantaloupe?" She moved her chair back and got up from the table.

"I can't eat another bite," Carol said.

"Me neither," Robert said. "I'm fine." He seemed to want to go on with what they were talking about, and then he stopped. "Nick, sometime I'll come down here and go fishing with you. When's the best time to go?"

"Do it," Nick said. "You're welcome to come anytime. Come over and stay as long as you'd like. July is the best month. But August is good too. Even the first week or two of September." He started to say something about how swell it was fishing in the evenings, when most of the boats had gone in. He started to say something about the time he'd hooked a big one in the moonlight.

Robert seemed to consider this for a minute. He drank some of his coffee. "I'll do it. I'll come this summer—in July, if that's all right."

"It's fine," Nick said.

"What will I need in the way of equipment?" Robert said, interested.

"Just bring yourself," Nick said. "I have plenty of gear."

"You can use my pole," Joanne said.

"But then you couldn't fish," Robert said. And suddenly that was the end of the talk about fishing. Somehow, Nick could see, the prospect of sitting together in a boat for hours on end made Robert and him both feel uneasy. No, frankly he couldn't see any more for their relationship than sitting here in this nice kitchen twice a year, eating breakfast and lingering over coffee. It was pleasant enough, and it was just enough time spent together. More than this was just not in the cards. Lately he'd even passed up an occasional trip to Seattle with Joanne, because he knew she'd want to stop at the end of the day at Carol and Robert's for coffee. Nick would make an excuse and stay home. He'd say he was too busy at the lumberyard that he managed. On one occasion, Joanne had spent the night with Carol and Robert, and when she came home, she seemed to Nick to be remote and thoughtful for a few days. When he asked her about the visit, she said it had been fine and that they'd sat up late after dinner talking. Nick knew they must have talked about Bill Daly; he was certain they had, and he found himself irritated for a few weeks. But so what if they'd talked about Daly? Joanne was Nick's now. Once he would have killed for her. He loved her still, and she loved him, but he didn't feel that obsessive now. No, he wouldn't kill for her now, and he had a hard time understanding how he'd ever felt that way in the first place. He didn't think that she—or anybody, for that matter—could ever be worth killing somebody else for.

Joanne stood up and began clearing the plates from the table. "Let me help," Carol said.

Nick put his arm around Joanne's waist and squeezed her, as if vaguely ashamed of what he'd been thinking. Joanne stood still, close to Nick's chair. She let him hold her. Then her face reddened slightly and she moved a little, and Nick let go of her.

The children, Jenny and Megan, opened the door and rushed into the kitchen carrying their skateboards. "There's a fire down the street," Jenny said.

"Somebody's house is burning," Megan said.

"A fire?" Carol said. "If it's a real fire, stay away from it."

"I didn't hear any fire trucks," Joanne said. "Did you guys hear fire trucks?"

"I didn't either," Robert said. "You kids go play now. We don't have much longer."

Nick stepped to the bay window and looked out, but nothing out of the ordinary seemed to be happening. The idea of a house fire on the block in clear, sunny weather at eleven in the morning was incomprehensible. Besides, there had been no alarms, no carloads of rubberneckers or clang of bells, or wail of sirens and hiss of air brakes. It seemed to Nick it had to be a part of a game the children were playing.

"This was a wonderful breakfast," Carol said. "I loved it. I feel like I could roll over and go to sleep."

"Why don't you?" Joanne said. "We have that extra room upstairs. Let the kids play, and you guys take yourselves a nap before starting off."

"Go ahead," Nick said. "Sure."

"Carol's just kidding, of course," Robert said. "We couldn't do anything like that. Could we, Carol?" Robert looked at her.

"Oh, no, not really," Carol said and laughed. "But every-thing was so good, as always. A champagne brunch without the champagne."

"The best kind," Nick said. Nick had quit drinking six years ago after being arrested for driving under the influence. He'd gone with someone to an AA meeting, decided that was the place for him, and then went every night, sometimes twice in one night, for two months, until the desire to drink left him, as he put it, almost as if it'd never been there. But even now, though he didn't drink, he still went to a meeting every once in a while.

"Speaking of drinking," Robert said. "Jo, do you remember Harry Schuster—*Dr.* Harry Schuster, a bone-marrow-transplant man now, don't ask me how—but do you remember the Christmas party that time when he got into the fight with his wife?"

"Marilyn," Joanne said. "Marilyn Schuster. I haven't thought of her in a long time."

"Marilyn, that's right," Robert said. "Because he thought she'd had too much to drink and was making eyes at—"

He paused just long enough for Joanne to say, "Bill."

"Bill, that's right," Robert said. "Anyway, first they had words, and then she threw her car keys on the living-room floor and said, 'You drive, then, if you're so goddamn safe, sane, and sober.' And so Harry—they'd come in two cars, mind, he'd been interning at the hospital—Harry went out and drove her car two blocks, parked it, and then came back for *his* car, and drove that about two blocks, parked, walked back to her car, drove it two blocks, walked to his own car and drove it a little farther, and parked and walked back to her car and drove that a few blocks, et cetera, et cetera."

They all laughed. Nick laughed too. It *was* funny. Nick had heard plenty of drinking stories in his time, but he'd never heard one that had this particular spin on it.

"Anyway," Robert said, "to make a long story short, as they say, he drove both cars home that way. It took him two or three hours to drive five miles. And when he got to the house, there was Marilyn, at the table with a drink in her hand. Somebody had driven her home. 'Merry Christmas,' she said when Harry came in the door, and I guess he decked her."

Carol whistled.

Joanne said, "Anybody could see those two weren't going to make it. They were in the fast lane. A year later they were both at the same Christmas party, only they had different partners by then."

"All the drinking and driving I did," Nick said. He shook his head. "I was only picked up once."

"You were lucky," Joanne said.

"Somebody was lucky," Robert said. "The other drivers on the road were lucky."

"I spent one night in jail," Nick said, "and that was enough. That's when I stopped. Actually, I was in what they call detox. The doctor came around the next morning—his name was Dr. Forester—and called each person into this little examining room and gave you the once-over. He looked in your eyes with his penlight, he made you hold out your hands, palms up, he took your pulse and listened to your heartbeat. He'd give you a little talking-to about your drinking, and then he'd tell you what time of the morning you could be released. He said I could leave at eleven o'clock. 'Doctor,' I said, 'could I leave earlier, please?' 'What's the big hurry?' he said. 'I have to be at church at eleven o'clock,' I said. 'I'm getting married.'"

"What'd he say to that?" Carol said.

"He said, 'Get the hell out of here, mister. But don't ever forget this, do you hear?' And I didn't. I stopped drinking. I didn't even drink anything at the wedding reception that afternoon. Not a drop. That was it for me. I was too scared. Sometimes it takes something like that, a real shock to your nervous system, to turn things around."

"I had a kid brother who was nearly killed by a drunk driver," Robert said. "He's still wired up and has to use a metal brace to get around."

"Last call for coffee," Joanne said.

"Just a little, I guess," Carol said. "We really have to collect those kids and get on the road."

Nick looked toward the window and saw several cars pass by

on the street outside. People hurried by on the sidewalk. He remembered what Jenny and the other child had said about a fire, but for God's sake, if there were a fire there'd be sirens and engines, right? He started to get up from the table, and then he didn't.

"It's crazy," he said. "I remember when I was still drinking and I'd just had what they call an alcoholic seizure—I'd fallen and hit my head on a coffee table. Lucky for me I was in the doctor's office when it happened. I woke up in a bed in his office, and Peggy, the woman I was married to at the time, she was leaning over me, along with the doctor and the doctor's nurse. Peggy was calling my name. I had this big bandage round my head—it was like a turban. The doctor said I'd just had my first seizure, but it wouldn't be my last if I kept on drinking. I told him I'd got the message. But I just said that. I had no intention of quitting then. I told myself and my wife that it was my nerves—stress—that had caused me to faint.

"But that night we had a party, Peggy and me. It was something we'd planned for a couple of weeks, and we didn't see how we could call it off at the last minute and disappoint everybody. Can you imagine? So we went ahead and had the party, and everybody came, and I was still wearing the bandage. All that night I had a glass of vodka in my hand. I told people I'd cut my head on the car door."

"How much longer did you keep drinking?" Carol said.

"Quite a while. A year or so. Until I got picked up that night."

"He was sober when I met him," Joanne said, and blushed, as if she'd said something she shouldn't.

Nick put his hand on Joanne's neck and rested his fingers there. He picked up some of the hair that lay across her neck and rubbed it between his fingers. Some more people went by the window on the sidewalk. Most of the people were in shirtsleeves and blouses. A man was carrying a little girl on his shoulders.

"I quit drinking about a year before I met Joanne," Nick said, as if telling them something they needed to know.

"Tell them about your brother, honey," Joanne said.

Nick didn't say anything at first. He stopped rubbing Joanne's neck and took his hand away.

"What happened?" Robert said, leaning forward.

Nick shook his head.

"What?" Carol said. "Nick? It's okay—if you want to tell us, that is."

"How'd we get onto this stuff, anyway?" Nick said.

"You brought it up," Joanne said.

"Well, what happened, you see, was that I was trying to get sober, and I felt like I couldn't do it at home, but I didn't want to have to go anyplace, like to a clinic or a recovery place, you know, and my brother had this summer house he wasn't using— this was in October—and I called him and asked him if I could go there and stay for a week or two and try to get myself together again. At first he said yes. I began to pack a suitcase and I was thinking I was glad I had family, glad I had a brother and that he was going to help me. But pretty soon the phone rang, and it was my brother, and he said—he said he'd talked it over with his wife, and he was sorry—he didn't know how to tell me this, he said—but his wife was afraid I might burn the place down. I might, he said, drop off with a cigarette burning in my fingers, or else leave a burner turned on. Anyway, they were afraid I would catch the house on fire, and he was sorry but he couldn't let me stay. So I said okay, and I unpacked my suitcase."

"Wow," Carol said. "Your own brother did that. He forsook you," she said. "Your own brother."

"I don't know what I'd have done, if I'd been in his shoes," Nick said.

"Sure you do," Joanne said.

"Well, I guess I do," Nick said. "Sure. I'd have let him stay there. What the hell, a house. What's that? You can get insurance on a house."

"That's pretty amazing, all right," Robert said. "So how do you and your brother get along these days?"

"We don't, I'm sorry to say. He asked me to lend him some money a while back, and I did, and he repaid me when he said he would. But we haven't seen each other in about five years. It's been longer than that since I've seen his wife."

"Where are all these *people* coming from?" Joanne said. She got up from the table and went over to the window and moved the curtain.

"The kids said something about a fire," Nick said.

"That's silly. There can't be a fire," Joanne said. "Can there?"

"Something's going on," Robert said.

Nick went to the front door and opened it. A car slowed and then pulled up alongside the curb in front of the house and parked. Another car drove up and parked across the street. Small groups of people moved past down the sidewalk. Nick went out into the yard, and the others—Joanne, Carol, and Robert—followed him. Nick looked up the street and saw the smoke, a crowd of people, and two fire engines and a police car parked at the intersection. Men were training hoses on the shell of a house—the Carpenter house, Nick saw at a glance. Black smoke poured from the walls, and flames shot from the roof. "My God, there's a fire all right," he said. "The kids were right."

"Why didn't we hear anything?" Joanne said. "Did you hear anything? I didn't hear anything."

"We'd better go down and see about the girls, Robert," Carol said. "They might get in the way somehow. They might get too close or something. Anything could happen."

The four of them started down the sidewalk. They fell in with some other people who were walking at an unhurried pace. They walked along with these other people. Nick had the feeling that they could have been on an outing. But all the while, as they kept their eyes on the burning house, they saw firemen pouring water onto the roof of the house, where flames kept breaking through. Some other firemen were holding a hose and aiming a stream of water through a front window. A fireman wearing a helmet with straps, a long black coat, and black knee-high boots was carrying an ax and moving around toward the back of the house.

They came up to where the crowd of people stood watching. The police car had parked sideways in the middle of the road, and they could hear the radio crackling inside the car, over the sound of the fire as it ripped through the walls of the house. Then Nick spotted the two girls, standing near the front of the crowd, holding their skateboards. "There they are," he said to Robert. "Over there. See them?"

They made their way through the crowd, excusing themselves, and came up beside the girls.

"We told you," Jenny said. "See?" Megan stood holding her skateboard in one hand and had the thumb of her other hand planted in her mouth.

"Do you know what happened?" Nick said to the woman beside him. She was wearing a sun hat and smoking a cigarette.

"Vandals," she said. "That's what somebody told me, anyway."

"If they can catch them, they ought to kill them, if you ask me," said the man standing next to the woman. "Or else lock them up and throw away the key. These people are traveling in Mexico and don't even know they won't have a house to live in when they come back. They haven't been able to get in touch with them. Those poor people. Can you imagine? They're going to come home and find out they don't have a house to live in any longer."

"It's going!" the fireman with the ax shouted. "Stand back!"

Nobody was close to him or to the house. But the people in the crowd moved their feet, and Nick could feel himself grow tense. Someone in the crowd said, "Oh my God. My God."

"Look at it," someone else said.

Nick edged closer to Joanne, who was staring intently at the fire. The hair on her forehead appeared damp. He put his arm around her. He realized, as he did it, that he'd touched her this way at least three times that morning.

Nick turned his head slightly in Robert's direction and was

surprised to see Robert staring at him instead of the house. Robert's face was flushed, his expression stern, as if everything that had happened—arson, jail, betrayal, and adultery, the over-turning of the established order—was Nick's fault and could be laid on his doorstep. Nick stared back, his arm around Joanne, until the flush left Robert's face and he lowered his eyes. When he raised them again, he didn't look at Nick. He moved closer to his wife, as if to protect her.

Nick and Joanne were still holding each other as they watched, but there was that familiar feeling Nick would have from time to time, as she absently patted his shoulder, that he didn't know what she was thinking.

"What are you thinking?" he asked her.

"I was thinking about Bill," she said.

He went on holding her. She didn't say any more for a minute, and then she said, "I think about him every now and then, you know. After all, he was the first man I ever loved."

He kept holding her. She let her head rest on his shoulder and went on staring at the burning house.

Call if You Need Me

We had both been involved with other people that spring, but when June came and school was out we decided to let our house for the summer and move from Palo Alto to the north coast country of California. Our son, Richard, went to Nancy's grandmother's place in Pasco, Washington, to live for the summer and work toward saving money for college in the fall. His grandmother knew the situation at home and had begun working on getting him up there and locating him a job long before his arrival. She'd talked to a farmer friend of hers and had secured a promise of work for Richard baling hay and building fences. Hard work, but Richard was looking forward to it. He left on the bus in the morning of the day after his high school graduation. I took him to the station and parked and went inside to sit with him until his bus was called. His mother had already held him and cried and kissed him good-bye and given him a long letter that he was to deliver to his grandmother upon his arrival. She was at home now finishing last-minute packing for our own move and waiting for the couple who were to take our house. I bought Richard's ticket, gave it to him, and we sat on one of the benches in the station and waited. We'd talked a little about things on the way to the station.

"Are you and Mom going to get a divorce?" he'd asked. It was Saturday morning, and there weren't many cars.

"Not if we can help it," I said. "We don't want to. That's why we're going away from here and don't expect to see anyone all summer. That's why we've rented our house for the summer and rented the house up in Eureka. Why you're going away, too,

63

I guess. One reason anyway. Not to mention the fact that you'll come home with your pockets filled with money. We don't want to get a divorce. We want to be alone for the summer and try to work things out."

"You still love Mom?" he said. "She told me she loves you."

"Of course I do," I said. "You ought to know that by now. We've just had our share of troubles and heavy responsibilities, like everyone else, and now we need time to be alone and work things out. But don't worry about us. You just go up there and have a good summer and work hard and save your money. Consider it a vacation too. Get in all the fishing you can. There's good fishing around there."

"Waterskiing too," he said. "I want to learn to water-ski."

"I've never been waterskiing," I said. "Do some of that for me too, will you?"

We sat in the bus station. He looked through his yearbook while I held a newspaper in my lap. Then his bus was called and we stood up. I embraced him and said, "Don't worry, don't worry. Where's your ticket?"

He patted his coat pocket and then picked up his suitcase. I walked him over to where the line was forming in the terminal, then I embraced him again and kissed him on the cheek and said good-bye.

"Good-bye, Dad," he said, and turned from me so I wouldn't see his tears.

I drove home to where our boxes and suitcases were waiting in the living room. Nancy was in the kitchen drinking coffee with the young couple she'd found to take our house for the summer. I'd met the couple, Jerry and Liz, graduate students in math, for the first time a few days before, but we shook hands again, and I drank a cup of coffee that Nancy poured. We sat around the table and drank coffee while Nancy finished her list of things they should look out for or do at certain times of the month, the first and last of each month, where they should send any mail, and the like. Nancy's face was tight. Sun fell through the curtain onto the table as it got later in the morning.

Finally, things seemed to be in order and I left the three of them in the kitchen and began loading the car. It was a furnished house we were going to, furnished right down to plates and cooking utensils, so we wouldn't need to take much with us from this house, only the essentials.

I'd driven up to Eureka, 350 miles north of Palo Alto, on the north coast of California, three weeks before and rented us the furnished house. I went with Susan, the woman I'd been seeing. We stayed in a motel at the edge of town for three nights while I looked in the newspaper and visited realtors. She watched me as I wrote out a check for the three months' rent. Later, back at the motel, in bed, she lay with her hand on her forehead and said, "I envy your wife. I envy Nancy. You hear people talk about 'the other woman' always and how the incumbent wife has the privileges and the real power, but I never really understood or cared about those things before. Now I see. I envy her. I envy her the life she'll have with you in that house this summer. I wish it were me. I wish it were us. Oh, how I wish it were us. I feel so crummy," she said. I stroked her hair.

Nancy was a tall, long-legged woman with brown hair and eyes and a generous spirit. But lately we had been coming up short on generosity and spirit. The man she'd been seeing was one of my colleagues, a divorced, dapper, three-piece-suit-and-tie fellow with graying hair who drank too much and whose hands, some of my students told me, sometimes shook in the classroom. He and Nancy had drifted into their affair at a party during the holidays, not too long after Nancy had discovered my own affair. It all sounds boring and tacky now—it is boring and tacky—but during that spring it was what it was, and it consumed all of our energies and concentration to the exclusion of everything else. Sometime in late April we began to make plans to rent our house and go away for the summer, just the two of us, and try to put things back together, if they could be put back together. We each agreed we would not call or write or otherwise be in touch with the other parties. So we made arrangements for Richard, found the couple to look after our house, and I had looked at a map and driven north from San Francisco and found Eureka, and a realtor who was willing to rent a furnished house to a respectable middle-aged married couple for the summer. I think I even used the phrase "second honeymoon" to the realtor, God forgive me, while Susan smoked a cigarette and read tourist brochures out in the car.

I finished storing the suitcases, bags, and cartons in the trunk and backseat and waited while Nancy said a final good-bye on the porch. She shook hands with each of them and turned and came toward the car. I waved to the couple, and they waved back. Nancy got in and shut the door. "Let's go," she said. I put the car in gear and we headed for the freeway. At the light just before the freeway we saw a car ahead of us come off the freeway trailing a broken muffler, the sparks flying. "Look at that," Nancy said. "It might catch fire." We waited and watched until the car managed to pull off the road onto the shoulder.

We stopped at a little café off the highway near Sebastopol. Eat and Gas, the sign read. We laughed at the sign. I pulled up in front of the café and we went inside and took a table near a window in the back. After we ordered coffee and sandwiches, Nancy touched her forefinger to the table and began tracing lines in the wood. I lit a cigarette and looked outside. I saw rapid movement, and then I realized I was looking at a hummingbird in the bush beside the window. Its wings moved in a blur of motion and it kept dipping its beak into a blossom on the bush.

"Nancy, look," I said. "There's a hummingbird."

But the hummingbird flew at this moment and Nancy looked and said, "Where? I don't see it."

"It was just there a minute ago," I said. "Look, there it is. Another one, I think. It's another hummingbird."

We watched the hummingbird until the waitress brought our order and the bird flew at the movement and disappeared around the building.

"Now that's a good sign, I think," I said. "Hummingbirds. Hummingbirds are supposed to bring luck."

"I've heard that somewhere," she said. "I don't know where I heard that, but I've heard it. Well," she said, "luck is what we could use. Wouldn't you say?"

"They're a good sign," I said. "I'm glad we stopped here."

She nodded. She waited a minute, then she took a bite of her sandwich.

We reached Eureka just before dark. We passed the motel on the highway where Susan and I had stayed and had spent the three nights two weeks before, then turned off the highway and took a road up a hill overlooking the town. I had the house keys in my pocket. We drove over the hill and for a mile or so until we came to a little intersection with a service station and a grocery store. There were wooded mountains ahead of us in the valley, and pastureland all around. Some cattle were grazing in a field behind the service station. "This is pretty country," Nancy said. "I'm anxious to see the house."

"Almost there," I said. "It's just down this road," I said, "and over that rise." "Here," I said in a minute, and pulled into a long driveway with hedge on either side. "Here it is. What do you think of this?" I'd asked the same question of Susan when she and I had stopped in the driveway.

"It's nice," Nancy said. "It looks fine, it does. Let's get out."

We stood in the front yard a minute and looked around. Then we went up the porch steps and I unlocked the front door and turned on the lights. We went through the house. There were two small bedrooms, a bath, a living room with old furniture and a fireplace, and a big kitchen with a view of the valley.

"Do you like it?" I said.

"I think it's just wonderful," Nancy said. She grinned. "I'm glad you found it. I'm glad we're here." She opened the refrigerator and ran a finger over the counter. "Thank God, it looks clean enough. I won't have to do any cleaning."

"Right down to clean sheets on the beds," I said. "I checked. I made sure. That's the way they're renting it. Pillows even. And pillowcases too."

"We'll have to buy some firewood," she said. We were standing in the living room. "We'll want to have a fire on nights like this."

"I'll look into firewood tomorrow," I said. "We can go shopping then, too, and see the town."

She looked at me and said, "I'm glad we're here."

"So am I," I said. I opened my arms and she moved to me. I held her. I could feel her trembling. I turned her face up and kissed her on either cheek. "Nancy," I said.

"I'm glad we're here," she said.

We spent the next few days settling in, taking trips into Eureka to walk around and look in store windows, and hiking across the pastureland behind the house all the way to the woods. We bought groceries and I found an ad in the newspaper for firewood, called, and a day or so afterwards two young men with long hair delivered a pickup truckload of alder and stacked it in the carport. That night we sat in front of the fireplace after dinner and drank coffee and talked about getting a dog.

"I don't want a pup," Nancy said. "Something we have to clean up after or that will chew things up. That we don't need. But I'd like to have a dog, yes. We haven't had a dog in a long time. I think we could handle a dog up here," she said.

"And after we go back, after summer's over?" I said. I rephrased the question. "What about keeping a dog in the city?"

"We'll see. Meanwhile, let's look for a dog. The right kind of dog. I don't know what I want until I see it. We'll read the classifieds and we'll go to the pound, if we have to." But though we went on talking about dogs for several days, and pointed out dogs to each other in people's yards we'd drive past, dogs we said we'd like to have, nothing came of it, we didn't get a dog.

Nancy called her mother and gave her our address and telephone number. Richard was working and seemed happy, her mother said. She herself was fine. I heard Nancy say, "We're fine. This is good medicine."

One day in the middle of July we were driving the highway near the ocean and came over a rise to see some lagoons that were closed off from the ocean by sand spits. There were some people fishing from shore, and two boats out on the water.

I pulled the car off onto the shoulder and stopped. "Let's see what they're fishing for," I said. "Maybe we could get some gear and go ourselves."

"We haven't been fishing in years," Nancy said. "Not since that time Richard was little and we went camping near Mount Shasta. Do you remember that?"

"I remember," I said. "I just remembered, too, that I've missed fishing. Let's walk down and see what they're fishing for."

"Trout," the man said, when I asked. "Cutthroats and rainbow trout. Even some steelhead and a few salmon. They come in here in the winter when the spit opens and then when it closes in the spring, they're trapped. This is a good time of the year for them. I haven't caught any today, but last Sunday I caught four, about fifteen inches long. Best eating fish in the world, and they put up a hell of a fight. Fellows out in the boats have caught some today, but so far I haven't done anything."

"What do you use for bait?" Nancy asked.

"Anything," the man said. "Worms, salmon eggs, whole-kernel corn. Just get it out there and leave it lay on the bottom. Pull out a little slack and watch your line."

We hung around a little longer and watched the man fish and watched the little boats *chat-chat* back and forth the length of the lagoon.

"Thanks," I said to the man. "Good luck to you."

"Good luck to you," he said. "Good luck to the both of you."

We stopped at a sporting goods store on the way back to town and bought licenses, inexpensive rods and reels, nylon line, hooks, leaders, sinkers, and a creel. We made plans to go fishing the next morning.

But that night, after we'd eaten dinner and washed the dishes and I had laid a fire in the fireplace, Nancy shook her head and said it wasn't going to work.

"Why do you say that?" I asked. "What is it you mean?"

"I mean it isn't going to work. Let's face it." She shook her head again. "I don't think I want to go fishing in the morning, either, and I don't want a dog. No, no dogs. I think I want to go up and see my mother and Richard. Alone. I want to be alone. I miss Richard," she said and began to cry. "Richard's my son, my baby," she said, "and he's nearly grown and gone. I miss him."

"And Del, do you miss Del Shraeder too?" I said. "Your boyfriend. Do you miss him?"

"I miss everybody tonight," she said. "I miss you too. I've missed you for a long time now. I've missed you so much you've gotten lost somehow, I can't explain it. I've lost you. You're not mine any longer."

"Nancy," I said.

"No, no," she said. She shook her head. She sat on the sofa in front of the fire and kept shaking her head. "I want to fly up and see my mother and Richard tomorrow. After I'm gone you can call your girlfriend."

"I won't do that," I said. "I have no intention of doing that."

"You'll call her," she said.

"You'll call Del," I said. I felt rubbishy for saying it.

"You can do what you want," she said, wiping her eyes on her sleeve. "I mean that. I don't want to sound hysterical. But I'm going up to Washington tomorrow. Right now I'm going to go to bed. I'm exhausted. I'm sorry. I'm sorry for both of us, Dan. We're not going to make it. That fisherman today. He wished us good luck." She shook her head. "I wish us good luck too. We're going to need it."

She went into the bathroom and I heard water running in the tub. I went out and sat on the porch steps and smoked a cigarette.

70

It was dark and quiet outside. I looked toward town and could see a faint glow of lights in the sky and patches of ocean fog drifting in the valley. I began to think of Susan. A little later, Nancy came out of the bathroom and I heard the bedroom door close. I went inside and put another block of wood on the grate and waited until the flames began to move up the bark. Then I went into the other bedroom and turned the covers back and stared at the floral design on the sheets. Then I showered, dressed in my pajamas, and went to sit near the fire-place again. The fog was outside the window now. I sat in front of the fire and smoked. When I looked out the window again, something moved in the fog and I saw a horse grazing in the front yard.

I went to the window. The horse looked up at me for a minute, then went back to pulling up grass. Another horse walked past the car into the yard and began to graze. I turned on the porch light and stood at the window and watched them. They were big white horses with long manes. They'd gotten through a fence or an unlocked gate from one of the nearby farms. Somehow they'd wound up in our front yard. They were larking it, enjoying their breakaway immensely. But nervous, too; I could see the whites of their eyes from where I stood behind the window. Their ears kept rising and falling as they tore out clumps of grass. A third horse wandered into the yard, and then a fourth. It was a herd of white horses, and they were grazing in our front yard.

I went into the bedroom and woke Nancy. Her eyes were red and the skin around the eyes was swollen. She had her hair up in curlers, and a suitcase lay open on the floor near the foot of the bed.

"Nancy," I said. "Honey, come and see what's in the front yard. Come and see this. You must see this. You won't believe it. Hurry up."

"What is it?" she said. "Don't hurt me. What is it?"

"Honey, you must see this. I'm not going to hurt you. I'm

71

sorry if I scared you. But you must come out here and see something."

I went back into the other room and stood in front of the window, and in a few minutes Nancy came in tying her robe. She looked out the window and said, "My God, they're beautiful. Where'd they come from, Dan? They're just beautiful."

"They must have gotten loose from around here somewhere," I said. "One of these farm places. I'll call the sheriff's department pretty soon and let them locate the owners. But I wanted you to see this first."

"Will they bite?" she said. "I'd like to pet that one there, the one that just looked at us. I'd like to pat that one's shoulder. But I don't want to get bitten. I'm going outside."

"I don't think they'll bite," I said. "They don't look like the kind of horses that'll bite. But put a coat on if you're going out there; it's cold."

I put my coat on over my pajamas and waited for Nancy. Then I opened the front door and we went outside and walked into the yard with the horses. They all looked up at us. Two of them went back to pulling up grass. One of the other horses snorted and moved back a few steps, and then it, too, went back to pulling up grass and chewing, head down. I rubbed the forehead of one horse and patted its shoulder. It kept chewing. Nancy put out her hand and began stroking the mane of another horse. "Horsey, where'd you come from?" she said. "Where do you live and why are you out tonight, Horsey?" she said, and kept stroking the horse's mane. The horse looked at her and blew through its lips and dropped its head again. She patted its shoulder.

"I guess I'd better call the sheriff," I said.

"Not yet," she said. "Not for a while yet. We'll never see anything like this again. We'll never, never have horses in our front yard again. Wait a while yet, Dan."

A little later, Nancy was still out there moving from one horse to another, patting their shoulders and stroking their manes, when one of the horses moved from the yard into the driveway

72

and walked around the car and down the driveway toward the road, and I knew I had to call.

In a little while the two sheriff's cars showed up with their red lights flashing in the fog and a few minutes later a fellow in a sheepskin coat driving a pickup with a horse trailer behind it. Now the horses shied and tried to get away, and the man with the horse trailer swore and tried to get a rope around the neck of one horse.

"Don't hurt it!" Nancy said.

We went back in the house and stood behind the window and watched the deputies and the rancher work on getting the horses rounded up.

"I'm going to make some coffee," I said. "Would you like some coffee, Nancy?"

"I'll tell you what I'd like," she said. "I feel high, Dan. I feel like I'm loaded. I feel like, I don't know, but I like the way I'm feeling. You put on some coffee and I'll find us some music to listen to on the radio and then you can build up the fire again. I'm too excited to sleep."

So we sat in front of the fire and drank coffee and listened to an all-night radio station from Eureka and talked about the horses and then talked about Richard, and Nancy's mother. We danced. We didn't talk about the present situation at all. The fog hung outside the window and we talked and were kind with one another. Toward daylight I turned off the radio and we went to bed and made love.

The next afternoon, after her arrangements were made and her suitcases packed, I drove her to the little airport where she would catch a flight to Portland and then transfer to another airline that would put her in Pasco late that night.

"Tell your mother I said hello. Give Richard a hug for me and tell him I miss him," I said. "Tell him I send love."

"He loves you too," she said. "You know that. In any case, you'll see him in the fall, I'm sure."

I nodded.

"Good-bye," she said and reached for me. We held each other. "I'm glad for last night," she said. "Those horses. Our talk. Everything. It helps. We won't forget that," she said. She began to cry.

"Write me, will you?" I said. "I didn't think it would happen to us," I said. "All those years. I never thought so for a minute. Not us."

"I'll write," she said. "Some big letters. The biggest you've ever seen since I used to send you letters in high school."

"I'll be looking for them," I said.

Then she looked at me again and touched my face. She turned and moved across the tarmac toward the plane.

Go, dearest one, and God be with you.

She boarded the plane and I stayed around until its jet engines started, and in a minute the plane began to taxi down the runway. It lifted off over Humboldt Bay and soon became a speck on the horizon.

I drove back to the house and parked in the driveway and looked at the hoofprints of the horses from last night. There were deep impressions in the grass, and gashes, and there were piles of dung. Then I went into the house and, without even taking off my coat, went to the telephone and dialed Susan's number.

FIVE ESSAYS AND
A MEDITATION

My Father's Life

My dad's name was Clevie Raymond Carver. His family called him Raymond and friends called him C. R. I was named Raymond Clevie Carver Jr. I hated the "Junior" part. When I was little my dad called me Frog, which was okay. But later, like everybody else in the family, he began calling me Junior. He went on calling me this until I was thirteen or fourteen and announced that I wouldn't answer to that name any longer. So he began calling me Doc. From then until his death, on June 17, 1967, he called me Doc, or else Son.

When he died, my mother telephoned my wife with the news. I was away from my family at the time, between lives, trying to enroll in the School of Library Science at the University of Iowa. When my wife answered the phone, my mother blurted out, "Raymond's dead!" For a moment, my wife thought my mother was telling her that I was dead. Then my mother made it clear *which* Raymond she was talking about and my wife said, "Thank God. I thought you meant *my* Raymond."

My dad walked, hitched rides, and rode in empty boxcars when he went from Arkansas to Washington State in 1934, looking for work. I don't know whether he was pursuing a dream when he went out to Washington. I doubt it. I don't think he dreamed much. I believe he was simply looking for steady work at decent pay. Steady work was meaningful work. He picked apples for a time and then landed a construction laborer's job on the Grand Coulee Dam. After he'd put aside a little money, he bought a car and drove back to Arkansas to help his folks, my grandparents, pack up for the move west. He said later that they were about to starve down there, and this wasn't meant as a figure of speech. It was during that short while in Arkansas, in a town called Leola, that my mother met my dad on the sidewalk as he came out of a tavern.

"He was drunk," she said. "I don't know why I let him talk to me. His eyes were glittery. I wish I'd had a crystal ball." They'd met once, a year or so before, at a dance. He'd had girlfriends before her, my mother told me. "Your dad always had a girlfriend, even after we married. He was my first and last. I never had another man. But I didn't miss anything."

They were married by a justice of the peace on the day they left for Washington, this big, tall country girl and a farmhand turned construction worker. My mother spent her wedding night with my dad and his folks, all of them camped beside the road in Arkansas.

In Omak, Washington, my dad and mother lived in a little place not much bigger than a cabin. My grandparents lived next door. My dad was still working on the dam, and later, with the huge turbines producing electricity and the water backed up for a hundred miles into Canada, he stood in the crowd and heard Franklin D. Roosevelt when he spoke at the construction site. "He never mentioned those guys who died building that dam," my dad said. Some of his friends had died there, men from Arkansas, Oklahoma, and Missouri.

He then took a job in a sawmill in Clatskanie, Oregon, a little town alongside the Columbia River. I was born there, and my mother has a picture of my dad standing in front of the gate to the mill, proudly holding me up to face the camera. My bonnet is on crooked and about to come untied. His hat is pushed back on his forehead, and he's wearing a big grin. Was he going in to work or just finishing his shift? It doesn't matter. In either case, he had a job and a family. These were his salad days.

In 1941 we moved to Yakima, Washington, where my dad went to work as a saw filer, a skilled trade he'd learned in Clatskanie. When war broke out, he was given a deferment because his work was considered necessary to the war effort. Finished lumber was in demand by the armed services, and he kept his saws so sharp they could shave the hair off your arm.

After my dad had moved us to Yakima, he moved his folks into the same neighborhood. By the mid-1940s the rest of my dad's family—his brother, his sister and her husband, as well as uncles, cousins, nephews, and most of their extended family and friends—had come out from Arkansas. All because my dad came out first. The men went to work at Boise Cascade, where my dad worked, and the women packed apples in the canneries. And in just a little while, it seemed—according to my mother— everybody was better off than my dad. "Your dad couldn't keep money," my mother said. "Money burned a hole in his pocket. He was always doing for others."

The first house I clearly remember living in, at 1515 South Fifteenth Street, in Yakima, had an outdoor toilet. On Halloween night, or just any night, for the hell of it, neighbor kids, kids in their early teens, would carry our toilet away and leave it next to the road. My dad would have to get somebody to help him bring it home. Or these kids would take the toilet and stand it in somebody else's backyard. Once they actually set it on fire. But ours wasn't the only house that had an outdoor toilet. When I was old enough to know what I was doing, I threw rocks at the other toilets when I'd see someone go inside. This was called bombing the toilets. After a while, though, everyone went to indoor plumbing until, suddenly, our toilet was the last outdoor one in the neighborhood. I remember the shame I felt when my third-grade teacher, Mr. Wise, drove me home from school one day. I asked him to stop at the house just before ours, claiming I lived there.

I can recall what happened one night when my dad came home late to find that my mother had locked all the doors on him from the inside. He was drunk, and we could feel the house shudder as he rattled the door. When he'd managed to force open a window, she hit him between the eyes with a colander and knocked him out. We could see him down there on the grass. For years afterward, I used to pick up this colander—it was as heavy as a rolling pin—and imagine what it would feel like to be hit in the head with something like that.

It was during this period that I remember my dad taking me into the bedroom, sitting me down on the bed, and telling me that I might have to go live my with Aunt LaVon for a while. I couldn't understand what I'd done that meant I'd have to go away from home to live. But this, too—whatever prompted it—must have blown over, more or less, anyway, because we stayed together, and I didn't have to go live with her or anyone else.

I remember my mother pouring his whiskey down the sink. Sometimes she'd pour it all out and sometimes, if she was afraid of getting caught, she'd only pour half of it out and then add water to the rest. I tasted some of his whiskey once myself. It was terrible stuff, and I don't see how anybody could drink it.

After a long time without one, we finally got a car, in 1949 or 1950, a 1938 Ford. But it threw a rod the first week we had it, and my dad had to have the motor rebuilt.

"We drove the oldest car in town," my mother said. "We could have had a Cadillac for all he spent on car repairs." One time she found someone else's tube of lipstick on the floorboard, along with a lacy handkerchief. "See this?" she said to me. "Some floozy left this in the car."

Once I saw her take a pan of warm water into the bedroom where my dad was sleeping. She took his hand from under the covers and held it in the water. I stood in the doorway and watched. I wanted to know what was going on. This would make him talk in his sleep, she told me. There were things she needed to know, things she was sure he was keeping from her.

Every year or so, when I was little, we would take the North Coast Limited across the Cascade Range from Yakima to Seattle and stay in the Vance Hotel and eat, I remember, at a place called the Dinner Bell Café. Once we went to Ivar's Acres of Clams and drank glasses of warm clam broth.

In 1956, the year I was to graduate from high school, my dad quit his job at the mill in Yakima and took a job in Chester, a little sawmill town in northern California. The reasons given at the time for his taking the job had to do with a higher hourly wage and the vague promise that he might, in a few years' time, succeed to the job of head filer in this new mill. But I think, in the main, that my dad had grown restless and simply wanted to try his luck elsewhere. Things had gotten a little too predictable for him in Yakima. Also, the year before, there had been the deaths, within six months of each other, of both his parents.

But just a few days after graduation, when my mother and I were packed to move to Chester, my dad penciled a letter to say he'd been sick for a while. He didn't want us to worry, he said, but he'd cut himself on a saw. Maybe he'd got a tiny sliver of steel in his blood. Anyway, something had happened and he'd had to miss work, he said. In the same mail was an unsigned postcard from somebody down there telling my mother that my dad was about to die and that he was drinking "raw whiskey."

When we arrived in Chester, my dad was living in a trailer that belonged to the company. I didn't recognize him immediately. I guess for a moment I didn't want to recognize him. He was skinny and pale and looked bewildered. His pants wouldn't stay up. He didn't look like my dad. My mother began to cry. My dad put his arm around her and patted her shoulder vaguely, like he didn't know what this was all about, either. The three of us took up life together in the trailer, and we looked after him as best we could. But my dad was sick, and he couldn't get any better. I worked with him in the mill that summer and part of the fall. We'd get up in the mornings and eat eggs and toast while we listened to the radio, and then go out the door with our lunch pails. We'd pass through the gate together at eight in the morning, and I wouldn't see him again until quitting time. In November I went back to Yakima to be closer to my girlfriend, the girl I'd made up my mind I was going to marry.

He worked at the mill in Chester until the following February, when he collapsed on the job and was taken to the hospital. My mother asked if I would come down there and help. I caught a bus from Yakima to Chester, intending to drive them back to Yakima. But now, in addition to being physically sick, my dad was in the midst of a nervous breakdown, though none of us knew to call it that at the time. During the entire trip back to Yakima, he didn't speak, not even when asked a direct question. ("How do you feel, Raymond?" "You okay, Dad?") He'd communicate, if he communicated at all, by moving his head or by turning his palms up as if to say he didn't know or care. The only time he said anything on the trip, and for nearly a month afterward, was when I was speeding down a gravel road in Oregon and the car muffler came loose. "You were going too fast," he said.

Back in Yakima a doctor saw to it that my dad went to a psychiatrist. My mother and dad had to go on relief, as it was called, and the county paid for the psychiatrist. The psychiatrist asked my dad, "Who is the President?" He'd had a question put to him that he could answer. "Ike," my dad said. Nevertheless, they put him on the fifth floor of Valley Memorial Hospital and began giving him electroshock treatments. I was married by then and about to start my own family. My dad was still locked up when my wife went into this same hospital, just one floor down, to have our first baby. After she had delivered, I went upstairs to give my dad the news. They let me in through a steel door and showed me where I could find him. He was sitting on a couch with a blanket over his lap. *Hey*, I thought. *What in hell is happening to my dad?* I sat down next to him and told him he was a grandfather. He waited a minute and then he said, "I feel like a grandfather." That's all he said. He didn't smile or move. He was in a big room with a lot of other people. Then I hugged him, and he began to cry.

Somehow he got out of there. But now came the years when he couldn't work and just sat around the house trying to figure what next and what he'd done wrong in his life that he'd wound up like this. My mother went from job to crummy job. Much later she referred to that time he was in the hospital, and those years just afterward, as "when Raymond was sick." The word *sick* was never the same for me again.

In 1964, through the help of a friend, he was lucky enough to be hired on at a mill in Klamath, California. He moved down there by himself to see if he could hack it. He lived not far from the mill, in a one-room cabin not much different from the place he and my mother had started out living in when they went west. He scrawled letters to my mother, and if I called she'd read them aloud to me over the phone. In the letters, he said it was touch and go. Every day that he went to work, he felt like it was the most important day of his life. But every day, he told her, made the next day that much easier. He said for her to tell me he said hello. If he couldn't sleep at night, he said, he thought about me and the good times we used to have. Finally, after a couple of months, he regained some of his confidence. He could do the work and didn't think he had to worry that he'd let anybody down ever again. When he was sure, he sent for my mother.

He'd been off from work for six years and had lost everything in that time—home, car, furniture, and appliances, including the big freezer that had been my mother's pride and joy. He'd lost his good name too—Raymond Carver was someone who couldn't pay his bills—and his self-respect was gone. He'd even lost his virility. My mother told my wife, "All during that time Raymond was sick we slept together in the same bed, but we didn't have relations. He wanted to a few times, but nothing happened. I didn't miss it, but I think he wanted to, you know."

During those years I was trying to raise my own family and earn a living. But, one thing and another, we found ourselves having to move a lot. I couldn't keep track of what was going down in my dad's life. But I did have a chance one Christmas to tell him I wanted to be a writer. I might as well have told him I wanted to become a plastic surgeon. "What are you going to write about?" he wanted to know. Then, as if to help me out, he said, "Write about stuff you know about. Write about some of those fishing trips we took." I said I would, but I knew I wouldn't. "Send me what you write," he said. I said I'd do that, but then I didn't. I wasn't writing anything about fishing, and I didn't think he'd particularly care about, or even necessarily understand, what I was writing in those days. Besides, he wasn't a reader. Not the sort, anyway, I imagined I was writing for.

Then he died. I was a long way off, in Iowa City, with things still to say to him. I didn't have the chance to tell him good-bye, or that I thought he was doing great at his new job. That I was proud of him for making a comeback.

My mother said he came in from work that night and ate a big supper. Then he sat at the table by himself and finished what was left of a bottle of whiskey, a bottle she found hidden in the bottom of the garbage under some coffee grounds a day or so later. Then he got up and went to bed, where my mother joined him a little later. But in the night she had to get up and make a bed for herself on the couch. "He was snoring so loud I couldn't sleep," she said. The next morning when she looked in on him, he was on his back with his mouth open, his cheeks caved in. *Gray-looking*, she said. She knew he was dead—she didn't need a doctor to tell her that. But she called one anyway, and then she called my wife.

Among the pictures my mother kept of my dad and herself during those early days in Washington was a photograph of him standing in front of a car, holding a beer and a stringer of fish. In the photograph he is wearing his hat back on his forehead and has this awkward grin on his face. I asked her for it and she gave it to me, along with some others. I put it up on my wall, and each time we moved, I took the picture along and put it up on another wall. I looked at it carefully from time to time, trying to figure out some things about my dad, and maybe myself in the process. But I couldn't. My dad just kept moving further and further away from me and back into time. Finally, in the course of another move, I lost the photograph. It was then that I tried to recall it, and at the same time make an attempt to say something about my dad, and how I thought that in some important ways we might be alike. I wrote the poem when I was living in an apartment house in an urban area south of San Francisco, at a time when I found myself, like my dad, having trouble with alcohol. The poem was a way of trying to connect up with him.

PHOTOGRAPH OF MY FATHER IN HIS
TWENTY-SECOND YEAR

October. Here in this dank, unfamiliar kitchen
I study my father's embarrassed young man's face.
Sheepish grin, he holds in one hand a string
of spiny yellow perch, in the other
a bottle of Carlsbad beer.

In jeans and denim shirt, he leans
against the front fender of a 1934 Ford.
He would like to pose bluff and hearty for his posterity,
wear his old hat cocked over his ear.
All his life my father wanted to be bold.

But the eyes give him away, and the hands
that limply offer the string of dead perch
and the bottle of beer. Father, I love you,
yet how can I say thank you, I who can't hold my
   liquor either,
and don't even know the places to fish?

The poem is true in its particulars, except that my dad died in June and not October, as the first word of the poem says. I wanted a word with more than one syllable to it to make it linger a little. But more than that, I wanted a month appropriate to

85

what I felt at the time I wrote the poem—a month of short days and failing light, smoke in the air, things perishing. June was summer nights and days, graduations, my wedding anniversary, the birthday of one of my children. June wasn't a month your father died in.

After the service at the funeral home, after we had moved outside, a woman I didn't know came over to me and said, "He's happier where he is now." I stared at this woman until she moved away. I still remember the little knob of a hat she was wearing. Then one of my dad's cousins—I didn't know the man's name—reached out and took my hand. "We all miss him," he said, and I knew he wasn't saying it just to be polite.

I began to weep for the first time since receiving the news. I hadn't been able to before. I hadn't had the time, for one thing. Now, suddenly, I couldn't stop. I held my wife and wept while she said and did what she could do to comfort me there in the middle of that summer afternoon.

I listened to people say consoling things to my mother, and I was glad that my dad's family had turned up, had come to where he was. I thought I'd remember everything that was said and done that day and maybe find a way to tell it sometime. But I didn't. I forgot it all, or nearly. What I do remember is that I heard our name used a lot that afternoon, my dad's name and mine. But I knew they were talking about my dad. *Raymond*, these people kept saying in their beautiful voices out of my childhood. *Raymond*.

On Writing

Back in the mid-1960s, I found I was having trouble concentrating my attention on long narrative fiction. For a time I experienced difficulty in trying to read it as well as in attempting to write it. My attention span had gone out on me; I no longer had the patience to try to write novels. It's an involved story, too tedious to talk about here. But I know it has much to do now with why I write poems and short stories. Get in, get out. Don't linger. Go on. It could be that I lost any great ambitions at about the same time, in my late twenties. If I did, I think it was good it happened. Ambition and a little luck are good things for a writer to have going for him. Too much ambition and bad luck, or no luck at all, can be killing. There has to be talent.

Some writers have a bunch of talent; I don't know any writers who are without it. But a unique and exact way of looking at things, and finding the right context for expressing that way of looking, that's something else. *The World According to Garp* is, of course, the marvelous world according to John Irving. There is another world according to Flannery O'Connor, and others according to William Faulkner and Ernest Hemingway. There are worlds according to Cheever, Updike, Singer, Stanley Elkin, Ann Beattie, Cynthia Ozick, Donald Barthelme, Mary Robison, William Kittredge, Barry Hannah, Ursula K. Le Guin. Every great or even every very good writer makes the world over according to his own specifications.

It's akin to style, what I'm talking about, but it isn't style alone. It is the writer's particular and unmistakable signature on everything he writes. It is his world and no other. This is one

87

of the things that distinguishes one writer from another. Not talent. There's plenty of that around. But a writer who has some special way of looking at things and who gives artistic expression to that way of looking: that writer may be around for a time.

Isak Dinesen said that she wrote a little every day, without hope and without despair. Someday I'll put that on a three-by-five card and tape it to the wall beside my desk. I have some three-by-five cards on the wall now. "Fundamental accuracy of statement is the ONE sole morality of writing." Ezra Pound. It is not everything by ANY means, but if a writer has "fundamental accuracy of statement" going for him, he's at least on the right track.

I have a three-by-five up there with this fragment of a sentence from a story by Chekhov: ". . . and suddenly everything became clear to him." I find these words filled with wonder and possibility. I love their simple clarity, and the hint of revelation that's implied. There is mystery, too. What has been unclear before? Why is it just now becoming clear? What's happened? Most of all—what now? There are consequences as a result of such sudden awakenings. I feel a sharp sense of relief—and anticipation.

I overheard the writer Geoffrey Wolff say "No cheap tricks" to a group of writing students. That should go on a three-by-five card. I'd amend it a little to "No tricks." Period. I hate tricks. At the first sign of a trick or a gimmick in a piece of fiction, a cheap trick or even an elaborate trick, I tend to look for cover. Tricks are ultimately boring, and I get bored easily, which may go along with my not having much of an attention span. But extremely clever chichi writing, or just plain tomfoolery writing, puts me to sleep. Writers don't need tricks or gimmicks or even necessarily need to be the smartest fellows on the block. At the risk of appearing foolish, a writer sometimes needs to be able to just stand and gape at this or that thing—a sunset or an old shoe—in absolute and simple amazement.

Some months back, in the *New York Times Book Review*, John Barth said that ten years ago most of the students in his fiction writing seminar were interested in "formal innovation," and this no longer seems to be the case. He's a little worried that writers are going to start writing mom-and-pop novels in the 1980s. He worries that experimentation may be on the way out, along with liberalism. I get a little nervous if I find myself within earshot of somber discussions about "formal innovation" in fiction writing. Too often "experimentation" is a license to be careless, silly or imitative in the writing. Even worse, a license to try to brutalize or alienate the reader. Too often such writing gives us no news of the world, or else describes a desert landscape and that's all—a few dunes and lizards here and there, but no people; a place uninhabited by anything recognizably human, a place of interest only to a few scientific specialists.

It should be noted that real experiment in fiction is original, hard earned and cause for rejoicing. But someone else's way of looking at things—Barthelme's, for instance—should not be chased after by other writers. It won't work. There is only one Barthelme, and for another writer to try to appropriate Barthelme's peculiar sensibility or *mise en scène* under the rubric of innovation is for that writer to mess around with chaos and disaster and, worse, self-deception. The real experimenters have to MAKE IT NEW, as Pound urged, and in the process have to find things out for themselves. But if writers haven't taken leave of their senses, they also want to stay in touch with us, they want to carry news from their world to ours.

It's possible, in a poem or a short story, to write about commonplace things and objects using commonplace but precise language, and to endow those things—a chair, a window curtain, a fork, a stone, a woman's earring—with immense, even startling power. It is possible to write a line of seemingly innocuous dialogue and have it send a chill along the reader's spine— the source of artistic delight, as Nabokov would have it. That's the kind of writing that most interests me. I hate sloppy or haphazard writing whether it flies under the banner of experimentation or else is just clumsily rendered realism. In Isaac Babel's wonderful short story "Guy de Maupassant" the narrator has this to say about the writing of fiction: "No iron can stab the heart with such force as a period put just at the right place." This too ought to go on a three-by-five.

Evan Connell said once that he knew he was finished with a short story when he found himself going through it and taking out commas and then going through the story again and putting commas back in the same places. I like that way of working on something. I respect that kind of care for what is being done. That's all we have, finally, the words, and they had better be the right ones, with the punctuation in the right places so that they can best say what they are meant to say. If the words are heavy with the writer's own unbridled emotions, or if they are imprecise and inaccurate for some other reason—if the words are in any way blurred—the reader's eyes will slide right over them and nothing will be achieved. The reader's own artistic sense will simply not be engaged. Henry James called this sort of hapless writing "weak specification."

I have friends who've told me they had to hurry a book because they needed the money, their editor or their wife was leaning on them or leaving them—something, some apology for the writing not being very good. "It would have been better if I'd taken the time." I was dumbfounded when I heard a novelist friend say this. I still am, if I think about it, which I don't. It's none of my business. But if the writing can't be made as good as it is within us to make it, then why do it? In the end, the satisfaction of having done our best, and the proof of that labor, is the one thing we can take into the grave. I wanted to say to my friend, for heaven's sake go do something else. There have to be easier and maybe more honest ways to try and earn a living. Or else just do it to the best of your abilities, your talents, and then don't justify or make excuses. Don't complain, don't explain.

In an essay called, simply enough, "Writing Short Stories," Flannery O'Connor talks about writing as an act of discovery.

O'Connor says she most often did not know where she was going when she sat down to work on a short story. She says she doubts that many writers know where they are going when they begin something. She uses "Good Country People" as an example of how she put together a short story whose ending she could not even guess at until she was nearly there:

> When I started writing that story, I didn't know there was going to be a Ph.D. with a wooden leg in it. I merely found myself one morning writing a description of two women that I knew something about, and before I realized it, I had equipped one of them with a daughter with a wooden leg. As the story progressed, I brought in the Bible salesman, but I had no idea what I was going to do with him. I didn't know he was going to steal that wooden leg until ten or twelve lines before he did it, but when I found out that this was what was going to happen, I realized that it was inevitable.

When I read this some years ago it came as a shock that she, or anyone for that matter, wrote stories in this fashion. I thought this was my uncomfortable secret, and I was a little uneasy with it. For sure I thought this way of working on a short story somehow revealed my own shortcomings. I remember being tremendously heartened by reading what she had to say on the subject.

I once sat down to write what turned out to be a pretty good story, though only the first sentence of the story had offered itself to me when I began it. For several days I'd been going around with this sentence in my head: "He was running the vacuum cleaner when the telephone rang." I knew a story was there and that it wanted telling. I felt it in my bones, that a story belonged with that beginning, if I could just have the time to write it. I found the time, an entire day—twelve, fifteen hours even—if I wanted to make use of it. I did, and I sat down in the morning and wrote the first sentence, and other sentences promptly began to attach themselves. I made the story just as I'd make a poem;

one line and then the next, and the next. Pretty soon I could see a story, and I knew it was my story, the one I'd been wanting to write.

I like it when there is some feeling of threat or sense of menace in short stories. I think a little menace is fine to have in a story. For one thing, it's good for the circulation. There has to be tension, a sense that something is imminent, that certain things are in relentless motion, or else, most often, there simply won't be a story. What creates tension in a piece of fiction is partly the way the concrete words are linked together to make up the visible action of the story. But it's also the things that are left out, that are implied, the landscape just under the smooth (but sometimes broken and unsettled) surface of things.

V. S. Pritchett's definition of a short story is "something glimpsed from the corner of the eye, in passing." Notice the "glimpse" part of this. First the glimpse. Then the glimpse given life, turned into something that illuminates the moment and may, if we're lucky—that word again—have even further-ranging consequences and meaning. The short story writer's task is to invest the glimpse with all that is in his power. He'll bring his intelligence and literary skill to bear (his talent), his sense of proportion and sense of the fitness of things: of how things out there really are and how he sees those things—like no one else sees them. And this is done through the use of clear and specific language, language used so as to bring to life the details that will light up the story for the reader. For the details to be concrete and convey meaning, the language must be accurate and precisely given. The words can be so precise they may even sound flat, but they can still carry; if used right, they can hit all the notes.

Fires

Influences are forces—circumstances, personalities, irresistible as the tide. I can't talk about books or writers who might have influenced me. That kind of influence, literary influence, is hard for me to pin down with any kind of certainty. It would be as inaccurate for me to say I've been influenced by everything I've read as for me to say I don't think I've been influenced by any writers. For instance, I've long been a fan of Ernest Hemingway's novels and short stories. Yet I think Lawrence Durrell's work is singular and unsurpassed in the language. Of course, I don't write like Durrell. He's certainly no "influence." On occasion it's been said that my writing is "like" Hemingway's writing. But I can't say his writing influenced mine. Hemingway is one of the many writers whose work, like Durrell's, I first read and admired when I was in my twenties.

So I don't know about literary influences. But I do have some notions about other kinds of influences. The influences I know something about have pressed on me in ways that were often mysterious at first glance, sometimes stopping just short of the miraculous. But these influences have become clear to me as my work has progressed. These influences were (and they still are) relentless. These were the influences that sent me in this direction, onto this spit of land instead of some other—that one over there on the far side of the lake, for example. But if the main influence on my life and writing has been a negative one, oppressive and often malevolent, as I believe is the case, what am I to make of this?

*

Let me begin by saying that I'm writing this at a place called Yaddo, which is just outside of Saratoga Springs, New York. It's afternoon, Sunday, early August. Every so often, every twenty-five minutes or so, I can hear upwards of thirty thousand voices joined in a great outcry. This wonderful clamor comes from the Saratoga racecourse. A famous meet is in progress. I'm writing, but every twenty-five minutes I can hear the announcer's voice coming over the loudspeaker as he calls the positions of the horses. The roar of the crowd increases. It bursts over the trees, a great and truly thrilling sound, rising until the horses have crossed the finish line. When it's over, I feel spent, as if I too had participated. I can imagine holding pari-mutuel tickets on one of the horses who finished in the money, or even a horse who came close. If it's a photo finish at the wire, I can expect to hear another outburst a minute or two later, after the film has been developed and the official results posted.

For several days now, ever since arriving here and upon first hearing the announcer's voice over the loudspeaker, and the excited roar from the crowd, I've been writing a short story set in El Paso, a city where I lived for a while some time ago. The story has to do with some people who go to a horse race at a track outside of El Paso. I don't want to say the story has been waiting to be written. It hasn't, and it would make it sound like something else to say that. But I needed something, in the case of this particular story, to push it out into the open. Then after I arrived here at Yaddo and first heard the crowd, and the announcer's voice over the loudspeaker, certain things came back to me from that other life in El Paso and suggested the story. I remembered that track I went to down there and some things that took place, that might have taken place, that *will* take place—in my story anyway—two thousand miles away from here.

So my story is under way, and there is that aspect of "influences." Of course, every writer is subject to this kind of influence. This is the most common kind of influence—*this* suggests that,

94

that suggests something else. It's the kind of influence that is as common to us, and as natural, as rainwater.

But before I go on to what I want to talk about, let me give one more example of influence akin to the first. Not so long ago in Syracuse, where I live, I was in the middle of writing a short story when my telephone rang. I answered it. On the other end of the line was the voice of a man who was obviously a black man, someone asking for a party named Nelson. It was a wrong number and I said so and hung up. I went back to my short story. But pretty soon I found myself writing a black character into my story, a somewhat sinister character whose name was Nelson. At that moment the story took a different turn. But happily it was, I see now, and somehow knew at the time, the right turn for the story. When I began to write that story, I could not have prepared for or predicted the necessity for the presence of Nelson in the story. But now, the story finished and about to appear in a national magazine, I see it is right and appropriate and, I believe, aesthetically correct, that Nelson be there, and be there with his sinister aspect. Also right for me is that this character found his way into my story with a coincidental rightness I had the good sense to trust.

I have a poor memory. By this I mean that much that has happened in my life I've forgotten—a blessing for sure—but I have these large periods of time I simply can't account for or bring back, towns and cities I've lived in, names of people, the people themselves. Large blanks. But I can remember some things. Little things—somebody saying something in a particular way; somebody's wild, or low, nervous laughter; a landscape; an expression of sadness or bewilderment on somebody's face; and I can remember some dramatic things—somebody picking up a knife and turning to me in anger; or else hearing my own voice threaten somebody else. Seeing somebody break down a door, or else fall down a flight of stairs. Some of those more dramatic kinds of memories I can recall when it's necessary. But I don't have the kind of memory that can bring entire conversations back to the present, complete with all the gestures and nuances of real speech; nor can I recall the furnishings of any room I've ever spent time in, not to mention my inability to remember the furnishings of an entire household. Or even very many specific things about a racetrack—except, let's see, a grandstand, betting windows, closed-circuit TV screens, masses of people. Hubbub. I make up the conversations in my stories. I put the furnishings and the physical things surrounding the people into the stories as I need those things. Perhaps this is why it's sometimes been said that my stories are unadorned, stripped down, even "minimalist." But maybe it's nothing more than a working marriage of necessity and convenience that has brought me to writing the kind of stories I do in the way that I do.

None of my stories really *happened*, of course—I'm not writing autobiography—but most of them bear a resemblance, however faint, to certain life occurrences or situations. But when I try to recall the physical surroundings or furnishings bearing on a story situation (what kind of flowers, if any, were present? did they give off any odor? etc.), I'm often at a total loss. So I have to make it up as I go along—what the people in the story say to each other, as well as what they do then, after thus and so was said, and what happens to them next. I make up what they say to each other, though there may be, in the dialogue, some actual phrase, or sentence or two, that I once heard given in a particular context at some time or other. That sentence may even have been my starting point for the story.

When Henry Miller was in his forties and was writing *Tropic of Cancer*, a book, incidentally, that I like very much, he talks about trying to write in this borrowed room, where at any minute he may have to stop writing because the chair he is sitting on may be taken out from under him. Until fairly recently, this state of affairs persisted in my own life. For as long as I can remember, since I was a teenager, the imminent removal of the chair from under me was a constant concern. For years and years my wife and I met ourselves coming and going as we tried to keep a roof over our heads and put bread and milk on the table. We had no money, no visible, that is to say, marketable skills—nothing that we could do toward earning anything better than a get-by living. And we had no education, though we each wanted one very badly. Education, we believed, would open doors for us, help us get jobs so that we could make the kind of life we wanted for ourselves and our children. We had great dreams, my wife and I. We thought we could bow our necks, work very hard, and do all that we had set our hearts to do. But we were mistaken.

I have to say that the greatest single influence on my life, and on my writing, directly and indirectly, has been my two children. They were born before I was twenty, and from beginning to end of our habitation under the same roof—some nineteen years in all—there wasn't any area of my life where their heavy and often baleful influence didn't reach.

In one of her essays Flannery O'Connor says that not much needs to happen in a writer's life after the writer is twenty years old. Plenty of the stuff that makes fiction has already happened to the writer before that time. More than enough, she says. Enough things to last the writer the rest of his creative life. This is not true for me. Most of what now strikes me as story "material" presented itself to me after I was twenty. I really don't remember much about my life before I became a parent. I really don't feel that anything happened in my life until I was twenty and married and had the kids. Then things started to happen.

In the mid-1960s I was in a busy laundromat in Iowa City trying to do five or six loads of clothes, kids' clothes, for the most part, but some of our own clothing, of course, my wife's and mine. My wife was working as a waitress for the University Athletic Club that Saturday afternoon. I was doing chores and being responsible for the kids. They were with some other kids that afternoon, a birthday party maybe. Something. But right then I was doing the laundry. I'd already had sharp words with an old harridan over the number of washers I'd had to use. Now I was waiting for the next round with her, or someone else like her. I was nervously keeping an eye on the dryers that were in operation in the crowded laundromat. When and if one of the dryers ever stopped, I planned to rush over to it with my shopping basket of damp clothes. Understand, I'd been hanging around in the laundromat for thirty minutes or so with this basketful of clothes, waiting my chance. I'd already missed out on a couple of dryers—somebody'd gotten there first. I was getting frantic. As I say, I'm not sure where our kids were that afternoon. Maybe I had to pick them up from someplace, and it was getting late, and that contributed to my state of mind. I did know that even if I could get my clothes into a dryer it would still be another hour or more before the clothes would dry, and I could sack them up and go home with them, back to our apartment in married-student housing. Finally a dryer came to a stop. And I was right there when it did. The clothes inside quit tumbling and lay still. In thirty seconds or so, if no one showed up to claim them, I planned to get rid of the clothes and replace them with my own. That's the law of the laundromat. But at that minute a woman came over to the dryer and opened the door. I stood there waiting. This woman put her hand into the machine and took hold of some items of clothing. But they weren't dry enough, she decided. She closed the door and put two more dimes into the machine. In a daze I moved away with my shopping cart and went back to waiting. But I remember thinking at that moment, amid the feelings of helpless frustration that had me close to tears, that nothing—and, brother, I mean nothing—that ever happened to me on this earth could come anywhere close, could possibly be as important to me, could make as much difference, as the fact that I had two children. And that I would always have them and always find myself in this position of unrelieved responsibility and permanent distraction.

I'm talking about real *influence* now. I'm talking about the moon and the tide. But like that it came to me. Like a sharp breeze when the window is thrown open. Up to that point in my life I'd gone along thinking, what exactly, I don't know, but that things would work out somehow—that everything in my life I'd hoped for or wanted to do was possible. But at that moment, in the laundromat, I realized that this simply was not true. I realized—what had I been thinking before?—that my life was a small-change thing for the most part, chaotic, and without much light showing through. At that moment I felt—I knew—that the life I was in was vastly different from the lives of the writers I most admired. I understood writers to be people who didn't spend their Saturdays at the laundromat and every waking hour subject to the needs and caprices of their children. Sure, sure, there've been plenty of writers who have had far more serious impediments to their work, including imprisonment, blindness, the threat of torture or of death in one form or another. But knowing this was no consolation. At that moment—I swear all of this took place there in the laundromat—I could see nothing ahead but years more of this kind of responsibility and perplexity. Things would change some, but they were never really going to get better. I understood this, but could I live with it? At that moment I saw accommodations would have to be made. The sights would have to be lowered. I'd had, I realized later, an insight. But so what? What are insights? They don't help any. They just make things harder.

For years my wife and I had held to a belief that if we worked hard and tried to do the right things, the right things would happen. It's not such a bad thing to try and build a life on. Hard work, goals, good intentions, loyalty, we believed these were virtues and would someday be rewarded. We dreamt when we had the time for it. But, eventually, we realized that hard work and dreams were not enough. Somewhere, in Iowa City maybe, or shortly afterwards, in Sacramento, the dreams began to go bust.

The time came and went when everything my wife and I held sacred, or considered worthy of respect, every spiritual value, crumbled away. Something terrible had happened to us. It was something that we had never seen occur in any other family. We couldn't fully comprehend what had happened. It was erosion, and we couldn't stop it. Somehow, when we weren't looking, the children had got into the driver's seat. As crazy as it sounds now, they held the reins, and the whip. We simply could not have anticipated anything like what was happening to us.

During these ferocious years of parenting, I usually didn't have the time, or the heart, to think about working on anything very lengthy. The circumstances of my life, the "grip and slog" of it, in D. H. Lawrence's phrase, did not permit it. The circumstances of my life with these children dictated something else. They said if I wanted to write anything, and finish it, and if ever I wanted to take satisfaction out of finished work, I was going to have to stick to stories and poems. The short things I could sit down and, with any luck, write quickly and have done with. Very early, long before Iowa City even, I'd understood that I would have a hard time writing a novel, given my anxious inability to focus on anything for a sustained period of time. Looking back on it now, I think I was slowly going nuts with frustration during those ravenous years. Anyway, these circumstances dictated, to the fullest possible extent, the forms my writing could take. God forbid, I'm not complaining now, just giving facts from a heavy and still bewildered heart.

If I'd been able to collect my thoughts and concentrate my energy on a novel, say, I was still in no position to wait for a payoff that, if it came at all, might be several years down the road. I couldn't see the road. I had to sit down and write something I could finish now, tonight, or at least tomorrow night, no later, after I got in from work and before I lost interest. In those days I always worked some crap job or another, and my wife did the same. She waitressed or else was a door-to-door sales-woman. Years later she taught high school. But that was years later. I worked sawmill jobs, janitor jobs, deliveryman jobs, service station jobs, stockroom boy jobs—name it, I did it. One summer, in Arcata, California, I picked tulips, I swear, during the daylight hours, to support us; and at night after closing, I cleaned the inside of a drive-in restaurant and swept up the parking lot. Once I even considered, for a few minutes anyway—the job application form there in front of me—becoming a bill collector!

In those days I figured if I could squeeze in an hour or two a day for myself, after job and family, that was more than good enough. That was heaven itself. And I felt happy to have that hour. But sometimes, one reason or another, I couldn't get the hour. Then I would look forward to Saturday, though sometimes things happened that knocked Saturday out as well. But there was Sunday to hope for. Sunday, maybe.

I couldn't see myself working on a novel in such a fashion, that is to say, no fashion at all. To write a novel, it seemed to me, a writer should be living in a world that makes sense, a world that the writer can believe in, draw a bead on, and then write about accurately. A world that will, for a time anyway, stay fixed in one place. Along with this there has to be a belief in the essential *correctness* of that world. A belief that the known world has reasons for existing, and is worth writing about, is not likely to go up in smoke in the process. This wasn't the case with the world I knew and was living in. My world was one that seemed to change gears and directions, along with its rules, every day. Time and again I reached the point where I couldn't see or plan any further ahead than the first of next month and gathering together enough money, by hook or by crook, to meet the rent and provide the children's school clothes. This is true.

I wanted to see tangible results for any so-called literary efforts of mine. No chits or promises, no time certificates, please. So I purposely, and by necessity, limited myself to writing things I knew I could finish in one sitting, two sittings at the most. I'm talking of a first draft now. I've always had patience for rewriting. But in those days I happily looked forward to the rewriting as it took up time which I was glad to have taken up. In one regard

I was in no hurry to finish the story or the poem I was working on, for finishing something meant I'd have to find the time, and the belief, to begin something else. So I had great patience with a piece of work after I'd done the initial writing. I'd keep something around the house for what seemed a very long time, fooling with it, changing this, adding that, cutting out something else.

This hit-and-miss way of writing lasted for nearly two decades. There were good times back there, of course; certain grown-up pleasures and satisfactions that only parents have access to. But I'd take poison before I'd go through that time again.

The circumstances of my life are much different now, but now I *choose* to write short stories and poems. Or at least I think I do. Maybe it's all a result of the old writing habits from those days. Maybe I still can't adjust to thinking in terms of having a great swatch of time in which to work on something—anything I want!—and not have to worry about having the chair yanked out from under me, or one of my kids smarting off about why supper isn't ready on demand. But I learned some things along the way. One of the things I learned is that I had to bend or else break. And I also learned that it is possible to bend and break at the same time.

I'll say something about two other individuals who exercised influence on my life. One of them, John Gardner, was teaching a beginning fiction writing course at Chico State College when I signed up for the class in the fall of 1958. My wife and I and the children had just moved down from Yakima, Washington, to a place called Paradise, California, about ten miles up in the foothills outside of Chico. We had the promise of low-rent housing and, of course, we thought it would be a great adventure to move to California. (In those days, and for a long while after, we were always up for an adventure.) Of course, I'd have to work to earn a living for us, but I also planned to enroll in college as a part-time student.

Gardner was just out of the University of Iowa with a Ph.D. and, I knew, several unpublished novels and short stories. I'd never met anyone who'd written a novel, published or otherwise. On the first day of class he marched us outside and had us sit on the lawn. There were six or seven of us, as I recall. He went around, asking us to name the authors we liked to read. I can't remember any names we mentioned, but they must not have been the right names. He announced that he didn't think any of us had what it took to become real writers—as far as he could see none of us had the necessary *fire*. But he said he was going to do what he could for us, though it was obvious he didn't expect much to come of it. But there was an implication too that we were about to set off on a trip, and we'd do well to hold onto our hats.

I remember at another class meeting he said he wasn't going to mention any of the big-circulation magazines except to sneer at them. He'd brought in a stack of "little" magazines, the literary quarterlies, and he told us to read the work in those magazines. He told us that this was where the best fiction in the country was being published, and all of the poetry. He said he was there to tell us which authors to read as well as teach us how to write. He was amazingly arrogant. He gave us a list of the little magazines he thought were worth something, and he went down the list with us and talked a little about each magazine. Of course, none of us had ever heard of these magazines. It was the first I'd ever known of their existence. I remember him saying during this time, it might have been during a conference, that writers were made as well as born. (Is this true? My God, I still don't know. I suppose every writer who teaches creative writing and who takes the job at all seriously has to believe this to some extent. There are apprentice musicians and composers and visual artists—so why *not* writers?) I was impressionable then, I suppose I still am, but I was terrifically impressed with everything he said and did. He'd take one of my early efforts at a story and go over it with me. I remember him as being very patient, wanting me to understand what he was trying to show me, telling me over and over how important it was to have the right words saying what I wanted them to say. Nothing vague or blurred, no smoked-glass prose. And he kept drumming at me the importance of using—I don't know how else to say it—common language, the language of normal discourse, the language we speak to each other in.

Recently we had dinner together in Ithaca, New York, and I reminded him then of some of the sessions we'd had up in his office. He answered that probably everything he'd told me was wrong. He said, "I've changed my mind about so many things." All I know is that the advice he was handing out in those days was just what I needed at that time. He was a wonderful teacher. It was a great thing to have happen to me at that period of my life, to have someone who took me seriously enough to sit down and go over a manuscript with me. I knew something crucial was happening to me, something that mattered. He helped me to see how important it was to say exactly what I wanted to say and nothing else; not to use "literary" words or "pseudo-poetic" language. He'd try to explain to me the difference between saying something like, for example, "wing of a mead-owlark" and "meadowlark's wing." There's a different sound and feel, yes? The word "ground" and the word "earth," for instance. Ground is ground, he'd say, it means *ground*, dirt, that kind of stuff. But if you say "earth," that's something else, that word has other ramifications. He taught me to use contractions in my writing. He helped show me how to say what I wanted to say and to use the minimum number of words to do so. He made me see that absolutely everything was important in a short story. It was of consequence where the commas and periods went. For this, for that—for his giving me the key to his office so I would have a place to write on the weekends—for his putting up with my brashness and general nonsense, I'll always be grateful. He was an influence.

Ten years later I was still alive, still living with my children, still writing an occasional story or poem. I sent one of the occasional stories to *Esquire* and in so doing hoped to be able to forget about it for a while. But the story came back by return mail, along with a letter from Gordon Lish, at that time the fiction editor for the magazine. He said he was returning the story. He was not apologizing that he was returning it, not returning it "reluctantly"; he was just returning it. But he asked to see others. So I promptly sent him everything I had, and he just as promptly sent everything back. But again a friendly letter accompanied the work I'd sent to him.

At that time, the early 1970s, I was living in Palo Alto with my family. I was in my early thirties and I had my first white-collar job—I was an editor for a textbook publishing firm. We lived in a house that had an old garage out back. The previous tenants had built a playroom in the garage, and I'd go out to this garage every night I could manage after dinner and try to write something. If I couldn't write anything, and this was often the case, I'd just sit in there for a while by myself, thankful to be away from the fracas that always seemed to be raging inside the house. But I was writing a short story that I'd called "The Neighbors." I finally finished the story and sent it off to Lish. A letter came back almost immediately telling me how much he liked it, that he was changing the title to "Neighbors," that he was recommending to the magazine that the story be purchased. It was purchased, it did appear, and nothing, it seemed to me, would ever be the same. *Esquire* soon bought another story, and then another, and so on. James Dickey became poetry editor of the magazine during this time, and he began accepting my poems for publication. In one regard, things had never seemed better. But my kids were in full cry then, like the racetrack crowd I can hear at this moment, and they were eating me alive. My life soon took another veering, a sharp turn, and then it came to a dead stop off on a siding. I couldn't go anywhere, couldn't back up or go forward. It was during this period that Lish collected some of my stories and gave them to McGraw-Hill, who published them. For the time being I was still off on the siding, unable to move in any direction. If there'd once been a fire, it'd gone out.

Influences. John Gardner and Gordon Lish. They hold irredeemable notes. But my children are it. Theirs is the main influence. They were the prime movers and shapers of my life and my writing. As you can see, I'm still under their influence, though the days are relatively clear now, and the silences are right.

John Gardner:
The Writer as Teacher

A long time ago—it was the summer of 1958—my wife and I and our two baby children moved from Yakima, Washington, to a little town outside of Chico, California. There we found an old house and paid twenty-five dollars a month rent. In order to finance this move, I'd had to borrow a hundred and twenty-five dollars from a druggist I'd delivered prescriptions for, a man named Bill Barton.

This is by way of saying that in those days my wife and I were stone broke. We had to eke out a living, but the plan was that I would take classes at what was then called Chico State College. But for as far back as I can remember, long before we moved to California in search of a different life and our slice of the American pie, I'd wanted to be a writer. I wanted to write, and I wanted to write anything—fiction, of course, but also poetry, plays, scripts, articles for *Sports Afield*, *True*, *Argosy*, and *Rogue* (some of the magazines I was then reading), pieces for the local newspaper—anything that involved putting words together to make something coherent and of interest to someone besides myself. But at the time of our move, I felt in my bones I had to get some education in order to go along with being a writer. I put a very high premium on education then—much higher in those days than now, I'm sure, but that's because I'm older and have an education. Understand that nobody in my family had ever gone to college or for that matter had got beyond the mandatory eighth grade in high school. I didn't *know anything*, but I knew I didn't know anything.

So along with this desire to get an education, I had this very strong desire to write; it was a desire so strong that, with the encouragement I was given in college, and the insight acquired, I kept on writing long after "good sense" and the "cold facts"—the "realities" of my life—told me, time and again, that I ought to quit, stop the dreaming, quietly go ahead and do something else.

That fall at Chico State I enrolled in classes that most freshman students have to take, but I enrolled as well for something called Creative Writing 101. This course was going to be taught by a new faculty member named John Gardner, who was already surrounded by a bit of mystery and romance. It was said that he'd taught previously at Oberlin College but had left there for some reason that wasn't made clear. One student said Gardner had been fired—students, like everyone else, thrive on rumor and intrigue—and another student said Gardner had simply quit after some kind of flap. Someone else said his teaching load at Oberlin, four or five classes of freshman English each semester, had been too heavy and that he couldn't find time to write. For it was said that Gardner was a real, that is to say a practicing, writer—someone who had written novels and short stories. In any case, he was going to teach CW 101 at Chico State, and I signed up.

I was excited about taking a course from a real writer. I'd never laid eyes on a writer before, and I was in awe. But where were these novels and short stories, I wanted to know. Well, nothing had been published yet. It was said that he couldn't get his work published and that he carried it around with him in boxes. (After I became his student, I was to see those boxes of manuscript. Gardner had become aware of my difficulty in finding a place to work. He knew I had a young family and cramped quarters at home. He offered me the key to his office. I see that gift now as a turning point. It was a gift not made casually, and I took it, I think, as a kind of mandate—for that's what it was. I spent part of every Saturday and Sunday in his office, which is where he kept the boxes of manuscript. The boxes were stacked up on the floor beside the desk. *Nickel Mountain*, grease-penciled on one of the boxes, is the only title I recall. But it was in his office, within sight of his unpublished books, that I undertook my first serious attempts at writing.)

When I met Gardner, he was behind a table at registration in the women's gym. I signed the class roster and was given a course card. He didn't look anywhere near what I imagined a writer should look like. The truth is, in those days he looked and dressed like a Presbyterian minister, or an FBI man. He always wore a black suit, a white shirt, and a tie. And he had a crewcut. (Most of the young men my age wore their hair in what was called a "DA" style—a "duck's ass"—the hair combed back along the sides of the head onto the nape and plastered down with hair oil or cream.) I'm saying that Gardner looked very square. And to complete the picture he drove a black four-door Chevrolet with black-wall tires, a car so lacking in any of the amenities it didn't even have a car radio. After I'd got to know him, had been given the key, and was regularly using his office as a place to work, I'd be at his desk in front of the window on a Sunday morning, pounding away on his typewriter. But I'd be watching for his car to pull up and park on the street out in front, as it always did every Sunday. Then Gardner and his first wife, Joan, would get out and, all dressed up in their dark, severe-looking clothes, walk down the sidewalk to the church where they would go inside and attend services. An hour and a half later I'd be watching for them as they came out, walked back down the sidewalk to their black car, got inside and drove away.

Gardner had a crewcut, dressed like a minister or an FBI man, and went to church on Sundays. But he was unconventional in other ways. He started breaking the *rules* on the first day of class; he was a chain smoker and he smoked continuously in the classroom, using a metal wastebasket for an ashtray. In those days, nobody smoked in a classroom. When another faculty member who used the same room reported on him, Gardner merely remarked to us on the man's pettiness and narrow-mindedness, opened windows, and went on smoking.

For short story writers in his class, the requirement was one story, ten to fifteen pages in length. For people who wanted to write a novel—I think there must have been one or two of these souls—a chapter of around twenty pages, along with an outline of the rest. The kicker was that this one short story, or the chapter of the novel, might have to be revised ten times in the course of the semester for Gardner to be satisfied with it. It was a basic tenet of his that a writer found what he wanted to say in the ongoing process of *seeing* what he'd said. And this seeing, or seeing more clearly, came about through revision. He *believed* in revision, endless revision; it was something very close to his heart and something he felt was vital for writers, at whatever stage of their development. And he never seemed to lose patience rereading a student story, even though he might have seen it in five previous incarnations.

I think his idea of a short story in 1958 was still pretty much his idea of a short story in 1982; it was something that had a recognizable beginning, middle, and end to it. Once in a while he'd go to the blackboard and draw a diagram to illustrate a point he wanted to make about rising or falling emotion in a story— peaks, valleys, plateaus, resolution, *dénouement*, things like that. Try as I might, I couldn't muster a great deal of interest or really understand this side of things, the stuff he put on the blackboard. But what I did understand was the way he would comment on a student story that was undergoing class discussion. Gardner might wonder aloud about the author's reasons for writing a story about a crippled person, say, and leaving out the fact of the character's crippledness until the very end of the story. "So you think it's a good idea not to let the reader know this man is crippled until the last sentence?" His tone of voice conveyed his disapproval, and it didn't take more than an instant for everyone in class, including the author of the story, to see that it wasn't a good strategy to use. Any strategy that kept important and necessary information away from the reader in the hope of overcoming him by surprise at the end of the story was cheating.

In class he was always referring to writers whose names I was not familiar with. Or if I knew their names, I'd never read the work. Conrad. Céline. Katherine Anne Porter. Isaac Babel. Walter Van Tilburg Clark. Chekhov. Hortense Calisher. Curt Harnack. Robert Penn Warren. (We read a story of Warren's called "Blackberry Winter." For one reason or another, I didn't care for it, and I said so to Gardner. "You'd better read it again," he said, and he was not joking.) William Gass was another writer he mentioned. Gardner was just starting his magazine, *MSS*, and was about to publish "The Pedersen Kid" in the first issue. I began reading the story in manuscript, but I didn't understand it and again I complained to Gardner. This time he didn't tell me I should try it again, he simply took the story away from me. He talked about James Joyce and Flaubert and Isak Dinesen as if they lived just down the road, in Yuba City. He said, "I'm here to tell you who to read as well as teach you how to write." I'd leave class in a daze and make straight for the library to find books by these writers he was talking about.

Hemingway and Faulkner were the reigning authors in those days. But altogether I'd probably read at the most two or three books by these fellows. Anyway, they were so well known and so much talked about, they couldn't be all that good, could they? I remember Gardner telling me, "Read all the Faulkner you can get your hands on, and then read all of Hemingway to clean the Faulkner out of your system."

He introduced us to the "little" or literary periodicals by bringing a box of these magazines to class one day and passing them around so that we could acquaint ourselves with their names, see what they looked like and what they felt like to hold in the hand. He told us that this was where most of the best fiction in the country and just about all of the poetry was appearing. Fiction, poetry, literary essays, book reviews of recent books, criticism of *living* authors *by* living authors. I felt wild with discovery in those days.

For the seven or eight of us who were in his class, he ordered heavy black binders and told us we should keep our written work in these. He kept his own work in such binders, he said, and of course that settled it for us. We carried our stories in those binders and felt we were special, exclusive, singled out from others. And so we were.

I don't know how Gardner might have been with other students when it came time to have conferences with them about their work. I suspect he gave everybody a good amount of attention. But it was and still is my impression that during that period he took my stories more seriously, read them closer and more carefully, than I had any right to expect. I was completely unprepared for the kind of criticism I received from him. Before our conference he would have marked up my story, crossing out unacceptable sentences, phrases, individual words, even some of the punctuation; and he gave me to understand that these deletions were not negotiable. In other cases he would bracket sentences, phrases, or individual words, and these were items we'd talk about, these cases were negotiable. And he wouldn't hesitate to add something to what I'd written—a word here and there, or else a few words, maybe a sentence that would make clear what I was trying to say. We'd discuss commas in my story as if nothing else in the world mattered more at that moment— and, indeed, it did not. He was always looking to find something to praise. When there was a sentence, a line of dialogue, or a narrative passage that he liked, something that he thought "worked" and moved the story along in some pleasant or unexpected way, he'd write "Nice" in the margin, or else "Good!" And seeing these comments, my heart would lift.

It was close, line-by-line criticism he was giving me, and the reasons behind the criticism, why something ought to be this way instead of that; and it was invaluable to me in my development as a writer. After this kind of detailed talk about the text, we'd talk about the larger concerns of the story, the "problem" it was trying to throw light on, the conflict it was trying to grapple with, and how the story might or might not fit into the grand scheme of story writing. It was his conviction that if the words in the story were blurred because of the author's insensitivity, carelessness, or sentimentality, then the story suffered from a tremendous handicap. But there was something even worse and something that must be avoided at all costs: if the words and the sentiments were dishonest, the author was faking it, writing about things he didn't care about or believe in, then nobody could ever care anything about it.

A writer's values and craft. This is what the man taught and what he stood for, and this is what I've kept by me in the years since that brief but all-important time.

Gardner's *On Becoming a Novelist*, which he completed before his sudden death on 14 September 1982, seems to me to be a wise and honest assessment of what it is like and what is necessary to become a writer and stay a writer. It is informed by common sense, magnanimity, and a set of values that is not negotiable. Anyone reading it must be struck by the absolute and unyielding honesty of the author, as well as by his good humor and high-mindedness. Throughout the book, if you notice, the author keeps saying: "it has been my experience. . . ." It was his experience—and it has been mine, in my role as a teacher of creative writing—that certain aspects of writing can be taught and handed over to other, usually younger, writers. This idea shouldn't come as a surprise to any person seriously interested in education and the creative act. Most good or even great conductors, composers, microbiologists, ballerinas, mathematicians, visual artists, astronomers, or fighter pilots learned their business from older and more accomplished practitioners. Taking classes in creative writing, like taking classes in pottery or medicine, won't in itself make anyone a great writer, potter, or doctor—it may not even make the person *good* at any of these things. But Gardner was convinced that it wouldn't hurt your chances, either.

One of the dangers in teaching or taking creative writing classes lies—and here I'm speaking from my experience again—in the overencouragement of young writers. But I learned from Gardner to take that risk rather than err on the other side. He gave and kept giving, even when the vital signs fluctuated wildly, as they do when someone is young and learning. A young writer certainly needs as much, I would even say more, encouragement than young people trying to enter other professions. And it ought to go without saying that the encouragement must always be honest encouragement and never hype. What makes this book particularly fine is the quality of its encouragement.

Failure and dashed hopes are common to us all. The suspicion that we're taking on water and that things are not working out in our life the way we'd planned hits most of us at some time or another. By the time you're nineteen you have a pretty good idea of some of the things you're *not* going to be; but more often, this sense of one's limitations, the really penetrating understanding, happens in late youth or early middle age. No teacher or any amount of education can make a writer out of someone who is constitutionally incapable of becoming a writer in the first place. But anyone embarking on a career, or pursuing a calling, risks setback and failure. There are failed policemen, politicians, generals, interior decorators, engineers, bus drivers, editors, literary agents, businessmen, basket weavers. There are also failed and disillusioned creative writing teachers and failed and disillusioned writers. John Gardner was neither of these, and the reasons why are to be found in *On Becoming a Novelist*.

My own debt is great and can only be touched on in this brief context. I miss him more than I can say. But I consider myself the luckiest of men to have had his criticism and his generous encouragement.

Left to right: Tobias Wolff, Raymond Carver and Richard Ford.

Friendship

Boy, are these guys having fun! They're in London, and they've just finished giving a reading to a packed house at the National Poetry Centre. For some time now critics and reviewers who write for the British papers and magazines have been calling them "Dirty Realists," but Ford and Wolff and Carver don't take this seriously. They joke about it just as they joke about a lot of other things. They don't feel like part of a group.

It's true they are friends. It's also true they share some of the same concerns in their work. And they know many of the same people and sometimes publish in the same magazines. But they don't see themselves as belonging to, or spearheading, a movement. They are friends and writers having a good time together, counting their blessings. They know luck plays a part in all this, and they know they're lucky. But they're as vain as other writers and think they deserve any good fortune that comes their way—though often as not they're surprised when it happens. Between them they have produced several novels, books of short stories and poems, novellas, essays, articles, screenplays and reviews. But their work, and their personalities, are as different as sea breezes and salt water. It is these differences, along with the similarities, and something else hard to define that make them friends.

The reason they're in London and having such a big time together and not back home where they belong in Syracuse, New York (Wolff), or Coahoma, Mississippi (Ford), or Port Angeles, Washington (Carver), is that they all have books coming out in England within days of each other. Their books are not that much alike—at least I don't feel so—but what the work does have in common, I believe, is that it is uncommonly good and of some importance to the world. And I would go on thinking this even if, God forbid, we should ever cease being friends.

But when I look again at this picture that was taken three years ago in London, after a fiction reading, my heart moves, and I'm nearly fooled into thinking that friendship is a permanent thing. Which it is, up to a point. Now, clearly, the friends in the picture are enjoying themselves and having a good time together. The only serious thing on their minds is that they're wondering when this photographer will finish his business so that they can leave and go about their business of having more fun together. They've made plans for the evening. They don't want this time to end. They're not much looking forward to night and fatigue and the gradual—or sudden—slowing down of things. Truth is, they haven't seen each other for a long time. They're having such a good time being together and being themselves—being friends, in short—they'd like things to just go on like this. To last. And they will. Up to a point, as I said.

That point is Death. Which, in the picture, is the farthest thing from their minds. But it's something that's never that far away from their thinking when they're alone and not together and having fun, as they were that time in London. Things wind down. Things *do* come to an end. People stop living. Chances are that two of the three friends in this picture will have to gaze upon the remains—the *remains*—of the third friend, when that time comes. The thought is grievous, and terrifying. But the only alternative to burying your friends is that they will have to bury you.

I'm brought to ponder such a dreary matter when I think about friendship, which is, in at least one regard anyway, like marriage—another shared dream—something the participants have to believe in and put their faith in, trusting that it *will* go on forever.

As with a spouse, or a lover, so it is with your friends: you remember when and where you met. I was introduced to Richard Ford in the lobby of a Hilton Hotel in Dallas where a dozen or so writers and poets were being housed and fed. A mutual friend—there's a web—the poet Michael Ryan, had invited us to a literary festival at Southern Methodist University. But until the day I got on the plane in San Francisco, I didn't know if I had the nerve to fly to Dallas. After a destructive six-year alcoholic binge, I was venturing out of my hole for the first time since having stopped drinking a few months before. I was sober but shaky.

Ford, however, emanated confidence. There was an elegance about his bearing, his clothes, even his speech—which was poised and courtly and southern. I looked up to him, I think. Maybe I even wished I could be him since he was so clearly everything I was not! Anyway, I'd just read his novel, *A Piece of My Heart*, and loved it and was glad to be able to tell him so. He expressed enthusiasm for my short stories. We wanted to talk more but the evening was breaking up. We had to go. We shook hands again. But the next morning, early, we met in the hotel dining room and shared a table for breakfast. Richard ordered, I recall, biscuits and country ham along with grits and a side of gravy. He said "Yes, ma'am" or "No, ma'am" and "Thank you, ma'am" to the waitress. I liked the way he talked. He let me taste his grits. We told each other things, talking through breakfast, coming away feeling we'd known each other, as they say, for a long time.

During the next four or five days we spent as much time together as we could. When we said good-bye on the last day, he invited me to visit him and his wife in Princeton. I figured my chances of ever getting to Princeton were, to put it mildly, slim, but I said I looked forward to it. Still, I knew I'd made a friend, and a good friend. The kind of friend you'd go out of your way for.

Two months later, in January 1978, I found myself in Plainfield, Vermont, on the campus of Goddard College. Toby Wolff, looking every bit as anxious and alarmed as I must have looked, had the cell-like room next to my cell in a condemned barracks building that had formerly been used to house rich kids looking for an alternative to the usual college education. We were there, Toby and I, for a two-week residency and were then expected to go home and work with five or six graduate students through the mail, helping them to write short stories. It was thirty-six degrees below zero, eighteen inches of snow lay on the ground, and Plainfield was the coldest place in the country.

No one, it seems to me, could have been more surprised to find himself at Goddard College in Vermont in January than Toby or I. In Toby's case he was there only because the writer who was supposed to be on board had to cancel at the last minute because of illness. But the writer had suggested Toby in his stead. And not only did Ellen Voigt, the director of the program, invite Toby, sight unseen, but miracle of miracles, she took a chance on a recovering alcoholic still in the early stages of getting well.

The first two nights in the barracks, Toby had insomnia and couldn't sleep. But I liked the way he didn't complain and could even joke about having given up sleep. And I was drawn to him too, I think, because of what I sensed to be his vulnerability; in certain ways he was even more vulnerable than I was, and that's saying something. We were in the company of writers, fellow faculty members, who were, some of them, among the most distinguished in the country. Toby didn't have a book out, though he had published several stories in the literary magazines. I'd published a book, a couple in fact, but I hadn't written anything in a long time and didn't feel much like a writer. I remember waking up at five one morning, suffering my own anxieties, to find Toby at the kitchen table eating a sandwich and drinking some milk. He looked deranged and as if he hadn't slept in days, which he hadn't. We were glad of each other's uneasy company. I made us some cocoa and we began to talk. It seemed important to be telling each other things there in the kitchen that morning; it was still dark outside and so cold we could hear the trees snap from time to time. From the little window over the sink we could see the northern lights.

For the remaining days of the residency, we hung out when we could, taught a class on Chekhov together and laughed a lot. We both felt we'd been down on our luck, but felt too that our luck just might be changing. Toby said I should come and see him if ever I got to Phoenix, and of course I said sure. Sure. I mentioned to him that I'd met Richard Ford not too long before, who, it turned out, was good friends with Toby's brother, Geoffrey, a man I was to meet and become friends with myself a year or so later. The web again.

In 1980 Richard and Toby became friends. I like it when my friends meet, take a liking to each other and establish their own friendship. I feel all the more enriched. But I can recall Richard's reservation, just before meeting Toby: "I'm sure he's a good guy," Richard said. "But I don't *need* any more friends in my life right now. I have all the friends I can accommodate. I can't do right by my old friends as it is."

I've had two lives. My first life ended in June 1977, when I stopped drinking. I didn't have many friends left by then, mostly casual acquaintances and drinking pals. I'd lost my friends. Either they'd faded away—and who could blame them?—or else they'd simply plummeted out of sight and, more's the pity, I don't think I even missed them or noted their passing.

Would I choose, saying I had to choose, a life of poverty and ill health, if that was the only way I could keep the friends I have? No. Would I give up my place on the lifeboat, that is to say, die, for any one of my friends? I hesitate, but again the answer is an unheroic no. They wouldn't, any of them, for me either, and I wouldn't have it any other way. We understand each other perfectly in this, and in most other ways as well. Partly we're friends because we *do* understand that. We love each other, but we love ourselves a little more.

Back to the picture. We're feeling good about ourselves and about other things in our life as well. We like being writers.

There's nothing else on earth we'd rather be, though we've all been something else too at one time or another. Still, we like it enormously that things have worked out so that we can be together in London. We're having fun, you see. We're friends. And friends are supposed to have a good time when they get together.

Meditation on a Line from Saint Teresa

There is a line of prose from the writings of Saint Teresa which seemed more and more appropriate as I thought toward this occasion, so I want to offer a meditation on that sentence. It was used as an epigraph to a recent collection of poems by Tess Gallagher, my dear friend and companion who is here with me today, and I take the line from the context of her epigraph.

Saint Teresa, that extraordinary woman who lived 373 years ago, said: "Words lead to deeds. . . . They prepare the soul, make it ready, and move it to tenderness."

There is clarity and beauty in that thought expressed in just this way. I'll say it again, because there is also something a little foreign in this sentiment coming to our attention at this remove, in a time certainly less openly supportive of the important connection between what we say and what we do: "Words lead to deeds. . . . They prepare the soul, make it ready, and move it to tenderness."

There is something more than a little mysterious, not to say—forgive me—even mystical about these particular words and the way Saint Teresa used them, with full weight and belief. True enough, we realize they appear almost as echoes of some former, more considered time. Especially the mention of the word "soul," a word we don't encounter much these days outside of church and perhaps in the "soul" section of the record store.

"Tenderness"—that's another word we don't hear much these days, and certainly not on such a public, joyful occasion as this. Think about it: when was the last time you used the word or heard it used? It's in as short a supply as that other word, "soul."

There is a wonderfully described character named Moiseika in Chekhov's story "Ward No. 6" who, although he has been consigned to the madhouse wing of the hospital, has picked up the habit of a certain kind of tenderness. Chekhov writes: "Moiseika likes to make himself useful. He gives his companions water, and covers them up when they are asleep; he promises each of them to bring him back a kopeck, and to make him a new cap; he feeds with a spoon his neighbor on the left, who is paralyzed."

Even though the word tenderness isn't used, we feel its presence in these details, even when Chekhov goes on to enter a disclaimer by way of this commentary on Moiseika's behavior: "He acts in this way, not from compassion nor from any consid-erations of a humane kind, but through imitation, unconsciously dominated by Gromov, his neighbor on the right hand."

In a provocative alchemy, Chekhov combines words and deeds to cause us to reconsider the origin and nature of tenderness. Where does it come from? As a deed, does it still move the heart, even when abstracted from humane motives?

Somehow, the image of the isolate man performing gentle acts without expectation or even self-knowledge stays before us as an odd beauty we have been brought to witness. It may even reflect back upon our own lives with a questioning gaze.

There is another scene from "Ward No. 6" in which two characters, a disaffected doctor and an imperious postmaster, his elder, suddenly find themselves discussing the human soul.

"And you do not believe in the immortality of the soul?" the postmaster asks suddenly.

"No, honored Mihail Averyanitch; I do not believe it, and have no grounds for believing it."

"I must own I doubt it too," Mihail Averyanitch admits. "And yet I have a feeling as though I should never die. Oh, I think to myself: 'Old fogey, it is time you were dead!' But there is a little voice in my soul says: 'Don't believe it; you won't die.'"

The scene ends but the words linger as deeds. "A little voice in the soul" is born. Also the way we have perhaps dismissed certain concepts about life, about death, suddenly gives over unexpectedly to belief of an admittedly fragile but insistent nature.

Long after what I've said has passed from your minds, whether it be weeks or months, and all that remains is the sensation of having attended a large public occasion, marking the end of one significant period in your lives and the beginning of another, try then, as you work out your individual destinies, to remember that words, the right and true words, can have the power of deeds.

Remember too, that little-used word that has just about dropped out of public and private usage: tenderness. It can't hurt. And that other word: soul—call it spirit if you want, if it makes it any easier to claim the territory. Don't forget that either. Pay attention to the spirit of your words, your deeds. That's preparation enough. No more words.

EARLY STORIES

Furious Seasons

That duration which maketh Pyramids
pillars of snow, and all that's past a moment.

SIR THOMAS BROWNE

Rain threatens. Already the tops of the hills across the valley are obscured by the heavy gray mist. Quick shifting black clouds with white furls and caps are coming from the hills, moving down the valley and passing over the fields and vacant lots in front of the apartment house. If Farrell lets go his imagination he can see the clouds as black horses with flared white manes and, turning behind, slowly, inexorably, black chariots, here and there a white-plumed driver. He shuts the screen door now and watches his wife step slowly down the stairs. She turns at the bottom and smiles, and he opens the screen and waves. In another moment she drives off. He goes back into the room and sits down in the big leather chair under the brass lamp, laying his arms straight out along the sides of the chair.

It is a little darker in the room when Iris comes out of her bath wrapped in a loose white dressing gown. She pulls the stool out from under the dresser and sits down in front of the mirror. With her right hand she takes up a white plastic brush, the handle inset with imitation pearl, and begins combing out her hair in long, sweeping, rhythmical movements, the brush passing down through the length of the hair with a faint squeaking noise. She holds her hair down over the one shoulder with her left hand and makes the long, sweeping, rhythmical movements with the right.

She stops once and switches on the lamp over the mirror. Farrell takes up a glossy picture magazine from the stand beside the chair and reaches up to turn on the lamp, fumbling against the parchment-like shade in his hunt for the chain. The lamp is two feet over his right shoulder and the brown shade crackles as he touches it.

It is dark outside and the air smells of rain. Iris asks if he will close the window. He looks up at the window, now a mirror, seeing himself and, behind, Iris sitting at the dresser watching him, with another, darker Farrell staring into another window beside her. He has yet to call Frank and confirm the hunting trip for the next morning. He turns the pages. Iris takes down the brush from her hair and taps it on the dresser edge.

"Lew," she says, "you know I'm pregnant?"

Under the lamplight the glossy pages are open now to a halftone, two-page picture of a disaster scene, an earthquake, somewhere in the Near East. There are five almost fat men dressed in white, baggy pants standing in front of a flattened house. One of the men, probably the leader, is wearing a dirty white hat that hangs down over one eye giving him a secret, malevolent look. He is looking sideways at the camera, pointing across the mess of blocks to a river or a neck of the sea on the far side of the rubble. Farrell closes the magazine and lets it slide out of his lap as he stands. He turns out the light and then, before going on through to the bathroom, asks: "What are you going to do?" The words are dry, hurrying like old leaves into the dark corners of the room and Farrell feels at the same instant the words are out that the question has already been asked by someone else, a long time ago. He turns and goes into the bathroom.

It smells of Iris; a warm, moist odor, slightly sticky; New Spring talc and King's Idyll cologne. Her towel lies across the back of the toilet. In the sink she has spilled talcum. It is wet now and pasty and makes a thick yellow ring around the white sides. He rubs it out and washes it into the drain.

He is shaving. By turning his head, he can see into the living room. Iris in profile sitting on the stool in front of the old dresser. He lays down the razor and washes his face, then picks up the razor again. At this moment he hears the first few drops of rain spatter against the roof . . .

After a while he turns out the light over the dresser and sits down again in the big leather chair, listening to the rain. The rain comes in short, fluttery swishes against his window. The soft fluttering of a white bird.

His sister has caught it. She keeps it in a box, dropping in flowers for it through the top, sometimes shaking the box so they can hear it fluttering its wings against the sides until one morning she shows him, holding out the box, there is no fluttering inside. Only a lumpy, scraping sound the bird makes as she tilts the box from one side to the other. When she gives it to him to get rid of he throws box and all into the river, not wanting to open it for it has started to smell funny. The cardboard box is eighteen inches long and six inches wide and four inches deep, and he is sure it is a Snowflake cracker box because this is what she used for the first few birds.

He runs along the squashy bank following. It is a funeral boat and the muddy river is the Nile and it will soon run into the ocean but before that the boat will burn up and the white bird will fly out and into his father's fields someplace where he will hunt out the bird in some thick growth of green meadow grass, eggs and all. He runs along the bank, the brush whipping his pants, and once a limb hits him on the ear, and it still hasn't burned. He pulls loose some rocks from the bank and begins throwing them at the boat. And then the rain begins; huge, gusty, spattering drops that belt the water, sweeping across the river from one shore to the other.

Farrell had been in bed for a number of hours now, how long he could not be sure. Every so often he raised up on one shoulder, careful not to disturb his wife, and peered across to her night-stand trying for a look at the clock. Its side was turned a little too much in his direction and raising as he does on one shoulder, being as careful as possible, he could see only that the yellow hands say 3:15 or 2:45. Outside the rain came against his window. He turned on his back, his legs spread wide under the sheet barely touching his wife's left foot, listening to the clock on the nightstand. He pulled down into the quilts again and then because it was too hot and his hands were sweating, he threw back the close covers, twisting his fingers into the sheet, crushing it between his fingers and knotting it against his palms until they felt dry.

Outside the rain came in clouds, lifting up in swells against the faint yellow outside light like myriads of tiny yellow insects coming furiously against his window, spitting and rippling. He turned over and slowly began working himself closer to Lorraine until her smooth back touched his chest. For a moment he held her gently, carefully, his hand lying in the hollow of her stomach, his fingers slipped under the elastic band of her underpants, the fingertips barely touching the stiff, brush-like hair below. An odd sensation then, like slipping into a warm bath and feeling himself a child again, the memories flooding back. He moved his hand and pulled away, then eased out of bed and walked to the streaming window.

It was a huge, foreign dream night outside. The street lamp a gaunt, scarred obelisk running up into the rain with a faint yellow light holding to its point. At its base the street was black, shiny. Darkness swirled and pulled at the edges of the light. He could not see the other apartments and for a moment it was as if they'd been destroyed, like the houses in the picture he'd been looking at a few hours ago. The rain appeared and disappeared against the window like a dark veil opened and closed. Down below it flooded at the curbs. Leaning closer until he could feel the cold drafts of air on his forehead from the bottom of the window, he watched his breath make a fog. He had read someplace and it seemed he could remember looking at some picture once, perhaps *National Geographic*, where groups of brown-skinned people stood around their huts watching the frosted sun come up. The caption said they believed the soul was visible in the breath, that they were spitting and blowing into the palms of their hands, offering their souls to God. His breath disappeared while he watched, until only a tiny circle, a dot remained, then nothing. He turned away from the window for his things.

He fumbled in the closet for his insulated boots, his hands tracing the sleeves of each coat until he found the rubber slick waterproof. He went to the drawer for socks and long underwear, then picked up his shirt and pants and carried the armload through the hallway into the kitchen before turning on the light. He dressed and pulled on his boots before starting the coffee. He would have liked to turn on the porch light for Frank but somehow it didn't seem good with Iris out there in bed. While the coffee perked he made sandwiches and when it had finished he filled a thermos, took a cup down from the cupboard, filled it, and sat down near the window where he could watch the street. He smoked and drank the coffee and listened to the clock on the stove squeaking. The coffee slopped over the cup and the brown drops ran slowly down the side onto the table. He rubbed his fingers through the wet circle across the rough tabletop.

He is sitting at the desk in his sister's room. He sits in the straight-backed chair on a thick dictionary, his feet curled up beneath the seat of the chair, the heels of his shoes hooked on the rung. When he leans too heavily on the table one of the legs picks up from the floor and so he has had to put a magazine under the leg. He is drawing a picture of the valley he lives in. At first he meant to trace a picture from one of his sister's schoolbooks, but after using three sheets of paper and having it still not turn out right, he has decided to draw his valley and his house. Occasionally he stops drawing and rubs his fingers across the grainy surface of the table.

Outside, the April air is still damp and cool, the coolness that comes after the rain in the afternoon. The ground and the trees and the mountains are green and steam is everywhere, coming off the troughs in the corral, from the pond his father made, and out of the meadow in slow, pencil-like columns, rising off the river and going up over the mountains like smoke. He can hear his father shouting to one of the men and he hears the man swear and shout back. He puts his drawing pencil down and slips off the chair. Down below in front of the smokehouse he sees his father working with the pulley. At his feet there is a coil of brown rope and his father is hitting and pulling on the pulley bar trying to swing it out and away from the barn. On his head he wears a brown wool army cap and the collar of his scarred leather jacket is turned up exposing the dirty white lining. With a final blow at the pulley he turns around facing the men. Two of them, big, red-faced Canadians with greasy flannel hats, dragging the sheep toward his father. Their fists are balled deep into the wool and one of them has his arms wrapped around the front legs of the sheep. They go toward the barn, half dragging, half walking the sheep on its hind legs like some wild dance. His father calls out again and they pin the sheep against the barn wall, one of the men straddling the sheep, forcing its head back and up toward his window. Its nostrils are dark slits with little streams of mucus running down into its mouth. The ancient, glazed eyes stare up at him for a moment before it tries to bleat, but the sound comes out a sharp squeaking noise as his father cuts it off with a quick, sweeping thrust of the knife. The blood gushes out over the man's hands before he can move. In a few moments they have the animal up on the pulley. He can hear the dull crank-crank-crank of the pulley as his father winds it even higher. The men are sweating now but they keep their jackets fastened up tight.

Starting right below the gaping throat his father opens up the brisket and belly while the men take the smaller knives and begin cutting the pelt away from the legs. The gray guts slide out of the steaming belly and tumble onto the ground in a thick coil. His father grunts and scoops them into a box, saying something about bear. The red-faced men laugh. He hears the chain in the bathroom rattle and then the water gurgling into the toilet. A moment later he turns toward the door as footsteps approach. His sister comes into the room, her body faintly steaming. For an instant she is frozen there in the doorway with the towel around her hair, one hand holding the ends together and the other on the doorknob. Her breasts are round and smooth-looking, the nipples like the stems of the warm porcelain fruit on the living room table. She drops the towel and it slides down, pulling at her neck, touching across her breasts and then heaping up at her foot. She smiles, slowly puts the hand to her mouth and pulls the door shut. He turns back to the window, his toes curling up in his shoes.

Farrell sat at the table sipping his coffee, smoking again on an empty stomach. Once he heard a car in the street and got up quickly out of the chair, walking to the porch window to see. It started up the street in second then slowed in front of his house, taking the corner carefully, water churning half up to its hubs, but it went on. He sat down at the table again and listened to the electric clock on the stove squeaking. His fingers tightened around the cup. Then he saw the lights. They came bobbing down the street out of the darkness; two close-set signal lanterns on a narrow prow, the heavy white rain falling across the lights, pelting the street ahead. It splashed down the street, slowed, then eased in under his window.

He picked up his things and went out on the porch. Iris was there, stretched out under the twisted pile of heavy quilts. Even as he hunted for a reason for the action, as if he were detached somehow, crouched on the other side of her bed watching himself go through this, at the same time knowing it was over, he moved toward her bed. Irresistibly he bent down over her figure, as if he hung suspended, all senses released except that of smell, he breathed deeply for the fleeting scent of her body, bending until his face was against her covers he experienced the scent again, for just an instant, and then it was gone. He backed away, remembered his gun, then pulled the door shut behind him. The rain whipped into his face. He felt almost giddy clutching his gun and holding onto the banister, steadying himself. For a minute, looking down over the porch to the black, ripply sidewalk, it was as though he were standing alone on a bridge someplace, and again the feeling came, as it had last night, that this had already happened, knowing then that it would happen again, just as he somehow knew now. "Christ!" The rain cut at his face, ran down his nose and onto his lips. Frank tapped the horn twice and Farrell went carefully down the wet, slippery stairs to the car.

"Regular downpour, by God!" Frank said. A big man, with a thick quilted jacket zipped up to his chin and a brown duck-bill cap that made him look like a grim umpire. He helped move things around in the backseat so Farrell could put his things in.

Water ran up against the gutters, backed up at the drains on the corners and now and then they could see where it had flooded over the curbs and into a yard. They followed the street to its end and then turned right onto another street that would take them to the highway.

"This is going to slow us down some, but, Jesus, think what it's going to do to them geese!"

Once again Farrell let go and saw them, pulling them back from that one moment when even the fog had frozen to the rocks and so dark it could as well have been midnight as late afternoon when they started. They come over the bluff, flying low and savage and silent, coming out of the fog suddenly, spectrally, in a swishing of wings over his head and he is jumping up trying to single out the closest, at the same moment pushing forward his safety, but it is jammed and his stiff, gloved finger stays hooked into the guard, pulling against the locked trigger. They all come over him, flying out of the fog across the bluff and over his head. Great strings of them calling down to him. This was the way it happened three years ago.

He watched the wet fields fall under their lights and then sweep beside and then behind the car. The windshield wipers squeaked back and forth.

Iris pulls her hair down over the one shoulder with her left hand while the other wields the brush. Rhythmically the brush makes its sweeping movement through the length of the hair with a faint squeaking noise. The brush rises quickly again to the side of the head and repeats the movement and the sound. She has just told him she is pregnant.

Lorraine has gone to a shower. He has still to call Frank and confirm the hunting trip. The glossy picture of the magazine he holds in his lap is open to the scene of a disaster. One of the men in the picture, evidently the leader, is pointing over the disaster scene to a body of water.

"What are you going to do?" He turns and goes on through to the bathroom. Her towel hangs over the back of the toilet and the bathroom smells of New Spring talc and King's Idyll cologne. There is a yellow pasty ring of talcum powder in the sink that he must rub out with water before he shaves. He can look through to the living room where she sits combing her hair. When he has washed his face and dried, just after he has picked up the razor again, the first raindrops strike the roof.

He looked at the clock on the dashboard but it had stopped. "What time is it?"

"Don't pay any attention to that clock there," Frank said, lifting his thumb off the wheel to indicate the big glowing yellow clock protruding from the dash. "It's stopped. It's 6:30. Did your wife say you had to be home at a certain time?" He smiled.

Farrell shook his head but Frank would not be able to see this. "No. Just wondered what time it was." He lit a cigarette and slumped back in his seat, watching the rain sweep into the car lights and splash against the window.

They are driving down from Yakima to get Iris. It started to rain when they hit the Columbia River highway and by the time they got through Arlington, it was a torrent.

It is like a long sloping tunnel, and they are speeding down the black road with the thick matted trees close overhead and the water cascading against the front of the car. Lorraine's arm extends along the back of the seat, her hand resting lightly on his left shoulder. She is sitting so close that he can feel her left breast rise and fall with her breathing. She has just tried to dial something on the radio, but there is too much static.

"She can fix up the porch for a place to sleep and keep her things," Farrell says, not taking his eyes off the road. "It won't be for long."

Lorraine turns toward him for a moment leaning forward a little in the seat, placing her free hand on his thigh. With her left hand she squeezes her fingers into his shoulder then leans her head against him. After a while she says: "You're all mine, Lew. I hate to think of sharing you even for a little while with anybody. Even your own sister."

The rain lets up gradually and often there are no trees at all over their heads. Once Farrell sees the moon, a sharp, stark yellow crescent, shining through the mist of gray clouds. They leave the woods and the road curves and they follow it into a valley that opens onto the river below. It has stopped raining and the sky is a black rug with handfuls of glistening stars strewn about.

"How long will she stay?" Lorraine asks.

"A couple of months. Three at the most. The Seattle job will be open for her before Christmas." The ride has made his stomach a little fluttery. He lights a cigarette. The gray smoke streams out of his nose and is immediately pulled out through the wing window.

The cigarette began to bite the tip of his tongue and he cracked the window and dropped it out. Frank turned off the highway and onto a slick blacktop that would take them to the river. They were in the wheat country now, the great fields of harvested wheat rolling out toward the dimly outlined hills beyond and broken every so often by a muddy, churned-looking field glimmering with little pockets of water. Next year they would be in plant and in the summer the wheat would stand as high as a man's waist, hissing and bending when the wind blew.

"It's a shame," Frank said, "all this land without grain half the time with half the people in the world starving." He shook his head. "If the government would keep its fingers off the farm we'd be a damn sight better off."

The pavement ended in a jag of cracks and chuckholes and the car bounced onto the rubbery, black pitted road that stretched like a long black avenue toward the hills.

"Have you ever seen them when they harvest, Lew?"

"No."

The morning grayed. Farrell saw the stubble fields turned into a cheat-yellow as he watched. He looked out the window at the sky where gray clouds rolled and broke into massive, clumsy chunks. "The rain's going to quit."

They came to the foot of the hills where the fields ended, then turned and drove along at the edge of the fields following the hills until they came to the head of the canyon. Far below at the very bottom of the stone-ribbed canyon lay the river, its far side covered by a bank of fog.

"It's stopped raining," Farrell said.

Frank backed the car into a small, rocky ravine and said it was a good enough place. Farrell took out his shotgun and leaned it against the rear fender before taking out his shell bag and extra coat. Then he lifted out the paper sack with the sandwiches and his hand closed tightly around the warm, hard thermos. They walked away from the car without talking and along the ridge before starting to drop down into one of the small valleys that opened into the canyon. The earth was studded here and there with sharp rocks or a black, dripping bush.

The ground sogged under his feet, pulled at his boots with every step, and made a sucking noise when he released them. He carried the shell bag in his right hand, swinging it like a sling, letting it hang down by its strap from his hand. A wet breeze off the river blew against his face. The sides of the low bluffs overlooking the river down below were deeply grooved and cut back into the rock, leaving table-like projections jutting out, marking the high-water lines for thousands of years past. Piles of naked white logs and countless pieces of driftwood lay jammed onto the ledge like cairns of bones dragged up onto the cliffs by some giant bird. Farrell tried to remember where the geese came over, three years ago. He stopped on the side of a hill just where it sloped into the canyon and leaned his gun on a rock. He pulled bushes and gathered rocks from nearby and walked down toward the river after some of the driftwood to make a blind.

He sat on his raincoat with his back against a hard shrub, his knees drawn up to his chin, watching the sky whiten and then blue a little and the clouds run with the wind. Geese were gabbling somewhere in the fog on the other side of the river. He rested and smoked and watched the smoke whip out of his month. He waited for the sun.

It is four in the afternoon. The sun has just gone behind the gray, late afternoon clouds leaving a dwarfed half-shadow that falls across the car following him as he walks around to open the door for his wife. They kiss.

Iris and he will be back for her in an hour and forty-five minutes, exactly. They are going by the hardware store and then to the grocery. They will be back for her at 5:45. He slides in behind the wheel again and in a moment, seeing his chance, eases out into the traffic. On the way out of town he must stop and wait for every red light, finally turning left onto the secondary, hitting the gas so hard that they both lean back a little in the seat. It is 4:20. At the forks they turn onto the blacktop, orchards on both sides of the road. Over the tops of the trees, the low brown hills and beyond, the blue-black mountains crowned with white. From the close rows of trees, shadows, blackening into the shoulders, creep across the pavement in front of the car. New boxes are jumbled together in white piles at the end of each orchard row, and up against the trees or pushed into the limbs, some leaning in the crotches, are the ladders. He slows the car and stops, pulling off onto the shoulder close enough to one of the trees so that all Iris has to do is open her door and she can reach the limb. It scrapes against the door as she releases it. The apples are heavy and yellow, and sweet juice spurts into his teeth as he bites into one.

The road ends and they follow the dust-covered hard-track right up to the edge of the hills where the orchards stop. He can still go farther, though, by turning onto the bank road that follows the irrigation canal. The canal is empty now and the steep dirt banks are dry and crumbling. He has shifted the car into second. The road is steeper, driving is more difficult and slower. He stops the car under a pine tree outside a water gate where the canal comes down out of the hills to slide into a circular cement trough. Iris lays her hand in his lap. It is nearly dark. The wind is blowing through the car and once he hears the tops of the trees creaking.

He gets out of the car to light a cigarette, walking to the rim of the hill overlooking the valley. The wind has strengthened; the air is colder. The grass is sparse under his feet and there are a few flowers. The cigarette makes a short, twisting red arc as it spins down into the valley. It is six o'clock.

The cold was bad. The dead numbness of the toes, the cold slowly working its way up into the calves of his legs and setting in under his knees. His fingers too, stiff and cold even though they were balled into his pockets. Farrell waited for the sun. The huge clouds over the river turned, breaking up, shaping and reshaping while he watched. At first he barely noticed the black line against the lowest clouds. When it crossed into sight he thought it was mosquitoes, close up against his blind, and then it was a far-off dark rent between cloud and sky that moved closer while he watched. The line turned toward him then and spread out over the hills below. He was excited but calm, his heart beating in his ears urging him to run, yet his movements slow and ponderous as if heavy stones hung to his legs. He inched up on his knees until his face pressed into the brush wall and turned his eyes toward the ground. His legs shook and he pushed his knees into the soft earth. The legs grew suddenly numb and he moved his hand and pushed it into the ground up over his fingers, surprised at its warmth. Then the soft gabble of geese over his head and the heavy, whistling push of wings. His finger tightened around the trigger. The quick, rasping calls; the sharp upward jerk of ten feet as they saw him. Farrell was on his feet now, pulling down on one goose before swinging to another, then again quickly onto a closer one, following it as it broke and cut back over his head toward the river. He fired once, twice, and the geese kept flying, clamoring, split up and out of range, their low forms melting into the rolling hills. He fired once more before dropping back to his knees inside the blind. Somewhere on the hill behind him and a little to the left he heard Frank shooting, the reports rolling down through the canyon like sharp whip snaps. He felt confused to see more geese getting off the river, stringing out over the low hills and rising up the canyon, flying in V formations for the top of the canyon and the fields behind. He reloaded carefully, pushing the green, ribbed #2s up into the breech, pumping one of the shells into the chamber with a hollow, cracking sound. Yet six shells would do the job better than three. He quickly loosened the plug from the underbarrel of the gun and dropped the coil spring and the wooden plug into his pocket. He heard Frank shoot again, and suddenly there was a flock gone by he hadn't seen. As he watched them he saw three more coming in low and from the side. He waited until they were even with him, swinging across the side of the hill thirty yards away, their heads swinging slowly, rhythmically, right to left, the eyes black and glistening. He raised to one knee, just as they passed him, giving them a good lead, squeezing off an instant before they flared. The one nearest him crumpled and dived straight into the ground. He fired again as they turned, seeing the goose stop as if it had run into a wall, flailing against the wall trying to get over it before turning over, head downward, wings out, to slowly spiral down. He emptied his gun at the third goose even when it was probably out of range, seeing it stop the charge on the fifth shot, its tail jerking hard and settling down, but its wings still beating. For a long time he watched it flying closer and closer to the ground before it disappeared into one of the canyons.

Farrell laid the two geese on their backs inside the blind and stroked their smooth white undersides. They were Canadian geese, honkers. After this it didn't matter too much that the geese that flew came over too high or went out someplace else down the river. He sat against the shrub and smoked, watching the sky whirl by over his head. Sometime later, perhaps in the early afternoon, he slept.

When he woke he was stiff, cold and sweating and the sun was gone, the sky a thickening gray pall. Somewhere he could hear geese calling and going out, leaving those strange sharp echoes in the valleys, but he could see nothing but wet, black hills that ended in fog where the river should have been. He wiped his hand over his face and began to shiver. He stood up. He could see the fog rolling up the canyon and over the hills, closing off and hemming in the land, and he felt the breath of the cold damp air around him, touching his forehead and cheeks and lips. He broke through the blind getting out and started running up the hill.

He stood outside the car and pressed the horn in a continual blast until Frank ran up and jerked his arm away from the window.

"What's the matter with you? Are you crazy or something?"

"I have to go home, I tell you!"

"*Jesus* Christ! Well, *Jesus* Christ! Get in then, get in!"

They were quiet then but for Farrell's asking twice the time before they were out of the wheat country. Frank held a cigar between his teeth, never taking his eyes from the road. When they ran into the first drifting patches of fog he switched on the car lights. After they turned onto the highway the fog lifted and layered somewhere in the dark over the car, and the first drops of rain began hitting the windshield. Once three ducks flew in front of the car lights and pitched into a puddle beside the road. Farrell blinked.

"Did you see that?" Frank asked.

Farrell nodded.

"How do you feel now?"

"Okay."

"You get any geese?"

Farrell rubbed the palms of his hands together, interlacing his fingers, finally folding them into his lap. "No, I guess not."

"Too bad. I heard you shooting." He worked the cigar to the other side of his mouth and tried to puff, but it had gone cold. He chewed on it for a minute then laid it in the ashtray and glanced at Farrell.

"'Course it's none of my affair, but if it's something you're worried about at home . . . My advice is not to take it too seriously. You'll live longer. No gray hairs like me." He coughed, laughed. "I know, I used to be the same way. I remember . . ."

Farrell is sitting in the big leather chair under the brass lamp watching Iris comb out her hair. He is holding a magazine in his lap whose glossy pages are open to the scene of a disaster, an earthquake, somewhere in the Near East. Except for the small light over the dresser it is dark in the room. The brush moves quickly through her hair in long, sweeping, rhythmical movements, causing a faint squeaking noise in the room. He has yet to call Frank and confirm the hunting trip for the next morning. There is a cold, moist air coming in through the window from the outside. She is tapping the brush against the edge of the dresser. "Lew," she says, "you know I'm pregnant?"

Her bathroom smell sickens him. Her towel lies across the back of the toilet. In the sink she has spilled talcum. It is wet now and pasty and makes a thick, yellow ring around the white sides. He rubs it out and washes it into the drain.

He is shaving. By turning his head he can see into the living room. Iris in profile sitting on the stool in front of the old dresser. She is combing her hair. He lays down the razor and washes his face, then picks up the razor again. At this moment he hears the first few drops of rain spatter against the roof . . .

He carries her out to the porch, turns her face to the wall, and covers her up. He goes back into the bathroom, washes his hands, and stuffs the heavy, blood-soaked towel into the clothes hamper. After a while he turns out the light over the dresser and sits down again in his chair by the window, listening to the rain.

Frank laughed. "So it was nothing, nothing at all. We got along fine after that. Oh, the usual bickering now and then but when she found out just who was running the show, everything was all right." He gave Farrell a friendly rap on the knee.

They drove into the outskirts of town, past the long line of motels with their blazing red, blinking, neon lights, past the cafés with steamy windows, the cars clustered in front, and past the small businesses, dark and locked until the next day. Frank turned right at the next light, then left, and now they were on Farrell's street. Frank pulled in behind a black and white car that had SHERIFF'S OFFICE painted in small white letters across the trunk. In the lights of their car they could see another glass inside the car inset with a wire screen making the backseat into a cage. Steam rose from the hood of their car and mixed with the rain.

"Could be he's after you, Lew." He started to open the door, then chuckled. "Maybe they've found out you were hunting with no license. Come on, I'll turn you in myself."

"No. You go on, Frank. That's all right. I'll be all right. Wait a minute, let me get out!"

"Christ, you'd really think they were after you! Wait a minute, get your gun." He rolled down the window and passed out the shotgun to Farrell. "Looks like the rain's never going to let up. See you."

"Yeah."

Upstairs all the lights of his apartment were turned on and blurred figures stood frieze-like at the windows looking down through the rain. Farrell stood behind the sheriff's car holding onto the smooth, wet tail fin. Rain fell on his bare head and worked its way down under his collar. Frank drove a few yards up the street and stopped, looking back. Farrell holding onto the tail fin, swaying a little, with the fine impenetrable rain coming down around him. The gutter water rushed over his feet, swirled frothing into a great whirlpool at the drain on the corner and rushed down to the center of the earth.

The Hair

He worked at it with his tongue for a while then sat up in bed and began picking at it with his fingers. Outside it was going to be a nice day and some birds were singing. He tore off a corner of the matchbook and scraped in between his teeth. Nothing. He could still feel it. He ran his tongue over his teeth again from back to front, stopping when he got to the hair. He touched all around it then stroked it with his tongue where it threaded in between two of the front teeth, followed it in an inch or so to the end and smoothed it against the roof of his mouth. He touched it with his finger.

"Uuuk—Christ!"

"What's the matter?" his wife asked, sitting up. "We oversleep? What time is it?"

"I've got something in my teeth. Can't get it out. I don't know . . . feels like a hair."

He went into the bathroom and glanced at the mirror, then washed his hands and face with cold water. He turned on the shaving lamp over the mirror.

"I can't see it but I know it's there. If I could just get hold of it maybe I could pull it out."

His wife came into the bathroom, scratching her head and yawning. "You get it, honey?"

He ground his teeth together, squeezed his lips down against his teeth until his fingernails broke the skin.

"Just a minute. Let me see it," she said, moving closer. He stood under the light, mouth open, twisting his head back and forth, wiping his pajama sleeve over the glass as it fogged up.

146

"I don't see anything," she said.

"Well, I can feel it." He turned off the light and started running water in the tub. "The hell with it! Forget it. I've got to get ready for work."

He decided to walk downtown since he didn't want any breakfast and still had plenty of time to get to work. Nobody had a key except the boss and if he got there too early he'd only have to wait. He walked by the empty corner where he usually caught the bus. A dog he'd seen around the neighborhood before had his leg cocked, pissing on the bus stop sign.

"Hey!"

The dog quit pissing and came running over to him. Another dog that he didn't recognize came trotting up, sniffed at the sign, and pissed. Golden, slightly steaming as it ran down the sidewalk.

"Hey—get out of here!" The dog squirted a few more drops then both dogs crossed the street. They almost looked like they were laughing. He threaded the hair back and forth through his teeth.

"Nice day now, isn't it, huh?" the boss asked. He opened the front door, raised the shade.

Everyone turned to look back outside and nodded, smiling.

"Yes it is, sir, just a beautiful day," someone said.

"Too nice to be working," someone else said, laughed with the others.

"Yes it is. It is at that," the boss said. He went on up the stairs to open up Boys Clothing, whistling, jingling his keys.

Later on when he came up from the basement and was taking his break in the lounge, smoking a cigarette, the boss came in wearing a short-sleeved shirt.

"Hot today, isn't it, huh?"

"Yes it is, sir." He'd never noticed before that the boss had such hairy arms. He sat picking his teeth, staring at the thick tufts of black hair that grew in between the boss's fingers.

"Sir, I was wondering—if you don't think I can, that's all right, naturally, but if you think so, without putting anybody in a bind, I mean—I'd like to go home. I don't feel so well."

"Mmm. Well, we can make it all right, of course. That's not the point, of course." He took a long drink of his Coke, kept looking at him.

"Well then, that's all right then, sir. I'll make it. I was just wondering."

"No, no, that's all right now. You go on home. Call me up tonight, let me know how you are." He looked at his watch, finished his Coke. "Ten twenty-five. Say 10:30. Go on home now, we'll call it 10:30."

Out in the street he loosened his collar and began to walk. He felt strange walking around town with a hair in his mouth. He kept touching it with his tongue. He didn't look at any of the people he met. In a little while he began to sweat under his arms and could feel it dripping through the hair into his undershirt. Sometimes he stopped in front of the showroom windows and stared at the glass, opening and closing his mouth, fishing around with his finger. He took the long way home, down through the Lions Club park where he watched the kids play in the wading pool and paid fifteen cents to an old lady to go through the little zoo and see the birds and animals. Once after he had stood for a long time looking through the glass at the giant Gila monster, the creature opened one of its eyes and looked at him. He backed away from the glass and went on walking around the park until it was time to go home.

He wasn't very hungry and only drank some coffee for supper. After a few swallows he rolled his tongue over the hair again. He got up from the table.

"Honey, what's the matter?" his wife asked. "Where you going?"

"I think I'm going to go to bed. I don't feel so well."

She followed him into the bedroom, watched while he undressed. "Can I get you something? Maybe I should call the doctor? I wish I knew what was the matter."

"That's all right. I'll be all right." He pulled up the covers over his shoulders and turned over, closing his eyes.

She pulled the shade. "I'll straighten up the kitchen a little, then I'll be back."

It felt better just to stretch out. He touched his face and thought he might have a fever. He licked his lips and touched the end of the hair with his tongue. He shivered. After a few minutes, he began to doze but woke suddenly and remembered about calling the boss. He got slowly out of bed and went out to the kitchen.

His wife was at the draining board doing dishes. "I thought you were asleep. Honey? You feel better now?"

He nodded, picked up the phone and got Information. He had a kind of bad taste in his mouth as he dialed.

"Hello. Yes, sir, I think I feel better. Just wanted you to know I'll be at work tomorrow. Right. Eight thirty, sharp."

After he got back in bed he smoothed his tongue over his teeth again. Maybe it was just something he could get used to. He didn't know. Just before he went to sleep, he'd almost stopped thinking about it. He remembered what a warm day it had been and those kids out wading—how the birds were singing that morning. But once during the night he yelled out and woke up sweating, almost choking. No, no, he kept saying, kicking his feet against the covers. It scared his wife and she didn't know what was the matter.

The Aficionados

They are sitting in the shade at a small iron patio table drinking wine out of heavy metal cups.

"Why should you feel this way now?" he asks her.

"I don't know," she says. "It always makes me sad when it comes. It's been such a short year, and I don't even know any of the others." She leans forward and reaches for his hand, but he is too quick for her. "They seem so, so unprofessional." From her lap she takes her napkin and wipes her lips in a way that has become detestable to him this last month. "We won't talk about it anymore," she says. "We still have three hours yet. We won't even think about it."

He shrugs and looks past her towards the open windows with their blanket-like squares of white sky, out into the street, taking it all in. Dust covers the low, powdery buildings and fills the street.

"What will you wear?" he asks, not turning around.

"How can you talk about it so?" She slumps back in her chair, interlacing her fingers, twisting the lead ring around her index finger.

There are no other patrons on the patio and in the street nothing moves.

"I'll probably wear white, as usual. But, I might not. I won't!"

He smiles, then drains his cup, tasting, at the bottom, the almost bitter pieces of soft leaves that touch against his lips. "Should we go?"

He pays for the wine and counts out an additional five thousand pesos to the shopkeeper. "This is for you."

The old woman hesitates, looks at the younger woman and then with a birdlike frightened movement scrabbles up the bills and pushes them, crinkling, into a front pocket. "*Gracias.*" She bows stiffly, and respectfully touches her forehead.

The patio is dark and has a smell like rotting wood. There are squat black arches encircling it and one of these opens onto the street. It is noon. The pallid dead brilliance makes him dizzy for a minute. Heat ripples rise from the adobe walls that close in the narrow street. His eyes water and the air is dry and hot on his face.

"Are you all right?" She takes his arm.

"Yes. Just a minute." From a street very close to them, a band is playing. The music streams up and over the roofless buildings, melting against the heat over his head. "We should see this."

She frowns. It is the same frown she makes when someone tells her there are few young men interested in the Arena nowadays. "If you wish, darling."

"I do. Come on, aren't you going to indulge me on my last afternoon?"

She clutches his arm tighter and they go slowly down the street in the shade of a low wall, the music moving closer as they near the end of the street. When he was a child the band used to play several times a year, then twice a year for a long time, and now they play and march only one time in the year. Suddenly the soft, fluffed dust in front of his feet spouts, and he kicks up a brown spider that clings to the toe of his huarache before he kicks it away.

"Should we pretend?" he asks.

Her eyes have followed the spider and now they turn to him, flat and gray-filmed, motionless under her damp forehead. Her lips purse: "Pretend?"

On an impulse, he kisses her. Her lips are dry and cracked and he kisses her hard and presses her against the hot brick wall. The band shrieks and clangs and passes across at the end of the street, pauses, and moves on. Fainter now as it tramps along then turns off onto another street.

"Like it was when we first met and I was a struggling young disciple. You remember?" He remembers, anyway. Long, hot afternoons at the Arena; practicing, practicing, perfecting—every action, every thought, every grace. The blood thrill and rush of excitement as his compadres finished, one by one. He was one of the lucky ones and the dedicated. Then he'd moved up at last among the few eligibles, then above them even.

"I remember," she says.

This last year as his wife she might remember and perhaps she might remember this afternoon. For a moment he lets himself think about the afternoon.

"It was good—it was," she says. Her eyes are cold and clouded, flat into her face like the eyes of a snake he'd killed once in the mountains in the blind season.

They come to the end of the street and stop. It is quiet and the only sound that reaches them is a dry rattling, gagging cough coming from somewhere down the street in the direction of the band. He looks at her and she shrugs before they turn down the street. They walk by some old men sitting in doorways, the doors boarded up behind them, their big dusty sombreros pulled down over their faces, legs drawn up tight and folded against their chests or sticking out into the street. The coughing starts again, dry and thick as if it comes from under the ground, the throat tubed full of dirt. He listens and looks closely at the men.

She points into a narrow passageway at a bareheaded small gray man squeezed in between the two buildings. The man opens his mouth . . . and makes a cough.

He turns her around to him. "How many of us have you lived with?"

"Why . . . five or six. I'd have to think. Why do you ask?"

He shakes his head. "Do you remember Luis?"

She pulls her arm out of his, her heavy bracelet making a dull chinking sound. "He was my first. I loved him."

"He taught me almost everything . . . I needed to know." He

chews on his lip and the sun presses like a hot flat stone on his neck. "Do you remember Jorge?"

"Yes." They are walking again and she takes his arm once more. "A good man. Like you a little, but I didn't love him. Please, let's not talk about it anymore."

"All right. I think I'd like to walk down to the plaza."

Vacant-eyed men and women stare at them as they pass. They sag against the doors or crouch in the dark alcoves and some gaze dully at them from low windows. They walk farther, away from the town and out onto the plain. All around them are mortar blocks and chunks of old limed white cement and broken, grainy bits and pieces that crush under their feet. Over everything a thick coat of dust. The plated sun shimmers white and blinding above their heads, burning the garments into their sticky backs.

"We should go back," she says, squeezing his arm a little.

"Pretty soon." He points at the thin, wash-yellow flowers stretching up in the dark crack of a broken block of cement roadway. They are standing in the Zocalo, the Great Square, facing the ruins of the Metropolitan Cathedral. Bordering the square is a line of powdery brown mounds with a single hole in the side of each, facing them. Beyond the mounds, brown rows of adobe houses that run and spread toward the hills until only the tops of the tallest houses are visible. Then a long up-and-down line of gray humped hills that stretch as far as he can see down the valley. The hills have always reminded him of great-breasted reclining women but it all seems strange now, and dirty.

"Please, love," she says, "let's go back now and drink a little wine while there's time."

From the Arena the band has struck up, a few strains jagging over and across the plain to them. He listens. "Yes. We mustn't be late." He looks at the ground and stirs the dust with his heel. "All right, yes, let's go and have a little wine." He bends and picks the small cluster of yellow flowers for her.

They go to Manuel's and when Manuel sees them sit down

at one of his tables he first salutes and then goes to the cellar and brings out their last bottle of dark wine.

"You will be at the Arena this afternoon, Manuel?"

Manuel studies a crack that runs down the length of the wall behind the table. "*Si.*"

"Don't feel that way, my friend. It's not so bad. Look." He tilts his cup and lets the warm wine run down his throat. "I'm happy? What would be the sense of it if I were not happy? That the moment should be perfect, there should be joy and consent on the part of all persons concerned." He smiles at him; no hard feelings. "This is the way it has always been, so you see—I must be happy. And so should you, my friend. We're all in this together." He finishes another cup and wipes his sweaty palms on his pants. Then he gets up and shakes hands with Manuel. "We must go. Good-bye, Manuel."

At the entrance to their quarters she clings to him, whispering and stroking his neck. "I do love you! I love only you." She pulls him to her, her fingers digging into his shoulders, pulling his face to hers. And then she turns and runs for the entrance.

He shouts: "You'll have to hurry if you're going to dress!"

Now he is walking in the late afternoon green shadows and now crossing a deserted square, his sandaled feet settling into the hot crumbly dirt. For a moment the sun has gone behind a skein of white clouds and when he comes onto the street leading to the Arena, it is very pale and light and there are no shadows. Silent, small groups of people shuffle down the street but they keep their eyes away and show no recognition when he passes them. In front of the Arena a group of dusty men and women is already waiting. They stare at the ground or at the white-laced sky, and a few of them have their mouths open with the backs of their heads almost touching the shoulders, swaying back and forth like ragged stalks of corn as they follow the clouds. He uses a side entrance and goes directly to the dressing room.

He lies on the table, his face turned toward the dripping white candle, watching the women. Their distorted slow movements flicker on the wall as they undress him, rubbing his body with oils and scent before dressing him again in the white rough-textured garment. Dirt walls close in the narrow room and there is barely space for the table and the six women who hover over him. A wrinkled, oily brown face peers into his, blowing a wet breath of old food, the breath scraping in her throat. The lips crack farther until they part, open and close over hoarse ancient syllables. The others pick it up as they help him off the table and lead him into the Arena.

He lies down quickly on the small platform, closes his eyes and listens to the chanting of the women. The sun is bright against his face and he turns his head away. The band flares up, much closer, somewhere inside the Arena, and for a moment he listens to that. The chanting drops suddenly to a murmur, then stops. He opens his eyes and turns his head first to one side and then to the other. For an instant all the faces are focused on him, heads craning forward. He closes his eyes to the sight. Then the dull *chink* of a heavy bracelet close to his ear, and he opens his eyes. She is standing over him dressed in a white robe and holding the long shiny obsidian knife. She bends closer, the cluster of flowers woven into her hair—bending lower over his face as she blesses his love and devotion and asks his forgiveness.

"Forgive me."

"What is the use?" he whispers. Then, as the knife point touches his chest he screams, "I forgive you!"

And the people hear and settle back in their seats, exhausted, as she cuts out his heart and holds it up to the lustrous sun.

Poseidon and Company

He saw nothing only suddenly the wind stiffened and blew mist up off the sea and over his face, taking him by surprise. He'd been dreaming again. Using his elbows, he worked a little closer to the edge that overlooked the beach and raised his face out toward the sea. The wind struck his eyes, bringing tears. Down below, the other boys were playing war but their voices sounded watery and far away, and he tried not to listen. Over the voices came the squeak of the gulls, out where the sea thundered on the rocks below the temple. Poseidon's temple. He lay again on his stomach and turned his face a little to one side, waiting.

On his back the sun slipped away and a chill broke over his legs and shoulders. Tonight he would lie wrapped in his cover and remember these few minutes of felt time, day fading. It was different than standing in Naiad's cave up in the hills, someone holding his hand under the water that trickled steadily out of the crack in the rock. It had been dripping for no one knows how long, they said. Different too than wading in the surf up to his knees, feeling the strange pull. That was time too, but not the same. They'd told him about that, about when to wade and when to stay off the beach. But this was something of his own and every afternoon he lay on his stomach up over the sea and waited for the change, the prickly passage of time across his back.

Out loud, tasting the sea salt on his lips as he did so, he said a few verses into the wind, new ones that he'd heard last night. Some of the words he liked he rolled over again in his mouth. Below, he heard Aias curse another boy and invoke one of the gods. Was it true, what men told of the gods? He remembered every song he'd heard, every story handed down and recited at night around the fire, as well as all the eyewitness accounts. Still, he had heard some men speak of the gods with disrespect, even disbelief, so that it was hard to know what to believe anymore. Someday he'd leave here and find out for himself. He'd walk over the hills to Eritrea where the trading ships came in. Maybe he'd even be able to board one of them and go wherever it was they go, the places men talked about.

Below, the voices were louder and one of the boys was crying jerkily against the clatter of their sticks on the shields. He raised up onto his knees to listen and swayed blindly, dizzy with memory and idea as the evening wind carried up the angry voices. He could hear Achilles yelling loudest of all as the two groups ran back and forth over the beach. Then his own name was called, and he lay down quickly to keep out of sight. Nearer, his sister called again. Now the steps behind him and he sat up all at once, discovered.

"There you are!" she said. "I had to walk all this way for you! Why didn't you come home? You never do anything you're supposed to." She came closer. "Give me your hand!"

He felt her hands take his and begin to pull him. "No!" he said, shaking. He jerked free and with the stick he sometimes called Spear began to feel his way down the trail.

"Well, you'll see, little man who thinks he's so big," she said. "Your time's coming, Mama said."

Bright Red Apples

"I can't make water, Mommy," Old Hutchins said, coming out of the bathroom with tears in his eyes.

"Close your barn door, Pa!" Rudy shouted. The old man disgusted him and his hand twitched in anger. He leaped out of his chair and looked around for his boomerang. "Have you seen my boomerang, Ma?"

"No, I haven't," Mother Hutchins said patiently. "Now you just behave yourself, Rudy, while I see to your pa. You just heard him say he can't make water. But close your barn door, Daddy, like Rudy says."

Old Hutchins sniffled but did as he was told. Mother Hutchins came over to him with a worried look, holding her hands in her apron.

"It's just what Dr. Porter said would happen, Mommy," Old Hutchins said, sagging against the wall and looking as if he were going to die right then. "I'll get up one morning, he said, and not be able to make water."

"Shut up!" Rudy shouted. "Shut up! Talk, talk, talk, dirty talk all day long. I've had enough of it!"

"You keep quiet now, Rudy," Mother Hutchins said feebly, moving back a step or two with Old Hutchins in her arms.

Rudy began stalking up and down the linoleum-covered floor of the sparsely furnished but tidy living room. His hands jumped in and out of his hip pockets as he threw menacing looks at Old Hutchins, who hung limply in Mother Hutchins's arms.

At the same time, a warm smell of fresh apple pie drifted in from the kitchen and made Rudy lick his lips hungrily, reminded him, even in the midst of his great anger, that it was nearly snack time. Now and then he glanced nervously out of the corner of his eye at his older brother Ben, who sat in a heavy oak chair in the corner near the treadle-operated sewing machine. But Ben never raised his eyes from his worn copy of *Restless Guns*.

Rudy couldn't figure Ben. He kept tramping up and down the living room, from time to time knocking over a chair or breaking a lamp. Mother Hutchins and Old Hutchins inched back toward the bathroom. Rudy stopped suddenly and glared at them, then looked at Ben again. He just couldn't figure Ben. He couldn't figure any of them, but he could figure Ben even less than the others. He wanted Ben to notice him sometimes, but Ben always had his nose in a book. Ben read Zane Grey, Louis L'Amour, Ernest Haycox, Luke Short. Ben thought Zane Grey, Louis L'Amour, and Ernest Haycox were all right, but not as good as Luke Short. He thought Luke Short was the best of the lot. He'd read Luke Short's books forty or fifty times. He had to have something to pass the time. Ever since his rigging had come loose seven or eight years ago when he was topping trees for Pacific Lumber, he'd had to have something to pass the time. Since then he could only move the upper part of his body; also, he seemed to have lost the power of speech. Anyway, he had never uttered a word since the day of the fall. But then he'd always been a quiet boy when he was living at home before; no bother at all. Still no bother, his mother maintained, if she was asked. Quiet as a mouse and needed very little seeing to.

Besides, on the first of each month Ben got a little disability check in the mail. Not much, but enough for them all to live on. Old Hutchins had quit work when the disability checks started coming. He didn't like his boss was the reason he gave at the time. Rudy had never left home. He'd never finished high school, either. Ben had finished high school but Rudy was a high school dropout. Now he was afraid of being drafted. The idea of being drafted made him very nervous. He didn't at all like the idea of being drafted. Mother Hutchins had always been a house-wife and a homemaker. She was not very shrewd but she knew how to make ends meet. Once in a while, though, if they ran short before the end of the month, she had to walk into town with a nice box of apples on her back and sell them for a dime each on the corner in front of Johnson's Pharmacy. Mr. Johnson and the clerks knew her and she always gave Mr. Johnson and the clerks a shiny red apple that she polished against the front of her dress.

Rudy began making violent slashes and sword thrusts in the air, grunting as he gouged and chopped. He seemed to have forgotten about the old couple cowering in the passageway.

"Now, dear, don't you worry," Mother Hutchins said faintly to Old Hutchins. "Dr. Porter'll put you right. Why, a prostrate operation is, is an everyday occurrence. Look at Prime Minister MacMillian. Remember Prime Minister MacMillian, Daddy? When he was prime minister and had his prostrate operation he was up and around in no time. No time. Now you just cheer up. Why—"

"Shut up! Shut up!" Rudy made a frightening lunge toward them, but they drew back farther into the narrow passageway. Fortunately, Mother Hutchins had enough strength left to whistle up Yeller, a shaggy giant of a dog, who immediately ran into the room from the back porch and put his paws up on Rudy's narrow chest, pushing him back a step or two.

Rudy retreated slowly, appalled at the dog's rank breath. On his way through the living room he picked up Old Hutchins's prized possession, an ashtray made from the hoof and foreleg of an elk, and hurled the smelly thing out into the garden.

Old Hutchins began to cry again. His nerves were gone. Ever since Rudy's vicious attack upon his life a month ago, his nerves, which weren't good to begin with, had gone.

What had happened was this: Old Hutchins was taking a bath when Rudy sneaked up and threw the RCA Victrola into the bathtub. It could have been serious, fatal even, if in his haste Rudy hadn't forgot to plug it in. As it was, Old Hutchins had received a bad bruise on his right thigh when the Victrola had made its flying entry through the open door. That was just after Rudy had seen a movie in town called *Goldfinger*. Now they were more or less on guard at all moments, but especially whenever Rudy ventured into town. Who could tell what ideas he might pick up at the movies? He was very impressionable. "He's at a very impressionable age," Mother Hutchins said to Old Hutchins. Ben never said anything, one way or the other. Nobody could figure Ben, not even his mother, Mother Hutchins.

Rudy stayed in the barn just long enough to devour half the pie, then put a halter on Em, his favorite camel. He led her out the back door and safely through the elaborate network of snares, covered pits and traps, laid for the careless and the unwary. Once clear, he pulled Em's ear and commanded her to kneel, mounted, and was off.

He clop-clopped out across the back forty, up into the dry, sage-covered foothills. He stopped once on a little rise to look back at the old homestead. He wished he had some dynamite and a plunger to blow it right off the landscape—like Lawrence of Arabia had done with those trains. He hated the sight of it, the old homestead. They were all crazy down there anyway. They wouldn't be missed. Would he miss them? No, he wouldn't miss them. Besides, there would still be the land, the apples. Damn the land and the apples anyway! He wished he had some dynamite.

He turned Em into a dry arroyo. With the sun bearing down fiercely on his back, he cantered to the end of the box canyon. He stopped and dismounted and, behind a rock, uncovered the canvas that held the big Smith & Wesson service revolver, the burnoose and the headgear. He dressed and then stuck the revolver in his sash. It fell out. He stuck it in again and it fell out again. Then he just decided to carry it in his hand, though it was heavy and it would be hard to guide Em. It would call for a skillful bit of maneuvering on his part, but he thought he could do it. He thought he was up to it.

Back at the farm, he left Em in the barn and made his way to the house. He saw the elk-leg ashtray still in the garden, a few flies working away on it, and he sneered; the old man had been afraid to come out and retrieve it. But it gave him an idea.

He burst in on them in the kitchen. Old Hutchins, sitting rather comfortably at the kitchen table and stirring his coffee and cream, looked completely stunned. Mother Hutchins was at the stove, putting in another pie.

"Apples, apples, apples!" Rudy shrieked. He followed this outburst with a wild laugh, waving his Colt .45 around in the air, then herded them into the living room. Ben looked up with a slight show of interest, and then went back to his book. It was Luke Short's *Rawhide Trail*.

"This is it," Rudy said, his voice rising. "This is it, this is it, this is it!"

Mother Hutchins kept puckering her lips—almost as if expecting a kiss—trying to whistle up Yeller, but Rudy only laughed and hooted. He pointed at the window with the barrel of his Winchester. "There's Yeller," he said. Mother Hutchins and Old Hutchins both looked to see Yeller trotting into the orchard with the ashtray in his mouth. "There's your old Yeller," Rudy said.

Old Hutchins groaned and fell with a painful clump to his knees. Mother Hutchins got down beside him but cast an imploring look in Rudy's direction. Rudy was about four feet away from her, just to the right of the red Naugahyde footstool.

"Rudy, now you wouldn't do anything now, dear, you'd be sorry for later. You wouldn't hurt me or your pa, would you, Rudy?"

"He ain't a pa to me—ain't, ain't, ain't," said Rudy, dancing around the living room with an occasional glance at Ben, who, since his initial momentary flicker of interest in the proceedings, hadn't stirred himself again.

"Shouldn't say ain't, Rudy," Mother Hutchins gently reproved.

"Son," Old Hutchins stopped sniffling for a minute, "you

wouldn't hurt a poor old helpless broken-down old man with a prostrate condition, would you? Huh?"

"Stick it out here, stick it out here and I'll blow it off for you," Rudy said, waving the ugly snub-nosed barrel of his .38 right under Old Hutchins's rather large nose. "I'll show you what I'll do for you!" He waved it there from side to side a minute longer, then danced off again. "No, no, I wouldn't shoot you. Shooting's too good for you." But he fired a burst from the BAR into the kitchen wall just to show them he meant business.

Ben raised his eyes. He had a soft, indolent look to his face. He stared at Rudy a minute without recognition, then went back to his book. He was in a fine room in a Virginia City hotel called The Palace. Downstairs there were three or four angry men waiting for him at the bar, but right now he was going to enjoy the first bath he'd had in three months.

Rudy faltered a minute, then looked around wildly. His eyes fell on the grandfather railroad ticktock clock that had been in the family seven years. "You see that clock there, Ma? When the b-big hand gets on the little hand there's going to be an explosion. Wham! Foom! Up she goes, everything! Ballou!" With this he bounded out the front door and jumped off the porch.

He sat down behind an apple tree a hundred yards from the house. He intended to wait until they were all assembled on the front porch: Mother Hutchins, Old Hutchins, even Ben; all assembled there with the few pitiful accumulations they hoped to preserve, and then he would pick them off quickly, one by one. He swept the porch with his scope, putting the cross hairs on the window, a wicker chair, a cracked flowerpot drying in the sun on one of the porch steps. Then he took a long breath and settled down to wait.

He waited and waited, but they didn't come. A small band of California mountain quail began to work their way down through the orchard, stopping every now and then to pick at a fallen apple, or to look around the base of a tree for a nice juicy grub. He kept watching them and pretty soon was no longer watching the porch. He sat very still behind the tree, almost without breathing, and they didn't see him and came closer and closer, talking soft quail talk between themselves as they picked at the apples and sharply scrutinized the ground. He leaned forward slightly and strained his ears to overhear what they were saying. The quail were talking about Vietnam.

It was too much for Rudy. He could've cried. He flapped his arms at the quail, said "Who!" Ben, Vietnam, apples, prostrate: what did it all mean? Was there a connection between Marshal Dillon and James Bond? Oddjob and Captain Easy? If so, where did Luke Short fit it? And Ted Trueblood? His mind reeled.

With a last, forlorn glance at the empty porch, he placed the shiny, recently blued barrels of the 12-gauge double into his mouth.

FRAGMENT OF A NOVEL

from The Augustine Notebooks

"No way, sugar," she said, looking at him steadily. "No way at all. Not on your life."

He shrugged. He sipped from the glass of lemon fix without looking at her.

"You must be crazy, it's true." She looked around at the other tables. It was ten o'clock in the morning and, at this time of year, there were not many tourists left on the island. Most of the tables in the courtyard were empty and on some of the tables waiters had stacked chairs.

"Are you crazy? Is it really true, then?"

"Forget it," he said. "Let it alone."

A peacock had wandered in from the marketplace which was next to the nearly empty courtyard where they sat at their table drinking the lemon fixes. The peacock stopped at a spigot near the edge of the courtyard and held its beak under the dripping tap. As it drank, its throat rippled up and down. Then the peacock walked slowly around some empty tables and headed in their direction. Halprin threw a wafer onto the flagstones. The bird picked it to bits there on the flagstones and ate the pieces without once looking up at them.

"You remind me of that peacock," he said.

She stood up and said, "I think you might just as well stay here. I think you've had it, anyway. I think you've lost your mind. Why don't you just kill yourself and get it over with?" She waited a minute longer, holding her purse, and then she walked away between the empty tables.

He signaled the waiter, who had watched everything. In a minute the waiter put another bottle of lemon fix and a clean glass in front of him. After pouring what was left of her drink into his glass, the waiter took away her bottle and glass without saying anything.

Halprin could see the bay and their ship from where he sat. The harbor was too shallow for a ship of its size to enter, so it had anchored a quarter mile out, behind the breakwater, and they had come ashore that morning on a tender. The entrance to the bay was narrow and had, more than two thousand years ago, given rise to the legend that, in even more ancient days, the Colossus itself had straddled the entrance to the harbor—one mammoth bronze leg on either side of the harbor entrance. Some of the postcards for sale in the marketplace depicted a gigantic cartoon Colossus with boats going and coming between its legs.

In a little while, she came back to the table and sat down as if nothing had happened. Every day that passed, they hurt each other a little more. Every day now they grew more used to wounding each other. At night, with this knowledge, their love-making had become vicious and unbridled, their bodies coming together like knives clashing in the dark.

"You weren't serious, were you?" she said. "You didn't mean what you said? About staying here, you know, and all the rest?"

"I don't know. Yes, I said it, didn't I? I'm serious about it."

She continued to look at him.

"How much money do you have?" he asked.

"Not a cent. Nothing. You have everything, sugar. You're carrying it all. I can't believe this has happened to me, but I don't even have enough to buy cigarettes."

"I'm sorry. Well," he said after a minute, "if we just wouldn't look or act or even talk like broken-down Hemingway characters. That's what I'm afraid of," he said.

She laughed. "Jesus, if that's all you're afraid of," she said.

"You have your typewriter," she said.

"That's true, and they must sell paper here, and pens or pencils.

Here, here's a pen, for instance. I have a pen right here in my pocket." He scribbled some sharp vertical lines on the paper coaster. "It works." He grinned for the first time.

"How long would it take?" she said and waited.

"I don't have any idea. Maybe six months, maybe longer. I've known people who . . . Probably longer. I've never done it before, as you know." He drank from his glass and didn't look at her. His breathing had slowed.

"I don't think we can make it," she said. "I don't think you, I don't think we have it in us."

"Frankly, I don't think we do, either," he said. "I'm not asking or forcing you to stay. The ship won't leave for another five or six hours, you can make up your mind before that. You don't have to stay. I'll divide up the money, of course. I'm sorry about that. I don't want you to stay unless you're sure you want to stay. But I think I will stay. My life is half over, more than half over. The only, the only really extraordinary thing to happen to me in, I don't know, years, was to fall in love with you. That's the only really extraordinary thing in years. That other life is over now, and there's no going back. I don't believe in gestures, not since I was a kid, before I married Kristina, but this would be a gesture of some sort, I suppose. Call it that, if you want. That is, if I pull it off. But I think I might if I stay. I know it sounds crazy. I don't know, though, about us. I'd like you to stay. You know what you mean to me. But you must do what's right for you from now on. In my more lucid moments"—he turned the glass in his hand— "I think it's true, it's over for us. Why, just look at me! My hands are shaking, for Christ's sake." He put his hands out over the table so she could see. He shook his head. "In any case, there's somebody out there waiting for you. If you want to go."

"Just like you were waiting."

"Yes, just like I was waiting, that's true."

"I want to stay," she said after a minute. "If it doesn't work, if it isn't going to work, we'll know, we'll be able to see in a little while, a week or two. I can always go then."

169

"Anytime," he said. "I won't try to hold you."

"You will," she said. "If I decide to go, one way or another you'll try to hold me. You'll do that."

They watched a flock of pigeons turn with a rush of wings overhead and then wheel toward the ship.

"Let's go for it, then," she said and touched the back of his left hand where it held his glass. His right hand was in his lap, clenched.

"You stay, I'll stay, we'll both stay together, okay? Then we'll see. Sugar?"

"Okay," he said. He got up from the table and sat down again. "Okay, then." His breathing was all right once more. "I'll speak to someone about getting our stuff off the ship and applying for a refund for the rest of the trip. Then I'll divide all the money between us. We'll divide the money today. We'll both feel better about that. We'll get a hotel for tonight, divide the money, and then look for a place tomorrow. But you're probably right, you know: I am crazy. Sick and crazy." He was serious as he said this.

She began to cry. He stroked her hand and felt tears come to his own eyes. He took her hands. She nodded slowly as the tears continued to run from her eyes.

The waiter turned his back on them abruptly. He moved to the sink and after a minute began to wash and dry some glasses and hold them up to the light.

A thin, moustached man with carefully combed hair—Halprin recognized him from the ship; the man had boarded with them at Piraeus—pulled out a chair and sat down at one of the empty tables. He hung his jacket over the back of one of the chairs, rolled the cuffs of his sleeves back once, and lighted a cigarette. He looked briefly in their direction—Halprin was still holding her hands, she was still crying—and then looked away.

The waiter arranged a small white towel over his arm and went over to the man. At the edge of the courtyard, the peacock turned its head slowly from side to side and regarded them all with cold, brilliant eyes.

He sipped coffee and remembered beginnings. Imagine, he thought, and the next time he looked it was clearly noon. The house was quiet. He got up from the table and went to the door. Women's voices carried in from the street. Flowers of all kinds grew around the steps—big, puffy flowers, drooping red and yellow flowers mainly, with a few shapely purple ones as well. He shut the door and headed down the street for cigarettes. He didn't whistle, but he let his arms swing as he moved down the steep, cobbled street. The sun fell squarely off the sides of the white buildings and made him squint. *Augustine.* What else? Simple. No diminutive either, ever. He had never called her anything but: Augustine. He kept walking. He nodded at men, women, and horses alike.

He drew aside the bead curtains over the door and went inside. The young barman, Michael, wearing a black armband, was leaning on his elbows on the bar, a cigarette between his lips, talking to George Varos. Varos was a fisherman who had lost his left hand in an accident. He still went out now and then but since he was unable to handle the nets, he said he no longer felt right going out in the boats. He spent his days selling sesame rolls that looked like doughnuts. Two broomsticks stacked with sesame rolls leaned against the counter next to Varos. The men looked at him and nodded.

"Cigarettes and a lemon fix, please," he said to Michael. He took the cigarettes and his drink to a small table near the window where he could see the bay. Two small boats moved up and down with the motion of the waves. The men in the boats sat staring down into the water without moving or talking, while the boats moved up and down on the waves.

He sipped the drink and smoked and in a little while he took the letter out of his pocket and commenced to read. Now and then he stopped and looked out the window at the boats. The men at the counter went on talking.

*

"That's a start, for sure," she said. She had put her arms around his shoulders, her breasts just grazing his back. She was reading what he had written.

"It's not bad, sugar," she said. "No, it's not bad at all. But where was I when this was taking place? Was this yesterday?"

"What do you mean?" He glanced over the pages. "You mean this, *the house was quiet*? Maybe you were asleep. I don't know. Or out shopping. I don't know. Is it important? All I say is— the house was quiet. I don't need to go into your whereabouts right now.

"I never nap in the morning, or in the middle of the day either, for that matter." She made a face at him.

"I don't think I have to account in this for your whereabouts at every minute. Do you think? What the hell."

"No, I mean, I'm not making anything out of it. I mean, it's just strange, you know, that's what I mean." She waved her hand at the pages. "You know what I mean."

He got up from the table and stretched and looked out the window at the bay.

"Do you want to work some more?" she said. "Lord, we don't have to go to the beach. That was just a suggestion. I'd rather see you work some more, if that's what you want."

She had been eating an orange. He could smell the orange on her breath as she leaned over the table and looked seriously at the pages once more. She grinned and ran her tongue over her lips. "Well," she said. "So. Well, well."

He said, "I want to go to the beach. That's enough for today. That's enough for now, anyway. Maybe tonight I'll do something. I'll fool around with this tonight, maybe. I've started, that's the main thing. I'm the compulsive type; I'll go on now. Maybe it'll work itself out. Let's go to the beach."

She grinned again. "Good," she said. She put her hand on his cock. "Good, good, good. How is our little friend today?" She stroked his cock through his trousers. "I'd hoped you'd start today," she said. "I thought you might today for some reason,

I don't know why. Let's go, then. I'm happy today, this minute. I can't tell you. It's as if . . . I feel happier today than I've felt in a long, long time. Maybe—"

"Let's not think maybe or anything," he said. He reached under the halter and touched her breast, took the nipple between his fingers and rolled it back and forth. "We'll take one day at a time, that's what we decided. One day, then the next day, then the next." The nipple began to stiffen under his fingers.

"When we come back from swimming we'll do things to each other," she said. "Unless, of course, you want to put off swimming until later?"

"I'm easy," he said. Then, "No, wait, I'll put my trunks on. When we're at the beach maybe we'll tell each other about what we're going to do to each other when we get back here. Let's go ahead and go to the beach now while the sun's out. It may rain. Let's go ahead and go."

She began to hum something as she put some oranges into a little bag.

Halprin slipped on his trunks. He put the sheets of paper and the ballpoint pen into the cupboard. He stared into the cupboard a minute and then, the humming gone, turned slowly.

She stood in front of the open door in her shorts and halter, the long black hair hanging down over her shoulders from under the white straw sun hat. She held the oranges and the straw-covered water bottle against her breasts. She looked at him a minute, and then she winked, grinned, and cocked her hip.

His breath went out of him and his legs felt weak. For a minute he was afraid of another seizure. He saw the wedge of blue sky behind her and the darker blue, shining blue, water of the bay, the small waves rising and falling. He closed his eyes and opened them. She was still there, grinning. *What we do matters, brother,* he remembered Miller saying long ago. There came to him an empty tugging in his stomach, then he felt his jaws simply tighten of their own accord until he ground his teeth and felt his face might tell her things he himself didn't yet know. He felt light-headed, but all senses on the alert: he could smell the broken orange in the room, could hear a fly drone and then bump the window near the bed. He heard flowers around the steps, their long stems moving against each other in the warm breeze. Gulls called and waves rose and then fell on the beach. He felt at the edge of something. It was as if things he had never understood before might now suddenly be made clear to him.

"Crazy about you," he said. "Crazy about you, baby. Baby."

She nodded.

"Close the door," he said. His cock began to rise against the swimming trunks.

She put her things on the table and pushed the door shut with her foot. Then she took off her hat and shook her hair.

"Well, well, well," she said and grinned again. "Well, let me say hello to our friend," she said. "Not so little friend." Her eyes shone as she moved toward him and her voice had become languorous.

"Lie down," she said. "And don't move. Just lie down on the bed. And don't move. Don't move, hear."

OCCASIONS

On "Neighbors"

"Neighbors" first hit me as an idea for a story in the fall of 1970, two years after returning to the United States from Tel Aviv. While in Tel Aviv, we had for a few days looked after an apartment belonging to some friends. Though none of the high jinks in the story really occurred in the course of our apartment watching, I have to admit that I did do a bit of snooping in the refrigerator and liquor cabinet. I found that experience of entering and leaving someone else's empty apartment two or three times a day, sitting for a while in other people's chairs, glancing through their books and magazines and looking out their windows, made a rather powerful impression on me. It took two years for the impression to surface as a story, but once it did I simply sat down and wrote it. It seemed a fairly easy story to do at the time, and it came together very quickly after I went to work on it. The real work on the story, and perhaps the art of the story, came later. Originally the manuscript was about twice as long, but I kept paring it on subsequent revisions, and then pared some more, until it achieved its present length and dimensions.

In addition to the confusion or disorder of the central personality in the story—the main theme at work, I guess—I think that the story has captured an essential sense of mystery or strangeness that is in part due to the treatment of the subject matter, in this case the story's style. For it is a highly "stylized" story if it is anything, and it is this that helps give it its value.

With each subsequent trip to the Stones' apartment, Miller is drawn deeper and deeper into an abyss of his own making. The turning point in the story comes, of course, when Arlene insists that this time she will go next door alone and then, finally, Bill has to go and fetch her. She reveals through words and through appearance (the color in her cheeks is high and there is "white lint clinging to the back of her sweater") that she in turn has been doing pretty much the same kind of rummaging and prowling that he has been engaging in.

I think the story is, more or less, an artistic success. My only fear is that it is too thin, too elliptical and subtle, too inhuman. I hope this is not so, but in truth I do not see it as the kind of story that one loves unreservedly and gives up everything to; a story that is ultimately remembered for its sweep, for the breadth and depth and lifelike sentiment of its characters. No, this is a different kind of story—not better, maybe, and I surely hope no worse, different in any case—and the internal and external truths and values in the story do not have much to do, I'm afraid, with character, or some of the other virtues held dear in short fiction.

As to writers and writing that I like, I tend to find much more around that I like than dislike. I think there is all kinds of good stuff getting written and published these days in both the big and little magazines, and in book form. Lots of stuff that's not so good, too, but why worry about that? To my mind Joyce Carol Oates is the first writer of my generation, perhaps any recent generation, and we are all going to have to learn to live under that shadow, or spell—at least for the foreseeable future.

On "Drinking While Driving"

I'm not a "born" poet. Many of the poems I write I write because I don't always have the time to write fiction, my first love. An offshoot of this interest in fiction is that I'm interested in a story line, and as a result I suppose many of my poems are narrative in bent. I like poems that say something to me the first time around, although poems I like a lot, or don't like especially but can see value in, I'll read a second, third, and fourth time to see what makes them go. In all my poems I'm after a definite mood or ambience. I constantly use the personal pronoun, although many of the poems I write are sheer invention. Very often, however, the poems do have at least a slender base in reality, which is the case with "Drinking While Driving."

The poem was written a couple of years ago. I think it has a certain amount of tension, and I want to believe it's successful in presenting a sense of loss and faint desperation on the part of a narrator who seems—to me anyway—at dangerously loose ends. When I wrote the poem I was working an eight-to-five job in a more or less decent white-collar position. But, as always with a full-time job, there was not enough time to go around. For a while I wasn't writing or reading anything. It was an exaggeration to say "I haven't read a book in six months," but at the time I felt it was not far from the truth. Some while before the poem happened along I had read *The Retreat from Moscow* by Caulaincourt, one of Napoleon's generals, and once or twice during that period I had ridden around at night with my brother in his car, both of us feeling aimless and hemmed in and working on a pint bottle of Old Crow. Anyway, there were these vaguely remembered facts or traces in my head, along with my own very real feelings of frustration at the time, when I sat down to write the poem. I think some of all this came together.

I really can't tell you more about the poem or the process. I don't know how good the poem is, but I think it has merit. I can tell you it's one of my favorites.

On Rewriting

When I was asked if I'd like to write a foreword to this book [*Fires*], I said I didn't think so. But the more I thought on it, it seemed to me a few words might be in order. But not a foreword, I said. Somehow a foreword seemed presumptuous. Forewords and prefaces to one's own work, in fiction or poetry, ought to be reserved for literary eminences over the age of fifty, say. But maybe, I said, an afterword. So what follows then, for better or worse, are a few words after the fact.

The poems I've chosen to include were written between 1966 and 1982. Some of them first appeared in book form in *Near Klamath, Winter Insomnia*, and *At Night the Salmon Move*. I've also included poems that were written since the publication, in 1976, of *At Night the Salmon Move*—poems which have appeared in magazines and journals but not yet in a book. The poems have not been put into a chronological order. Instead, they have been more or less arranged into broad groups having to do with a particular way of thinking and feeling about things—a constellation of feelings and attitudes—that I found at work when I began looking at the poems with an eye toward collecting them for this book. Some of the poems seemed to fall naturally into certain areas, or obsessions. There were, for instance, a number of them that had to do in one way or another with alcohol; some with foreign travel and personages; others strictly concerned with things domestic and familiar. So this became the ordering principle when I went to arrange the book. For example, in 1972 I wrote and published a poem called "Cheers." Ten years later, in 1982, in a vastly different life and after many poems of a different nature entirely, I found myself writing and publishing a poem called "Alcohol." So when the time came to make a selection of poems for this book, it was the content, or obsession (I don't care for the word "theme"), which most often suggested where the poems would go. Nothing particularly noteworthy or remarkable about this process.

One final word: in nearly every instance the poems that appeared in the earlier books have been slightly, in some cases ever so slightly, revised. But they have been revised. They were revised this summer, and I think they've been made better in the process. But more about revision later.

The two essays were written in 1981, and I was asked to write them. In one case, an editor at the *New York Times Book Review* wanted me to write on "any aspect of writing" and the little piece "On Writing" was the result. The other came about through an invitation to contribute something to a book on "influences" called *In Praise of What Persists* which was being put together by Steve Berg of *American Poetry Review*, and Ted Solotaroff at Harper and Row. My contribution was "Fires"—and it was Noel Young's idea that we call this book after that title.

The earliest story, "The Cabin," was written in 1966, was collected in *Furious Seasons*, and was revised this summer for publication here. *Indiana Review* will publish the story in their fall 1982 number. A much more recent story is "The Pheasant," which will be published this month in a limited edition series by Metacom Press and will appear later this fall in *New England Review*.

I like to mess around with my stories. I'd rather tinker with a story after writing it, and then tinker some more, changing this, changing that, than have to write the story in the first place. That initial writing just seems to me the hard place I have to get to in order to go on and have fun with the story. Rewriting for me is not a chore—it's something I like to do. I think by nature I'm more deliberate and careful than I am spontaneous, and maybe that explains something. Maybe not. Maybe there's no connection except the one I'm making. But I do know that revising the work once it's done is something that comes naturally to me and is something I take pleasure in doing. Maybe I revise because it gradually takes me into the heart of what the story is *about*. I have to keep trying to see if I can find that out. It's a process more than a fixed position.

There was a time when I used to think it was a character defect that made me have to struggle along like this. I don't think this way any longer. Frank O'Connor has said that he was always revising his stories (this after sometimes taking the story through twenty or thirty rewrites in the first place) and that someday he'd like to publish a revised book of his revisions. To a limited extent, I've had that opportunity here. Two of the stories, "Distance" and "So Much Water So Close to Home" (from the original eight stories that made up *Furious Seasons*), were first published in book form in *FS* and were then included in *What We Talk about When We Talk about Love*. When Capra approached me about reprinting, between two covers, *Furious Seasons* and *At Night the Salmon Move*—both books were then out of print—the idea of this book began to take hold. But I was in something of a quandary about these two particular stories Capra wanted to include. They had both been largely rewritten for the Knopf book. After some deliberation, I decided to stay fairly close to the versions as they first appeared in the Capra Press book, but this time hold the revisions to a minimum. They *have* been revised again, but not nearly so much as they once were. But how long can this go on? I mean, I suppose there is, finally, a law of diminishing returns. But I can say now that I prefer the later versions of the stories, which is more in accord with the way I am writing short stories these days.

So all of the stories here have been reworked, to a greater or lesser degree; and they are somewhat different now than the original versions published either in magazines or in *Furious Seasons*. I see this as an instance in which I am in the happy position of being able to make the stories better than they were.

At least, God knows, I *hope* they're better. I think so anyway. But, truly, I've seldom seen a piece of prose, or a poem—my own or anyone else's—that couldn't be improved upon if it were left alone for a time.

I'm grateful to Noel Young for giving me the opportunity, and the initiative, to look at the work once more and see what could be done with it.

On the *Dostoevsky* Screenplay

In early September 1982, the director Michael Cimino called
to ask if I would be willing to rework a screenplay on the life
of Dostoevsky. After we talked and I'd expressed interest, we
decided to talk further, once the business side of things had been
worked out. His agent contacted my agent, an agreement was
made, and then Cimino and I arranged to meet for dinner in New
York. At the time I was teaching at Syracuse University and the
semester was under way. I was also writing the last story for
Cathedral, and editing and arranging the work that would go into
Fires. I didn't know where I was going to find the time to work
on a screenplay, but I'd decided it was something I wanted to do.

I called Tess Gallagher, who was spending that fall out in
Port Angeles, Washington. She was on leave from her teaching
duties at Syracuse so she could help attend to her father, who was
dying of lung cancer. I asked if she wanted to work with me.
This project had to be done in a hurry and I knew I wouldn't
have time to do research or reread the novels. Tess agreed to help.
She would research and write new scenes where necessary and
edit what I'd done. In general she would co-rewrite with me—
or, as it turned out, cowrite an entirely new script.

Cimino and I met for dinner at Paul and Jimmy's, an Italian
restaurant near Gramercy Park. After dinner, we got down to
business: Dostoevsky. Cimino said he wanted to make a movie
about a great writer. In his opinion, it hadn't been done before.
He cited *Doctor Zhivago* as an example of what he didn't want
to do. As we talked about the movie, I recalled that Zhivago, the
writer-physician, is seen only once in the film trying to write

something. It is winter, the height of the Bolshevik civil war, and Zhivago and Lara, his mistress, are hiding out in an isolated *dacha*. (In case anyone has forgotten, Omar Sharif and Julie Christie played these roles in the film.) There is a scene with Zhivago at a desk, wearing woolen gloves against the cold, trying to write a poem. The camera moves in for a big close-up on the poem. Granted, the writing of poetry or fiction is not in itself exactly show-stopping material. Cimino wanted to keep Dostoevsky the novelist visible throughout. His idea was that the dramatic, often melodramatic, circumstances of Dostoevsky's life, played out against the obsessive composition of the novels, offered a wonderful opportunity for a movie.

Carlo Ponti, who wanted to produce the Dostoevsky film, had already made a movie in Russia in the early 1970s called *Sunflower* starring his wife, Sophia Loren, and Marcello Mastroianni. Ponti was friendly with Soviet filmmakers and had friends among some members of the political leadership. As a result, Cimino hoped to be able to shoot on location in Russia, including Siberia and other areas normally closed to westerners.

I was thinking about the script when I asked if the Russians would want to exercise censorship of any sort. Cimino said no, they intended to be cooperative in this matter. In the first place, it was the centennial year of Dostoevsky's death. (Actually that was 1981.) They were hoping for a big film down the road to celebrate the man and his work. There'd be no censorship. The film wouldn't even be processed in Russian film laboratories; instead, each day's "rushes" would be sent out to France.

At this point Cimino took out the script, a thick manuscript in a black folder, and put it on the table. I picked it up and flipped through some pages, reading a few lines to get an idea of it. Even dipping into it like that, I could tell at once this wasn't a happy prospect. "Is there a story line here?" I asked. "Does it have a dramatic narrative?" Cimino shook his head. "That's one of its problems. But I think there's a spiritual development to it." He said that and didn't bat an eye. I was impressed. I could go on that, but what I'd been scanning hardly seemed like English, and it wasn't just that there were a lot of Russian names. "Maybe after you've read it you'll just want to throw up your hands and forget it," Cimino said. The script had a strange look to it—dismayingly long passages of narrative occasionally interspersed with dialogue. I'd never seen a film script, but this didn't even vaguely resemble my idea of such a work. But knowing, as he did, that I'd never seen one before, polished or otherwise (I'd warned him beforehand), Cimino had brought one along for me so that I would have a clear idea of the correct form. (When I looked at the sample screenplay he'd brought along, I had to ask what the letters INT. and EXT. stood for. "Interior" and "exterior," he explained. V.O. and OS.? "Voice-over" and "offscreen.") I went back up to Syracuse the next day and began work.

Spiritual development or not, the work turned out to be inconsistent with everything I knew about Dostoevsky's life. I was baffled and didn't know where to start. It did cross my mind that it might be better if I simply "threw up my hands." Working night and day, with time away from it only long enough to meet my classes, I roughed out a long savage draft which I immediately sent to Tess. Meanwhile, in preparation, she had read all the biographies she could get her hands on, as well as *Crime and Punishment*, *The Gambler*, *The House of the Dead*, and *The Diary of Polina Suslova*. She went to work, adding many new scenes and expanding everywhere. Then she copied the work and sent it back to me. I went to work on it again. It was retyped once more, and again it went back to Tess who did still more work. I remember her telephone calls at odd hours to talk about Dostoevsky. Now and again she read me a scene she had just pulled out of the typewriter. The script came back to me and once more I worked on it. It was typed again and then again. By this time it was late November and the script was 220 pages long—prohibitive, that's the only word for it. (An average screenplay falls somewhere between 90 and 110 pages; a rough estimate for gauging the length of a film is a page a minute. And

Cimino is not one to speed up the process. His screenplay for *Heaven's Gate* was 140 pages in length; the resulting film was nearly four hours long.)

Despite everything that had been going on in our respective lives, Tess and I had been working like crazy on the script during this period. "I wish it had come at any time but this," she told me during one of our many phone conversations. But she was excited about it, too. "Just imagine," she said once. "Dostoevsky! We're making him *live* again." Her own father was losing his battle with cancer, and I was aware of the background of daily loss she worked against. "Dostoevsky gives me courage in all this," she said to me. "And he lets me cry, too."

At the end of November, I sent the completed script to Cimino. Would anyone besides Tess and me feel it was as good as we thought? However, Cimino called at once to tell me how pleased and surprised he was with what had happened. Despite its length—he'd never seen a screenplay as long as our *Dostoevsky*—he was immensely happy with the result.

I don't know when or even if the screenplay will ever be turned into a movie. Cimino tells me that Carlo Ponti has moved from Los Angeles, presumably back to Europe, has dropped out of sight and is not making any efforts on behalf of producing the script. Cimino has put the 220-page screenplay aside and moved on to other projects.

When I was invited to join the "Back-to-Back Series" I thought it might prove interesting if we could extract some material from the screenplay and present it in a coherent fashion. We excerpted material from the early pages of the script as St. Petersburg is torn by revolution and Dostoevsky is visiting a young writer in the mental ward of a hospital. Then we move to the time just after Dostoevsky's arrest and confinement on charges of treason. Along with several coconspirators, he faced a death sentence. (Interestingly enough, Vladimir Nabokov's grandfather was one of the judges in the case.) Then we skip and pick up the story just after Dostoevsky's sentence has been commuted and he's in prison awaiting deportation to Siberia.

After the scenes in Siberia, we jump ahead and pick up the narrative ten years later, after Dostoevsky's return to St. Petersburg and his involvement with Polina Suslova, the woman Dostoevsky drew on to create the heroine for *The Gambler*.

The last section deals with Dostoevsky and Anna Grigoryevna, the woman who became his second wife. (His first died of tuberculosis two years after his return from Siberia to St. Petersburg.) Anna went to work for Dostoevsky as a stenographer, fell in love with him, and married him. She saw to it that Dostoevsky's last years, the period of *The Possessed* and *The Brothers Karamazov*, were years of peace and tranquility.

On "Bobber" and Other Poems

Every poem I've written has been, for me, an occasion of the first order. So much so, I believe, that I can remember the emotional circumstances that were at work when I wrote the poem, my physical surroundings, even what the weather was like. If pressed, I think I could come close to recalling the day of the week. At least, in most instances, I can remember whether the poems were written during the week or on a weekend. Most certainly I can remember the particular time of day I wrote them—morning, midday, afternoon or, once in a great while, late at night. This kind of recall is not true of the short fiction I write, especially the stories I wrote early in my career. When I look back at my first book of stories, for example, I have to glance over the copyright dates to even get a fix on the year the stories were published, and from that I can guess—give or take a year or two—when they must have been written. It's only in a few isolated instances that I can recall anything in particular, or out of the ordinary, about when I wrote them, let alone what I was feeling at the time I did so.

I don't know why it is that I recall so clearly the time and circumstances surrounding each poem, yet don't recall much about the composition of these stories. I think partly it has to do with the fact that, in truth, I feel the poems are closer to me, more special, more of a gift received than my other work, even though I know, for sure, that the stories are no less a gift. It could be that I put a more intimate value finally on the poems than I do the stories.

My poems are of course not literally true—the events didn't

actually happen, or at least the stuff in the poems didn't happen in the way I say it does. But, like most of my fiction, there is an autobiographical element to the poems. Something resembling what happens in them did happen to me at some time or another, and the memory stayed with me until it found expression. Or often what is being described in the poem was to some degree a reflection of my state of mind at the time of writing it. I suppose in a large way then the poems *are* more personal than my stories and hence more "revealing."

In poetry, my own or someone else's, I like narrative. A poem doesn't have to tell a story with a beginning, middle and end, but for me it has to keep moving, it has to step lively, it has to spark. It may move in any direction at all—back in time, far into the future, or it may veer off onto some overgrown trail. It may even cease to be earthbound and go out seeking habitation with the stars. It might speak in a voice from beyond the grave or travel with salmon, wild geese, or locusts. But it isn't static. It *moves*. It moves and though it may have mysterious elements at work in it, its development is intrinsic, one thing suggesting something else. It shines—or at any rate I hope it shines.

Each of my poems that the editor has seen fit to include in this anthology touches upon a real-life concern or situation that pressed upon my life with some degree of urgency when that particular poem was written. To that degree I suppose the poems could be called narrative or story poems for they are always *about* something. They have a "subject." One of the things each one is "about" is what I thought and felt at the time I wrote it. Each poem preserves a specific moment in time; and when I look at one I can see the frame of mind I was in at the time I wrote it. Reading my poems now, I am in a very real sense looking back over a rough, but true map of my past. So in a way they are helping hold together my life, and I like that idea.

"Bobber," the oldest poem in the group, was written one fine June morning in a motel room in Cheyenne, Wyoming, on my way from Berkeley to Rock Island, Illinois. A year and a half later, in the fall of 1969, I was living in Ben Lomond, California, a few miles north of Santa Cruz, and it was there I wrote "Prosser." I woke up one morning thinking about my father. He'd been dead for two years, but had appeared that night in the margins of a dream I'd had. I tried to pin something down from the dream, but couldn't. But that morning I began to think about him and began to recall some hunting trips we'd made together. Then I clearly remembered the wheat fields we'd hunted over together, and I recalled the town of Prosser, a little place where we often stopped for something to eat in the evening once we'd finished hunting. It was the first town we came to after we left the wheat field country, and I suddenly remembered how the lights would appear to us at night, just as they do in the poem. I wrote it quickly and, seemingly, effortlessly. (This may be one of the reasons I'm especially fond of this poem. But if I were ever asked which is the favorite of any poem I've written, this one would be it.) A few days later that same week I wrote the poem "Your Dog Dies." That one, too, came quickly and didn't seem to require much revision.

"Forever" was different. I wrote the poem in 1970, just before Christmas, in a workroom in a garage in Palo Alto; and it was a poem that I must have written fifty or sixty times before I felt I had it right. I remember that when I wrote the first draft it was raining hard outside. I had this worktable set up in the garage, and every now and then I would look out of the little garage window toward the house. It was late at night. Everyone inside the house was asleep. The rain seemed a part of that "Forever" I was approaching in my mind.

"Looking for Work" was written the following August, in the afternoon, in an apartment house in Sacramento during a confusing and difficult summer. My children and my wife had gone to the park. The temperature was nearly a hundred degrees, and I was barefoot and in swimming trunks. When I walked across the tile floors of the apartment, my feet left tracks.

"Wes Hardin" was also written in Sacramento. But it came

a few months later, in October, and in a different residence, a house on a dead-end road called, if you can believe it, Lunar Lane. It was early in the morning, eight o'clock or so, and my wife had just left the house to drop the children off at school and go on to her job. I had the day in front of me, a rare day in which to write, but instead of trying to write anything I picked up a book that had come in the mail and began to read about outlaws of the Old West. I came to a photograph of John Wesley Hardin and stopped there. In a little while, I roughed out the poem.

"Marriage" is the most recent poem in this particular group of poems and was written in a two-room apartment in Iowa City in April 1978. My wife and I had been separated for months. But we had gotten back together on a trial basis for what, as it turned out, would prove to be a very short time. But we were trying once more to see if we could put our marriage back together. Our children, both of them grown now, were someplace in California, pretty much on their own. Still, I was worried about them. I was also worried about myself and my wife and our marriage of twenty-some years that we were making one final effort to preserve. I was alive with apprehensions of all sorts. I wrote the poem in the evening, my wife in one room and I in the other. The fears I was experiencing found a place to go.

The reconciliation didn't work out, but that's another story.

On "For Tess"

In its way, this poem is a kind of love letter to my wife, the poet and short story writer Tess Gallagher. At the time I wrote the poem, in March 1984, I was spending time by myself in our house in Port Angeles, Washington. Prior to March I'd been in Syracuse, New York, where we live most of the time and where Tess teaches at the university. But in September 1983, my publisher had brought out *Cathedral*, a book of my short stories. After the book was published, there was such an extended hubbub for a while—a period of time that stretched right on into the new year—that I was thrown off my stride and couldn't seem to find my way back into my work. And this literary commotion came in addition to the usual social activities we normally engage in when living in Syracuse—dinners with friends, movies, concerts, fiction and poetry readings at the university.

In many regards, it was a "high" time, a good time, certainly, but frustrating for me as well: I was finding it hard to get back to my work. It was Tess who, seeing my frustration, suggested I go out alone to our house in Port Angeles in hopes of finding the necessary peace and quiet that I felt I needed to begin writing again. I headed west with the intention of writing fiction once I'd arrived. But after I'd settled into the house and been still for a while, I began, much to my surprise, to write poems. (I say "surprise" because I hadn't written a poem in over two years and didn't know if I ever would again.)

Though "For Tess" is not, strictly speaking, "autobiographical"—I hadn't used a red Daredevil lure to fish with for years and do not carry Tess's dad's pocketknife with me; and I didn't go fishing on the day the poem seems to be taking place; nor was I "followed for a while" by a dog named "Dixie"—all of the things taking place in the poem *had* happened at one time or another, and I remembered, and I put these details into the poem. But—and this is important—the emotion in the poem, the sentiment (not to be confused, ever, with sentimentality)— the sentiment is true in every line, and it is given in clear and precise language. Further, the details in the poem are lively and specific. And insofar as the narrative or storytelling aspect is concerned, I think the poem is authentic and convincing. (I don't have much patience with poems that use rhetoric to keep them going, or unengaged abstract pseudopoetic language. I tend to shy away from the abstract and rhetorical in literature, as well as in life.)

"For Tess" tells a little story *and* captures a moment. Remember that a poem is not simply an act of self-expression. A poem or a story—any literary work that presumes to call itself art—is an act of communication between the writer and reader. Anyone can express himself, or herself, but what writers and poets want to do in their work, more than simply *express* themselves, is communicate, yes? The need is always to translate one's thoughts and deepest concerns into language which casts these thoughts and concerns into a form—fictional or poetic—in the hope that a reader might understand and experience those same feelings and concerns. Other understandings and feelings contributed by the reader always accompany a piece of writing. That's inevitable and even desirable. But if the main cargo of what the writer had to give is left at the depot, then that piece of writing, to my way of thinking, has largely failed. I think I'm right in feeling that being understood is a fundamental assumption that every good writer makes or rather a goal that he or she works toward.

A final note. Not only did I attempt to capture and hold—that is to say, make permanent—a specific moment through a pro- gression of specific details—I realized, halfway through the poem, that what I was writing was nothing less than a love poem. (One of the few love poems I've ever written, by the way.) For, not only was I addressing the poem *to* Tess, the woman who has shared my life for the past ten years, giving her some "news" of my life in Port Angeles—here I'm thinking of Ezra Pound's remark that "literature is news that stays news"—but I was taking the occasion to say that I was grateful to her for coming into my life when she did, back in 1977. She made an immense difference and helped change my life in profound ways.

That's one of the things I was trying to "say" in the poem. And I'm pleased if I reached her and, because of that, touched other readers as well—gave them a little of the real emotion I was feeling when I wrote the poem.

On "Errand"

In early 1987 an editor at E. P. Dutton sent me a copy of the newly published Henri Troyat biography, *Chekhov*. Immediately upon the book's arrival, I put aside what I was doing and started reading. I seem to recall reading the book pretty much straight through, able, at the time, to devote entire afternoons and evenings to it.

On the third or fourth day, nearing the end of the book, I came to the little passage where Chekhov's doctor—a Badenweiler physician by the name of Dr. Schwöhrer, who attended Chekhov during his last days—is summoned by Olga Knipper Chekhov to the dying writer's bedside in the early morning hours of July 2, 1904. It is clear that Chekhov has only a little while to live. Without any comment on the matter, Troyat tells his readers that this Dr. Schwöhrer ordered up a bottle of champagne. Nobody had asked for champagne, of course; he just took it upon himself to do it. But this little piece of human business struck me as an extraordinary action. Before I really knew what I was going to do with it, or how I was going to proceed, I felt I had been launched into a short story of my own then and there. I wrote a few lines and then a page or two more. How did Dr. Schwöhrer go about ordering champagne and at that late hour at this hotel in Germany? How was it delivered to the room and by whom, etc.? What was the protocol involved when the champagne arrived? Then I stopped and went ahead to finish reading the biography.

But just as soon as I'd finished the book I once again turned my attention back to Dr. Schwöhrer and that business of the champagne. I was seriously interested in what I was doing. But what *was* I doing? The only thing that was clear to me was that I thought I saw an opportunity to pay homage—if I could bring it off, do it rightly and honorably—to Chekhov, the writer who has meant so much to me for such a long time.

I tried out ten or twelve openings to the piece, first one beginning and then another, but nothing felt right. Gradually I began to move the story away from those final moments back to the occasion of Chekhov's first public hemorrhage from tuberculosis, something that occurred in a restaurant in Moscow in the company of his friend and publisher, Suvorin. Then came the hospitalization and the scene with Tolstoy, the trip with Olga to Badenweiler, the brief period of time there in the hotel together before the end, the young bellman who makes two important appearances in the Chekhov suite and, at the end, the mortician who, like the bellman, isn't to be found in the biographical account.

The story was a hard one to write, given the factual basis of the material. I couldn't stray from what had happened, nor did I want to. As much as anything, I needed to figure out how to breathe life into actions that were merely suggested or not given moment in the biographical telling. And, finally, I saw that I needed to set my imagination free and simply invent within the confines of the story. I knew as I was writing this story that it was a good deal different from anything I'd ever done before. I'm pleased, and grateful, that it seems to have come together.

On *Where I'm Calling From*

I wrote and published my first short story in 1963, twenty-five years ago, and have been drawn to short story writing ever since. I think in part (but only in part) this inclination toward brevity and intensity has to do with the fact that I am a poet as well as a story writer. I began writing and publishing poetry and fiction at more or less the same time, back in the early 1960s when I was still an undergraduate. But this dual relationship as poet and short story writer doesn't explain everything. I'm hooked on writing short stories and couldn't get off them even if I wanted to. Which I don't.

I love the swift leap of a good story, the excitement that often commences in the first sentence, the sense of beauty and mystery found in the best of them; and the fact—so crucially important to me back at the beginning and even now still a consideration—that the story can be written and read in one sitting. (Like poems!)

In the beginning—and perhaps still—the most important short story writers to me were Isaac Babel, Anton Chekhov, Frank O'Connor and V. S. Pritchett. I forget who first passed along a copy of Babel's *Collected Stories* to me, but I do remember coming across a line from one of his greatest stories. I copied it into the little notebook I carried around with me everywhere in those days. The narrator, speaking about Maupassant and the writing of fiction, says: "No iron can stab the heart with such force as a period put just at the right place."

When I first read this it came to me with the force of revelation. This is what I wanted to do with my own stories: line up the right words, the precise images, as well as the exact and correct punctuation so that the reader got pulled in and involved in the story and wouldn't be able to turn away his eyes from the text unless the house caught fire. Vain wishes perhaps, to ask words to assume the power of actions, but clearly a young writer's wishes. Still, the idea of writing clearly with authority enough to hold and engage the reader persisted. This remains one of my primary goals today.

My first book of stories, *Will You Please Be Quiet, Please?*, did not appear until 1976, thirteen years after the first story was written. This long delay between composition, magazine and book publication was due in part to a young marriage, the exigencies of child rearing and blue-collar laboring jobs, a little education on the fly—and never enough money to go around at the end of each month. (It was during this long period, too, that I was trying to learn my craft as a writer, how to be as subtle as a river current when very little else in my life was subtle.)

After the thirteen-year period it took to put the first book together and to find a publisher who, I might add, was most reluctant to engage in such a cockeyed enterprise—a first book of stories by an unknown writer!—I tried to learn to write fast when I had the time, writing stories when the spirit was with me and letting them pile up in a drawer; and then going back to look at them carefully and coldly later on, from a remove, after things had calmed down, after things had, all too regrettably, gone back to "normal."

Inevitably, life being what it is, there were often great swatches of time that simply disappeared, long periods when I did not write any fiction. (How I wish I had those years back now!) Sometimes a year or two would pass when I couldn't even think about writing stories. Often, though, I was able to spend some of that time writing poems, and this proved important because in writing the poetry the flame didn't entirely putter out, as I sometimes feared it might. Mysteriously, or so it would seem to me, there would come a time to turn to fiction again. The circumstances in my life would be right or at least improved and the ferocious desire to write would take hold of me, and I would begin.

I wrote *Cathedral*—eight of these stories are reprinted here—in a period of fifteen months. But during that two-year period before I began to work on those stories, I found myself in a period of stocktaking, of trying to discover where I wanted to go with whatever new stories I was going to write and how I wanted to write them. My previous book, *What We Talk about When We Talk about Love*, had been in many ways a watershed book for me, but it was a book I didn't want to duplicate or write again. So I simply waited. I taught at Syracuse University. I wrote some poems and book reviews, and an essay or two. And then one morning something happened. After a good night's sleep, I went to my desk and wrote the story "Cathedral." I knew it was a different kind of story for me, no question. Somehow I had found another direction I wanted to move toward. And I moved. And quickly.

The new stories that are included here, stories which were written after *Cathedral* and after I had intentionally, happily, taken "time out" for two years to write two books of poetry, are, I'm sure, different in kind and degree from the earlier stories. (At the least I think they're different from those earlier stories, and I suspect readers may feel the same. But any writer will tell you he wants to believe his work will undergo a metamorphosis, a sea change, a process of enrichment if he's been at it long enough.)

V. S. Pritchett's definition of a short story is "something glimpsed from the corner of the eye, in passing." First the glimpse. Then the glimpse given life, turned into something that will illuminate the moment and just maybe lock it indelibly into the reader's consciousness. Make it a part of the reader's own experience, as Hemingway so nicely put it. Forever, the writer hopes. Forever.

If we're lucky, writer and reader alike, we'll finish the last line or two of a short story and then just sit for a minute, quietly. Ideally, we'll ponder what we've just written or read; maybe our hearts or our intellects will have been moved off the peg just a little from where they were before. Our body temperature will have gone up, or down, by a degree. Then, breathing evenly and steadily once more, we'll collect ourselves, writers and readers alike, get up, "created of warm blood and nerves" as a Chekhov character puts it, and go on to the next thing: Life. Always life.

INTRODUCTIONS

Steering by the Stars

This collection of eleven poems and two short stories from Syracuse University's creative writing program—work from both graduate and undergraduate writers is included—is a writing sampler from the program. I think it's good work, and I'm willing to stand behind my choices. Another editor might have chosen, indeed, would have chosen, some different poems as well as different stories. But that's one of the things that help make teaching creative writing interesting and this particular writing program a most interesting one to be associated with: we're all of us, students and faculty, different kinds of writers with different tastes, as unlike one another as you'd want to imagine.

What we do all have in common is an uncommon love of good writing and a desire to encourage it when we see it. We share as well, all of us, a willingness to talk about our ideas of writing, and the courage to put those ideas into practice. We find we're able to talk, sometimes even sensibly, about a piece of writing—in some cases work so new it's just come out of the typewriter the week before. We're able, because of the special circumstance of community, to sit around a seminar table or a table in a beer-and-pizza joint, and talk about what's good or bad in a story or poem, to praise this and discourage that. Sure, bad poems and bad stories turn up in writing classes, but, Lord, that's no secret or disgrace: bad writing can turn up anywhere. The most common form of badness is the writer misusing the language, being careless about what he is trying to say and how he is trying to say it or using the language only to convey some kind of fast-forward information better left to the daily papers or the talking heads on the evening news. When he does this, the other writers around him will say so, if their opinion is solicited. If the emotion in the poem or the story is sheer hype, something trumped up, or just confused and smeary, or if the writer is writing about something he really doesn't care about one way or the other, or if he doesn't have anything much to write about and is simply finding that overwhelming in itself, be it a poem or a short story, why then his fellow writers, the other students and the faculty, will call him to account. The other writers in the writing community can help keep the young writer straight.

A good creative writing teacher can save a good writer a lot of time. I think he can save a bad writer a lot of time too, but we don't need to go into that. Writing is tough and lonely work, and wrong paths can be easily taken. If we are doing our job, creative writing teachers are performing a necessary negative function. If we are any good as teachers, we should be teaching the young writers how not to write and teaching them to teach themselves how not to write. In his *ABC of Reading*, Ezra Pound says that "fundamental accuracy of statement is the ONE sole morality of writing." But if you take the word "accuracy" to mean honesty in the use of the language, saying exactly what you mean in order to achieve exactly the results you want to achieve, then honesty in the student's writing can be helped and encouraged and maybe even taught.

Writing is hard and writers need all the help and honest encouragement they can get. Pound was a writing teacher for Eliot, Williams, Hemingway (Hemingway was taking instruction from Gertrude Stein at the same time), Yeats, and dozens of lesser-known poets and fiction writers. In turn, Yeats—by Pound's own admission—became Pound's writing teacher in later years. Nothing odd about this. If they're any good, creative writing teachers are always learning from their students.

Don't get me wrong. This is not an apology for nor by any means an attempt at a justification for the existence of creative writing programs. I don't think they need one in the slightest. As

I see it, the only essential difference between what any of those other writers did and what we're trying to do here at Syracuse University is that we're simply involved in a more formalized endeavor. That's all. We have here the makings of a literary community. Every creative writing program around the country that's worth its salt has a sense of itself in this manner, a sense of a literary community at work. You know what I'm talking about. (But a lot of writers don't get along well in the community. That's fine too.)

In a creative writing program there exists, or most certainly should exist, this sense of a shared community, people banded together with fairly similar interests and goals—a group of kinfolk, if you will. If you're in a writing program and want to partake of it, it's there. But the mere fact of this group just being there in the same town or city can help palliate a little the young writer's sense of loneliness, which sometimes borders on a feeling of genuine isolation. There's always a feeling of dread excitement that fills you when you go into the room where it's done, or not done, and sit down in front of the empty page. It doesn't help to know that your fellow writers are doing the same thing, maybe even at the same time. But it does help, I'm convinced, that if something comes out of that time spent in that room alone, you know that there is somebody there in the community who wants to see what you've done, somebody who'll be pleased if you're doing something right and true, and disappointed if you're not. In any case, he'll tell you what he thinks—if you ask him. Of course, this is not enough by any means. But it can help. Meanwhile, your muscles will grow stronger, your skin thicken, and you can begin to grow the winter coat of hair that might help sustain you in the cold and difficult journey ahead. With luck, you'll learn to steer by the stars.

All My Relations

The next best thing to writing your own short story is to read someone else's short story. And when you read and reread, as I did, 120 of them back to back in a fairly short span of time (January 25 to February 25), you come away able to draw a few conclusions. The most obvious is that clearly there are a great many stories being written these days, and generally the quality is good—in some cases even exceptional. (There are plenty of stories that aren't so good, by both "known" and "unknown" writers, but why talk about these? So what if there are? So what? We do what we can.) I want to remark on the good stories I read and say why I think they're good and why I chose the twenty I did. But first a few words about the selection process itself.

Shannon Ravenel, who has been the annual editor for this series since 1977, read 1,811 short stories from 165 different periodicals—a big increase over previous years, she tells me. From her reading she sent 120 for my consideration. As editor, my job was to pick twenty stories for inclusion. But I had liberty in making my selections: I didn't have to take all or, conceivably, any of the 120 that arrived one morning by Express Mail—an event that brought conflicting emotions, as they say, on my part. For one thing, I was writing a story of my own, and I was nearly finished with it. Of course I wanted to go on without interruption. (As usual, when working on a story, this one felt like the best I'd ever write. I was loath to turn my attention from it to the 120 others that waited for some sign from me.) But I was also more than a little interested in knowing just which 120 stories I now had in my possession. I leafed through the stories then and there, and while I didn't read any of them that day, or even the next, I noted the names of the authors, some of whom were friends or acquaintances, others belonging to writers I knew by name only, or by name *and* some prior work. But, happily, most of the stories were by writers I didn't know, writers I'd never heard of—unknowns, as they're called, and as they indeed are to the world at large. The magazines the stories had come from were nearly as diverse and as numerous as the writers. I say *nearly*. Stories from the *New Yorker* predominated, and this is as it should be. The *New Yorker* not only publishes good stories—on occasion wonderful stories—but, by virtue of the fact that they publish every week, fifty-two weeks a year, they bring out more fiction than any other magazine in the country. I took three stories that had first appeared in that magazine. The other magazines I selected from are represented with one story each.

In November 1984, when I was invited to serve as this year's editor, I made plans to begin my own list of "best" come January 1985. And in the course of my reading last year I came across a dozen or so that I liked exceedingly well, stories that excited me enough to put them aside for a later reading. (In the final analysis, being excited by a story is the only acceptable criterion for including it in a collection of this kind, or for publishing the story in a magazine in the first place.) I kept these stories in a folder with the intention of rereading them this January or February, when I knew I would be looking at the other 120. And most often, in 1985, when I read something I liked, something that stirred me enough to put it by for later, I wondered— a stray thought—if I'd see that same story turn up in Shannon Ravenel's choices.

Well, there was some duplication. A few of the stories I'd flagged were among those she sent along. But most of the stories I'd noted were not, for whatever reasons, included among those 120. In any event, I had liberty, as I've said, to take what I wanted from her selections, as well as include what I wanted from my own reading. (I could, I suppose, if I'd been willful, or out of my mind, have selected twenty stories entirely of my own choosing, had none of the stories she sent pleased me.) Now— and this is the last set of figures, just about, that you'll hear on the matter—the breakdown went as follows: of the 120 stories I received in the mail, I selected twelve, all beauties, for inclusion. I found eight other beauties from my own reading.

I'd like to make claims for these twenty as being *the* best stories published in the United States and Canada in 1985. But since I know there will be some people who won't agree with this and since I know, too, that another editor would have chosen differently, with possibly two or three notable exceptions, I'd better say instead that I believe these twenty are among the best stories published in 1985. And I'll go on to say the obvious: under someone else's editorship, this would be a different book with an entirely different feel and composition to it. But this is only as it should be. For no editor puts together a collection such as this without bringing to it his or her own biases and notions of what makes a good story a good story. What works in a short story? What convinces us? Why am I moved, or perturbed, by this story? Why do some stories seem good the first time around but don't hold up on rereading? (I read every story I've included here at least four times; if I found myself still interested, still *excited* by the story after I'd read it a fourth time, I figured it might be a story I wanted to see in the book.)

There were other biases at work. I lean toward realistic, "life-like" characters—that is to say, people—in realistically detailed situations. I'm drawn toward the traditional (some would call it old-fashioned) methods of storytelling: one layer of reality unfolding and giving way to another, perhaps richer layer; the gradual accretion of meaningful detail; dialogue that not only reveals something about character but advances the story. I'm not very interested, finally, in haphazard revelations, attenuated characters, stories where method or technique is all—stories, in short, where nothing much happens, or where what *does* happen merely confirms one's sour view of a world gone out of control.

Too, I distrust the inflated language that some people pile on when they write fiction. I believe in the efficacy of the concrete word, be it noun or verb, as opposed to the abstract or arbitrary or slippery word—or phrase, or sentence. I tried to steer away from stories that, in my terms, didn't seem to be *written* well, stories where the words seemed to slide into one another and blur the meaning. If that happens, if the reader loses his way and his interest, for whatever reason, the story suffers and usually dies.

Abjure carelessness in writing, just as you would in life.

The present volume is not to be seen as a holding action against slipshod writing or poorly conceived and executed stories. But it does, by virtue of its contents, stand squarely against that brand of work. I believe it is safe to say that the day of the campy, or crazy, or trivial, stupidly written account of inconsequential acts that don't count for much in the world has come and gone. And we should all be grateful that it *has* passed on. I deliberately tried to pick stories that rendered, in a more or less straightforward manner, what it's like out there. I wanted the stories I selected to throw some light on what it is that makes us and keeps us, often against great odds, recognizably human.

Short stories, like houses—or cars, for that matter—should be built to last. They should also be pleasing, if not beautiful, to look at, and everything inside them should *work*. A reader searching for "experimental" or "innovative" stories won't find them here. (Along with Flannery O'Connor, I admit to being put off by something that "looks funny" on the page.) Donald Barthelme's "Basil from Her Garden" is the closest thing anyone will find to the experimental or avant-garde. But Barthelme is the exception in this, as he is in all things: his oftentimes "funny-looking" stories are properly inimitable, and this is as good a touchstone as any for picking stories you want to preserve. His stories are also, in some strange way, quite often moving, which is another touchstone.

Since I mentioned Barthelme, I'm brought to remark on a final item in the selection process. On the one hand, you have stories of the first order by some of the best, and best-known, living

American and Canadian writers—which is to say, stories by some of the best writers in the English language. On the other hand, you have a few equally wonderful stories from unknown, or virtually unknown, writers. And the editor of this collection is supposed to pick twenty and no more for his book. A plethora of riches. But what if there are two "equally wonderful" stories, and finally you're making the last selection, and there's room in the book for, say, only one of those? Which story is to be included? Should the interests of the great or well-known authors be looked after over and above the interests of the lesser known? Should extraliterary considerations ever apply? Happily, I can say it never came to that, quite. In the one or two instances when it seemed headed in that direction, I picked a story of quality by an unknown writer. But finally—in every case, really—the stories I selected were, in my estimation, the best stories available, "name" and prior achievements notwithstanding.

Yet looking back, I see it's turned out that many, if not the majority, of my selections fell on younger, lesser-known writers. Jessica Neely, say. Who is she, and how does she come to write a story as beautiful as "Skin Angels"? Look at this irresistible first sentence: "In the beginning of the summer my mother memorized the role of Lady Macbeth four mornings a week and worked the late shift in Geriatrics." Or Ethan Canin. Why have I read only one short story by him before now? What is his fine story "Star Food" doing in a "city magazine" like *Chicago*—a magazine, I'm told, that doesn't plan to publish fiction any longer. And this writer David Michael Kaplan. His name rings a bell, faintly. I think so, anyway. (Maybe I'm thinking of another writer, a poet or a fiction writer who uses three names and who has a name that sounds like David Michael Kaplan.) In any event, "Doe Season" is an amazing piece of work. What a joy, what a great pleasure it was to come across this story and to be able to reprint it in the company of such other fine stories. Or take, for instance, another unknown writer, Mona Simpson, and her superb "Lawns" with *her* irresistible first sentence, "I steal." Take another writer whose work I was not familiar with, Kent Nelson. His wonderful story "Invisible Life" has to do, in part, with the new beginnings some people are always trying to make.

A further admission. I confess to not having read David Lipsky before this. Surely he's published other work. Have I been asleep and missed some stories of his, or maybe even a novel or two? I don't know. I do know I intend to pay attention from now on if I see his name over a short story. "Three Thousand Dollars" is, well, there's nothing in the book quite like it. Which is partly, but only partly, the point I'm trying to make.

James Lee Burke. Here's another writer I didn't know the first thing about. But he's written a story called "The Convict" that I'm proud to have in this collection. There's a remarkable evocation of a particular time and place at work in the story (as there is with each story I picked, which is undoubtedly one of the reasons I was attracted to begin with; a sense of place, location, *setting* being as important to me as it is). But there is the strong personal drama of the young narrator and his father, Will Broussard, who tells the boy, "You have to make choices in this world."

Choices. Conflict. Drama. Consequences. *Narrative.*

Christopher McIlroy. Where in the world did he come from? How does he know so much about alcohol, ranch life, *pastry*, and the dreary existence of the reservation Indians—not to mention the secrets of the human heart?

Grace Paley, of course, is Grace Paley—fundamental reading to short story readers. She has been doing inimitable work for nearly thirty years. I'm pleased to be able to include her splendid story "Telling." And Alice Munro, the distinguished Canadian short story writer. For some years she's been quietly writing some of the best short fiction in the world. "Monsieur les Deux Chapeaux" is a good example.

Are we our brothers' keepers? Before answering, read Munro's story and "The Rich Brother," an unforgettable story by Tobias Wolff. "Where is he? Where is your brother?" is the question Donald, the rich brother, has to answer at the conclusion.

And there's Ann Beattie's scrupulously written and singular story "Janus," which is given entirely in narrative.

Some of the writers whose work I was to one degree or another familiar with before I selected their stories include Joy Williams, Richard Ford, Thomas McGuane, Frank Conroy, Charles Baxter, Amy Hempel, Tess Gallagher—the last an established poet. (Fact: short stories are closer in spirit to poems than they are to novels.)

What do these writers have in common so far as the stories in this anthology are concerned?

For one thing they are, each of them, concerned with writing accurately, that is to say, thoughtfully and carefully, about recognizable men and women and children going about the sometimes ordinary business of living, which is, as we all know, not always an easy matter. And they are writing, in most cases, not just about living and getting by, but about *going on*, sometimes against the odds, sometimes even prevailing against the odds. They are writing, in short, about things that count. What counts? Love, death, dreams, ambition, growing up, coming to terms with your own and other people's limitations. Dramas every one, and dramas played out against a larger canvas than might be apparent on first glance.

Talk about bias! I see now that each of the stories in the book has to do, in one way or another, with family, with other people, with community. "Real people" in the guise of fictional characters inhabit the stories, make decisions for good or evil (mostly good), and reach a turning point, which in some cases is a point of no return. In any case, things will never be the same for them again. The reader will find grown-up men and women in the stories—husbands, wives, fathers and mothers, sons and daughters, lovers of every stripe including one poignant father-daughter relationship (Mona Simpson's "Lawns"). The characters in the stories are people you're likely to be familiar with. If they're not kin, or your immediate neighbors, they live on a nearby street, or else in a neighboring town, or maybe even the next state over.

(I'm talking about a real state now, a place on the map, not just a state of mind.) The Pima Indian reservation in Arizona, for instance. Or else northern California, the Eureka and Mendocino counties area in particular; the high tableland country around Victory, Montana; a small town in northern Vermont. Or else they live in New York, or Berkeley, or Houston, or just outside New Orleans—not such exotic places finally, when all is said and done. The people in the stories are not terribly exotic, either. We've seen them in the cities, towns, and countrysides I've just mentioned, or else on TV, talking to the news commentator, bearing witness, telling how it feels to have survived, to have come through, after the house was carried away in the flood, or the fourth-generation farm has been foreclosed on by the FHA. They are people who've been struck and altered by circumstance and who are about to turn this way or that, depending.

I'm saying the people in the stories are very much like us, in our better—and worse—moments. In "Gossip," Frank Conroy has his narrator say and, more importantly, understand the following: "Everyone was connected in a web . . . pain was part of the web, and yet despite it, people loved one another. That's what you found out when you got older." The people in the stories make decisions, as we all do, that affect the way they will live their lives ever after. In "Communist," Richard Ford's young narrator, Les, says, "I felt the way you feel when you are on a trestle all alone and the train is coming, and you know you have to decide." He does decide, and nothing is the same for him afterward.

The train *is* coming, and we have to decide. Is this true, or is this true? "There're limits to everything, right?" says Glen, the ex-CIA man, the mother's boyfriend in the story, the goose hunter, the "communist."

Right.

In his story, "All My Relations"—a title, incidentally, that could serve as an overall title for this collection—Christopher McIlroy has his rancher, Jack Oldenburg, say these words to

Milton, concerning Milton's self-destructive drinking: "Drawing the line helps you. It's not easy living right. . . . The right way is always plain, though we do our best to obscure it."

In "Today Will Be a Quiet Day," the little gem of a story by Amy Hempel, the dad who is trying to raise his two precocious kids and do the right "dad" things on a rainy Sunday afternoon has this to say about a father's concerns: "You think you're safe . . . but it's thinking you're invisible because you closed your eyes." Hempel also has one of the best and simplest descriptions of happiness I've ever read: "He doubted he would ever feel— not better, but *more* than he did now."

From "Sportsmen," Thomas McGuane's fine story that takes place in the 1950s in a little town on the shore of Lake Erie, we share a strange meal with two teenagers, one of whom has suffered a broken neck in a diving accident:

> I had to feed Jimmy off the point of my Barlow knife, but we ate two big ducks for breakfast and lunch at once. . . .
>
> "Fork me some of that there duck meat," said Jimmy Meade in his Ohio voice. . . .
>
> [Later] I wrap Jimmy's blanket up under his chin.

And in David Lipsky's "Three Thousand Dollars" there is the following little exchange:

> "I just don't want to be a burden."
>
> "You are," she says. "But it's OK. I mean, I'm your mother, and you're supposed to be my burden."

You see what I'm saying? I'm not sure what I'm saying, but I think I know what I'm trying to get at. Somehow, and I feel strongly about this, these twenty stories are connected, they belong together—at least to my way of thinking—and when you read them I hope you'll see what I mean.

Putting together a collection such as this lets the reader in on what it is, in the way of short stories at least, that the editor likes and holds dear to his heart. Which is fine. One of the things I feel strongly about is that while short stories often tell us things we don't know anything about—and this is good, of course—they should also, and maybe more importantly, tell us what *everybody* knows but what nobody is talking about. At least not publicly. Except for the short story writers.

Of the writers included here, Grace Paley is the one who has been at it the longest. Her first book of stories appeared in 1959. Donald Barthelme published his first book five years later, in 1964. Alice Munro, Frank Conroy, Ann Beattie, Thomas McGuane, Joy Williams—they've also been working at this trade for a while. Two writers who have come to prominence recently are Richard Ford and Tobias Wolff. I don't in the least worry about the other, newer writers. Charles Baxter. Amy Hempel. David Lipsky. Jessica Neely. David Michael Kaplan. Tess Gallagher. James Lee Burke. Mona Simpson. Christopher McIlroy. Kent Nelson. Ethan Canin. They're fine writers, each of them, and I have the feeling they're stickers as well. I think they've found the road and will keep to it.

Of course, if this collection was anything like the other *Best American* collections or like *Prize Stories: The O. Henry Awards*, odds are that many of the writers I've included would never be seen or heard from again. (If you don't believe this, go look at the table of contents of any of the major anthologies for the past several years. Open the 1976 *Best American* collection or the 1966 edition and see how many names you recognize.) The more established writers I've included will, I'm sure, go on producing work of distinction. But, as I've said, I don't plan to worry about the newer writers in this book finding their way. I have the feeling they've pretty much done that already.

Writers write, and they write, and they go on writing, in some cases long after wisdom and even common sense have told them to quit. There are always plenty of reasons—good, compelling reasons, too—for quitting, or for not writing very much or very seriously. (Writing is trouble, make no mistake, for everyone involved, and who needs trouble?) But once in a great while lightning strikes, and occasionally it strikes early in the writer's life. Sometimes it comes later, after years of work. And sometimes, most often, of course, it never happens at all. Strangely, it seems, it may hit people whose work you can't abide, an event that, when it occurs, causes you to feel there's no justice whatsoever in the world. (There isn't, more often than not.) It may hit the man or woman who is or was your friend, the one who drank too much, or not at all, who went off with someone's wife, or husband, or sister, after a party you attended together. The young writer who sat in the back of the class and never had anything to say about anything. The dunce, you thought. The writer who couldn't, not in one's wildest imaginings, make anyone's list of top ten possibilities. It happens sometimes. The dark horse. It happens, lightning, or it doesn't happen. (Naturally, it's more fun when it does happen.) But it will never, never happen to those who don't work hard at it and who don't consider the act of writing as very nearly the most important thing in their lives, right up there next to breath, and food, and shelter, and love, and God.

I hope people will read these stories for pleasure and amusement, for solace, courage—for whatever reasons people turn to literature—and will find in them something that will not just show us how we live now (though a writer could do worse than set his sights on this goal), but something else as well: a sense of union maybe, an aesthetic feeling of correctness; nothing less, really, than beauty given form and made visible in the incomparable way only short stories can do. I hope readers will find themselves interested and maybe even *moved* from time to time by what they find herein. Because if short story writing, along with the reading of short stories, doesn't have to do with any of these matters, then what is it we are all doing, what is it we are about, pray tell? And why are we gathered here?

The Unknown Chekhov

After reading "The Lady with the Dog," Maxim Gorky wrote that, in comparison, "work by other writers seems coarse, written with a log instead of a pen. Everything else has stopped seeming truthful."

Ask any thoughtful reader—a student or teacher of literature, a critic or another writer, and you will find agreement: Chekhov is the greatest short story writer who ever lived. There are good reasons why people feel this way. It is not only the immense number of stories he wrote—few, if any, writers have ever done more—it is the awesome frequency with which he produced masterpieces, stories that shrive us as well as delight and move us, that lay bare our emotions in ways only true art can accomplish.

People sometimes speak of Chekhov's "saintliness." Well, he wasn't a saint, as anyone who has read a biography of him can tell you. What he was, in addition to being a great writer, was a consummate artist. He once admonished another writer: "Your laziness stands out between the lines of every story. You don't work on your sentences. You must, you know. That's what makes art."

Chekhov's stories are as wonderful (and necessary) now as when they first appeared. They present, in an extraordinarily precise manner, an unparalleled account of human activity and behavior in his time; and so they are valid for all time. Anyone who reads literature, anyone who believes, as one must, in the transcendent power of art, sooner or later has to read Chekhov. And just now might be a better time than any.

Fiction of Occurrence and Consequence

(WITH TOM JENKS)

The excellent becomes the permanent.

ARISTOTLE

When we began the work of assembling short stories for this book, one of our criteria—unspoken, but there nonetheless—was that a story's narrative interest would be one of the deciding factors in our selections. We also felt that we were not out to be democratic in our selections, or even representative. There was only so much space in the anthology after all, and a limit to the number of stories we could include. Decisions had to be made that were not always easy. But aside from this, however, we were simply not interested in putting before the reader further samples of what some have called "postmodern" or "innovative" fiction, and others have hailed as "the new fiction"—self-reflexive, fabulist, magical realist, as well as all mutations, offshoots, and fringe movements thereof. We were interested in stories that had not only a strong narrative drive, with characters we could respond to as human beings, but stories where the effects of language, situation, and insight were intense and total—short stories which on occasion had the ambition of enlarging our view of ourselves and the world.

A tall order, indeed. But isn't it true that with any great, or even really good, short story (or any other singular work of literary art), just something like this does often happen? We think the thirty-six short stories included herein are ample evidence that it *is* possible for stories to produce such salutary effects; and in our selections we aimed for work that aspired to nothing less—stories of consequence that in some important way bear witness to our own lives. In any event, in light of our sensibilities and according to our criteria, time and again we found ourselves moved and exhilarated as we read and selected the work that follows.

It's our view, and one not held lightly, certainly not defensively, that the best short stories of the past thirty years can stand alongside the best of those of earlier generations—the several generations of writers represented, say, in *Short Story Masterpieces*, that excellent book edited by Robert Penn Warren and Albert Erskine. In its way, this present collection may be seen as a companion volume to that earlier book. Most important in this regard, the bias of this collection, as in the other, is toward the lifelike—that is to say, toward realistically fashioned stories that may even in some cases approximate the outlines of our own lives. Or, if not our own, at least the lives of fellow human beings—grown-up men and women engaged in the ordinary but sometimes remarkable business of living and, like ourselves, in full awareness of their mortality.

In the last thirty years there was, on the part of many writers, a radical turning away from the concerns and techniques of realism—a turning away from the "manners and morals" that Lionel Trilling correctly saw as the best subject matter for fiction. In place of realism, a number of writers—writers of considerable skill and stature, some of them—substituted the surreal and the fantastic. A smaller and less talented group mixed the weird and the far-out with a relentless and sometimes disquieting nihilism. Now it seems that the wheel has rolled forward again and fiction that approximates life—replete with recognizable people, and motive, and plot, and drama—fiction of *occurrence* and *consequence* (the two are inseparable), has reasserted itself with a reading public that has grown tired of the fragmentary, or bizarre. Fiction that asks that the reader give up too much—in some cases deny—what reason, common sense, the emotions, and a sense of right and wrong tell him—is seemingly in retreat these days.

No one should be surprised then at the resurgence, not to say new dominance, of realistic fiction, that most ancient of story-telling modes. This book might be seen as a celebration of, and a tribute to, the lasting power of narrative short fiction. We further feel we have gathered together some of the best stories recently produced by this oldest of literary traditions, work that we like to think has as good a chance as any, and better than most, of withstanding "the tooth of time."

A notable difference between *Short Story Masterpieces* and this book is that fully a third of the thirty-six stories in the earlier collection are by writers from England and Ireland. When we were establishing some ground rules to determine how we planned to go about selecting stories for this anthology, we decided early on to include works by American writers only. There was, we felt, plenty of significant work on this side of the Atlantic from which to choose. We also decided not to include stories by writers who were already included in *Short Story Masterpieces*. Thus, Peter Taylor, Eudora Welty, and John Cheever, some of whose best work was published after 1954 (the year *Short Story Masterpieces* appeared), were reluctantly left out.

In one respect, at least, it would seem that life was simpler in the literary world of the early 1950s: Warren and Erskine didn't have to talk about "postmodernism" or any of the other "isms"—including "realism." They didn't find it necessary to explain the reasons that lay behind their choices, or articulate their taste and methodology. They simply discussed good and great stories—masterpieces, by their definition—and masters of the form. The word *masterpieces* meant something in those days and signaled a benchmark of excellence that most readers (and writers) could agree on. No one had to debate the concept itself, or the wisdom of applying such a term to select examples of serious, imaginative writing. The editors found two dozen stories by American writers, spanning fifty years or more of American life and literary endeavor, and they put these stories alongside a dozen stories by their English and Irish counterparts of roughly the same period. They had their book. We limited ourselves to American writers only, as has been noted, and our selections cover thirty-three years—1953 to 1986, to be exact—surely the most climactic, and traumatic, period in American literary history. Traumatic, in part, because it has been a time during which the currency of narrative fiction has fluctuated wildly and been variously assailed from several quarters. Now is as good a time as any, perhaps, to try to reestablish the term *masterpiece* as it applies to singular stories with a narrative durability, within a discernible *narrative* tradition.

As we considered the merits of each story, we asked ourselves at how deep a level of feeling and insight the writer was operating. How compelling, and coherent, was the writer's *sincerity* (Tolstoy's word, and one of his criteria for excellence) toward his material? Great fiction—good fiction—is, as any serious reader knows, intellectually and emotionally significant. And the best fiction ought to have, for want of a better word, *heft* to it. (The Romans used the word *gravitas* when talking about work of substance.) But whatever one wants to call it (it doesn't even need naming), everyone recognizes it when it declares itself. When a reader finishes a wonderful story and lays it aside, he should have to pause for a minute and collect himself. At this moment, if the writer has succeeded, there ought to be a unity of feeling and understanding. Or, if not a unity, at least a sense that the disparities of a crucial situation have been made available in a new light, and we can go from there. The best fiction, the kind of fiction we're talking about, should bring about this kind of response. It should make such an impression that the work, as Hemingway suggested, becomes a part of the reader's experience. Or else, and we're serious, why should people be asked to read it? Further—why write it? In great fiction (and this *is* true, and we mustn't fool ourselves that it's otherwise), there is always the "shock of recognition" as the human significance of the work is revealed and made manifest. When, in Joyce's words, the soul of the story, its "whatness, leaps to us from the vestment of its appearance."

In his "Introduction to the Works of Guy de Maupassant," Tolstoy wrote that talent is "the capacity to direct intense concentrated attention on the subject . . . a gift of seeing what others have not seen." We think the writers included in these pages have done this, have directed "intense concentration" on their subject, seeing clearly and forcefully what others have not seen. On the other hand, considering some of these stories and their insistence on depicting the "familiar," we think something else is just as often at work—another definition of "talent," perhaps. We'd like to suggest that talent, even genius, is also *the gift of seeing what everyone else has seen, but seeing it more clearly, from all sides*. Art in either case.

The writers in this book have talent, and they have it in abundance. But they have something else as well: they can all tell a good story, and good stories, as everyone knows, have always been in demand. In the words of Sean O'Faolain, a contributor to the earlier book, the stories that follow have "a bright destination." We hope readers will be affected by more than a few of these and will perhaps find occasion to laugh, shudder, marvel—in short, be *moved*, and maybe even a little haunted by some of the lives represented here.

On Contemporary Fiction

I'm interested in the diverse brands of work being done these days in the short story form by a large and increasingly significant number of writers. Many of these writers, some of whom are quite talented and have already produced work of real distinction, have publicly declared they may never write any novels—that is to say, they have little or no interest in writing novels. Should they? they seem to want to add. Who says? Short stories will do nicely, thank you. If money enters into it (and when, at some bottom-line level, does it ever not?), it ought to be said that advances presently paid for collections of short stories are as large, though some would say as modest, as those paid for novels by writers of comparable stature. An author who publishes a collection of stories can expect to sell, generally speaking, roughly the same number of copies as his or her novelist counterpart. And, besides, as anyone can tell you, it's mainly the short story writers who are being talked about these days. Some people would even say it's where the so-called "cutting edge" is to be found.

Has there ever been a time like the present for short story writers? I don't think so. Not to my knowledge, at any rate. It wasn't long ago, as recently as ten years back, say, that a short story writer had a distressingly hard time trying to place a first book. (I'm not saying it's an easy matter now, I'm only saying it was even harder ten years ago.) The commercial publishers, expert in ascertaining what the public wanted, knew there wasn't an audience out there, felt sure there wasn't a readership for short fiction, so they dragged their corporate heels when it came to publishing stories. That unrewarding enterprise was, they figured, better left—like poetry—to a few small independent presses, and an even fewer number of university presses.

A vastly different situation exists today, as everyone knows. Not only are the small presses and university presses continuing to publish collections, the truth in fact is that first collections (or second or third) are now regularly issued in significant numbers by large mainstream publishers—and just as regularly, and prominently, reviewed in the media. Short stories are flourishing.

To my mind, perhaps the best, certainly the most variously interesting and satisfying work, even, just possibly, the work that has the greatest chance of enduring, is being done in the short story. "Minimalism" vs. "Maximalism." Who cares finally what they want to call the stories we write? (And who isn't tired to death by now of that stale debate?) Short stories will continue to attract more attention, and more readers, insofar as the writers of them continue to produce work of genuine interest and durability, work that merits the attention, and approval, of increasingly large numbers of perceptive readers.

The current profusion in the writing and publishing of short stories is, so far as I can see, the most eventful literary phenomenon of our time. It has provided the tired blood of mainstream American letters with something new to think about and even—any day now, I suspect—something to take off from. (Where it's going, of course, is anybody's guess.) But whether or not such a claim can be permitted, the fact is the resurgence of interest in the short story has done nothing less than revitalize the national literature.

On Longer Stories

After reading, over a period of days, the nineteen stories chosen by the editors of this collection, I asked myself, "What am I remembering? What *should* I remember from these stories?" I think this has to be one of the tests of first-rate storytelling: are voice, situation, character and details handled so that they are memorable? And maybe, just maybe, even indelible. It so happens, in this case, that humor also played a large part in lifting the story I chose for first place out of the ranks of some otherwise fine and vigorous work. When I say humor I am not talking about "ha-ha" funny, either, although that sometimes enters in. Who doesn't feel the world brighten when they've had a few good from-the-belly laughs? But what I'm appreciating here is the irreverence of the young which leads to a special kind of lightness and hilarity as soon as it comes into contact with so-called "adult" seriousness.

In "The Expendables," by Antonya Nelson, the story I selected for first place in the collection, we see clearly too what it is that the best young writers have to offer—a kind of pizzazz, the love of undercurrent, of voyeuristic intensity, a bewildered fascination with ritual as it has been undermined in our time, yet sustained, too, in an oddly moving way. We also witness familial relationships from the bottom up.

The narrator of this story, a young man in charge of parking cars at his older sister's second wedding (this time to a mafioso character), is someone trying to get a bead on what it is to grow up and make life-changing decisions. He's aware of lives lived quite differently from those of his household as he observes an extended family of Gypsies who live across the street. On the day of his sister's wedding, there happens to be a funeral going on at the house of the Gypsies. The young man sees a coffin carried in and later he watches the cortege move down the street toward the nearby cemetery. Probably the energy and mystery of these juxtapositions—wedding and funeral, the business world of the young man's hotel-owning father which borders the inexplicable mingling of the Gypsies on their paved-over lawn—go a long way toward adding dimension to a story which is disarmingly frontal in its telling. Add to this the narrator's spontaneity of spirit and his uncanny sense of times past, present and future as they overlap, and you begin to see what's special in this story. There's a strong sense of scene coupled with the interior negotiations of the narrator. This leads to first-rate passages like the following in which the speaker cruises his cousin's Spitfire through the cemetery where he first learned to drive:

> The roadway was one lane and curved through the various sections of dead people the way I imagined the German autobahn cutting through that country. Everywhere we drove, crows flew out in waves before us, as if from the sheer power of the Spitfire's engine. It was dark enough to turn on the headlights, but I liked driving in the dusk. I felt I could actually be headed somewhere instead of only in a long convoluted circle.

Here, without the writer's having laid it on, we are brought as readers to acknowledge the "convoluted circle" as it relates to life-and-death matters at large.

There are things that make the best stories hold up under a second reading, and one of these has to do with the inner circuitry between the actions and the meanings. In the story I've been discussing, one of these moments comes when the narrator notices how "pasty" his sister, the bride, looks. Her ex-husband then tries to reassure her, and, through him, the writer makes a verbal bridge to the neighboring funeral scene: "We'll rouge you before the big event," the ex-husband tells Yvonne. "We'll rouge you good." It's one of the pleasures of reading—picking up on the crossovers in the weave, and the best writers are working, as the jazz pianist Cecil Taylor says, not just horizontally, but vertically too—all of it effortlessly, intuitively.

How compelling is the voice in the story at hand? That's another test of mine. Like most readers, I turn away from a whine or from the overly self-involved. I don't waste time on smart alecks either. There has to be something at stake, something important working itself out from sentence to sentence. But, as with Chekhov's stories, I prefer the light touch in this matter of how consequence is delivered. In "The Expendables" the central dilemma isn't really the sister's wedding to a jerk, but a sense of her disappearance as someone the narrator felt close to in his childhood who "always knew exactly what you meant when you said something." It also more deeply involves the young man's sudden glimpse into his father's defeat so that the son actually takes on the father's hardships for a few desperate moments: "I *was* him, I was my father and his life was happening to me."

Likewise, in the story I've ranked second, "Bringing Joboy Back" by Paul Scott Malone, a strong aspect of the writing is how it draws the reader into a life whose burdens we begin to experience with empathy. The story negotiates a world all too familiar for women and for the black woman of this story in particular, a world in which trust and unspoken loyalties are sacrificed by male characters who use and misuse this female legacy as if it were their birthright. Hardly a new theme or revelation, but Malone makes it poignant by creating in Ruby, the main character, a woman we don't just feel sorry for, but someone in whom we may recognize a striving against odds which intersects our own lives. A richness of texture and an ear for dialogue make this story stay in my mind. It is also encouraging to see a man representing a woman's situation so confidently and truly, just as I felt glad to find a woman assuming fully the voice of the young man in "The Expendables." A writer's ability to shed and assume sexual identities other than his or her own has inevitably to affect what we know and discover.

In my third choice, "Writing in the Dark" by Sandra Dorr, we meet a girl whose father fought in World War II. Through the girl's relationship to her father we experience the terror and uncertainty of war, and the gap between what a child knows and what children are asked, often unreasonably, to endure in the lives of the parents they join. The story is a sensual and suggestive portrait of a family complex which includes the father's mother, Clara, who has been left childlike by mental illness, yet who, in the narrator's imagination, retains an unassailable richness and vitality of being. Here again we sense the importance of young writers who are often moved to reveal extremities, realities at either end of the spectrum—the gratuitously cruel or the phenomenon of innocence preserved against odds.

For short stories, all three of these stories are somewhat long, as are several others chosen by the editors, and it leads me to make a generalization about this collection and perhaps about story writing in America at large in 1988. It seems to me that there must be a healthy ambition afoot to extend the reach of stories past the ten-to-fifteen-page manuscript, perhaps toward a scope which takes advantage of what have been more novelistic strategies. In many of the stories included here we get a sense of characters more fully drawn and placed within a community or an extended family spectrum. The time-sense is less truncated than in the so-called "traditional narrative," and we experience instead a feeling of times intersecting and overlapping for which added length seems a prerequisite. Primary and secondary characters as well as alternate lines of action are more likely to be developed in the longer short story.

When I think of three of Chekhov's longer stories which I admire—"In the Ravine," "The Lady with a Lapdog," and "Ward No. 6" (which is sometimes called a novella)—I realize that the incentive to aspire to the rangier story has been there all along. It's possible that the constraints of the so-called "well-made" poem experienced in the last several years have also begun to be felt in the arena of the short story to some degree. That is, if this collection is any clue to what's developing, young writers may have begun to prefer—or at least to explore—a more elastic territory for the short story, one that also dispenses, to some degree, with conclusiveness, and opts instead for the strengths of what we might call the tapestry of relationship and event. Granted, some unwieldy and patently boring stuff may be one of the hazards of such ambition. But, for the writer with guts and talent, the results can sometimes be invigorating for the whole prospect of the short story. In an essay on writing, I once advised story writers to "Get in, get out. Don't linger." I still think that holds as a pretty fair rule for the short stories I most enjoy reading. But we like to find ourselves surprised and liberated from our so-called "rules of thumb," so it's in such a spirit that I discover myself in a state of curiosity about the emergence of the long short story, a form I've worked with from time to time myself. I see this longer form as an important characteristic of the best stories in this anthology, and they have set me to wondering what is ahead for the short story in its current period of growth.

At the same time I focus on longer stories I realize there is no lack of fine representation here for the short story which holds to around fifteen manuscript pages and under. Ursula Hegi's story, "Saving a Life," about a young woman who dares herself toward the painful undertow of her dead mother's passion for swimming in the river, has a wonderful economy and physical exactness about it. Michael Blaine's "Suits" is a charmer. Its narrator is lively and wistful in a way that makes us remember when we were young, somebody's niece or nephew, son or daughter, and life was more overheard and conjectured about than lived. "In the Garden" by Gordon Jackson brings together elements of mystery with those of the quotidian. It involves a young man's loss of innocence when he realizes the promiscuity of the young girl who has just put the moves on him in the dark during a power outage at the Big Boy where they work.

Each of these stories centers around a loss which is made palpable and moving in a few scenes. In each there is something the narrator passionately desires. In other words, the stories I'm talking about are stories which *had* to be written, and this is already a high recommendation. The editors tell me they have made these choices in order to honor new and emerging writers. I too look at this anthology as a chance to experience new writers who are gaining a purchase on subject matter that belongs particularly to the young—stories which question and reevaluate the legacies of their elders. At the same time, I'm sensing the freedom of the young, that willingness to take chances; and this, truly, is a breath of fresh air for us all, writers and readers alike.

BOOK REVIEWS

Big Fish, Mythical Fish

The big ones always get away. Think of Nick Adams's lunker in "Big Two-Hearted River" and those heartbreakingly big line-busting trout in Norman Maclean's *A River Runs through It*. Think of the archetypal fish story of them all, *Moby Dick*. The big ones get away, they have to, and when they do it brings you to grief. Usually. This new book by William Humphrey is the tale of a man who hooks and then loses the Big One, but who does not come to grief. Instead, he finds his life enlarged and enriched by the experience, and so are we by the telling.

In the best fiction—and William Humphrey has written his fair share—the central character, the hero or heroine, is also the "moved" character, the one to whom something happens in the story that *makes a difference*. Something happens that changes the way that character looks at himself and hence the world. At the end of *My Moby Dick*, when the author tells us he is a changed man, we believe him. We have watched from beginning to end his dealings with a fish the size and appearance of which seem an awesome reminder of God's presence in this world. It is a fish that causes the author to know love, fear, admiration, and a profound sense of the mysteriousness of this life.

It was given to "Bill"—as the author calls himself—and to no other man, to bear witness to a brown trout, "very possibly the record trout"—very possibly the largest brown trout in this world, or the next. I God! (That's an expression some of the east Texas characters in Humphrey's fictions are fond of using

My Moby Dick by William Humphrey. New York: Doubleday, 1978.

when they want to express amazement—or disbelief.)

Just how big is this fish? Where in the wide world is this extraordinary pursuit taking place? How come we've never heard of Bill's fish before now? Something this big should have made the newspapers, not just the record books.

All this took place some years ago, Bill tells us, in the Berkshires, on a little slip of a stream dear to the hearts of Melville and the Hawthornes by the name of Shadow Brook. Bill speculates that the great fish must have washed downstream from a lake called Stockbridge Bowl during a flood. Stockbridge Bowl is near Tanglewood, the summer home of the Boston Symphony Orchestra. Once while Bill is casting for the big fellow he hears the distant thunder of Beethoven's "Ode to Joy" rolling down from Tanglewood. "The music seemed to be coming from light-years off, and so vast was the number of voices in the choir that had been assembled, it sounded like the hosts of heaven: ethereal harmony, music of the spheres." Bill writes like this when he's under the big fish's influence. Listen:

> Out of the water he rose again like a rocket—out and out, and there still was more to him, no end to him. More bird than fish he seemed as he hovered above the water, his spots and spangles patterned like plumage. I half expected to see his sides unfold and spread in flight, as though, like the insects he fed upon, he had undergone metamorphosis and hatched. His gleaming wetness gave an iridescent glaze to him, and as he rose into the sunshine his multitudinous markings sparkled as though he were studded with jewels. . . . Then, giving himself a flip like a pole-vaulter's, down he dove, parting the water with a wallop that rocked the pool to its edges.

Not only is this maybe the largest trout in America, it has the mark of Cain on it, the mark of the misbegotten, the rogue, the wounded. It is blind in one eye. "It was opaque, white, pupilless; it looked like the eye of a baked fish."

So just *how* big? you're still asking. Bill slips up on the fish where it is lying with its blind side next to the bank. He's brought Mrs. Humphrey along to corroborate this part of his tale, clever fellow, and hopes that none of his readers will be unchivalrous enough to doubt her word on the matter. Bill and Mrs. Humphrey get down on their bellies and Bill uses a carpenter's sliding rule. He tells us the fish is a little over forty-two inches in length, that the girth corresponds to his own thigh. He estimates its weight at thirty pounds, maybe larger. I God!

Bill is in thrall to this fish but is determined to kill it nevertheless, this fish that fills him with both pity and terror. (You don't *catch* a fish this size, you *kill* it.) He is a patient man with nothing very much else to do, it seems, and so he spends mornings, afternoons, and evenings watching the fish and observing its habits:

> I logged his comings and goings like an assassin establishing his victim's routine. He came always to the same feeding station, an eddy at the tail of the pool where a tiny feeder stream trickled in, like an old regular of a restaurant to the table reserved for him. . . . When I had fixed the hours at which he issued from his lair beneath the bridge, then I was there, prone on the bank beside his spot, waiting for him to come to breakfast at dawn, to dinner at dusk.

There is a boy who comes every day to the creek to watch Bill fruitlessly cast and cast his fly. He thinks Bill's dumb. He tells him so. They have little conversations about the fish and, by extension, the world at large. The boy is there on that fateful last day of the season (now is when you want to hear the music from Tanglewood) when Bill hooks into the Big One, Old Cyclops himself. The boy silently watches the brief, uneven contest, then, shaken, cries out angrily: "You had him and you let him get away!"

"The literature of angling falls into two genres," Humphrey writes, "the instructional and the devotional. The former is

written by fishermen who write, the latter by writers who fish."
This is a devotional book, filled with a loving and rare regard
for the mysteries of this world, and the other. It is a fine companion book to Humphrey's earlier work on salmon fishing, *The
Spawning Run*.

Barthelme's Inhuman Comedies

I've been an admirer of Donald Barthelme's stories since college, when I read his first collection, *Come Back, Dr. Caligari*. Everyone I knew at that time talked about Donald Barthelme, and for a while everyone tried to write like him. Donald Barthelme was our man, man! Some of those people are still trying to write stories like his, and with singular lack of success. His chief imitators were then, and are still, students of writing at colleges and universities across the country. The influence of Barthelme's stories has been considerable, but not always salutary, on young and not-so-young writers.

The imitations—no other word will do—are easy to recognize. Once in a while you see them in print somewhere, but most often you see them handed in in depressing numbers at writing workshop classes around the country where Barthelme stories are often studied and held up as models for young short story writers.

In these short fictions à la Barthelme, there is, almost without exception, a serious lack of interest and concern on the part of the author for his characters. The characters are dropped into silly situations where they are treated by their creators with the most extreme irony, or even downright contempt. They are never to be found in situations that might reveal them as characters with more or less normal human reactions. To allow the characters to express any emotion, unless it can be ridiculed, is unthinkable. It is impossible for the characters even to see, much less accept, responsibility for their actions. There is a feeling that anything

Great Days by Donald Barthelme. New York: Farrar, Straus & Giroux, 1979.

goes in the stories, that is, nothing in the story has to make sense, or has any more pertinence, value, or weight than anything else. This world is on the skids, man, so everything is relative, you know. Usually, the characters have no last names, often (as with the stories in *Great Days*) no first names either. The authors are determined to write fiction free from the responsibility of making any sense. They take it as given that there is no sense whatsoever to be made of this world, and so they are free to have their characters speak and act without any of the normal restraints of moral complication and consequence. In a word, there is absolutely no value to anything.

The imitators have picked up everything easy and obvious from Barthelme but they don't have his great talent, his genius for finding startling, original ways to say things about love and loss, triumph and despair. Disappointment and heartbreak are rife in the land, God knows, but if a writer writes about such matters and populates his fiction with whining, self-pitying creatures eaten up with unspecified angst, bitterness, and complaint, well, it isn't enough. Barthelme *is* different. His characters are never contemptible or mean-spirited. He can move you, and often make you laugh at the same time, can stir that emotion Camus called simply "fellow feeling"—notwithstanding the fact that the stories Barthelme writes are often the strangest-looking vehicles ever to come down the road. *Come Back, Dr. Caligari* was followed in 1967 by the little experimental novel *Snow White*. Then, in 1968, the strange and wonderful collection *Unspeakable Practices, Unnatural Acts*; *City Life*, more stories, in 1970. *Sadness*, another fine collection, appeared in 1972. *The Dead Father*, a novel, was published in 1975; *Amateurs*, yet another book of stories, in 1976. With these original works, Barthelme made a place for himself in the national literature and in so doing did honor to the practice of short story writing.

So I'm sorry to say I don't like his new book of stories, *Great Days*. The book isn't a profound disappointment, but it is a disappointment nevertheless. *Great Days* isn't going to cause one to lose regard for Barthelme, or detract from his considerable accomplishments, but it isn't going to help him along either. There is not a story in the collection of sixteen that has anywhere near the power, the complexity, the resonance of stories from his earlier collections, stories such as "The Indian Uprising," "The Balloon," "Robert Kennedy Saved from Drowning," "See the Moon?", "The Sandman," "Critique de la Vie Quotidienne," "Brain Damage," "Sentence," "Views of My Father Weeping." Seven of the stories in *Great Days* are "dialogues" between nameless pairs of male or female characters (although the gender is not always clear), disembodied voices stripped of everything save the willingness to babble.

From time to time Barthelme does engage your intellectual, literary fancy, and there are some funny, kooky one-liners here, but there are for a fact no innovative breakthroughs in this book, and he does not write about anything close or dear to the human heart. This last is the most serious drawback in the collection. The absence of anything remotely resembling the human in these stories is troubling. In this book he seems to be moving farther and farther away from what most concerns us, or what, I suggest, should concern us the most.

The two most interesting pieces in the book are not in the dialogue form. One is "The King of Jazz," starring Hokie Mokie and the challenger for the title, Hideo Yamaguchi, "the top trombone man in all of Japan." The other is a hilarious tale called "The Death of Edward Lear," a comic deathbed scene in which the nineteenth-century nonsense-verse writer has sent out invitations to witness his demise at "2:20 A.M., San Remo, the 29th of May, 1888."

In too many of the other stories the author is, I hate to say it, sounding like Donald Barthelme imitating Donald Barthelme. The technical virtuosity and the inventiveness are there, but most of the inventions seem strained this time around and bear little resemblance or relation to anything like "fellow feeling" and so, ultimately, are uninteresting in the extreme.

Rousing Tales

Jim Harrison is the author of three novels—*Wolf, A Good Day to Die,* and *Farmer*—as well as several distinguished books of poetry. *Farmer,* the best of his novels, is a fine, realistic study of a solitary man who hunts and fishes the good country of northern Michigan, earns a living off the land he works, has a love affair with a schoolteacher, reads a few good books, is exceptional only in that he is a decent, interesting man of some complexity—a man Harrison obviously feels close to and cares about. It's an honest book, scrupulously written. *Legends of the Fall* is a collection of three short novels—more properly, novellas—and appears four years after *Farmer.* It is Harrison at the height of his powers, and a book worth reading.

The best of these three works is a beautifully rendered story of just over ninety pages called "The Man Who Gave Up His Name." It's an extraordinary piece of writing, covering what might seem all-too-familiar territory: a change of life for a man in his early forties. But I think this novella can stand with the best examples the form has to offer—novellas by Conrad, Chekhov, Mann, James, Melville, Lawrence, and Isak Dinesen.

Nordstrom is the hero of "The Man Who Gave Up His Name." (All of the leading roles in these novellas are played by *heroes*—no other word will do. By the same token the bad guys *are* bad.) Nordstrom is a troubleshooting corporate executive in Los Angeles with roots, like all of Harrison's heroes, in rural

Legends of the Fall by Jim Harrison. New York: Delacorte Press/Seymour Lawrence, 1979.

areas of the Midwest. He gives it all up, career and family, and moves to the East Coast to take up a different kind of life—going to cooking school, for one thing. He has begun listening alone at night to stereo music as varied as Merle Haggard, Joplin's *Pearl*, the Beach Boys, Stravinsky's *The Rite of Spring*, Otis Redding, and The Grateful Dead. The life he gives up is one that he didn't so much lose faith in as one which he totally lost interest with. Like Tolstoy's Ivan Ilyich, he is overcome with the feeling of "What if what I've been doing all my life has been totally wrong?" Nordstrom has a wife, Laura, a splendidly interesting woman in her own right who is involved in film production, and a daughter, Sonia, a student at Sarah Lawrence. During Sonia's engagement party in New York City, which Nordstrom attends, he has a seemingly harmless altercation, after a few lines of cocaine, with a sinister trio: a black pimp and shake-down man named Slats, his white girlfriend Sarah, and their pal, a tough named Berto. After the extortion attempt, Nordstrom throws Berto from a hotel room window. Then he heads for the Florida Keys and a six-day-a-week job as fry cook for a little diner. He spends his mornings fishing for tarpon, and late at night after work he dances alone to his transistor radio. I don't know how to put this without sounding corny, but Nordstrom has found his measure of happiness on this earth.

I can't begin to do justice to the nuances of character and honest complexities of plot in this work. The writing is precise and careful. Ezra Pound may or may not be right in his assertion that fundamental accuracy of statement is the one sole morality of writing. John Gardner would likely disagree, but I think Gardner, too, would approve this story, not only for the beauty and accuracy of its language, its minute description of felt life, but for its wisdom and the lives it illuminates—including our own.

Each of these novellas is concerned with those basics of old-fashioned storytelling: plot, character, and action. In "Revenge," Cochran, left for dead off a backcountry road in northern

Mexico, is found and nursed back to health by a medical missionary named Diller. As Cochran slowly recovers his health, we are shown how he got himself into this fix: it was over a woman, another man's wife. Tibey (means "shark") Baldassaro Mendez is a rich, ruthless businessman who made his first million in narcotics and prostitution. Cochran, a tennis pal, falls in love with Tibey's wife, the beautiful, cultured Miryea—they meet in Tibey's library over a leather-bound copy of García Lorca's poetry. After several trysts in Cochran's apartment in Tucson, Cochran and Miryea try to go away for a few days to Cochran's cabin in Mexico, but they are trailed by Tibey and some of his henchmen. Cochran is beaten nearly to death, his car and cabin burned, and then "Tibey takes a razor from his pocket and deftly cuts an incision across Miryea's lips, the ancient revenge for a wayward girl." Now, several months later, Cochran's twofold quest begins: to have his revenge on Tibey, and to locate Miryea.

Tibey has put her into the meanest whorehouse in Durango, Mexico, where she is forcibly administered heroin. But she recovers enough to stab a man and is then moved to a secret asylum for "terminally insane women and girls." Several violent deaths later, part of a plot that often strains at the seams, Tibey and Cochran patch things up long enough to proceed to the asylum where Miryea is dying from, we can only assume, a broken heart.

Medical science cannot save her now. In the most primitive scene of a most primitive story, Cochran places a coyote tooth necklace around the dying woman's neck. Then: "she sang the song he knew so well in a throaty voice that only faintly surpassed the summer droning of a cicada. It was her death song and she passed from life seeing him sitting there as her soul billowed softly outward like a cloud parting. It began to rain and a bird in the tree above them crooned as if he were the soul of some Mayan trying to struggle his way back earthward."

Miryea then expires—no other word for it. Despite this

embarrassment, the epilogue that follows this scene is curiously moving, and the story itself is eminently worth your time.

The title story, "Legends of the Fall," is a virtuoso piece ranging in time back to the 1870s and touching down as recently as 1977. The story begins in Montana in October 1914, with three young brothers on their way to volunteer in the Canadian Army so they can fight in the Great War. The brothers are Alfred, the eldest, who will later become a U.S. senator from Montana; Tristan, the middle brother, who is the hero of this narrative and who, like Ahab, will curse God and so bring down upon his life the gravest kind of misfortunes; and Samuel, at eighteen the youngest, and a student at Harvard. Their father is William Ludlow, a wealthy rancher and retired cavalry officer who has seen duty under Custer. Here is a description of Custer from a work rich with description of man and nature: "Ludlow remembered Custer making an erratic speech to the troops with his long blond locks punctuated with clinging grasshoppers." The mother of these young men is an eastern socialite who spends most of each year going to concerts and taking lovers.

Samuel is killed in France (his heart is removed from the body by Tristan, encased in paraffin, and shipped back to Montana); Alfred is severely wounded; and Tristan goes crazy and begins to take German scalps. Later, after his return home, Tristan marries his Boston cousin, Susannah, and takes her out to the ranch. But, restless, he soon pulls up stakes and leaves for a ten-year stint at adventuring that takes him to Africa and South America on his own sailing vessel. He returns to Montana to find that his wife has divorced him and married Alfred. But Susannah, too, has gone crazy and is later committed and dies in an institution. Tristan marries a half-breed, and they have children and a few years of grace. But this happiness is shattered when his wife is accidentally killed by a Prohibition agent. (You don't curse God and get off scot-free.)

Tristan goes mad again for a while, then gets into whiskey-running in a big way. There are numerous bloody encounters with the vicious "Irish Gang" of San Francisco, including a murderous chase to Saratoga Springs, New York. The story ends with more violence back on the ranch in Montana, with the bad guys really getting it.

Despite a breakneck, mile-a-minute plot, this *is* a good tale—"rousing" is a word they used to use. Jim Harrison is good, and with this book he does honor to the old art of storytelling.

Bluebird Mornings, Storm Warnings

"Whole thing works on gravity. Heavy falls and the light floats away," says a wheat rancher, explaining how a threshing machine operates in "The Van Gogh Field," the title story in this startlingly original collection by William Kittredge, a book which won the 1979 St. Lawrence Award for Fiction. *Heavy falls and the light floats away*. And, a little later on in the same story: "What you do matters. What you do, right or wrong, has consequences, brother." I have to think this is true in life as well as in the best fiction. *What you do matters*. Listen up: these are wonderfully rendered stories about people and their actions, and the consequences of those actions. It is about a special and particular place in this country that has not had many writers speaking for it. I think of Wallace Stegner, Mary Beal, H. L. Davis, Walter Van Tilburg Clark. To this group of writers we can now add William Kittredge.

The West is a far country, indeed, but this is not the West as in West Coast, cities like San Francisco, Seattle, Portland, Vancouver; these cities, for all the influence they exert on the lives of Kittredge's people, may as well be on the European mainland. The West that figures in these stories runs from Red Bluff in north central California, through eastern Oregon into Idaho, Montana, and Wyoming. Drawing from the small towns and glens, tourist courts and spent farms, Kittredge presents us with a gallery of characters who are light-years away from the

The Van Gogh Field by William Kittredge. Columbia: University of Missouri Press, 1978.

American Dream, characters whose high hopes have broken down on them and gotten left behind like old, abandoned combines.

Kittredge knows the weather up there in his country, inside and outside. And the barometer is dropping fast; a man could get hurt, a man could get killed. They die, some of the people in these stories, of alcohol poisoning; or they get kicked to death by a horse, or crushed by a combine, or they burn to death in a car, drunk and sleeping beside the highway. Or else they're slaughtered by a strange kid "gone rotten" as in the novella "The Soap Bear," a brilliant, virtuoso piece of writing that puts me in mind of William Gass's "The Pedersen Kid" for its demonic intensity and its vivid depiction of a place. Listen to what follows. How would you like to have this one in your house, with the drop on you, after he's already committed murder five times over?

> "Your feet get cold," he said, "you put on your hat. There's a rule. Your head is like a refrigerator, so you have to turn it off to get your fingers and toes warm. So you put on your hat. . . ."
> He got up and went into the hallway where his lime-yellow stocking cap was stuffed into the pocket of his sheepskin coat, and pulled the cap down over his wet hair. "Now," he said, "I don't feel no pain, because my head is covered.
> "You got to do lots of things this way," he said, "with your head turned off."

Here are some of the places that figure in these stories: Vacaville, Nyall, Arlington, Horn Creek, Black Flat, Frenchglen, Mary's River, Corvallis, Prineville, Manteca, Davanero, Bakersfield, Shafter, Salem, Yakima, Paiute Creek, Klamath Falls, Tracy, Walla Walla, Donan, Red Bluff, McDermitt, Denio, Walker Lake, Bitterroot, Cody, Elk River, Clark Fork, Lompoc, Colorado Springs.

Some names: Clyman Teal, Robert Onnter, Jules Russel, Ambrose Vega, Davy Horse (so called "after his right leg was crushed against a rock-solid juniper gatepost by a stampeding green colt he tried to ride one Sunday afternoon when he was drunk, showing off for women"), Ben Alton, Corrie Alton, Steffanie Rudd, Jerome Bedderly, Oralie York, Red Yount, Lonnie, Cleve, Big Jimmy and "his running pal, Clarence Dunes," Virgil and Mac Banta, Sheriff Shirley Holland, his wife, Doris, Billy Kumar who is "dumber than rocks," Marly Prester, Amos Frantz who "kept a whore from Butte whose name was Annie," Dora and Slipper Count.

There's poetry in the naming of these places and people, but there is little poetry in the lives of the characters who populate Kittredge's stories. Or maybe there was a little, once, in the beginning, but then something happened—it was worked out of you, or you drank too much, too long, and it left you; and now you're worse off than ever because you still have to go through the motions, even though you know it's for nothing now, a senseless reminder of better days. Now, no matter what, even if your brother is being buried that day, killed in a barroom brawl, you still have to go out and feed the stock. If you don't feed them, they won't be fed. You have to do it. There are obligations. And maybe this same brother, you've just found out, is the father of the child your wife is carrying. This is going to take some figuring, adjustments are going to have to be made. This is from "Thirty-Four Seasons of Winter," one of the finest stories in the book.

If the characters in these stories listen to music, it's music by Waylon Jennings, Roger Miller, Loretta Lynn, Tom T. Hall singing "Spokane Motel Blues," Merle Haggard, Linda Ronstadt and "Party Doll," church music like "Rock of Ages" and "Nearer My God to Thee." If they read anything at all, they read the *Sporting News*. Besides, where most of them live, the big city newspapers, the papers from Seattle or Spokane or Portland or San Francisco, they're a day late getting there and so the gloomy horoscopes are a confirmation rather than a prediction.

One of the characters in "The Man Who Loved Buzzards" has had dreams that carry over from night to night. She lives with the certainty that if she can raise the money to get a better house and move away, the dreams will stop. She doesn't, and they don't, of course.

There's God's plenty of "dis-ease" in these stories, a phrase Camus used to describe a certain terrible kind of domesticity. Listen to this middle-aged man, a childless man into his twentieth year of marriage:

> How do you go to your own house when something has gone bad on the inside, when it doesn't seem like your place to live anymore, when you almost cannot recall living there although it was the place where you mostly ate and slept for all your grown-up life? Try to remember two or three things about living there. Try to remember cooking one meal. . . . Sometimes there is no choice but to walk into your own house. . . . And then there is a morning you walk in and take a look in your own house, like any traveler.

> "When I grew up," the kid said, "you knew my father, his name was Mac Banta down there in the Bitterroot."
> "I never knew anybody named Banta," Holland said.
> "Well, he was there anyway," the kid said, "and there was those spring mornings with the geese flying north and I would stand out on the lawn with the sun just coming up and the fence painted white around my mother's roses, and it would be what my father called a bluebird morning. . . . My sister would be there, and my mother and my father, and the birds playing in the lilac. Comes down to a world of hurt was what my father would say, and he would laugh because nothing could hurt you on those bluebird mornings."

Every great or even every really good writer makes the world over according to his own lights. Garp is right—John Irving is right. This area of the world, this part of our country, this scrupulously observed vision, this is the world according to Kittredge; and he writes of this land and its inhabitants with pity and terror, and, it must be said, love. These powerful stories are troubling and unforgettable. I urge your attention to them.

A Gifted Novelist at the Top of His Game

The publicity release for this book would remind us that Vance Bourjaily is one of America's major writers. I don't think this claim can be taken lightly. The proof of the matter lies in this compelling and relentlessly authentic work of art, *A Game Men Play*. It's his finest novel since *The Violated*, which up to now has been his best, and best-known, work.

A Game Men Play is a big book and one charged with acts of violence and dismay: you couldn't begin to count all the murders and "re-locations," the double and double-double dealings that occur in its pages. But, surprisingly, it is also—and this is more to our purpose—a long and profound, sometimes pastoral meditation on the human condition.

The settings are as various as any you'd want to conjure: the deck and cabin life of a Norwegian freighter on a voyage from San Francisco to Wellington, New Zealand; Caracas, Venezuela; St. Thomas in the Virgin Islands; an Argentinean horse ranch; the Greek islands of Crete and Corfu; Cairo and Alexandria; the Russian steppes and Vladivostok; Berlin during the Cold War; Thailand; Santiago, Chile; Honolulu; Montevideo, Uruguay; Yugoslavia during the German occupation; New Orleans; the high life and low of New York in the late 1970s. In many of these places we are witness to scrupulous renderings of violent acts, part of the vicious game some men play.

The novel is Conradian in its entanglement of motive and its intricacy of plot. It is filled with lore of all sorts: the raising,

A Game Men Play by Vance Bourjaily. New York: Dial Press, 1980.

training, and racing of horses; soldiering, mostly behind-the-lines guerrilla stuff, covert CIA activity; and as complete an inside look at the vile pursuits of terrorism as you'd ever want. But since I can only touch on the story's main lines, which will not begin to tell you what the novel is *about*, I want to say that it has to do with the not insignificant matters of courage, loyalty, love, friendship, danger, and self-reliance, and a man's lifetime journey of self-discovery.

The hero of this remarkable novel—and he *is* a hero, praise be—is a man of integrity and deep complexity; he has character, in the oldest and truest sense of that word. His name is C. K. "Chink" Peters (nicknamed because of the slightly slanted eyes he inherited from his mother, a Mongolian), and he is far and away Bourjaily's best fictional creation to date.

During World War II, Peters gained prominence as a young OSS agent tagged "Der Fleischwolf" (The Meat Grinder), and after the war found himself in the nascent CIA—the Agency, as it's called. Peters has written a small book on guerrilla warfare, and the book as well as its author have come to assume some fame in underground circles, mainly a radical IRA group whose members are fanatical but suave terrorists with European and Middle Eastern connections. Now forty-nine and free from involvement either domestic or Agency-related, Peters is living in a rooming house in San Francisco when the novel opens. He is about to sail for Wellington with a group of horses destined for a New Zealand breeder when he sees a television news account of the murders of Mary and Wendy Diefenbach in their New York apartment. He has not seen these girls since their childhood when their father, his friend, neighbor, and wartime commanding officer, Walden Diefenbach, took away Peters's wife. Diefenbach is now a UN ambassador-at-large, often mentioned as a potential secretary of state. Peters sends a telegram asking if there's anything he can do, waits, then goes ahead and sails.

Peters spends a lot of time talking to his horses, believe it, on the way to New Zealand; and so, in long flashbacks, we have the story of his life. Moving from past to present, this way and that, using the freighter as both metaphor for a journey and real oceangoing vessel, we follow him through prep school, where he goes on a wrestling scholarship but studies foreign languages, then enlistment in the military, army and Agency service. He later attends Yale and takes a degree in German medieval history. Happily married, he settles on the eastern seaboard to breed and race horses with Diefenbach as his country squire neighbor. This Diefenbach is a Machiavellian character with plenty of charm and intelligence who runs up against the IRA, whose agents set out to bring him down. Through a dreadful foul-up, his daughters become the victims instead.

In New Zealand, a cable from Diefenbach reaches Peters asking if he can come to New York and lend a hand in this horrible affair. What happens when Peters moves into the murdered girls' New York apartment takes up the second half of the book.

I've seldom read a novel that's offered up such rigorous and lasting pleasure. The people who populate this fine book will strike you not so much as characters but rather as common and uncommon men and women going about their lives, doing those things that may damn them forever—or that could raise them to something they might otherwise have not been capable of in this imperfect world, or in the hands of a lesser novelist.

Of course I won't give you the novel's ending. I can tell you that the plot turns, and then turns, and turns again. Until the last pages it has you, as they used to say, on the edge of your seat. For me, a discussion of the book brings to mind F. Scott Fitzgerald's invocation: "Draw your chair up close to the edge of the precipice and I'll tell you a story."

Vance Bourjaily is a writer of great gifts and originality, hard at work, as always, and in the fullness of his powers.

Fiction That Throws Light on Blackness

In a time when so much fiction is being written and published that doesn't seem to count for much, it should be said at once that this is a book about something—and something that matters. It has to do with the nature and meaning of friendship, love, obligation, responsibility, and behavior. Big concerns. But this is a big book, and one that throws light on—I'll say it once and without embarrassment—the human condition. It gives more than a passing glance at what Melville called "the blackness of darkness," but it helps hold back that darkness a little. It asks, early on and with all seriousness, How should a man act? And it's to his lasting credit that Yount has the intelligence and insight and very great literary skill to show us, page by page, the lives of the people who inhabit this fine book as they are revealed in all their glory and imperfection.

Fiction that counts is about people. Does this need saying? Maybe. Anyway, fiction is not, as some writers believe, the ascendance of technique over content. These days we also seem to be long on novels and short stories in which people are reduced to nameless or otherwise easily forgettable "characters," hapless creatures who have nothing much to do in this life or, even worse, go about doing unthinking and uncaring things to their own kind. In fiction that matters the significance of the action inside the story translates to the lives of people outside the story. Do we need to remind ourselves of this? In the best novels and short stories, goodness is recognized as such. Loyalty,

Hardcastle by John Yount. New York: Richard Marek, 1980.

love, fortitude, courage, integrity may not always be rewarded, but they are recognized as good or noble actions or qualities; and evil or base or simply stupid behavior is seen and held up for what it is: evil, base, or stupid behavior. There *are* a few absolutes in this life, some verities, if you will, and we would do well not to forget them.

Except for a frame of a few pages at the beginning and again at the end of the book—pages in which an old man appears with his grandchildren in Elkin, Kentucky, in the summer of 1979—the action of the novel takes place during the summer and fall of 1931 in that same Kentucky hill town. The hero is nineteen-year-old Bill Music, who has left his parents' worn-out farm in Shulls Mills, Virginia, to go to Chicago for a ninety-day course at Coin Electric. He had hoped to better his lot and earn a living as an electrician. But when he finds himself scavenging out of garbage cans because there are no jobs, he decides to give up his dream and head for home. Hunger forces him to leave the train just outside of Elkin. A mine guard named Regus Bone mistakes him for a "Communist" labor organizer, puts a gun in his face, and wants to place him under arrest. But Music is tired and hungry, and Bone, feeling sympathy, lets him recuperate a few days with him and his mother, Ella Bone. Music and Bone become friendly, and Music decides to hire on as a mine guard himself at the princely sum of three dollars a day.

It's dangerous work being a mine guard. Mine guards carry guns, as do some of the miners. Music and Bone pull their shift together and look after one another. On their days off from work they build a pigpen, go coon hunting, build and set rabbit traps, chop down a tree filled with bees and honey. Gradually, a deep friendship develops between the two men. Meanwhile, Music has fallen in love with a young mother and widow named Merlee. After a few months, Music becomes tired and ashamed of being a mine guard. Bone has also become disillusioned. They turn in their badges. But there comes, as we knew it must, the inevitable and fatal conflict with the Hardcastle Mining Company goons.

Bone is ambushed and killed. Music survives his friend. "And although he saw it come, the news of Regus's death didn't seem to reach all the areas of his understanding for months or even years afterward, so that it took a very long time to come to the end of his grief."

Music will marry Merlee and stay in Elkin to build a life. He doesn't go home again. Besides, "He suspects home is simply not a place at all, but a time, and when it's gone, it's gone forever."

Lionel Trilling has said that a great book reads us. Somewhere in my twenties I read this and pondered its meaning. What exactly was the man saying? It sounded wise, learned, insightful, and I wanted to be those things. When I finished reading *Hardcastle*, this remarkably generous but unsparing novel, I was reminded of Trilling's words and I thought, So this is what he was talking about. Yes. How true. This is what he meant, yes.

Brautigan Serves Werewolf Berries
and Cat Cantaloupe

The prose pieces that make up this uneven collection of prose pieces—it is not a "novel" by any definition of that word—range in length from a few lines to several pages. They are set in and around Livingston, Montana; Tokyo; and San Francisco. There is no ordering principle at work in the book; any selection could go anywhere and it wouldn't make the slightest difference. I think the first, and longest, piece is the best. It's called "The Overland Journey of Joseph Francl and the Eternal Sleep of His Wife Antonia in Crete, Nebraska." The other pieces have such titles as "Skylab at the Graves of Abbott and Costello," "Five Ice-Cream Cones Running in Tokyo," "Montana Traffic Spell," "A San Francisco Snake Story," "Werewolf Raspberries," "A Study in Thyme and Funeral Parlors," "Two Montana Humidifiers," "What Are You Going to Do with 390 Photographs of Christmas Trees?", "Cat Cantaloupe," "Chicken Fable," "Light On at the Tastee-Freez." You get an idea.

There are 131 of these, and some of them are really good, and they're like little astonishments going off in your hands. Some are so-so, take them or leave them. Others—I think too many—are just filling up space. These last, the space filler-uppers, make you wonder. I mean you want to ask, "Is there an editor in the house?" Isn't there someone around who loves this author more than anything, someone he loves and trusts in return, who could sit down with him and tell him what's good, even wonderful, in this farrago of bits and pieces, and what is lightweight, plain

The Tokyo-Montana Express by Richard Brautigan. New York: Delacorte Press/Seymour Lawrence, 1980.

silly stuff and better left unsaid, or in the notebooks?

Still wishing; one wishes there had been more to choose from. One wishes there had been 240 of these little things—or 390, like the number of Christmas tree photos; and then (still wishing) that the author had sat down with this good friend-trusted editor, and they had gone over all the pieces, looking at each piece as you would look at a poem, and looking at how many pieces stack up to make a *book*. One wishes that this imaginary editor-friend had been stern with the author now and again. "Look here, Richard! This one is just cutesy pie. And this one is finger exercise, laundry list jotting stuff. You want a good book? Keep that one out. But this one, now, this one's a keeper." And out of the 240, or 390, or even these original 131, maybe 90 or 100 had gone into the collection. It could have been a real book then, one filled with amazements and zingers. Instead, we have oh so many little reveries and gentle laid-back sweet notions that the author has been blessed with and saved up to share with us. But they don't need sharing, all of them.

Maybe none of this matters to the author. Maybe it's simply that we are either tuned into his wavelength, or we are not. If we're not, well, I suppose it could be said *tough luck*, so lump it. Or if our heads are where Brautigan's head is at, then perhaps everything and anything goes. What matter? But I have to believe—I don't *have* to believe anything; it's just a feeling I have—that Brautigan wants to write the very best he can, and write for grown-up men and women as well as just the easy-to-please younger set.

So you can take this book or leave it. It won't help you along any in this life, or hurt you, to read it. It won't change the way you look at things, or people, or make a dent of any size in your emotional life. It's gentle on the mind. It's 258 pages of reverie and impression, and some sparkly gleamings, of things past and present having to do with the author's life on "this planet Earth."

It's a book by Richard Brautigan called *The Tokyo-Montana Express*. It's not his best book by a long shot. But he must know this.

McGuane Goes After Big Game

Most of these essays are very good and a few are simply wonderful. Each has to do in some way with certain outdoor pursuits, chiefly fishing. In its highly personal depiction of particular landscapes, *An Outside Chance* belongs in the company of William Humphrey's *The Spawning Run* and *My Moby Dick*, Vance Bourjaily's *The Unnatural Enemy*, Norman Maclean's *A River Runs through It*, even Hemingway's *Green Hills of Africa*. For the record, let's call it a work of literature.

There are eighteen essays in the collection. They began to appear back in 1969, and they appeared off and on in magazines through the 1970s. They are, if you're interested, a patchy record of McGuane's life and interests this past decade while he was writing the books that established him as one of our better novelists. In an early piece called "Me and My Bike and Why," McGuane is living in California and writing about the vicissitudes of falling in love with and then buying a motorcycle. There is an affectionate give-and-take going on with his wife.

In "My Meadow Lark," set some years later in Key West, the author is suffering from "boat sickness"—a terrific yearning for a specially made craft called a Meadow Lark. The wife is still on the scene, still affectionate, and joined now by young Tom Jr. Still later, in a fine piece of work called "Roping, from A to B," we find the author participating in a jackpot roping contest out in Gardiner, Montana. Tom Jr. is there in the grandstand watching

An Outside Chance: Essays on Sport by Thomas McGuane. New York: Farrar, Straus & Giroux, 1980.

his father perform. Tom Jr.'s mother is there as well, but she has a new husband. Tom Sr. has a friend in the audience, a girl "up from Alabama."

"I don't know what this kind of thing indicates beyond the necessary, ecstatic resignation to the moment," McGuane says in another context.

Most of the essays detail various aspects of tarpon fishing, bone fishing, fishing for mutton snapper, permit fishing (permit being a mysterious hard-to-catch saltwater fish), rainbow and cutthroat trout fishing, and fishing for striped bass. One of the things I'll take away from the book is the image of the author standing on a rocky point facing the Atlantic Ocean and trying to land a striped bass in the dark while holding a flashlight in his mouth. There is an essay about a hunting dog named Molly, and there is another that has something to do with grouse and pheasant and waterfowl shooting; and there is "The Heart of the Game," maybe the centerpiece of the book—about deer and antelope hunting, meditation and metaphysics. Other essays include one about a horse named Chink's Benjibaby; motorcycle racing; being a kid and hunting for lost golf balls to sell; the Golden Gate Angling and Casting Club in San Francisco, where the casters have to watch out for the muggers—and a couple of essays about just messing around outside in general.

But fishing predominates and McGuane takes his fishing seriously. He's talking now about losing a large fish: "it joined that throng of shades, touched and unseen, that haunt the angler—fish felt and lost, big ones that got away that are the subject of levity to nonanglers but of a deeper emotion to the angler himself." And here is a description of the author's state of mind while fishing in a beautiful, remote region of western Canada: "While it had lasted [the fish's rise], all of British Columbia that existed had been the few square inches around my dry fly." McGuane is a catch-and-release fisherman, but fishermen of any persuasion can share these feelings.

"Inevitably, what actually happened is indescribable," the

author tells us. Maybe this is true of most profound experiences. But McGuane has gone the distance in trying to describe those experiences.

In *An Outside Chance* McGuane's batting .370 or better. He is not Ted Williams or Ty Cobb. Nor is he Ernest Hemingway. But he has written a good and true book, and I have a strong feeling "Papa" would have approved.

Richard Ford's Stark Vision of Loss, Healing

The surface action of this remarkable book can be described as follows: Harry Quinn, an ex-Marine and Vietnam veteran, and his girlfriend, Rae—like Quinn, a drifter—are in Oaxaca, Mexico, after a seven-month separation, to try to get Rae's brother, Sonny, out of prison. Sonny is behind bars because he has been apprehended with two pounds of cocaine in his possession. But with a smart lawyer, $10,000, iron resolution and some luck, the necessary document of release can be obtained and Sonny will be freed. Quinn and Rae will maybe pick up the pieces of their scorched love affair and go on to whatever grainy things lie in store. But there's a hitch. Everyone has gradually come to believe that Sonny has "taken off" the people he works for. As the Mexican lawyer Bernhardt puts it: "They think he makes the deal and lets himself be arrested."

So there are complications. The complications are serious and often ugly. Everybody wants a piece of Sonny. (One of his fellow inmates actually cuts off his ear as a warning.) Add to this the fact that what seems to be a small-scale insurrection is breaking out in the city; and the soldiers and police are responding with a ruthless yet almost indifferent repression. At times there is such pressure it seems impossible that normal life can still be going on in the city. But Sonny's hope of release, his continued existence, in fact, is seen slipping away ever faster into a maelstrom of events that have gone out of control, so that finally his life seems to become a thing of no importance at all.

The Ultimate Good Luck by Richard Ford. Boston: Houghton Mifflin, 1981.

The Ultimate Good Luck is a page-turner of the first order, felicitously rendered in a prose style rare in contemporary fiction. Here is an example of what I'm talking about:

> In Vietnam Quinn had made a minor science of light-study. Light made all the difference in the way you performed and how you made out, since everything was a matter of seeing and not seeing. The right distribution of eastern gray and composite green on the surface of an empty paddy and a line of coconut palms could give you a loop, and for a special celestial moment you wouldn't be there at all, but be out of it, in an evening's haze of beach on Lake Michigan with teals like flecks of gray space skittering down the flyway toward Indiana, and the entire day would back up sweetly against a heavy wash of night air.

On a deeper level, the book is a meditation on love and comportment between two ordinary but "marginal" people, Rae and Quinn. (Bernhardt believes "Everyone is marginal," and there is plenty of evidence in the book to support this belief.) They are in their early thirties when they meet at a dog race at a Louisiana track, but both seem to be at the tag end of their lives, "wounded in their sex," to borrow D. H. Lawrence's phrase, unable to break through their own self-imposed barriers. They live together for a time in Louisiana, Quinn working seven-on and seven-off as a fitter for a pipe contractor while Rae stays in the trailer and listens to "mellowed-out music" and paints from magazines. They drift to California where Quinn works for a time repossessing new cars. Through a friend, he lands a job as a game warden out in Michigan, a place where he hopes he can find a "clear frame of reference." But in Michigan, Rae is desperately unhappy with the way things are going. At various points she cries out in frustration: "I couldn't ever tell what the hell your life was in behalf of. . . . I don't like the way you think about things. You look at everything like it disappears down a hole that nothing ever comes out of."

"Do you love me?" she said. She had begun to cry. "You don't like to say it, do you?" she said. "It scares you. You don't want to need it."

"I can take care of me" is Quinn's answer.

That's not enough for Rae, and she pulls out on him, and Quinn has a hard time with it. He comes to realize that: "when you *tried* to protect yourself completely and never suffer a loss or a threat, you ended up with nothing. Or worse, you ended up being absorbed right into nothing, into the very luckless thing you were most afraid of."

At the conclusion of this superb novel Quinn and Rae have come full circle, and the heart slows and then picks up again as they move out and away from the circle. But throughout we have been witness to a significant and I think, finally, transcending arc of human conduct.

Ford is a masterful writer. In its stark vision of utter loss followed by a last-ditch healing redemption, *The Ultimate Good Luck* belongs alongside Malcolm Lowry's *Under the Volcano* and Graham Greene's *The Power and the Glory*. I can't give this novel higher marks.

A Retired Acrobat Falls under
the Spell of a Teenage Girl

Lynne Sharon Schwartz is the author of *Rough Strife*, a novel published in 1980. In that book she chronicles twenty-some years of a marriage between two bright, educated, talented people. For some obscure reason, I don't know why, I had little interest in reading the book when it appeared. I suppose—terrible confession!—I wondered what on earth this writer could tell me about a relationship between a university mathematics professor (Caroline) whose specialty is knot theory, and a foundation executive (Ivan), that could be of fundamental interest to me. After all—understand I had read some of the reviews—their children did not come along until some years after the marriage; Caroline and Ivan had time and energy and means to pursue their own lives and careers. On the surface of things, it seemed located in a landscape that was all too familiar—and yet totally foreign.

But I'm happy to say I read the novel, and I thought it was stunning. On the evidence of that book alone I'd say Schwartz is one of our better novelists. So what could the author do for an encore, a year after *Rough Strife*, that could measure up to the fierce pleasures of the first novel? Probably nothing.

Let me say that *Balancing Acts* is not a disappointment. But it suffers by the inevitable comparisons to the first book. For me, it does not have the cutting edges of *Rough Strife*, nor the full and scrupulously drawn characters who sometimes act in a willful and even capricious manner and often against their own seeming best interests—just like real people often act. The book does not

Balancing Acts by Lynne Sharon Schwartz. New York: Harper & Row, 1981.

have the relentless drive and the occasional breath-stopping places of that first novel. It is a good book, but is not a great or even a particularly memorable book. I don't say this to disparage. Most good novels are just that—"good," not great, and not always memorable.

Max Fried is a seventy-four-year-old widower recovering from the effects of a massive heart attack who goes to live in a residence that, in the part of the country I come from, we used to call an "old folks home." But this is not your basic old folks home. This place is more tony, and it's called Pleasure Knolls Semi-Service Apartments for Senior Citizens. It is located in Westchester County, New York. In his other life, the rich and fulfilling life he had before retirement and old age, Max Fried was a circus acrobat, a high-wire artist who performed with his wife, Susie. Those gone circus days are of course the good old days; and the metaphor of the title has in part to do with Max's trying to accommodate his grim, semi-invalided present reality with the halcyon times of his youth under the big top. Not surprisingly, the best writing in the book occurs when the author is writing about events and situations that have taken place in that other life.

Now comes Alison Markman, a precocious thirteen-year-old whose life intersects with Max's at the local junior high school where Max has a temporary-help job coaching would-be acrobats. Alison is an aspiring writer who has journals filled with adolescent adventure stuff and nonsense. She sees gruff old Max as a figure of romance and mystery, and she develops this terrific crush.

I'm not giving anything away when I say the crush she has on him indirectly brings about his demise. Fueled by her association with Max and her dreams of escaping what she feels is a dreary home life, Alison decides to run away and join a circus. There is a pursuit scene to Madison Square Garden and then on to Penn Station. The pursuers include Max and his sweetheart and neighbor at Pleasure Knolls, Lettie; and Alison's parents, Josh and Wanda, who, quite understandably, can't comprehend what in the world is going on with their daughter. Alison is reunited with her parents. But the strain proves too much for Max, and he collapses and dies. But his death does not diminish us in any essential way. It is not unexpected, or tragic, or finally even untimely. He simply falls dead. Lettie has to pick up her own life, and Alison is back home with her parents, where a thirteen-year-old belongs. In the final chapter, Lettie and Alison meet over ice-cream sodas and talk about Max and about things in general.

Go ahead and read *Balancing Acts*. But if you do, make sure you also read *Rough Strife*, if you haven't already. And catch Lynne Schwartz's next novel.

"Fame Is No Good, Take It from Me"

I love the stories and tales in *Winesburg, Ohio*—most of them, at any rate, I love. And I love a handful or so of Sherwood Anderson's other short stories. I think his best stories are as good as any around. *Winesburg, Ohio* (which was written in a Chicago tenement, based on people he knew there, not in Ohio) is taught in colleges and universities throughout the land, as it should be. One or another of his stories turns up in every anthology of American short fiction. But, beyond this, there isn't a whole lot else of Anderson's that is read today. His poems are long gone. His novels, books of essays and articles, the autobiographical writings, the memoirs and the book of plays—everything else seems to have passed into a dimly lighted zone that hardly anyone enters any longer.

After having just finished the *Selected Letters*, I think "S.A."—as he sometimes signed off on his letters—would be the first person to shrug his shoulders and say, "What did you expect?" He knew he'd written one book, at least, that would have staying power. People said he had written an American classic in *Winesburg*, and he was inclined to go along with that opinion. He made his reputation on that work, published in 1919. But what of the work between then and 1941, when he died? Something happened, and everyone knew it. The change in his work, and in the way the critics treated him (the "deep sea thinkers," Anderson called them), began as early as 1925, signaled

Selected Letters by Sherwood Anderson, edited by Charles E. Modlin. Knoxville: University of Tennessee Press, 1984.

by the young Ernest Hemingway's patronizing letters and followed up by his ill-natured parody of Anderson, *The Torrents of Spring*. Within a year after the publication of *Dark Laughter* in 1925, Anderson found himself reading his literary obituary in magazines. He said the attacks didn't bother him. But they did. In a letter to Burton Emmett, a benefactor, he said they made him "sick to my soul." To John Peale Bishop, one of his critics, he wrote, "your suspicion that my own mind is like one of those gray towns out here is, I am afraid, profoundly true."

But Anderson had always considered writing a form of therapy, and he kept on writing, despite what the critics had to say. "Writing helped me to live—it still helps me that way," he wrote to Floyd Dell in 1920. Writing was a cure for the "disease called living." He'd had one serious nervous collapse when a mail-order business he'd helped start went bankrupt. The date for his breakdown is precisely given as November 28, 1912. But two months later he was back in harness. He went to work for an advertising firm in Chicago to support his wife and three children and wrote stories and novels at night, sometimes falling asleep at the kitchen table. In 1914 some of his work began appearing in the little magazines of the day; and in 1916 he published his first novel, *Windy McPherson's Son*. In that year he divorced his wife, left his children, remarried, and began what he hoped would be a new life. He was able to give up advertising work. But his finances were such that for much of the next twenty years he worried that he might have to go back into advertising. To supplement his income he took to the lecture platform and, in his last years, appeared at several writers' conferences. On occasion he found himself having to accept money under humiliating circumstances from a wealthy man, and then from the man's widow.

Meanwhile, he kept turning out books and had plans for dozens more. Some of the books that, maybe happily, never materialized include a book on the history of the Mississippi, children's books (the idea of writing a "child book" had appealed to him as early as 1919 and was to persist until shortly before his death), and books on "modern industry." From time to time in the letters, Anderson makes mention of one or another of these ideas, and this will be footnoted to the effect that "Anderson did not undertake this project." Nevertheless, work did pour from his typewriter. He could write eight or ten or twelve thousand words at a stretch. And then lie down and sleep "like a dead man." And then get up and work some more.

After *Winesburg* he was famous but at best it was a mixed blessing. In 1927 he wrote to his brother, the painter Karl Anderson, that he thought fame was detrimental to the artist. To a schoolteacher from Washington, D.C., who sent Anderson a check for twenty-five dollars with a request that he critique two of her stories, he wrote, "Fame is no good, my dear. Take it from me." And in 1930, in another letter to Burton Emmett, he said, "I do not want attention centered on me. If I could work the rest of my life unknown, unnoticed by those who make current opinion, I would be happier."

Like it or not, however, he was famous. But he was in the position of a sitting duck. Everybody who came along, from hack journalist to hack playwright, and assorted magazine writers who weren't worth a patch on his pants, could take a potshot. He lived in the long shadows thrown by his more glamorous and success-ful—and, ultimately, more interesting—contemporaries. And he could never forgive them, or himself, for this state of affairs.

He urged Roger Sergel, an English professor at the University of Pittsburgh who was asking for advice about writing, to "Keep it loose. Keep it loose." He felt that most writers fail because "they aren't at bottom storytellers. They have theories about writing, notions about style, often real writing ability, but they do not tell the story—straight out—bang." He once threw a novel out of a car window in the Ozarks and another out of a hotel room window in Chicago because the work wasn't "clear straightforward storytelling." He distrusted "technique" and what he called "cleverness" in writers. The truth is, he seemed to be a little put out with most of them, with the exception of Thomas Wolfe. In September 1937, he wrote to Wolfe, "I love your guts, Tom. You are one who is O.K." But Joyce, a "gloomy Irishman, . . . makes my bones ache. He's up the wrong tree or I'm an egg." Ezra Pound struck Anderson as "an empty man without fire." He thought it was "very depressing" that Sinclair Lewis received the Nobel Prize. And after the publication of Hemingway's *Green Hills of Africa*, he wrote to his friend, the actor-director Jasper Deeter, that he thought Hemingway had "got into a kind of romanticizing of the so-called real . . . a kind of ecstasy over elephant dung, killing, death, etc., etc. And then he talks about writing the perfect sentence—something of that sort. Isn't that rot?"

Anderson hadn't read *The Grapes of Wrath* when he met the young John Steinbeck in November 1939, but he wrote from Fresno to Lewis Galantière that he thought Steinbeck looked like "a truck driver on his day off." He went on to remark that the situation in the labor camps "is in no way different from what is going on all over the country," and attributed the great popularity of the book to the fact that it "localizes a situation that is universal." It's clear that he didn't like the star-bright attention that was being paid to Steinbeck at the time.

Anderson was born in Camden, Ohio, in 1876, but grew up mostly in Clyde, a little town near Cleveland. His father was a drifter who moved the family "whenever the rent came due." For years Anderson took whatever manual labor jobs he could find until he put on a different sort of collar and went into advertising. He had, he said, "cunning." He could "handle people, make them do as I please, be what I wanted them to be. . . . the truth is I was a smooth son of a bitch." But he knew firsthand the underbelly of small town life in mid-America; and he wrote about it better, and with more fidelity and sympathy, than any American writer before him—and most of them since his time. Small towns and small lives were his subject matter. He loved America, and things American, with a devotion that, even at this remove, I find touching. "I love this country," he will say in his letters. And, "God, how I love this country." His heart, and his abiding interests—and his true genius—were rooted in rural areas and with country people and their ways. This from a letter to Waldo Frank in 1919: "It was delightful to sit in the grandstand among the farmers, off for a day's vacation, and see the trotting and pacing races. The horses were beautiful as were also the fine steers, bulls, pigs and sheep on show in the exhibition sheds." In a letter to George Church, written in 1927, he said, "What I really want to do—my purpose in writing—is to grow eloquent again about this country— I want to tell you how the streams sound at night—how quiet it is—the sound the wind makes in the pines."

He thought the best thing he'd ever written was his short story "The Egg." In addition to this, his favorite stories were "The Untold Lie," "Hands," "Out of Nowhere into Nothing," "I Want to Know Why," and "I'm a Fool." At the very least I would add to this list "Death in the Woods" and "The Man Who Became a Woman."

With the one novel that made him some money, *Dark Laughter*, he bought himself a farm in Troutdale, Virginia. But he was a restless man, a true American wanderer, who couldn't stay in one place. From 1919 until his death in February 1941 from peritonitis, on board a ship bound for South America (where he hoped to "get out of one of the bigger cities and into a town of five or ten thousand and perhaps stay in such a town for some months"), he was all over this country. He lived and worked in New York, California, Virginia, Texas, Alabama, Wisconsin, Kansas, Arizona, Michigan, Colorado, Florida—forty or fifty different residences in all—with time out for trips to Europe and Mexico. It helped that he "adored" hotels. "Even the worst of hotel life is so good compared with family life." He found a particular hotel in Kansas City very much to his liking: "full of little ham actors, prize fighters, ballplayers, whores and auto sales-men on their uppers. Lord God what gaudy people. I love them."

He was a prolific letter writer. Most of the 201 letters that make up this collection are being published for the first time. An earlier book, *Letters of Sherwood Anderson*, edited by Howard Mumford Jones and including 401 letters, was published in 1953. And there is the easily accessible group of letters in *The Portable Sherwood Anderson* that Horace Gregory edited in 1949.

The Newberry Library in Chicago holds over five thousand Anderson letters, and this collection has provided the nucleus for the present selection. But the editor, Charles E. Modlin, has also chosen letters from twenty-three other institutions, as well as from private individuals, "reserved" letters that have only recently been made available. He has chosen well, the letters dealing about equally with personal and professional concerns. And there was plenty going on in Anderson's life on both counts. This volume alone maps the life of a unique American writer, one whose presence is still felt in the plain-talk, straightforward fiction of many of today's writers.

These letters go a long way toward bringing Sherwood Anderson into the full light, where he belongs. To be sure, they are not letters written in the grand tradition of Letters, with one eye aimed at the recipient and the other on posterity. Nor are they "tailored" to match the personality of the recipient. Some of them were written in longhand, and Anderson apologized for this. If I have any reservation, it is that there tends to be a sameness of tone that hangs over them. And I think the fact that he didn't use contractions in his writing helps contribute to their seemingly subdued, formal, even elegiac manner. Reading these letters, we learn some things about Anderson and his work. But, finally, one comes away with the feeling that this man who didn't often show his emotions is very much like one of his stoic characters—holding back, unable to speak his mind or bare his heart.

In 1939, a year and a half before his death, he wrote to Roger

Sergel about a new book he was starting: "I'm trying again. A man has to begin over and over . . . to try to think and feel only in the very limited field, the house on the street, the man at the corner drugstore."

He was a brave man and a good writer—estimable qualities in these days or any other.

Gaston Gallimard, the French publisher, had acquired the rights to *Winesburg* but didn't publish the book immediately. Finally, after several years, Anderson was in Paris and went to see the distinguished president of the firm.

"Is it a good book?" Gallimard asked Anderson.

"You're damn right it is," Anderson answered.

"Well, then, if it's good, it will still be good when we do publish it."

Anderson's best work is still good. He might have penned his own epitaph when he wrote, "I have written a few stories that are like stones laid along the highway. They have solidity and will stay there."

Coming of Age, Going to Pieces

In 1954, after surviving two plane crashes in Africa and being reported dead, Ernest Hemingway had the unique experience of being able to read his own obituaries. I was in my teens, barely old enough to have a driver's license, but I can remember seeing his picture on the front page of our evening newspaper, grinning as he held a copy of a paper with his picture and a banner head-line announcing his death. I'd heard his name in my high school English class, and I had a friend who, like me, wanted to write and who managed to work Hemingway's name into just about every conversation we had. But at the time I'd never read anything the man had written. (I was busy reading Thomas B. Costain, among others.) Seeing Hemingway on the front page, reading about his exploits and accomplishments, and his recent brush with death, was heady and glamorous stuff. But there were no wars I could get to even if I'd wanted to, and Africa, not to mention Paris, Pamplona, Key West, Cuba, even New York City, seemed as far away as the moon to me. Still, I think my resolve to be a writer was strengthened by seeing Hemingway's picture on the front page. So I was indebted to him even then, if for the wrong reasons.

Soon after the accidents in Africa, Hemingway, musing on his life, wrote, "The most complicated subject that I know, since I am a man, is a man's life." The search for Ernest Hemingway goes

Along with Youth: Hemingway, the Early Years by Peter Griffin. New York: Oxford University Press, 1985; and *Hemingway: A Biography* by Jeffrey Meyers. New York: Harper & Row, 1985.

on. It's almost twenty-five years since the writer, seriously ill, paranoid and despondent, suffering from loss of memory brought about by electroshock treatments during two successive confinements at the Mayo Clinic, blew his head away with a shotgun. Mary Welsh Hemingway, his fourth wife, asleep in the upstairs master bedroom of the Hemingway residence in Ketchum, Idaho, was awakened on the morning of July 2, 1961, by what she thought were the sounds of "a couple of drawers banging shut." Edmund Wilson best expressed the general sense of shock and diminishment after his death: "It is as if a whole corner of my generation had suddenly and horribly collapsed."

In the years since 1961 Hemingway's reputation as "the outstanding author since the death of Shakespeare" (John O'Hara's wildly extravagant assessment in praise of *Across the River and into the Trees*) shrank to the extent that many critics, as well as some fellow writers, felt obliged to go on record that they, and the literary world at large, had been bamboozled somehow: Hemingway was not nearly as good as had been originally thought. They agree that at least one, maybe two, of the novels (*The Sun Also Rises* and, possibly, *A Farewell to Arms*) might make it into the twenty-first century, along with a handful, five or six, perhaps, of his short stories. Death had finally removed the author from center stage and deadly "reappraisals" began taking place.

It is not entirely coincidental, either, that soon after his death a particular kind of writing began to appear in this country, writing that stressed the irrational and fabulous, the antirealist against the realist tradition. In this context, it might be worthwhile to remind ourselves what Hemingway believed good writing should do. He felt fiction must be based on actual experience. "A writer's job is to tell the truth," he wrote in his introduction to *Men at War*. "His standard of fidelity to the truth should be so high that his invention, out of his experience, should produce a truer account than anything factual can be." And he also wrote: "find what gave you the emotion; what the action was that gave you the excitement. Then write it down making it so clear that . . . it can become a part of the experience of the person who reads it."

Given his stature and influence, maybe the sharp reaction after his death was inevitable. But gradually, especially within the last decade, critics have been better able to separate the celebrity big-game hunter and deep-sea fisherman, the heavy-drinking bully and brawler, from the disciplined craftsman and artist whose work seems to me, with each passing year, to become more durable.

"The great thing is to last and get your work done," Hemingway said in *Death in the Afternoon*. And that, essentially, is what he did. Who was this man—by his own admission, "a son of a bitch"—whose novels and books of short stories changed forever the way fiction was written and, for a time, even the way people thought about themselves?

Peter Griffin's wonderful and intimate book, *Along with Youth: Hemingway, the Early Years* (the title is from one of Hemingway's early poems), supplies some of the answers. Mr. Griffin was a young Ph.D. student at Brown University when he wrote a short letter to Mary Hemingway telling her how important Hemingway's work had been to him at a difficult time in his life. She invited him to visit and promised full cooperation in writing this book, the first of three biographical volumes. Working a territory where a regiment of literary scholars and specialists have gone before, Mr. Griffin has uncovered a significant amount of new and revealing information. (Five previously uncollected short stories are also included.) Several chapters deal with Hemingway's early family life and relationships. His mother was an overbearing woman with pretensions to being a singer; his father was a prominent doctor who taught Hemingway to hunt and fish and gave him his first pair of boxing gloves.

But by far the larger and more important part of the book is devoted to Hemingway's coming of age as a reporter for the *Kansas City Star*, then as an ambulance driver for the Red Cross in Italy, where he was seriously injured by an Austrian mortar shell and machine-gun bullets. There is a long section devoted to his convalescence in a military hospital in Milan. While there he fell in love with a nurse from Pennsylvania named Agnes Kurowsky, who became the model for Catherine Barkley in *A Farewell to Arms*. (She jilted him for an Italian count.)

In 1919 he returned home to Oak Park, Illinois, wearing "a cock-feathered Bersaglieri hat, a knee-length officer's cape lined with red satin, and a British tunic decorated with ribbons of the Valor Medal and the War Cross." He had to use a cane to walk. He was a hero, and he signed up with a lecture agency to talk to civic groups about his experience in the war. When he was finally asked to leave home by his angry and bewildered parents (Hemingway didn't want to work at a job, liked to sleep in late and spend his afternoons shooting pool), he went to the peninsula country in Upper Michigan and then to Toronto, where he accepted room and board and eighty dollars a month from a wealthy family to tutor and "make a man out of" the family's retarded son.

From Toronto he moved to Chicago, where he shared rooms and a bohemian life with a friend named Bill Horne. He worked at a magazine called *Commonwealth Cooperative*, for which he wrote, in his words, "Boys' Personals, The Country Division, Miss Congress's fiction, bank editorials, children's stories, etc." At this time, Hemingway began meeting literary people like Sherwood Anderson and Carl Sandburg. He liked to read aloud and explain the poems of Keats and Shelley and once, in the company of Sandburg, who praised his "sensitive interpretation," he read from *The Rubáiyát of Omar Khayyám*. He was crazy about dancing and won a dance contest with a woman friend named Kate Smith. (She later married John Dos Passos.) In October 1920, he met another woman, eight years older than he, who would become his first wife—the remarkable Elizabeth Hadley Richardson.

In the nine months of their courtship—she was living in St. Louis while Hemingway was living and working in Chicago—

they each wrote over one thousand pages of letters. (Hadley's correspondence was made available to Mr. Griffin by Jack Hemingway, the son of Ernest and Hadley, who has also provided a foreword to this volume.) The passages Mr. Griffin quotes are intelligent, witty, often moving, and show her offering a shrewd and perceptive response to the stories, sketches and poems that the twenty-one-year-old Hemingway was sending her every week.

In one of the letters, she contrasts her own writing with his. She knew, she said, that her writing was filled with abstractions, whereas his was not. But there was something more. "In all of Ernest's sentences, the accents fell naturally on 'the correct quantitative place. . . . *I* have to scratch lines under important words.'" She praised his intuitive sense: "It is a most lovely thing—intuition—inside dead sure of stuff. A very obvious example of it is . . . ideas just appearing in your mind that make you understand the way things are." It was, she felt, the basis for his work. She encouraged their plan to go to Europe and felt it would be just the thing for his writing: "Why, you will write like a great wonderful breeze bringing strong whiffs from all sorts of interior places. You'll give birth before I will, and for you Paris is the place to do it."

At the end of April 1921, Hemingway told her he was beginning his first novel, a book with "real people, talking and saying what they think." The young man who was the hero of the novel would be called Nick Adams. Hadley wrote back: "Thank the lord some young one is gonna write something young and beautiful; someone with the clean, muscular freshness of young things right in him at the moment of writing. You go ahead. I'm wild over the idea." His style, she observed, "eliminated everything except what is necessary and strengthening. [It] is the outcome of a deep feeling and not just intellection. . . . You've got a good ear for rhythm and tone and lines. Do you realize how many important threads you're weaving your life with these days? Honey, you're doing some of the best things you've ever done in your I life . . . I'm completely under its power. . . .

Simple—but as fine as the finest chain mail." But she warned him too: "it takes a lot . . . to hold yourself down to truthfulness in an art. And up to the day of your death you'll probably find yourself slipping with technical ease into poor psychology. But no one has a better chance to be honest than you because you've the will to be." "Honestly," she wrote, "you're doing marvels of stirring, potent stuff. . . . Don't let's ever die . . . let's go on together."

Mr. Griffin's biography closes just as the newly married couple, armed with letters of introduction to Gertrude Stein and Ezra Pound, are about to sail for France. It brings to life the young Hemingway with all his charm, vitality, good looks, passionate dedication to writing, like nothing else I've ever read about the man.

Quite a different Ernest Hemingway emerges from the pages of Jeffrey Meyers's *Hemingway: A Biography*. Mr. Meyers, a scholar and professional biographer, has written books on T. E. Lawrence, George Orwell, Katherine Mansfield, Siegfried Sassoon, Wyndham Lewis and D. H. Lawrence, to name a few. He seems to have read everything ever written on Hemingway and interviewed many of Hemingway's family members (with the notable exception of Mary Hemingway, who, quite tellingly, I think, refused to cooperate) as well as friends, cronies, and hangers-on.

Adulation is not a requirement for biographers, but Mr. Meyers's book fairly bristles with disapproval of its subject. What is especially disconcerting is his strong belief that, "Like his heroes Twain and Kipling, [Hemingway] never fully matured as an artist." This is more than a little dispiriting to read, but it's one of the premises of the book and it is sounded repeatedly as one reads dazedly on. Mr. Meyers talks briefly, and disapprovingly, about *Death in the Afternoon* (though he calls it "the classic study of bullfighting in English"), *Green Hills of Africa*, *Winner Take Nothing*, *Men without Women*, *To Have and Have Not*, *Across the River and into the Trees*, *Islands in the Stream*, *A Moveable Feast* (which he nonetheless maintains was Hemingway's "greatest work of nonfiction") and *The Old Man and the Sea*.

By and large the rest of the work, according to Mr. Meyers, is ruined by "an excessive display of vanity and self-pity . . . an inability to create a reflective character, a tendency to try to act out his fantasies." What's left? *The Sun Also Rises*, a dozen short stories (among them, "The Short Happy Life of Francis Macomber" and "The Snows of Kilimanjaro") and maybe *A Farewell to Arms* and *For Whom the Bell Tolls*. He seems to find it lamentable that Hemingway was not killed in one of the African crashes. Had he died, Mr. Meyers says, "over a cataract or among wild elephants, his reputation would have been even greater than it is today. He would have gone out in a literal blaze of glory . . . before he began to decline and waste away."

While the biographer doesn't, thank Heaven, mention fishing rods and penis envy in the same breath, his interpretation of Hemingway and the man's work is strictly Freudian. There is plenty of talk of "wounds"—not only the physical injuries Hemingway suffered, beginning with the shrapnel and machine-gun bullets in Italy in 1918, but the "wound" he sustained when jilted by Agnes Kurowsky. Another "wound" occurred when a suitcase of Hemingway's early work was stolen from Hadley's compartment while she was on a train from Paris to Switzerland; according to Mr. Meyers: "The loss was irrevocably connected in Hemingway's mind with sexual infidelity, and he equated the lost manuscripts with lost love."

It was an unfortunate and dismaying accident, but to the biographer it's clear that as a result Hadley was about to become the former Mrs. Hemingway. Yet not without guilt on Hemingway's part and guilt's sometimes exceedingly strange manifestations. Mr. Meyers writes: "Hemingway had three accidents, probably connected to his guilt, during the first year of marriage to Pauline [Pfeiffer]." And then this amazing statement: "Hemingway—like many ordinary men—had been engaged in an Oedipal struggle against his father for the possession of his mother. If the bullfight symbolizes sexual intercourse, as it clearly does in *The Sun Also Rises* ("the sword went in, and for just an instant he and the bull were one"), then the matador's triumphant domination of the bull at the moment of orgasmic death represents a virile defense against the threat of homosexuality."

Moving from Freud and the unconscious to the mundane (and flat-footed), consider some of these sentences: "Hemingway made a successful assault on the literary beachhead soon after reaching Paris." "Hemingway had a short fuse and a bad temper, liked to be considered a tough guy rather than a writer." "He was selfish and always put his books before his wives." "The two sides of Ernest's character came from his two parents." "Hemingway had four sisters (and, later, four wives)." "The world of war was attractive to him because it removed women, the greatest source of anxiety." There are hundreds more like these, of similar perspicacity. The book is very tough going indeed.

After his move to Key West in 1931 and the publication of *Death in the Afternoon*, Hemingway adopted the macho stance so often associated with the man and his work. He killed lions, water buffaloes, elephants, kudu, deer, bears, elk, ducks, pheasants, marlin, tuna, sailfish, trout. You name it, he caught it or shot it—everything that flew, finned, scooted, crawled or lumbered. He began to bluster and posture, encouraging people to call him "Papa," got into fistfights, became merciless to friends and enemies alike. Fitzgerald remarked perceptively that Hemingway "is quite as nervously broken down as I am but it manifests itself in different ways. His inclination is toward megalomania and mine toward melancholy." Damon Runyon said, "Few men can stand the strain of relaxing with him over an extended period."

Reading the depressing account of Hemingway's middle and late years, from 1940 on—the years of decline, as Mr. Meyers calls them—the reader is left to wonder not so much that he wrote anything of merit (Mr. Meyers thinks he did not, after *For*

Whom the Bell Tolls), but that he was able to write at all. He suffered numerous serious accidents and was subject to serious and debilitating illnesses, including alcoholism. (His son Jack says his father drank a quart of whiskey a day for the last twenty years of his life.) There is a three-page appendix cataloging major accidents and illnesses, including five concussions; a skull fracture; bullet and shrapnel wounds; hepatitis; hypertension; diabetes; malaria; torn muscles; pulled ligaments; pneumonia; erysipelas; amoebic dysentery; blood poisoning; cracked spinal disks; ruptured liver, right kidney and spleen; nephritis; anemia; arteriosclerosis; skin cancer; hemochromatosis; and first-degree burns. Once he shot himself through the leg trying to shoot a shark. At the time of his admission to the Mayo Clinic he suffered from "depression and mental collapse."

One grows weary of and ultimately saddened by the public Hemingway. But the private life of the man was no more edifying. The reader is battered with one display after another of mean-spiritedness and spite, of vulgar and shabby behavior. (After his break with his third wife, Martha Gellhorn, Hemingway wrote a scurrilous poem about her, which he liked to read aloud in company.) He carried on adulterous liaisons and, in his fifties, had embarrassing infatuations with girls not yet out of their teens. At one time or another he quarreled and broke with nearly all his friends, with members of his family, his former wives (with the exception of Hadley; he was still writing love letters to her years after they had divorced) and his sons and their wives. He fought bitterly with each of his sons; one, Gregory, he said he'd like to see hang. In his will he left an estate of $1.4 million, and disinherited the sons.

It is almost with a sense of relief that one reaches that awful morning of July 2, 1961, when Hemingway, recently released for the second time from the Mayo Clinic (against his wife's wishes; she felt he had "conned" his doctors), locates the key to the locked gun cabinet. By now everyone has suffered enough.

There's little in this book that Carlos Baker, in his 1969 biography, didn't say better. And Mr. Baker, despite his blind spots, was far more sympathetic to the work and, finally, more understanding of the man. It may well be that another full-scale biography needs to be written to augment Mr. Baker's and Mr. Meyers's work, but I don't think so. At least I for one am going to pass on reading it.

The only possible antidote for how you feel about Hemingway after finishing this book is to go back at once and reread the fiction itself. How clear, serene and solid the best work still seems; it's as if there were a physical communion taking place among the fingers turning the page, the eyes taking in the words, the brain imaginatively recreating what the words stand for and, as Hemingway put it, "making it a part of your own experience." Hemingway did his work, and he'll last. Any biographer who gives him less than this, granting the chaos of his public and personal life, might just as well write the biography of an anonymous grocer or a woolly mammoth. Hemingway, the writer—he's still the hero of the story, however it unfolds.

NOTES

Abbreviations Used in the Notes

AOU   *All of Us: The Collected Poems*, ed. William L. Stull (London: The Harvill Press, 1996; New York: Alfred A. Knopf, 1998)

F1   *Fires: Essays, Poems, Stories*, first edition (Santa Barbara, Calif.: Capra Press, 1983)

F2   *Fires: Essays, Poems, Stories*, second expanded edition (New York: Vintage Books, 1989; London: The Harvill Press, 1994)

RC   Raymond Carver

WICF   *Where I'm Calling From*, memorial reprint edition, with a foreword by RC (1988; New York: Atlantic Monthly Press, 1998; London: The Harvill Press, 1998)

UNCOLLECTED STORIES

KINDLING (7–20)
Text based on manuscripts found in Raymond Carver's home in Port Angeles, Washington. Published in slightly different form in *Esquire* [New York] 132, no. 1 (July 1999): 72–77.

WHAT WOULD YOU LIKE TO SEE? (21–37)
Text based on a single hand-corrected typescript found among the Raymond Carver papers in the William Charvat Collection of American Fiction at the Ohio State University Library. Published in the *Guardian* [London] 24 June 2000, 14.

DREAMS (38–48)
Text based on manuscripts found in Raymond Carver's home in Port Angeles, Washington. Published in slightly different form in *Esquire* [New York] 134, no. 2 (July 2000): 132–37.

VANDALS (49–62)
Text based on manuscripts found in Raymond Carver's home in Port Angeles, Washington. Published in slightly different form in *Esquire* [New York] 132, no. 4 (October 1999): 160–65.

CALL IF YOU NEED ME (63–74)
Text based on a single hand-corrected typescript found among the Raymond Carver papers in the William Charvat Collection of American Fiction at the Ohio State University Library. Published in slightly different form in *Granta* [London], no. 68 (winter 1999): 9–21.

FIVE ESSAYS AND A MEDITATION

MY FATHER'S LIFE (77–86)
Text from *F2*, 13–21. First published in *Esquire* [New York] 102, no. 3 (September 1984): 64–68. Reprinted as "Where He Was: Memories of My Father" in *Granta* [Cambridge, England], no. 14 (winter 1984): 19–28. Source for "Photograph of My Father in His Twenty-Second Year": *AOU*, 7.

ON WRITING (87–92)
Text from *F1*, 13–18. First published as "A Storyteller's Shoptalk" in *New York Times Book Review*, 15 February 1981, 9, 18. Reprinted in *Short Short Stories*, ed. Jack David and Jon Redfern (Toronto: Holt, Rinehart and Winston of Canada, 1982), 199–202.

FIRES (93–106)
Text from *F1*, 19–30. First published in *Antaeus* [New York], no. 47 (autumn 1982): 156–67. Published in slightly different form in *Syracuse Scholar* [Syracuse University] 3, no. 2 (fall 1982): 6–14. Reprinted in *In Praise of What Persists*, ed. Stephen Berg (New York: Harper & Row, 1983), 33–44.

After John Gardner's death in a motorcycle accident on 14 September 1982, an excerpt from "Fires" appeared under the title "John Gardner: A Trial by Fire for a Young Writer" in *Chicago Tribune Book World*, 26 September 1982, 1–2. To the excerpt RC added:

> Now, the news of his death having just reached me, I'm sitting here this morning trying to make sense out of the senseless—and of course I can't. My feeling of personal loss is terrific but in time I'll be able to accommodate that. (That's what I tell myself, anyway.) But his loss to the national literature is tremendous and incalculable.
>
> I'm trying to remember things. I remember the last time I saw him alive. It was last March, at his place in Susquehanna, Pennsylvania. We'd spent the night, Tess Gallagher and I, and John was taking leave of us that morning out in the drive. There was snow on the ground, but the weather wasn't so bad—the sun was out and I had my jacket over my arm. We

gave each other a hug. "Have a good trip back," he said. "Drive safely."

"You bet," I said.

Then he grinned, and I grinned. We were leading charmed lives, and we knew it. We'd talked about it the night before. He'd won his bout with cancer, and I'd won mine with alcohol. And we'd come a distance from Chico. "Good-bye, John," I said.

JOHN GARDNER: THE WRITER AS TEACHER (107–114)
First published as "John Gardner: Writer and Teacher" in *Georgia Review* [University of Georgia], 37, no. 2 (summer 1983): 413–19. Reprinted, in slightly different form, as RC's "Foreword" to Gardner's *On Becoming a Novelist* (New York: Harper & Row, 1983), xi–xix, and in *F2*, 40–47.

FRIENDSHIP (117–122)
Text and photograph from *Granta* [Cambridge, England], no. 25 (autumn 1988): 155–61.

MEDITATION ON A LINE
FROM SAINT TERESA (123–125)
Untitled statement from *Commencement* [15 May 1988] (West Hartford, Conn.: University of Hartford, 1988), 24–25. RC received an honorary Doctor of Letters degree from the University of Hartford at this graduation ceremony. The "Meditation" was his last-written work of prose.

EARLY STORIES

FURIOUS SEASONS (129–145)
Text from *Furious Seasons and Other Stories* (Santa Barbara, Calif.: Capra Press, 1977), 94–110. Previously published under the title "The Furious Seasons" in *December* [Western Springs, Ill.] 5, no. 1 (fall 1963): 31–41. An earlier version of this story, also titled "The Furious Seasons," appeared in *Selection* [Chico State College], no. 2 (winter 1960–61): 1–18, and was RC's first published short story.

THE HAIR (146–149)

Text from *Toyon* [Humboldt State College] 9, no. 1 (spring 1963): 27–30. This issue of *Toyon*, the Humboldt State College literary magazine, was edited by RC. A revised version of "The Hair" appeared in *Sundaze* [Santa Cruz, Calif.] 2, no. 6 (7–20 January 1972): n. pag. That version is reprinted in *Those Days: Early Writings by Raymond Carver*, ed. William L. Stull (Elmwood, Conn.: Raven Editions, 1987), 19–23.

THE AFICIONADOS (150–155)

Text from *Toyon* [Humboldt State College] 9, no. 1 (spring 1963): 5–9. RC published "The Aficionados" under the pseudonym "John Vale."

POSEIDON AND COMPANY (156–157)

Text from *Toyon* [Humboldt State College] 9, no. 1 (spring 1963): 24–25. A slightly different version of "Poseidon and Company" appeared in *Ball State Teachers College Forum* [Muncie, Ind.] 5, no. 2 (spring 1964): 11–12.

BRIGHT RED APPLES (158–164)

Text from *Gato Magazine* [Los Gatos, Calif.] 2, no. 1 (spring–summer 1967): 8–13.

FRAGMENT OF A NOVEL

FROM *THE AUGUSTINE NOTEBOOKS* (167–174)

Text from *Iowa Review* [University of Iowa] 10, no. 3 (summer 1979): 38–42. RC did not continue the novel beyond this point.

OCCASIONS

ON "NEIGHBORS" (177–178)

Untitled essay from *Cutting Edges: Young American Fiction for the '70s*, ed. Jack Hicks (New York: Holt, Rinehart and Winston, 1973), 528–29. Source for "Neighbors": *WICF*, 68–73.

ON "DRINKING WHILE DRIVING" (179–180)
Text from *New Voices in American Poetry*, ed. David Allan Evans
(Cambridge, Mass.: Winthrop Publishers, 1973), 44–45. Source for
"Drinking While Driving": *AOU*, 3.

ON REWRITING (181–184)
Published as RC's "Afterword" to *F1*, 187–89. RC's dates of composition for several works are unreliable.

ON THE *DOSTOEVSKY* SCREENPLAY (185–189)
RC's untitled introduction to *Dostoevsky: A Screenplay* by RC and Tess
Gallagher, Capra Back-to-Back Series V (Santa Barbara, Calif.: Capra
Press, 1985), 7–12. A slightly different version of this essay appeared in
NER/BLQ [*New England Review and Bread Loaf Quarterly*, Hanover,
N.H.] 6, no. 3 (spring 1984): 355–58.

ON "BOBBER" AND OTHER POEMS (190–193)
Published as "Occasions" in *The Generation of 2000: Contemporary
American Poets*, ed. William Heyen (Princeton, N. J.: Ontario Review
Press, 1984), 24–26. RC's dates of composition for several poems are
unreliable. Source for poems: *AOU*: "Bobber" (42), "Prosser" (33–34),
"Your Dog Dies" (6–7), "Forever" (48–49), "Looking for Work" (13,
237–38), "Wes Hardin: From a Photograph" (36–37), "Marriage"
(37–38).

ON "FOR TESS" (194–196)
Untitled essay from *Literary Cavalcade* [Scholastic, Inc., New York,
N.Y.] 39, no. 7 (April 1987): 8. Source for "For Tess": *AOU*, 138.

ON "ERRAND" (197–198)
Untitled essay from *The Best American Short Stories 1988*, selected from
U.S. and Canadian magazines by Mark Helprin with Shannon Ravenel
(Boston: Houghton Mifflin, 1988), 318–19. Source for "Errand":
WICF, 419–31.

ON *WHERE I'M CALLING FROM* (199–202)

First published as "A Special Message for the First Edition" in *Where I'm Calling From*, The Signed First Edition Society (Franklin Center, Pa.: The Franklin Library, 1988), n. pag. [vii–ix]. Reprinted as "Author's Foreword" to *WICF*, xi–xiv. RC in fact published his first short story, "The Furious Seasons," in 1960.

INTRODUCTIONS

STEERING BY THE STARS (205–207)

"Foreword" to *Syracuse Poems and Stories 1980*, selected by RC (Syracuse, N.Y.: Department of English, Syracuse University, 1980), iv–v. The quotation attributed to Ezra Pound ("fundamental accuracy of statement. . . .") is not to be found in Pound's *ABC of Reading* (1934). Contents: Andrew Abrahamson, "Five Places with Rob and Haines"; Brooks Haxton, "Thanksgiving Friday"; Anthony Robbins, "Kathy" and "Vita Nuova"; Marianne Loyd, "Everyone Has a Hobby"; Ron Block, "My Feral Child" and "Charles Billiter"; Penelope Phillips, "from *Minding the Heavens*" ("To Leonhard Euler"); Jay Grover-Rogoff, "Homage to Redon: Ophelia among the Flowers"; William C. Elkington, "Leech"; Allen Hoey, "When the Cows Come Down to Drink"; Nancy E. LeRoy, "The Red Couch"; David O'Meara, "A Country for Old Men."

ALL MY RELATIONS (208–218)

"Introduction" to *The Best American Short Stories 1986*, selected from U.S. and Canadian magazines by RC with Shannon Ravenel (Boston: Houghton Mifflin, 1986), xi–xx. Contents: Donald Barthelme, "Basil from Her Garden"; Charles Baxter, "Gryphon"; Ann Beattie, "Janus"; James Lee Burke, "The Convict"; Ethan Canin, "Star Food"; Frank Conroy, "Gossip"; Richard Ford, "Communist"; Tess Gallagher, "Bad Company"; Amy Hempel, "Today Will Be a Quiet Day"; David Michael Kaplan, "Doe Season"; David Lipsky, "Three Thousand Dollars"; Thomas McGuane, "Sportsmen"; Christopher McIlroy, "All My Relations"; Alice Munro, "Monsieur les Deux Chapeaux"; Jessica Neely, "Skin Angels"; Kent Nelson, "Invisible Life"; Grace Paley, "Telling"; Mona Simpson, "Lawns"; Joy Williams, "Health"; Tobias Wolff, "The Rich Brother."

THE UNKNOWN CHEKHOV (219)

Untitled statement on *The Unknown Chekhov: Stories and Other Writings*, trans. Avrahm Yarmolinsky (New York: Ecco Press, 1987), outside back wrapper.

FICTION OF OCCURRENCE AND CONSEQUENCE
(220–224)

"Introduction" to *American Short Story Masterpieces*, ed. RC and Tom Jenks (New York, Delacorte Press, 1987), xiii–xvi. The essay is signed off by both editors. Contents: James Baldwin, "Sonny's Blues"; Ann Beattie, "Weekend"; Gina Berriault, "The Bystander"; Vance Bourjaily, "The Amish Farmer"; Richard Brautigan, "1/3, 1/3, 1/3"; Harold Brodkey, "Verona: A Young Woman Speaks"; Carol Bly, "Talk of Heroes"; Raymond Carver, "Fever"; Evan S. Connell, "The Fisherman from Chihuahua"; Frank Conroy, "Midair"; E. L. Doctorow, "Willi"; Andre Dubus, "The Fat Girl"; Stanley Elkin, "A Poetics for Bullies"; Richard Ford, "Rock Springs"; Tess Gallagher, "The Lover of Horses"; John Gardner, "Redemption"; Gail Godwin, "Dream Children"; Lawrence Sargent Hall, "The Ledge"; Barry Hannah, "Water Liars"; Mark Helprin, "Letters from the *Samantha*"; Ursula K. Le Guin, "Ile Forest"; Bernard Malamud, "The Magic Barrel"; Bobbie Ann Mason, "Shiloh"; James Alan McPherson, "The Story of a Scar"; Leonard Michaels, "Murderers"; Arthur Miller, "The Misfits"; Joyce Carol Oates, "Where Are You Going, Where Have You Been?"; Flannery O'Connor, "A Good Man Is Hard to Find"; Grace Paley, "The Used-Boy Raisers"; Jayne Anne Phillips, "The Heavenly Animal"; David Quammen, "Walking Out"; Philip Roth, "The Conversion of the Jews"; James Salter, "Akhnilo"; John Updike, "The Christian Roommates"; Joy Williams, "The Wedding"; Tobias Wolff, "The Liar."

ON CONTEMPORARY FICTION (225–226)

Untitled contribution to "A Symposium on Contemporary American Fiction," *Michigan Quarterly Review* [University of Michigan] 26, no. 4 (fall 1987): 710–11.

ON LONGER STORIES (227–232)

"Introduction" to *American Fiction 88*, ed. Michael C. White and Alan Davis (Farmington, Conn.: Wesley Press, 1988), xi–xv. RC served as guest judge of this second annual American Fiction competition. Contents: Antonya Nelson, "The Expendables" (first prize); Paul Scott Malone, "Bringing Joboy Back" (second prize); Sandra Dorr, "Writing in the Dark" (third prize); Ursula Hegi, "Saving a Life"; Patricia Page, "Escapade"; Mary Elsie Robertson, "Parting Words"; Michael Blaine, "Suits"; Mark Vinz, "Almost October"; Donna Trussell, "Dream Pie"; Scott Driscoll, "Waiting for the Bus"; Pat Harrison, "The Winner"; Gordon Jackson, "In the Garden"; Toni Graham, "Jump!"; Michael Hettich, "Angels"; Patti Tana, "Harbor Island"; Ron Tanner, "The Hart House"; Stephen Tracy, "Fools' Experiments"; Lila Zeiger, "Fine Details"; Leslee Becker, "The Funny Part."

BOOK REVIEWS

BIG FISH, MYTHICAL FISH (235–238)

Title and text from *Chicago Tribune Book World*, 29 October 1978, 1, 6. A slightly different version of this review appeared as "A Man and His Fish" in *Texas Monthly*, December 1978, 222, 225.

BARTHELME'S INHUMAN COMEDIES (239–241)

Title from *Chicago Tribune Book World*, 28 January 1979, 1. Text from "Barthelme the Scribbler," *Texas Monthly*, March 1979, 162–63.

ROUSING TALES (242–246)

Title from *Chicago Tribune Book World*, 13 May 1979, 1. Text from untitled version in *San Francisco Review of Books* 5, no. 5 (October 1979): 23–24.

BLUEBIRD MORNINGS, STORM WARNINGS (247–251)

Title and text from *San Francisco Review of Books* 5, no. 2 (July 1979): 20–21. Reprinted in *American Book Review* 2, no. 2 (October 1979): 2, and *Quarterly West*, no. 10 (winter–spring 1980): 125–26. A shorter version of this review appeared as "*Van Gogh Field*: Troubling and Unforgettable Stories of the West," *Chicago Tribune*, 25 August 1979, sec. 1, p. 13. A later revision became RC's "Foreword" to *We Are Not in This Together: Stories by William Kittredge* (Port Townsend, Wash.: Graywolf Press, 1984), vii–x. The second quotation attributed to Kittredge ("What you do matters. . . .") is not to be found in "The Van Gogh Field" or any other story by Kittredge. Compare, however, the statement attributed to "Miller" in RC's unfinished novel, *The Augustine Notebooks*: "*What we do matters, brother . . .*" (173).

A GIFTED NOVELIST AT THE TOP OF HIS GAME
(252–254)

Title and text from *Chicago Tribune Book World*, 20 January 1980, 1. A slightly different version of this review appeared, untitled, in *San Francisco Review of Books* 5, no. 10 (March 1980): 10.

FICTION THAT THROWS LIGHT ON BLACKNESS
(255–257)

Title from *Chicago Tribune Book World*, 18 May 1980, 1, 10. Text from untitled version in *San Francisco Review of Books* 6, no. 1 (June 1980): 19.

BRAUTIGAN SERVES WEREWOLF BERRIES AND CAT CANTALOUPE (258–259)

Title and text from *Chicago Tribune Book World*, 26 October 1980, 3.

McGUANE GOES AFTER BIG GAME (260–262)

Title and text from *Chicago Tribune Book World*, 15 February 1981, 5. A shorter version of this review appeared, untitled, in *San Francisco Review of Books* 6, no. 4 (January–February 1981): 22.

RICHARD FORD'S STARK VISION OF LOSS, HEALING (263–265)

Title and text from *Chicago Tribune Book World*, 19 April 1981, 2. A slightly different version of this review appeared, untitled, in *San Francisco Review of Books* 6, no. 5 (March–April 1981): 29–30. In summarizing the novel, RC has rearranged the sequence of several passages.

A RETIRED ACROBAT FALLS UNDER
THE SPELL OF A TEENAGE GIRL (266–268)

Title and text from *Chicago Tribune Book World*, 5 July 1981, 1.

"FAME IS NO GOOD, TAKE IT FROM ME" (269–275)

Title and text from *New York Times Book Review*, 22 April 1984, 6–7.

COMING OF AGE, GOING TO PIECES (276–285)

Title and text from *New York Times Book Review*, 17 November 1985, 3,
51–52. RC's quotations from the letters of Hadley Richardson are
highly condensed, with a number of separate letters run together.
For Jeffrey Meyers's response to RC's review, see "Hemingway's
Biographer," *New York Times Book Review*, 8 December 1985, 85.